THE DEVIL'S KISS

There was nothing appealing about that sardonic face of his with its expressive black eyebrows, sharp nose, and those curious pointy-topped ears that in her mind defined him as Lucifer. No, there was only one thing about McAllister that worried her. His wide, sensual mouth. She gazed at it, shivering at the thought of it fastening on her own mouth. It had to be an illusion, that inviting mouth, because she was certain there was nothing more than a brute wearing it.

"Awright," she informed him grimly, "let's get on with it. What do I do here?"

"To start, you can stop looking like I'm going to strangle you. Relax, Callie." When she squeezed her eyes shut and braced herself, he sighed. "Oh, for the love of— Okay, just keep still. This won't hurt." She started when suddenly two hands framed her face to hold it steady. They were very large and very strong hands but surprisingly gentle. "Now we tip your head slightly just so. And my head goes here." She knew how close he was, for she felt his breath against her face. It was warm and dauntingly masculine.

"Callie," he whispered.

"What?" she croaked.

"Part your lips a little."

She obeyed, keeping her eyes tightly closed. In the next instant his mouth was on hers. He was kissing her! Slowly, softly. And, dear God, was that her kissing him back?

Other *Leisure* books by Jean Barrett:
ARCHER'S CROSSING
DELANEY'S CROSSING

McAllister's Crossing

Jean Barrett

LEISURE BOOKS NEW YORK CITY

To all of my readers;
You are very important to me.

A LEISURE BOOK®

June 2001

Published by

Dorchester Publishing Co., Inc.
276 Fifth Avenue
New York, NY 10001

ISBN 0-8439-4879-5

McAllister's
Crossing

Chapter One

The Oregon Trail—April, 1852

There was only one thing that Callie Burgess wanted. Only one thing that would make her happy. She longed to see the expression on Lincoln McAllister's face when she put a bullet through his murdering black heart. Which was precisely what she had sworn to do the minute she caught up with the viper. Callie had to admit, however, that she was having a bit of trouble achieving that intention. Well, maybe more than a bit.

She had been tracking McAllister for almost a week now, and her luck was running out. Early yesterday she had traded the last of her meager funds to a pair of renegade half-breeds for the information that the man she sought had passed them on the trail headed west. That part was encouraging because it meant she hadn't lost him. The rest was not encouraging. As of this morning her food was gone except for a little unappetizing hardtack, the water in her canteen was low, and she and her horse were dusty and drooping with exhaustion.

But Callie sure as hell was nowhere ready to give up and turn back to Missouri, even if the only thing not diminished was her supply of courage. That and her fierce resolve to punish Lincoln McAllister. That was why she was so impatient when her horse stopped in the middle of the trail and snorted unhappily.

"We got business, Apollo, and I don't aim for you to delay us in the executin' of it. Move on."

She dug her heels into his flanks, but the handsome chestnut remained at a stubborn standstill. Callie had a sudden feeling the horse maybe knew more than she did.

"Hey, you smell 'im out there watchin' us, Apollo? That what you tryin' to tell me?"

Shading her eyes against the glare of the afternoon sun, she scanned the terrain. The endless Kansas prairie rolled monotonously in every direction. There was not so much as a single tree on the horizon and no sign of life except for a lone hawk riding the thermals high overhead. And then she saw it! A plume of black smoke climbing into the cloudless sky from behind a low, distant ridge.

"Reckon you did smell somethin' at that!" she acknowledged excitedly.

Convinced that the source of the smoke was

Lincoln McAllister's campfire, she urged Apollo forward. This time the chestnut obeyed her, breaking into a trot. As they neared the ridge, Callie, too, could smell the smoke. But she realized now that there was too much of it to be a mere campfire. And there was something else. Something that worried her. She could hear the bark of gunfire. What in sweet hell was goin' on?

Exercising caution, Callie drew rein just before they topped the ridge. She flung herself from the saddle and crept forward clutching her rifle. Reaching the crown of the ridge, she dropped flat in the grass and examined the situation below her.

Well, damn! They was havin' a battle down there!

Far as she could tell, what with the roiling smoke from guns and a burning wagon together with the thick dust and the wild yells, a wagon train of emigrants was under siege. Weren't no Indians circling that caravan either. It appeared to be a band of white marauders looking for easy pickings.

The participants in the scene were far too busy to notice Callie's arrival. She might have slipped away without involving herself in any risk, but wagon trains headed west were sacred to Callie, and with good reason. She had once, long ago, been a member of such an expedition. There was no way she could not come to their defense.

Callie Burgess's skill with her Remington was legendary back in Horizon, Missouri. They said if a man had a mind to sport a gold earring, she could pierce his lobe for him from fifteen yards away and never touch a hair on his head. Not that anyone in Horizon had ever been tempted to put this boast to the test, but she *was* a darn good shot.

Callie proved it in the next several minutes, eliminating three of the attackers, then suddenly it was all over. The band, realizing they faced opposition from two directions, surrendered the fight and rode off with their wounded, disappearing over the horizon.

Coming to her feet, slapping the worst of the dust off her britches with the wide brim of her hat, Callie collected Apollo and headed down the slope. There was no one waiting to thank her. They were too occupied.

Turmoil ruled the corral as the emigrants struggled to deal with their wounded and to control the blazing wagon before the flames consuming its canvas spread to the other wagons. Her presence went unnoticed in the noise and commotion as she secured Apollo and joined them behind the barricades. Or so she thought.

Hoping they could spare her some grub and maybe even the latest word on that bastard Lincoln McAllister's whereabouts, Callie was on her way to find someone in authority when she was hailed by a voice that could have driven nails through steel.

"Hey, you there, sweet cheeks in the buckskins! Git over here and lend us a hand!"

Startled, she turned in the direction of the insistent voice. A few yards away, hands on her hips, was a buxom woman several years older than Callie. And this was no ordinary female, not with locks so unnaturally red. The fiery red hair, along with a painted mouth and a neckline that would have been defined as obscene by any respectable community's standards, told their own story. The only time that Callie had ever glimpsed a creature like this one, she'd been plying her trade in a room above the Good Times Saloon in Horizon.

"You decided yet, boy, whether t'haul that pretty butt o' yours over here where it's needed, or you gonna go on gapin' at me while a man bleeds to death?"

Scowling, Callie swiftly closed the distance between them. "I reckon, ma'am, one o' us is makin' a serious mistake."

The woman's penciled eyebrows lifted in amusement. "Oh, so it's a girl inside them britches, is it? Well, that makes two o' us now on this wagon train that's halfway interestin'. Come on, I need you."

Without further explanation, she turned and led the way to an area between two of the chained wagons. Callie, though resenting her brusqueness, was willing to follow, even if her reason for doing so was a silly one. Callie couldn't help it. Whether it was men, women, or flowers, she had a secret weakness for fragrances. And she sure did admire the perfume this woman wore, though it was a mite strong.

She was still clutching her Remington when she squatted down on the ground beside the redhead, who bent over a young man lying on his side.

11

"This here is Ned, our scout. How you doin', lover?"

Oh, Jeez, Callie thought, observing the boy's thin white face and the blood oozing through his trousers, *he looks real bad*.

There was fear in Ned's voice as he gazed pleadingly at the redhead. "Am I gonna die, ma'am?"

"Don't be a fool," she scoffed. "You was shot in the ass, not the chest. I need you to hold him down while I patch 'im up," she directed Callie.

Callie didn't object, but Ned was none too happy as the woman began to remove his trousers.

"Can't dress wounded flesh through your pants, Neddie. Been dyin' to git me a real look at this cute little posterior o' yours. Guess this here is my golden opportunity."

Callie watched Ned clench his jaw tight—either in pain or embarrassment, or maybe a combination of both—as the redhead eased the jean trousers over his narrow hips and down his skinny legs. But he made no protest.

"Got a name, buckskins?" the woman asked her.

"Callie Burgess."

"Mine's Pearl Slocum. Hope you ain't too fond o' these drawers, Ned. Gonna need to cut 'em away."

She reached for a pair of scissors inside a medicine basket on the ground beside her and began to snip at the blood-soaked flannel of the boy's underdrawers. Ned trembled. Callie

12

gripped his legs and tried to hold him steady while the other woman worked.

Glancing at her, Pearl chuckled. "You're whiter'n he is. Guess you got less talent for nursin' than straight shootin', huh?"

So someone *had* noticed her up on the ridge with her rifle, Callie thought.

"Now me," Pearl continued briskly as she exposed the wound on Ned's buttocks, "I got me a real skill with patchin'. Learned it by necessity in the houses where I worked. Some o' the customers, they could be mean . . . rough up the girls. Got so I could doctor 'em real good. Guess I don't need to explain just what kind of houses those was." Turning her head, she shouted behind her, "Hey, where's that water I asked you to favor me with?"

"Comin' up." A heavy woman appeared from the frenzy of activity that continued on all sides. The way she looked at Pearl made it obvious she didn't approve of her, but she must have had a grudging respect for the redhead's skills because she offered no argument as she placed a jug of water within Pearl's reach. "Ain't had time to heat it properly."

"This'll do. How's the wagon master?"

"They got the bullet out of him, but he ain't so good. Reverend's with him."

The woman retreated. Pearl began to carefully sponge the blood away from the scout's wound. "Don't know who'll pilot us to Oregon if we lose our wagon master. He's the only one what knows the route well enough to git us through." She leaned close to inspect the gash. "You're in

13

luck, Ned. Bullet didn't much more'n scrape you. Probably leave a scar, but that ain't bad. Somethin' for some tender young thing t'lovingly stroke for you one o' these days. Course, it's gonna be quite a while afore you're sittin' that pony o'yours ag'in, but all considered—"

"Pearl," Callie interrupted.

"Yeah?"

"He ain't hearin' you. Passed out when she brung the water."

"That so? Well, then, it ain't gonna be a problem dressin' this dimpled little cheek o' his."

The woman with the wide girth reappeared. "Hey, Pearl," she said sharply. "They're askin' for you on the other side of the corral. That stranger what wandered into camp earlier is down. Took a ball in the shoulder."

"Gonna have to wait his turn. I got me a bandagin' to finish here."

Stranger? Callie was immediately alert. She didn't have to ask for any name. It had to be Lincoln McAllister! He was here! She had finally caught up with the vile brute.

Pearl no longer had a need of her, and she was eager to settle her score with McAllister. Snatching up her rifle, Callie came to her feet and stormed across the corral.

There was no mistaking her objective. She found him seated on the ground, back propped against a wagon wheel, long legs stretched out in front of him. At the moment he looked as limp as day-old collard greens, body sagging, one hand pressing a bloodstained compress against the spot where his right arm joined his shoulder.

He wasn't aware of her arrival. His eyes were closed, and he didn't stir. Maybe, like the young scout, he had fainted in pain. There was no one tending him at the moment. They were alone. Callie was able to stand there and savor the sight of her target with grim pleasure.

She'd never met Lincoln McAllister, but they had provided her with a description of him back in Missouri. The description was an adequate one. Early thirties, tall and lean, black hair, a sharp nose. Trouble was, they had neglected to tell her just how ugly and unappealing this skunk was. He had angular features that needed a shave, a scar on his jaw, and clothes that were filthy. He obviously could use a bath. The cruel sonofabitch probably smelled bad, too, which was something else in his disfavor.

He must have sensed Callie staring at him with her naked rage, for his eyes drifted open, meeting her hard gaze. So he wasn't unconscious after all. Good. She wanted him fully aware of her raw hate when she sent him to hell.

It was aggravating, though. There should have been fear in those dark eyes of his, especially upon discovering her looming over him with her Remington pointed in the general direction of his groin. All she could see was a lazy insolence as his gaze climbed from her toes to her head and back down again. It was a bold gaze that stripped her to her young womanhood, and then decided it didn't like what it found. Callie's grip tightened angrily on the rifle.

"Something I can do for you?" His voice was deep and raspy and bore a faint trace of the

15

deep South. New Orleans, Callie figured. She'd heard of his Creole origins.

"Name's Callie Burgess," she informed him fiercely, "an' I'm here to put a bullet in you."

"Already got a bullet in me, Callie."

"But I guarantee this one ain't gonna miss your vitals."

His black eyebrows arched. It was a sardonic expression that, along with his narrow face and ears that were slightly pointed at their tops, made him look like Lucifer himself. Fittin, 'cause he was a devil.

"Uh-huh. You mind telling me what for? I'd kind of like to know before I breathe my last."

"You killed my pa, an' I'm payin' you back fer that."

"Seems fair enough." He was silently thoughtful for a few seconds before he drawled a casual, "Thing is, Callie, I've killed so many men in my long, bloody career that I've lost track of all their identities. How about refreshing my memory?"

"Hank Burgess. You shot him dead, 'long with his friend, Bud Colby, in that hotel room back in Independence."

"Ah, *that* Hank Burgess."

Was he laughing at her?

"I don't suppose you'd care to hear that I, uh, didn't—"

"Save your wind, mister, 'cause I wouldn't believe your dirty lies."

Callie was no fool. She had made certain of his guilt before coming after him. That crooked sheriff in Independence had let McAllister go because the two of them had once served in the army together. But the sheriff must have known there was no one else, not with the little maid in the hotel finding McAllister standing over their fresh bodies, his Colt still in his hand.

Besides, McAllister had the reputation of a ruthless killer. Callie had asked around, learned that he'd once served as a U.S. officer in the Mexican War, where he had disgraced his rank. No one knew the particulars, only that his deed was so sinful, he'd been court-martialed and dishonorably discharged. Following that, he'd committed a terrible crime in New Orleans, something so wicked that they said he was on the run from the law down there.

McAllister was a murderer all right, and if no one else would punish him, Callie was going to make certain that she did, whatever the consequences.

He must have seen by the determination in her eyes that she wasn't going to listen to him. "No, I guess not," he said. He shifted against the wagon wheel, grimacing over the discomfort of his wound against which he continued to hold the wadded bandana that served as a makeshift compress. "Well, if your mind is made up, I can't do much to stop you. Kind of helpless down here on the ground. Come on, get it over with."

Callie raised the rifle to the level of his chest, her finger on the trigger. Problem was, she couldn't bring herself to squeeze it.

"What are you waiting for?" he challenged.

Damn him, why wasn't he begging for his life, cursing her savagely, lunging at her in fury? Anything but this nonchalance he demonstrated

17

with that little smile on his wide mouth. She would have shot him through the heart without hesitation if it hadn't been for that smile. It somehow reminded her that she had a conscience.

Hell, she had promised herself she would show him no mercy, just as he had shown none to her pa and Bud Colby. Scum like Lincoln McAllister had no code of honor. Unfortunately, Callie Burgess did. She couldn't bring herself to shoot a man when he was down and helpless, even a mangy dog as undeserving as this one.

"Git to your feet," she ordered, nodding at the Colt strapped to his hip. "Gonna give you a chance to draw afore I drill you."

"Sorry, I can't oblige you," he apologized. "Even if I wasn't too weak at the moment to stand, my gun arm is useless. Afraid you'll have to execute me without the benefit of satisfying your sense of fair play."

He *knew*, blast his rotten soul. He knew she couldn't kill him like this. Lowering the muzzle of the rifle, she cursed him violently and at length. In her nineteen years of life, most of them rough ones, Callie had learned a lot of cuss words. And she blasted him with every one in her rich vocabulary.

When she was finally through, and standing there recovering her wind, he observed mildly, "I take that to mean I'm being given a reprieve."

"Mister, you'd better pray that wound takes a long time mendin', 'cause as soon as you're fit to hold a weapon ag'in, you're dead."

"Cheer up, Callie. Maybe I'll die from an infection."

"Oh, no, I ain't gonna be cheated like that!"

"Who's gettin' cheated?" demanded Pearl Slocum, who suddenly arrived on the scene bearing her medicine basket.

The redhead waited for one of them to explain, but Callie was silent. She had no intention of revealing her mission to any member of this wagon train. If they learned McAllister was a killer, they might take it into their heads to punish him themselves. Or maybe prevent her from exacting her revenge. Either way, she wasn't going to take the chance of losing him.

The bastard himself couldn't have been anxious for the wagon train to know the truth about him because he, too, withheld an explanation.

"All right," Pearl sniffed, gazing at them suspiciously, "so it ain't none o' my business. Guess this is, though." She knelt on the ground to examine McAllister's injury.

"The bullet is still in there," he said. "I can feel it."

"Gonna have to dig it out," she warned him. "Ain't gonna be pleasant."

"Looking forward to it." He smiled his devil's smile, but it was directed at Callie. She knew he referred not to the extraction of the bullet, but to the showdown she had promised him when he was sufficiently recovered.

"You up to helpin' me ag'in?" Pearl asked, cutting McAllister's shirt to expose an expanse of taut muscle where the bullet was lodged.

"A pleasure," Callie said as she joined her on

the ground, and she meant it. She wanted to be right here to watch him suffer. He deserved to suffer.

But he disappointed her. The business of Pearl probing for the bullet had to be excruciating. He never cried out; he never registered his pain as Callie hung on to him. All she saw in those black eyes meeting hers was a wry amusement. It taunted her. He was inhuman.

It was Pearl who did all the complaining, maybe just to distract her patient. She grumbled without letup throughout the whole process of removing the bullet, cleaning the wound, dressing it.

"Join us, sister, they sez. Bound for Oregon and new lives along the Willamette, they sez. Chance for lost souls like you and me to start over, they sez. Gonna be paradise in the west. Sure it is. Just looks and feels like hell, that's all.

"Well, it's been tough. Nothin' but hard times on this trek, and now we git ourselves attacked. Know why? Too many females, an' not enough men to protect us. There's a word for that."

"Vulnerable," McAllister muttered.

Pearl glanced at him in surprise, and Callie could see she was impressed by his vocabulary. "Yeah, I guess that's it. Like I say, too many women."

Callie, suddenly struck by the familiarity of her description, stared at Pearl. *Too many women.* Was it possible? "Leader," she said eagerly. "Who's yer leader?"

"Got a preacher in charge, but he ain't payin' the bills. There's a couple out in Oregon doin' that. Interested in helping women what need help. They used to bring the trains through theirselves once upon a time, so they tell me. Now just sponsor 'em. Name o' Delaney."

Callie smiled to herself. It *was* possible.

"You hear 'bout 'em?"

"Yeah, I heard 'bout 'em." Callie didn't offer to explain. Agatha and Cooper Delaney were too dear to her to casually share them with strangers.

Pearl nodded and began to fix a sling on McAllister's arm. "Looks like you'll be wearin' this until the wound has a chance to heal up a bit."

"Why?" he asked her, and Callie knew by the earnest tone in his voice that he wasn't referring to the sling. She had the feeling Pearl realized this too. The redhead didn't answer him.

"Why?" he persisted. "Why did that gang try to raid the wagon train? What were they after?"

Watching Pearl as she avoided the intense expression in McAllister's dark eyes, Callie knew she wasn't imagining it. The subject bothered the woman. Bothered her to a degree that she was fearful of discussing it.

Pearl shrugged. "Dunno."

"I can tell you what they were after, Mr. McAllister."

The voice came from behind them. A male voice so rich and mellow that Callie actually shivered with delight at the sound of it. Eager to put a face to that voice, she got to her feet and turned to face the speaker.

The sight of him stunned her. Never in all her nineteen years had Callie seen anything so beau-

21

tiful. The man was so perfect in form and face that he glowed. There was no other word for it. He positively *glowed*. Maybe it was an illusion, the sunlight turning his fair hair to gold, or the radiant gleam in his smiling blue eyes. Whatever it was, she couldn't keep herself from staring at him in an admiration that suddenly had her feeling all weak and squishy inside.

If he was aware of her awe, he was too polite to embarrass her. That devil, McAllister, had no such manners. Callie got all hot when he laughed at her derisively. She glared down at him, resenting his scorn. Pearl, too, was amused by Callie's breathless fascination, but hers was a kindly humor. She got to her feet and introduced the new arrival.

"Folks, this is our leader, the Reverend Mr. Gabriel Hawkins."

Gabriel, Callie thought, caressing the name inside her head. The Bible spoke of a head angel called Gabriel, didn't it? Fitting, because there was something so pure about this handsome man that she could hear a heavenly choir just looking at him. Listening to him, too, as he made his howdies to them in that musical voice, adding his gratitude for coming to their aid.

"After your effort on our behalf, Mr. McAllister," he went on, "I think I can trust you with an explanation. We're carrying a strongbox on the wagon train, funds destined for the missions in Oregon, and I believe those men somehow learned of its existence."

"Hope it's well hidden, Reverend."

"It is. I intend to see those funds delivered to

their destination, and thanks to you that's still possible."

Something funny about that, Callie thought. It wasn't in the nature of a skunk like Lincoln Mc-Allister to go and risk his skin helping out folks in trouble. He must have joined this wagon train for a purpose of his own, and instinct told her it was no good. Maybe he was after that strongbox for himself.

"That is, it will be possible," Gabriel amended his vow, "providing we can find our way."

McAllister nodded. "Yes, I heard your wagon master was down."

"We have every faith he'll recover, but at the present he's in no condition to lead us any-where. Which," the preacher added solemnly, "is why I'm here. I understand, Mr. McAllister, that you told one of our men you're familiar with the trail from your army days. If you're well enough, would you agree to substitute as our pilot until Tom Callahan is on his feet again?"

Callie anxiously watched Lincoln's face as he considered the proposition. Or *pretended* to consider it. "I might be persuaded to do that. Have to occupy myself somehow until my arm heals. I'm assuming, Reverend, you'll make it worth my while."

"Of course we'll pay you."

"Then I'm your man."

No way, Callie vowed. There was absolutely no way she was going to let Lincoln McAllister get away from her. She impulsively made up her mind. "Ain't got no scout either," she said swiftly. "Yer boy won't be ridin' or shootin' fer quite a spell, an' I'm real handy at both."

Pearl spoke up on her behalf. "I can vouch for that. Saw her in action on the ridge."

Gabriel glanced at Callie in surprise. "It's a little unconventional, I suppose, but we are in need." He considered her offer and then nodded decisively. "Yes, Miss Burgess, we would be pleased to have you as well."

It was a pleasure watching his face as he beamed at them, all gleaming teeth and welcoming blue eyes. And when he turned that saintly smile in her direction, as though he intended it to be a personal connection, Callie was lost.

For the first time in her life, she was aware of her womanhood. Deeply aware of both it and the desperate longing that accompanied it. She, Callie Burgess, was suddenly and completely smitten! Shoot, it made no sense either. She had no illusions about herself and what she was and all she wasn't, which made it crazy of her, downright hopeless, to want a man like Gabriel Hawkins, but there it was.

And, damn, it was a good thing she had this chance to play scout, because even if Lincoln McAllister wasn't reason enough for her to stick with the wagon train, the preacher was. She would do anything to be near him, and that included leaving Missouri behind her.

Wasn't really anything to go back to anyway, now that Pa was gone. A few measly acres that made poor farming and the miserable shack they'd called home. She had loved Pa, but he hadn't offered them much of an existence. He liked his drink and gaming too well for that.

Callie was ready for something else in her life, and she prayed that something would include Gabriel Hawkins. But she was suddenly seized by a horrible possibility. Could it be true? Pearl would know. She'd have to get Pearl alone to ask her.

That opportunity didn't occur until after sundown, and by then Callie was on fire with impatience. No help for it. The wagon train had been far too busy mending itself and securing the camp for the evening to permit any conversation.

When they finally got around to talking about anything, they were sharing a meal at Pearl's fire.

"Might as well attach yerself t'my rig while you're with us," the redhead had earlier invited her. "Way I see it, the both o' us is a couple o' misfits on this train. That makes us company fer each other."

Callie had gladly accepted her offer. 'Course, Pearl was a prostitute, or had been, and Callie could see that a lot of the other women in camp avoided her for that reason, but Callie didn't let that concern her. She already considered Pearl a friend, and that was rare. Having been practically an outcast herself back in Horizon, she didn't relate easily to other females, especially females she could confide in. Which was what she about to do now.

Devouring the last of her beans and bacon, she laid her tin plate on the ground beside her stool and leaned forward, hands planted on her knees. "Got sumpthin' t'ask you, Pearl."

"Ya got my ear."

Callie hesitated, afraid Pearl would laugh at her. "It's, um, 'bout the preacher. Is he, uh, taken? Y'know, like a wife or sumpthin'?"

Pearl didn't laugh. She drank coffee from her tin cup while Callie waited tensely for her reply. "Honey lamb," she finally said. "He ain't attached t'anything but his religion an' the welfare o' this here wagon train."

Callie was relieved but at the same time amazed. "Seems a man that sweet t'look at would've been spoken fer."

"Guess he's been too busy savin' souls."

Callie peered at her through the thickening twilight. "Doncha like 'im, Pearl?"

The redhead finished her coffee and shrugged. "Let's jest say I don't have a mind to get cozy with 'im."

"Why?"

" 'Cause the Gabriel Hawkinses o' this world have been tryin' t'change my wicked ways fer most o' my life, an' I like me just fine like I am."

"Thought you was wantin' t'change. Thought that's why you come on this trek."

"Maybe I did."

Pearl didn't want to talk about it, Callie saw. Something about the subject made her uncomfortable.

"How'd we come t'get on me?" the redhead said impatiently. "Thought we were discussin' this powerful hankerin' o' yours fer the preacher. Yeah, I saw you eyein' 'im like he was candy."

Callie was glad of the shadows hiding the sudden flush that stained her cheeks. "Reckon I'm an awful fool."

"Won't argue that, 'cause a woman has no sense when it comes to her heart."

"It's terrible, Pearl. I wanna please 'im like a woman goes about pleasin' a man so's he notices 'er, exceptin' I been this tomboy all my life. Dunno how t'be a girl. All I ever knowed was ridin', shootin', an' wearin' britches."

"Noticed that. Noticed yer real handy 'bout other things too. Saw you this afternoon showin' those two women how their water barrel wasn't properly lashed to their wagon. Also heard you tellin' that fella 'bout coverin' the hooves of his oxen with buffalo hide when the trail gets rough." Tipping her head to one side, she considered Callie with a shrewd expression on her painted face. "You been on a wagon train afore this, ain'tcha?"

Callie decided there was no reason why Pearl shouldn't know. "Fact is, I have. It were a long time ago. And me, I was this wild brat whose ma up and died sudden-like, leavin' 'er all alone in the world. See, I didn't know 'bout Pa then or how Ma had walked out on him just after I was born 'cause of some other woman. I guess he was as good as dead t'her after that, so I figgered I was an orphan. So did Agatha an' Cooper Delaney when they took me west with 'em."

"You speakin' o' the same Delaneys responsible fer this here wagon train o' ours?"

"Sure am." Callie gazed into the flickering fire, remembering that other life. "They was real good t'me. Took me inta their home after we got t'Oregon, treated me like I was their own. I figgered I'd be there fer always. Then one day Pa shows up outta nowhere. Been lookin' fer me all those years."

"Fetched you back east with 'im, huh?"

Callie nodded. "Yup. Convinced the Delaneys he'd be a lovin' father and took me back t'his farm in Horizon, Missouri. Not that it were much of a farm. Pa was real carin' an' he tried, but he wasn't so good when it come t'raisin' up a youngun. Had 'im a kind o' business, though, that put food on the table. When he was sober, anyways."

"Do I wanna know what this business was?"

"I ain't ashamed o' it," Callie said proudly, "even if folks did hold their noses when they seed us comin'."

"How bad could it be?"

"Manure. Pa an' I collected manure from the farms around, then bagged an' sold it fer fertilizer." Callie sometimes wondered if this was the reason why she had a secret fondness for pleasant fragrances. She supposed it was.

"Well, honey lamb, I ain't had folks hold their noses on me, but I sure had 'em crossin' the street t'get away from me, so I guess I know how rough things can be."

"That's a fact."

"So what became o' your old man?"

"Died." Callie wasn't prepared to go into the details, not when they involved Lincoln McAllister as they did.

"Uh-huh. An' now yer on yer own."

"I can take care o' myself."

"Guess ya can at that. Wouldn'ta picked up an' struck off on this trail otherwise. Lookin' for an adventure out west, are ya?"

"Somethin' like that," Callie mumbled.

Pearl laughed. It was a deep laugh, straight from the belly. "Honey lamb, the good Reverend Hawkins might accept people on faith, an' no questions asked, just like he went and done with you an' McAllister this afternoon. But Pearl Slocum ain't so trustin'. Weren't no accident the two o' you ridin' in here today outta nowhere, were it?"

"Don't know what ya mean."

"Doncha? Funny," she said perceptively, " 'cause I woulda said y'got business o' some kind with that man."

Callie didn't answer. She could feel Pearl gazing at her speculatively.

"All right," the redhead said. "It ain't my affair. But you watch yerself with 'im, girl. I know men, an' there's somethin' dangerous 'bout that one. He's all cool on the outside, even talks like he might've been brought up a gent, but inside 'im is a real fire of some kind. Wouldn't care t'see you git burned by it."

Chapter Two

Linc couldn't sleep. The wound in his arm was troubling him, throbbing with a persistent ache. He lay there on his bedroll, staring up at the stars and listening to the sounds of the camp settling down for the night.

"Everything all right here, O'Hara?"

He recognized the soft voice off in the darkness. It belonged to Gabriel Hawkins. The preacher was on his rounds, checking with the sentries he had posted outside the corral. The wagon train was exercising vigilance, making certain there were no more surprise attacks.

Better late than never, Linc supposed. In his opinion the clergyman was something of a cheerful fool, though a well-meaning one. Actually, Linc felt sorry for him.

Poor Hawkins. So blind he had no idea what

was in store for him. But Linc did. He hadn't missed the silly adoration lighting up Callie Burgess's freckled face like a bonfire the instant those hungry green eyes of hers had fastened on the preacher. She was just young enough and naive enough to actually think she stood a chance of winning him, and that meant the grubby creature would give the man no peace.

Come to think of it, he ought to be expressing his gratitude to Hawkins. Maybe the hellcat would be so busy chasing him, she'd leave Linc alone. Not that he was counting on it. He hadn't forgotten the lethal promise that stubborn little mouth of hers had issued to him. Callie Burgess was a complication he hadn't anticipated, and eventually he would have to do something about her, but right now he regarded her as more of a nuisance than a genuine threat.

A nuisance that he resented. She was feisty, headstrong, and about as attractive as measles with her untamed russet hair, and she had the language and manners of a bullwhacker. She was everything that Lincoln didn't admire in a woman. But none of that was why he resented her.

Fair or not, he begrudged Callie Burgess her robustness—a robustness he wished for the woman back in New Orleans who meant everything to him. Anne McAllister didn't possess that kind of exuberant health. She had suffered, she was delicate, but she was still the gentle beauty against whom he measured every other female. And he longed for her.

There was a daguerreotype hidden inside his

pack, the one possession that Linc prized. The hand of his uninjured arm was fumbling for it when the glow of an approaching lantern stopped him. His empty fingers withdrew from the pack as the lush figure of Pearl Slocum loomed above him.

"I make a practice of checking on my patients afore I turn in," she informed him. "You survivin'?"

Linc lifted his head from the bedroll. "I've felt better."

"Wound's painin' you, huh? Thought it might. 'Swhy I brung a bit o'medicine with me. Only let's keep it between ourselves. Don't reckon the reverend would approve."

She produced a bottle of whiskey from inside her shawl, uncorked it, and leaned down to hand it to him. Linc reached for it eagerly.

"Bless you and all your descendants!"

Tipping the bottle up to his mouth, he swigged from it as though it was no more potent than sugar water. The contents went down smoothly, making a welcome glow in his stomach.

"Hey," Pearl warned him. "Take it easy. You'll git yerself sicker'n you already are on that stuff."

Lowering the bottle, Linc laughed. "Not a chance. My father came from Scotland, and my mother was a Louisiana Creole. No two peoples breed stock that have stronger heads for liquor."

"That a fact?" she said dryly. "How they rate on tempers?"

"Hot," he admitted. "Any other questions?"

"Yeah. Providin' you ain't dealin' with a prize hangover tomorrow when we roll out ag'in, you gonna be well enough t'guide this parade?"

"My arm might be in a sling, Pearl, but my legs aren't. I'll be on my feet in the morning."

"Better be, 'cause the wagon master ain't showin' no signs yet of comin' 'round."

She reached for the whiskey, but Linc didn't want her to leave. Not just yet. He held the bottle away from her. "And you're real anxious for the wagon train to be under way again, aren't you, Pearl? You want to get away from this place. That band might come back, and the possibility of that makes you nervous."

She gazed at him, her eyes narrowing suspiciously. "What're you drivin' at, mister?"

"We both know those men aren't after the strongbox. They probably don't even know it's on the train. Know what I think? I think they want you and what you could give them. A piece of information far more valuable than a collection of mission funds."

"You're crazy!"

"Don't think so, Pearl. But that's all right. Your secret is safe with me. You can trust me not to pressure you about it." *For now*, he added to himself.

"That liquor's already gone t'yer head! It's got you dreamin' things!"

She snatched the bottle out of his hand. He watched the glow of her bobbing lantern as she turned around and made a fast retreat. This time he let her go. He had her worried, and for the time being that was all he could expect to achieve. He would approach her again, and in time he would wear her down. Get her to confide in him by offering a fair exchange. It was why he was here on the wagon train.

Linc stretched out again on the bedroll. The whiskey was already performing its magic. The throbbing in his arm was easing. He relaxed and closed his eyes.

Just before he drifted off, he reconsidered his other problem. Callie Burgess. He thought he knew now just how to handle her. Hawkins had unknowingly awakened a dormant sexuality in her, and Linc planned to use that vulnerability to his advantage.

Back down the trail several miles away was another camp. Its occupants, rolled in their blankets, were asleep on the ground. Only two of the rough company were still awake and sat huddled near the fire.

The elder of them, burly and bearded, had a brooding expression on his coarse face as he gazed into the twisting flames. His name was Judd Parsons, and he was the leader of the gang.

Or what was left of it, Judd thought sourly. They had buried two of their members out on the prairie, and by morning a third wounded man would probably join them. It didn't look as if he would make it.

As for the others . . . Well, he would lose them, too. The raid on the wagon train had failed, and they were angry. They had insisted on being paid off with the funds with which Judd had been provided. They would ride off at first light, likely heading back to Missouri and the nearest saloon.

"Weren't easy like we figgered, were it?" the man beside him observed in a gloomy voice. "Weren't easy."

Judd turned his head to consider his partner. The balding Ike Ritter had a nervous habit of repeating himself that Judd found irritating. He had to admit, though, the skinny runt was a loyal companion, not planning to desert him like those other weasels snoring in their blankets.

"Guess this is it," Ike went on in his thin, piping voice that reminded Judd of a squeaking mouse. "Guess we got no choice now exceptin' to give up. No choice."

"Shut yer trap, ya fool!" Judd growled at him. "I ain't about t'give up an' turn back. Hell, I'm just beginnin'."

"How we gonna do that? The money we got given us fer this chore is just 'bout gone. Ain't enough t'hire on other willin' guns, an' with just the two o'us we don't stand a prayer o' separatin' that whore from the wagon train. Don't stand a prayer."

"There's other ways o' gettin' to her and what she knows."

There was determination on Judd's brutish face as he stared into the fire. Pearl Slocum was the key to everything, the only key right now, and he wasn't about to lose her. The secret she was keeping was valuable, worth far more to them than Ike realized. It involved something Judd hadn't yet shared with his partner. Something that Judd had been instructed to do that was necessary but unpleasant. He supposed there would be time enough to tell Ike all about it when, and if, they were successful gaining what they had been sent to locate.

"What ways?" Ike asked. "What?"

"I don't know. I just know you and me is gonna shadow that wagon train from a safe distance. Bide our time an' wait fer an opportunity." His low chuckle carried a promise. "It's a long way t'Oregon, Ike. Anything can develop, 'specially if we see that it does."

This wasn't the Oregon Trail that Callie remembered. Changes had occurred since the rigorous crossing she had made with Agatha and Cooper back in 'forty-one. A number of those changes were apparent to her in the first few days she scouted for the wagon train, and others she learned about as the caravan approached the drier plains country.

They were welcome changes, for although the obstacles of a rugged terrain and the hardships of extreme weather still existed, the overland trail was no longer a desolate, nearly impossible challenge. The great tide of western expansion had been responsible for that. More forts had been erected along the route to serve the emigrants, ferries established at river crossings, shortcuts hacked through the wilderness.

Shoot, Callie thought, *it's almost a picnic.* An exaggeration, of course, but she encountered very few problems as she rode ahead of the train on Apollo's back, making sure the trail was safe while searching out game to fill their pots. She enjoyed those hours, solitary though they were. It made her feel good to see the clouds of bloom on the stunted cherry trees, to hear the yelp of prairie dogs, to test the wildflowers for the sweet scents that so pleased her, and to feel the wind as it caressed the surrounding oceans of waving grass. Her work was pleasant and uncomplicated.

Callie wished she could say the same for the time she spent back in camp. Frustration was what that was. Pure, unbearable frustration. No matter what she did to get close to Gabriel Hawkins—and she tried just about everything she could think of to interest him—he resisted.

"Gonna have prairie chicken tonight, Mr. Hawkins," she'd offered eagerly. "Me and Pearl would sure be pleased t'have you join us."

"Tempting, Callie, but I've already accepted an invitation for supper."

And on another occasion, "No trouble t'keep you company while you sit with the wagon master at his bedside this evenin', Mr. Hawkins."

"That's very kind of you, Callie, but I must decline. After a long day in the saddle, you need your rest."

And still again, "Ain't much of a hand with a needle and thread, Mr. Hawkins, but if you'd like my help with the tear in that coat—"

"Thank you, Callie, but I have it under control."

She couldn't stand it. She longed for his attention, for the chance to be near him, if for no other reason than just to gaze at him in all his handsome splendor. But he didn't see her need.

He didn't know she was aching to be alone with him.

And the worst of the whole thing, the *absolute* worst, was Lincoln McAllister. Because it seemed that whenever she tried to approach Gabriel, that villian was somewhere close by, watching her efforts with his taunting smile and one of those eyebrows of his lifted in mockery.

She knew he was silently ridiculing her. His kind had been doing that most of her life. Looking at her as if she was some unmannered critter that lived under a rock and wasn't entitled to the yearnings she kept hidden behind a shield of proud defiance. All right, so they were crazy yearnings, but she couldn't seem to help herself.

And because Lincoln McAllister was shrewd enough to see her weakness, she hated him more with each passing day. However, she did silently thank him on the evening when a miracle finally occurred. For once he was nowhere in evidence. Maybe that made all the difference, because this time when she approached Gabriel with her earnest plea to be of use, he didn't refuse her.

"Actually, Callie, there is something you can do for me."

She couldn't believe her luck. "Anything, Mr. Hawkins. You just name it."

"Perhaps I shouldn't request it since"—his rich voice lowered to a whisper she found deliriously exciting—"well, it does involve a certain necessary intimacy."

At last, at last, she thought gleefully. "Intimacy don't bother me none, Mr. Hawkins," she encouraged him happily. "I'm real good with intimate jobs."

He hesitated while she held her breath and gazed at his incredible face, marveling at the length and thickness of his eyelashes. Making up his mind, he smiled at her gratefully. Her heart soared. And then he told her.

"It's Mr. McAllister."

"Huh?"

"Mr. McAllister is, ah, overdue for a bath."

Callie stared at him in disbelief, her heart dropping to the vicinity of her knees. "Yer askin' me to give McAllister a bath?"

"It is a bit irregular, I know, to ask such a thing of a young female. But then, I don't imagine you've been sheltered from nature, have you? Besides," he assured her hastily, "I wouldn't dream of this requiring anything like a complete undressing."

"But couldn't somebody else—"

"No one else seems available at the moment. He is in need of the attention, Callie. We've had, uh, a complaint or two about it, you see, and with his good arm still in that sling . . . Well, you can understand the problem. I would help him myself, but Tom Callahan is asking for me again. Of course, if you'd rather not . . ."

It was out of the question! An unthinkable proposal! Lincoln McAllister, of all people! Why, she'd sooner bathe a razorback hog! And then she looked into Gabriel Hawkins's blue eyes with their irresistible appeal, and however outrageous the prospect was, she knew she couldn't bear to have him disappointed in her.

Fifteen minutes later, a towel slung over her shoulder, a bucket of water in either hand, and convinced she was out of her mind, Callie reluctantly approached McAllister where he was seated on a camp stool outside the corral. Looking up from the map he was consulting, he eyed the wooden buckets with amusement.

"Brought me supper, did you?"

"Got that right. I come t'slop the pig."

He laid aside the map. "Care to elaborate?"

"Folks complainin' you've gone ripe, McAllister. Guess you been standin' upwind o' them. This here is bath water, an' I'm aimin' t'apply it."

He grinned at her crookedly. "Were you elected, or did you volunteer?"

"What's it matter?"

"Because if you volunteered . . . well, that makes this an interesting proposition, Callie."

She glowered at him.

"I guess not. I guess you'd still rather shoot me than soap me."

"Oh, yeah," she said with grim pleasure, "but leastways you'll be clean when I finally do put that bullet in you."

"In that case . . ." He got to his feet, his hand on his belt buckle. "Uh, just how far are we talking about here?"

"Down to your drawers."

"Only that far, huh?"

"I ain't aimin' fer the rest, mister."

"Shame."

He stood there expectantly, his fingers still on his belt buckle. "What?" she demanded.

"The other arm is still useless in the sling, Cal-

40

lie. Can't manage this very well on my own."

Swearing under her breath, Callie glanced around. No one was in the vicinity; no one was interested in their activity. They were all busy preparing the evening meal. She banged the buckets down on the ground and moved toward the waiting McAllister, grumbling over what promised to be pure humiliation. She had yet to understand why, out of the whole wagon train, she should be the only one available to bathe him.

He was her enemy. It didn't seem right that she had to help him out of his clothes, touch him in places she didn't even care to think about, much less handle in a familiar way. But that was just what she had to do in the next several minutes as, together, they managed to remove his boots, trousers, and shirt. Worse was to follow. *Much* worse.

It began when he was finally stripped down to his drawers and standing there in front of her practically naked. She was suddenly, bewilderingly aware of his hard, lean masculinity. Of the breadth of his shoulders, the narrowness of his hips, the muscles of his thighs.

Her reaction to his blatant virility was unexpected and totally unwanted. Embarrassed and irritated with herself, she couldn't understand why she should find the sight of him in any way appealing, much less downright riveting. Not when he had killed her pa, not when she despised the very air he breathed. What in sweet tarnation had come over her?

"What's the matter?" he asked with that loathsome little smile. "Don't know where to begin?"

"Ain't nothin' the matter," she growled. "Git down on that stool ag'in where I can reach ya."

All right, she thought as she dipped a sponge into one of the buckets and fiercely lathered it with soap, so he had a fine, strong body. That didn't mean the man inside it was worth any silly flutters in her belly.

"This better?" he said, perching on the stool and offering himself for her assault with the sponge.

She glanced at him, wishing he hadn't spread his legs wide like that. It was disturbing to have to stand between them in order to get at him with the sponge. But she didn't want him imagining anything, so she didn't ask him to shift into a different position.

Instead, grunting her approval, Callie began with his face and neck, scrubbing vigorously with the sponge and wishing it was a brush with stiff wire bristles. She took particular pleasure in punishing those pointy ears of his. If she was hurting him, he didn't complain about it.

She had herself under control now. Or she did, anyway, until she moved to the area of his chest. There was hair there, a black, curling expanse of it. The sight of it, with beads of water clinging to it, started those flutters again deep inside her. And when the side of her hand brushed against his nipple, she got all hot and squirmy.

Don't mean nothin', she thought swiftly. *It's 'cause o' Gabriel. I wanna touch Gabriel in this way, an' on account o' I can't, I'm sufferin' through McAllister. That's all it is.*

"Underarms," he said.

"What?"

"Don't forget my underarms." He lifted his un-injured arm for her attention.

She didn't want to do his underarms. There was something too unsettling about those places. But she couldn't have him know that, so she washed him there as well, taking care around the sling and the bandaged wound.

Those black, sinful eyes of his followed her every stroke with the sponge—aware of her discomfort, taking pleasure in tormenting her.

She was relieved when she finished under his arms and leaned over to reach his back. Her buckskin shirt brushed against his face with the close contact. He sniffed suspiciously.

"Interesting perfume," he observed.

Callie flushed. When the sun was hot, and it had been throughout the day, it awakened the odor of manure that clung faintly to her buck-skins. An unpleasant, embarrassing legacy of her work with Pa.

"Guess I'm not the only one bearing an old stink, huh?"

"Leastways, it's an honest one," she snapped at him. "Not with blood on it, like yours." Why did he have to go and detect the one thing she hated about herself? Had she been able to afford replacements, she would have destroyed these buckskins long ago.

"I'll forgive you that one, Callie. Feels too good getting my back scrubbed to mind how that bel-ligerent little nose of yours twitches every time you blast me with an insult. Thing is, though,

43

you're neglecting another spot around the front here." He indicated his belly. "Think we ought to take care of this."

It was another unsafe area. She drew back in self-defense.

"You have an objection to navels, Callie?"

He was challenging her again, probably hoping she'd end up swooning like some dainty female. As if she ever would, she thought with a sniff.

Adding more soap to the sponge, she attacked his stomach, telling herself it was a form of revenge. It worked—until her hand came in contact with his warm, firm flesh again. There were whorls of black hair around his navel, and they brushed against her fingers, as though deliberately teasing her. The sensation jolted her.

"Ah, perfect," he said in a drowsy, suggestive voice. "Maybe when I get rid of this sling I can return the favor. Treat you to a slow, thorough bath of your own. What do you think, Callie?"

"That you ain't gonna have time fer that."

"That's right, I forgot. As soon as this sling is removed, you're going to fill me with lead. Hey, you haven't finished," he objected when she slapped the sponge into his good hand. "We haven't, uh, figured out how you're going to clean what's under the drawers."

"I'm drawin' the line at yer privates, mister. A lot of one-armed folks manage worse. Let's see if you can match 'em."

"Awkward, but if that's your decision . . ." The grin he wore was positively indecent as he lumbered to his feet, unloosened the tape in the waistband of his drawers, and slid the sponge inside.

A sensible woman would have turned her back on him. But that would have been an invitation for his cynical laughter, and she didn't want to hear that laugh. That was what she told herself anyway, as she watched his hand wrapped around the sponge moving slowly inside the drawers. In the end, mortified by the enticing images of what he might be stroking with that sponge, she lowered her gaze. The result, after all, was his deep, lewd chuckle.

"It's safe now, Callie. You can look."

She did. He was seated again on the stool, nodding toward the sponge he had dropped back into the bucket of soapy water. "Better get started on my legs," he said. "Got a lot of length to cover here."

She didn't want to touch his hard, hair-roughened legs. She didn't want to have anything more to do with this farcical bath. But she had promised the reverend. The sponge was in her hand again, and she was down on the ground and ready to lather his thighs when Gabriel appeared on the scene. There was a hearty smile on his handsome face.

"Any problems? No, I can see this is all going very well. I confess, McAllister, I had my misgivings when you made your request to me."

"What request?" Callie demanded sharply, surging to her feet.

"Why, that you should be the one to bathe him. I'll let you get on with it then."

He left them. Callie, feeling like a brainless little fool, glared down at McAllister, her green eyes blazing. He had deliberately asked that she be the one to bathe him just so he could use the opportunity to tease and taunt her. She was livid. *"You!"*

"You can't kill me, Callie. Not yet. I'm still wearing the sling, remember?"

"Mebbe I can't shoot ya, but I can drown ya!"

Picking up the bucket of rinse water, she dumped its contents over his head, shoved the sponge deep inside the waistband of his soaked drawers, and stormed away.

"Guess this means you're not going to towel me dry, huh?" he called after her.

In reply, she flipped the towel off her shoulder, flung it to the earth, ground it into the dust with her heel, and went on her way.

"Ya got a problem with my cookin'?"

Startled, Callie looked up from her supper plate to find Pearl Slocum's challenging gaze pinned on her. "I ain't got no complaints, Pearl. Yer dishes are always real tasty."

"That so? Then why ain'tcha eatin' that dried beef an' gravy, 'stead o' trailin' yer bread through it like it was day-old mush?"

Callie sighed. "Guess I got no appetite."

"Huh, that don't surprise me, way you been draggin' around camp lately. 'Pears t'me ya got a serious fever."

"I ain't ailin', Pearl."

"Honey lamb, there's fevers, an' there's fevers. An' yer ragin' variety, as I recollect, ya went an' caught from Gabriel Hawkins. Ain't gettin' no better either, is it?"

Callie shook her head sheepishly. "Guess I am a durn lovesick fool. Pearl, what am I gonna do? I keep tryin', but he ain't payin' no mind t'me."

"I ain't gonna be no party to this."

"Pearl, please," Callie begged her.

The redhead considered her plea for a few seconds, then blew out her cheeks in exasperation. "Seems like my life has been one mistake after another, an' here I go makin' the next one. But then, I never could stand t'see a poor dumb critter suffer. All right, ya got my attention."

Callie hunched forward eagerly. "So how do I go 'bout gettin' 'im interested in me?"

"Honey lamb, that oughta been clear from the start."

"Huh?"

"You're a mess, sugar. Ain't no man gonna find you appealin' lookin' like that. Time we got you outta those britches an' into a dress. I figger there's a woman under there somewhere. Let's find 'er an' see what happens when we offer 'er to the reverend."

Pearl's intention made Callie nervous. She had no experience being a woman, not the kind of woman Pearl was talking about. There had never been a need to be feminine; no man had ever been serious about her, or she about him—until now.

"Dunno, Pearl. I ain't exactly been in touch with that side o' me. Not lately, anyhow. Haven't been inside skirts in years. Don't even own a dress."

"I got me a trunk full. Know how to alter one of 'em, too. You willin'?"

Callie was in love and desperate, but there was something else. From the start she had admired Pearl Slocum in all her flamboyant finery, totally unmindful of its vulgarity, and the possibility of looking anywhere near that magnificent herself was awesome. She made up her mind. "I'm willin'."

"Then we're in business." Pearl got to her feet to add more buffalo chips to the fire. "Thing is, just puttin' you in skirts don't mean nothin' by itself. I'm figgerin' we need us an event t'get you all fancied up fer. Present ya, so to speak."

"Like what event, Pearl?"

"A party. Yeah, a real good-time party with dancin'."

"Pearl—"

" 'Course, there's gotta be a reason fer a party like that. Otherwise, the reverend might not go fer it."

"Pearl—"

"Too bad the Fourth o' July ain't here. Folks go wild when it comes t'celebratin' the Fourth." She was thoughtful for a few seconds. "Favorite holiday, huh? Well now, I think I just got me an inspiration fer that party. No need t'go into the particulars now, though, 'cause—"

"*Pearl,* you ain't listenin' t'me."

"Well, spit it out then."

"I can't dance."

Pearl stared at her. " 'Course you can. Everybody knows how t'dance."

48

"Not me. Leastways, not so's you'd call it dancin'. Never been to a real dance."

"All right. Then it's time we corrected that. I can teach ya some steps. 'Nough t'git by, anyway. Can't please a man lessen yer in his arms."

"Dancin'?"

"To start with. As t'what follows . . . well, guess we'd better leave that fer another discussion."

Callie, having second thoughts about her friend's proposed metamorphosis for her, began to panic. "Pearl, I'm scared. Lookit me. I ain't exactly material fer beautifyin'."

Hands on hips, the redhead gazed at her severely. "Honey lamb," she promised. "Time I'm finished with you, yer gonna be a sensation. An' we're gonna catch us a preacher."

Chapter Three

It was the most god-awful sight Linc had ever seen. Callie Burgess sashaying along the sandy floor of a dry ravine in a set of wide, fashionable hoops!

The thing that made it absurd were the buckskins. She still wore them. There were no skirts, no petticoats, just the bare frame of the hoops swinging from her waist, as if her pugnacious little figure had been encased in a bird cage.

Hunkered down on the edge of the ravine, Linc chewed on a long blade of grass and idly watched the comedy below. He wouldn't have missed this for anything.

"Come on," Pearl called to her pupil, "mosey toward me ag'in. Only this time put a little sass in it."

"I feel like a durn fool in this contraption!" Callie complained.

"Honey lamb, if you don' git over bein' awkward 'bout it, ain't no way yer gonna manage the night o' the dance. Now just come t'me easy-like."

Callie sauntered toward the redhead with a slow, exaggerated sway of her hips.

"Good, real good," Pearl encouraged her. "Make 'em think y'got somethin' worth dyin' fer under them hoops. What're you stoppin' fer?"

"Him!" Callie had come to a halt, her face flaming with embarrassment as she realized that the ravine was not as secluded as she'd imagined and that Lincoln was a witness to their private rehearsal.

"Pay 'im no mind," Pearl advised.

Linc took the blade of grass out of his mouth and grinned down at them. "Yes, just forget I'm here."

"Go away!" Callie shouted, hoping he would return to the wagon train, which was camped for the evening a few hundred yards away along the banks of the Little Blue River.

"Can't," he said casually, indicating his arm in the sling. "It's time for Pearl to change my dressing. But there's no hurry about it. You go on with your practicing."

He settled down on the rim of the ravine, prepared to wait. He knew Callie was incensed by his presence. It was deliberate, of course, calculated to keep her off balance. He figured that, if he continued to plague her like this at every

51

opportunity, she would be diverted from her intention to kill him long enough for him to get out of this sling, obtain what he was here for, and ride away from the wagon train still in one piece.

Except that if he pushed her too far, there was always the risk she would shoot him anyway, sling or no sling. On the other hand, if he ignored her, didn't keep her busy with his taunts, she would have time to brood about him and maybe not wait to kill him. Either way it was a gamble.

Linc refused to admit to himself that there might be another, clearer reason for his teasing—that, quite simply, he was enjoying himself. But it was impossible for him to entertain the notion that he might find the ridiculous Callie Burgess interesting on any level.

What Linc hadn't considered was that Callie refused to be a spectacle for his amusement. She proved that when she retrieved her Remington from where she had placed it behind a patch of oxeye daisies.

Whipping the rifle up to her shoulder, she aimed it at him with a sweet-voiced, "Sure would be obliged, mister, if you'd wait back at camp 'til Pearl can git there."

Gazing at the deadly muzzle of the rifle, he nodded slowly. "Believe at that I would be more comfortable in camp."

"Thought y'might."

She kept the rifle on him as he got to his feet and ambled toward the wagons. He chuckled to himself. If she thought he was intimidated by her, she was mistaken. He simply didn't want to risk anybody getting needlessly hurt, especially himself.

Callie glared after the retreating McAllister, wishing she could fill that arrogant backside of his with lead. But she couldn't. Not when he was defenseless, not when her shining Gabriel needed the bastard to guide the wagons. Oh, hell!

Pearl was growing impatient. "Ya gonna go on standin' there mutterin' over McAllister, or are we gittin' back t'business here?"

Callie put down her rifle. "I'm willin'. It's these hoops what ain't. They keep fightin' me. Pearl, you sure I need 'em?"

"If y'wanna be stylish fer Hawkins, y'do. Now let's try that waltz again I taughtcha."

For the next several minutes, with Pearl humming a popular melody while acting as her partner, Callie concentrated on the steps, dipping, turning, and this time managing not to stumble over her own feet. She was making progress, but one thing worried her.

"Pearl, you sure I oughta be doin' what you keep tellin' me I gotta do come time fer me t'dance with a man?"

"They like it," Pearl insisted.

"But I ain't never seen dancin' like that. I mean, where a woman rubs up ag'inst a man while they's movin' real close."

"Ya gotta give 'em a little sugar."

Callie didn't argue with her. After all, Pearl was experienced in the art of seduction so she must know what she was talking about. And if

53

men expected this sort of intimacy on the dance floor, then it must be acceptable.

Whatever it took to please Gabriel she was willing to do, but the road to alluring femininity was sure a tough one.

"Pearl," Callie said when they were taking a rest between measures, "got somethin' else t'ask ya. This here Oregon Freedom Day next week. That's the official date when Oregon got admitted t'the Union, only as a territory an' not as a state, right?"

Pearl snorted. "Now how'd I know 'bout somethin' like that?"

Callie stared at her. "But y'got everybody on the train excited 'bout it. All whipped up t'celebrate. They figger as how they oughta honor the freedom day of the land that's gonna be their new home. Are you sayin'—"

Pearl chuckled. "Yeah, I sorta made it up. Had to have some excuse fer a fancy dance, didn't I? But don't you worry 'bout it none. Could be there is a real Oregon Freedom Day. An' if not—" She shrugged. "Well, one just got born, and yer gonna be its center of attention."

Callie's hoops were no longer bare bones the night of the Oregon Freedom Day dance. The skeleton had been covered with flesh in the form of lacy petticoats and the ball gown Pearl had altered for her. And as far as Callie could tell, not having had the opportunity yet to look in the mirror, that silky flesh was a success, though she wasn't certain about the woman wearing it.

She could hardly contain her excitement

while she sat perched on a stool, a protective towel draped over her front as Pearl worked on her hair and face by the flickering light of a pair of oil lanterns.

"Stop yer squirmin'," Pearl commanded in her husky voice. "Be a fine sight if this here rouge ends up on yer chin and ears 'stead of yer mouth an' cheeks."

"Sorry, Pearl. I reckon it's this corset. Never wore one afore, an' these laces is awful tight."

"Need t'be. Otherwise, yer bosom wouldn't swell up enough."

"Pearl, what if it swells up right outta the top o' this neckline? Feels like it could."

"Yer safe—long as ya don't suck too deep a breath."

Callie concentrated on breathing carefully while she anticipated the evening ahead. She couldn't see the corral blazing with lanterns and campfires. Pearl had hung quilts over a line to give them privacy while they dressed, but she could hear the fiddlers tuning their instruments and the babble of voices inside the circle of wagons.

This was their first night beside the Platte River. It was a clear evening, the air mild, the sky thick with stars. Perfect weather for a major celebration, except—

"Pearl, what if somebody goes an' finds out this ain't the day Oregon got itself declared a territory? What if somebody already knows?"

"Then they woulda said, wouldn't they? Quit yer frettin' 'bout it. Only thing troublin' me," she muttered, dipping into the rouge pot, "is some

55

o' those louts is so happy 'bout Oregon's fine freedom, they been secretly nippin' since noon. Probably a little too eager by now, an' the Reverend Mr. Hawkins won't like that."

At the mention of Gabriel, everything else went out of Callie's head but her longing for his reaction when he laid eyes on her transformation. What would he say, how would he look? She could hardly wait for the moment.

For that matter, she was eager to view herself. But Pearl went on fussing over her for endless minutes. She was ready to bust her stays with impatience before the redhead pronounced her finished.

"Go and greet yerself, honey lamb," she said, whipping the towel from Callie's shoulders.

Pearl's most prized possession was a looking glass in a fancy gilt frame. The long mirror was propped up against the lowered tailboard of her wagon. Rising from the stool, Callie floated toward it. Long hours of practice enabled her by now to manage the hoops without difficulty. At least none that was apparent since the spreading skirts concealed any lingerging awkwardness.

She approached the mirror with a breathless apprehension. Would she be pleased with the results, or would she look like the world's worst fool? She felt like one as she peered into the glass, her stomach queasy from anxiety.

Oh, my!

For a long moment she stood rooted there in silent disbelief. She didn't recognize herself. How could she when that dazzling creature staring back at her was a stranger? This couldn't be Callie Burgess.

But it was her sure enough. Callie was awed. Overjoyed. Blinded by the miracle that Pearl had achieved.

The gown was a glossy, shimmering satin. *Red* satin. Not one of those tame, washed-out reds either but the kind of flaming scarlet that was certain to get a man's attention. And if that didn't succeed, the bodice would. It was so tight and low-cut that Callie wasn't sure where her skin ended and the dress began.

As for the skirts . . . well, they were about as elegant as skirts could be. Layers and layers of flounces and every one of them covered all over with silver loops and bows and crystal beads that winked in the glow of the lanterns.

There were plenty of other things that sparkled too. Callie's bare arms, throat, and ears were adorned with jewels of every size and hue. Of course, they weren't real jewels, but Callie knew they made a grand display just the same.

Why, Pearl had even wound strands of jewels in her hair. That hair was something all right! Pearl had tortured her wild russet length into a mass of curls and ringlets piled high on her head and crowned with a glittery star.

And her face . . . her face was beyond description. No longer was it freckled and ordinary. Her skin was smooth and white, her cheeks pink, her lips a sultry red. Pearl had done things with her eyes too. Things that made them mysterious and inviting.

"Oh, Pearl," Callie whispered, "I look just like one o' them fairy-tale princesses!"

Pearl, less splendid in emerald taffeta but equally impressive, was pleased. "Told you there was somethin' temptin' hidin' under them buckskins."

"An' you went and uncovered it fer me, Pearl. You sure enough did." She turned away from the mirror. "Only—"

"You got somethin' that don't satisfy you?"

"Oh, no, Pearl. Everything is real smart an' stylish."

"But?"

"Uh, you suppose I could have a dab of yer perfume? Seems t'call fer it. 'Sides," she confessed shyly, "I got this powerful fondness fer perfume. Always did."

Pearl chuckled. "Now how did a rough little darlin' like you end up with a female weakness like that?"

"Don't know. I figger it coulda had somethin' t'do with the manure business Pa and me had. All that handlin' o' stuff that were a long ways from bein' sweet. Anyways, I never let on 'bout my cravin' back in Horizon. They woulda tormented me somethin' fierce 'bout it."

Pearl nodded. "An' you had a reputation t'preserve."

"Well, bein' tough was the only way I knew t'survive. But this one time when I was a girl," she confided in a dreamy voice, "a customer o' Pa's gave me this little bottle o' scent. I didn't dare t'wear it, but I used t'take out the stopper when no one was lookin' an' just sniff at the stuff.

It were heaven. Kept it fer a long time. Leastways, 'til it all dried up."

"You tryin' t'make me bawl with them sad stories o' yours?" Pearl said gruffly. "Here, help
yourself." She produced her perfume from the
cosmetics box and handed it to Callie.

Callie removed the stopper and liberally applied the strong fragrance to several areas of her
bare skin.

"Easy with that," Pearl cautioned her. "Yer
s'pposed t'entice 'em, not drug 'em."

"Pearl, am I gonna entice the right man?"

"Let's hope so." She slid an encouraging arm
around Callie's waist. "But I know one thing fer
sure. Folks out there is gonna be in fer a real
surprise when they lay eyes on you."

Pearl was right. Callie did make a big impression
at the dance, though not exactly what they'd
planned. Her night of triumph encountered its
first problem the minute the two of them entered the corral arm in arm. There to challenge
them was a gaggle of women led by a pinch-
faced female with a figure as straight as a stick.
And just as flat.

Miss Parthenia Smyth prided herself that she
was not one of the wagon train's lost or battered
souls. She was a qualified teacher who had been
engaged to fulfill a position in Agatha Delaney's
new school. Miss Smyth was traveling to Oregon
for that purpose, no other, and her standards
were rigid ones. The five women with her, who
had become her loyal supporters even though
none of them had histories any more refined

than Pearl's or Callie's, admired Parthenia and were influenced by her.

When these women caught sight of Callie in all her garish, bosom-baring splendor, their shock was immediate and severe. They expressed it with gasps and various exclamations of outrage.

"She's wearing face paint!"

"*And* vulgar jewelry!"

"Not to mention that indecent neckline!"

"Wicked, all of it!"

Callie was stunned, Pearl incensed. Releasing Callie so that she could plant her hands on her hips, Pearl returned their fire, blasting them with a truth they would have preferred to forget.

"Well, if this don't beat all! Minnie Bird, I seem t'recollect you comin' outta the same house we once worked in together back in Chicago! Only difference is, you got kicked out fer bein' deceitful with the management, an' I got praised fer bein' straight with 'em. And you, Hattie Jackson! I hear tell you traveled a leaky riverboat on the Ohio, cheating folks at cards!

"What you smirkin' at, Flo Petrie? Everybody knows you lived in a shack down along the river in St. Louis, selling cheap liquor t'men whose pockets you went through when they was too drunk t'stand! You ain't no better than Minnie or Hattie! And neither are the rest o' you! So I'll thank all you respectable ladies not t'be givin' yerself airs you ain't earned!"

The women looked chagrined—all but Parthenia Smyth, who responded with a frigid, "My friends have changed because of the promise of new lives in Oregon. I suggest that both of you consider doing the same because I warn you, we won't tolerate any of your disreputable conduct here. Come, ladies."

The virtuous flock sailed away across the corral, leaving Callie hurt and bewildered. "Pearl, is there somethin' wrong with the way I look? 'Cause I figgered they'd be admirin' me."

" 'Course they do. But bein' a bunch o' jealous cats, they ain't gonna show it."

Privately, Pearl was concerned. Maybe this evening wasn't going to be as perfect for Callie as she'd planned. She frowned after the women, deciding that she'd better stay close to them. If they had trouble on their minds, she intended to prevent it. She patted Callie on the arm with an encouraging smile.

"Look, honey lamb, you don't need me anymore. You just go an' enjoy yerself."

Before Callie could stop her, the redhead drifted away in the direction of the departing women. Left alone, Callie was an instant target. Parthenia Smyth and her female supporters might not have approved of her, but the lusty young males on the wagon train lost no time in swarming around her eagerly.

"You sure are an eyeful in that dress, Callie."

"Warm evening. Let me get you a refreshment."

"They're fixin' to call the first dance. How about you steppin' out with me?"

They jostled and jockeyed to get close to her. Who would have thought that Callie Burgess, of all people, could turn out looking like this? And who would have guessed that hiding under those buckskins was this pair of luscious breasts fairly popping out of the red satin? Made a man go a little wild just gazing at them. Whooee!

Callie glowed, pleased by their attention. But there was only one man she wanted to impress. Where was he? She searched the gathering, but Gabriel was nowhere to be seen.

"Where's Mr. Hawkins?" she asked.

"Oh, he's gone to see to the wagon master. All the noise of the celebrating has got Tom Callahan restless."

Callie tried not to show her disappointment. "Ain't he gonna join us?"

"He'll be along when Callahan is quiet again. How about that dance?"

Several men around the camp led out their partners as the fiddlers began to saw a lively rendition of "Arkansas Traveler." Callie was eager to test her skills on the floor, but she shook her head. She wanted her first real dance to be memorable, and only one man could give her that. She would wait for Gabriel.

The young buck who had promised her a refreshment arrived breathlessly at her elbow and handed her a tin cup. "Here you go, Callie."

Accepting the cup, she started to drink from it. Then she paused, sniffing at its contents. "What's in here?" she asked suspiciously.

"It's just a lemonade punch, Callie."

"Ya certain o' that?" Unlike her pa, Callie had no head for liquor. Besides, she didn't want to risk offending Gabriel.

"Well, maybe a few spices," the young buck said innocently. "Nothing more'n that."

With her head lowered over the cup, Callie didn't see him wink at the others, who elbowed each other knowingly. She sipped the punch, too distracted by her longing for the Reverend Mr. Hawkins's arrival to know what she was tasting.

Her admirers kept pestering her to dance with them, all the while ogling her bosom. She ignored them and continued to scan the faces on all sides, afraid she would miss Gabriel. What was keeping him?

Callie went rigid when her roving gaze collided with Lincoln McAllister's. He was leaning negligently against a wagon on the far side of the corral. She had the uneasy feeling he had been watching her for some time and that he found the sight of her in her scarlet gown vastly amusing. He saluted her with a wolfish grin. Flushing in irritation, she turned away, resolved to put him out of her mind. She didn't want that varmint spoiling her evening.

The third dance was under way, and Callie, working on her second cup of punch, was on fire with impatience when Gabriel Hawkins finally appeared. His curiosity aroused by the crowd of males still collecting around Callie, he came to investigate.

"What's all the excitement here, gentlemen?"

"Let the reverend through," Callie demanded, trying to shove them out of the way. They fell back reluctantly, making a path.

She could see the amazement on Gabriel's

face when she was finally revealed to him. "Callie, is that you?"

"It's me all right, Mr. Hawkins."

She gazed at him nervously, waiting for his praise. He had never looked so handsome to her, tall and straight, his fair hair gleaming in the lantern light, his sky-blue eyes wide with disbelief. Shoot, he even smelled good, not like that skunk, McAllister. Probably tasted good too, though she guessed that was something she oughtn't to be thinking about. Leastways, not yet.

He wasn't saying anything. She prompted him with a shy, "Ya like it, Mr. Hawkins?"

"I hardly know what to think. It's, uh, very provocative."

Was that good? Callie thought it sounded good. The young bucks watching them had leers on their faces. She paid no attention to them, hoping Gabriel would ask her now to dance. When he didn't, when he just stood there staring at her, she helped him out with a bold, "Ain't danced yet, Mr. Hawkins. Been savin' my first one fer you."

Was that embarrassment she read on his perfect features? No, it couldn't be. Because he was going to tell her how pleased he was by her sacrifice. He was going to smile and lead her out for the next dance. It was going to happen.

But it didn't happen. Before he could offer his invitation, one of the women arrived on the scene. "Excuse me, Mr. Hawkins, but the wagon master is asking for you again."

"Then I must go back and comfort him." He

apologized to Callie. "I wish I could partner you, Callie, but it's not to be. Perhaps the next time."

He spoke with such earnest regret that Callie knew she was only imagining the relief in his eyes. She watched him go off with the woman who had brought him the message. She could have cried with disappointment. Why couldn't the wagon master hurry up and get well? It would solve all her problems. Then Gabriel would be available again, and she could get rid of that devil, McAllister.

"Now will you dance with me?" persisted the young man who stood closest to her.

"And I'm next," spoke up another admirer.

"Oh, all right," she said ungraciously, unaware that by this time she was beginning to slur her words a little.

She permitted herself to be led out into the center of the wagon-encircled camp, where the hard-packed earth served as a floor. Her partner's name was Caleb. She remembered hearing how proud he was of his thick moustache. At this point she was so depressed, she didn't care if he had a pointed beard and horns. She was grateful, however, that her first dance should turn out to be a waltz. Callie had gotten pretty good at waltzing.

They had taken a couple of turns around the floor when she suddenly remembered Pearl's instructions to her during their practice sessions. Give them a little sugar. That's what Pearl had called it.

Caleb was holding her so close that it wasn't difficult to wriggle her bosom against his thin chest. She heard him gulp, and his face turned a shade of deep red.

"What's a'matter?" she demanded. "Ain't I doin' it right?"

"Oh, yeah, Callie, you're doin' jest fine."

"Well, then, why ya lookin' so peculiar?"

"Jest wonderin' if I can have the next dance."

But there were too many others eager to have their turn with her. She gave each of them the sugar Pearl had advised. Why they should be so pleased by it Callie couldn't understand. It didn't affect her in the least, though she did enjoy the music and the steps. She even began to be cheerful about Gabriel, thinking he would turn up again and notice her popularity. Maybe he'd be jealous and insist she dance with him. That possibility excited her.

But Gabriel didn't reappear as she went on executing polkas and quadrilles and waltzes. The dancing made her hot so, when it was pressed on her again, she drank more lemon punch to cool down.

"This punch sure is popular with the young men," one of the women in charge of the refreshment table remarked to Pearl.

"Huh?" Pearl, who had been kept busy monitoring Parthenia Smyth and her supporters, paid little attention to the comment.

"They seem to empty the bowl almost as fast as I refill it," the woman explained.

This caught Pearl's attention. "What's in there?"

"Why, just lemonade and a few spices."

"Lemme sample that stuff." She sipped from

the dipper the woman handed to her. After one taste, she threw the dipper back into the bowl in disgust. "Them rascals been slipping whiskey in there when yer back was turned."

The woman stared at her, appalled.

"An' they been urgin' that brew on Callie like it was water."

Alarmed, Pearl looked around. Parthenia Smyth and her scandalized hens had had their heads together for some time, buzzing over the activity on the dance floor. But there had been no action from them. Until now.

While Pearl had been busy testing the punch, Parthenia had slipped away from her group. At this second she was storming like a crusader toward Callie and her current partner. Pearl made an effort to go to her friend's rescue, but there were too many dancers in her way. Frustrated, she found herself trapped among them.

The righteous Parthenia Smyth reached her objective, quivering with indignation. "This obscenity is intolerable!"

Callie's partner was too busy enjoying her cleavage to take notice of Parthenia's interruption, but Callie minded it. She didn't know what *obscenity* meant, but she was certain it was something nasty.

"Whatcha mean by—Hey, lemme go!" She paused to remove herself from her partner's arms. He let her go, his glazed eyes indicating he was in no condition to argue about it. Once free, Callie gave her full attention to Parthenia while her partner sneaked off to the punch bowl. "You tryin' t'tell me sumpthin'?"

"Young woman, your performance is brazen and lewd, a disgrace to this whole celebration! I demand that you take yourself back to your wagon this instant and—"

"Afraid she can't do that, ma'am," came a deep, raspy voice from off to the side. "Miss Burgess has promised this next waltz to me, and I intend to collect it."

Startled, both women stared at the tall, lean figure of Lincoln McAllister, who had arrived on the scene unnoticed. Callie's mouth fell open in surprise, but no words came out. Her head was spinning a little by now, probably from a combination of the warm evening and too much dancing. It didn't seem possible that skunk, McAllister, should come to her defense, so this couldn't actually be happening.

It was Parthenia who found her voice first. "That's absurd. Your arm is in a sling. How can you possibly dance with it?"

"Oh, I'll manage just fine with one arm. Unless," he added smoothly, the dark-eyed gaze he directed at her suddenly looking lethal, "you have some further objection. You don't, do you, ma'am?"

Parthenia started to sputter and then, as his gaze narrowed dangerously, she thought better of it. "I suppose you know what you're doing."

"I'm not certain I do, ma'am, but whatever it is, it ought to be entertaining. Now, if you'll excuse us—"

Before Callie could stop him, his good arm had firmly encircled her waist and he was whirling her into the "Barbara Allen" waltz.

Pearl, from where she had been trapped on the other side of the corral, watched Callie being swept way. She wasn't sure whether to be relieved that McAllister had saved her friend from trouble or whether to be worried that Callie had just gone from the frying pan into the fire.

"All right, McAllister," Callie demanded when she could speak again, "what's yer game?"

Linc wondered that himself. He had been observing her performance from the sidelines, amused by it and not caring a damn that she'd been naively waltzing her way to certain disaster. Then why had he impulsively come to the rescue of this little hellion, who was bad enough in buckskins but absolutely ridiculous decked out like a Bourbon Street whore? It worried him.

It worried him even more that he found the sight of her half-exposed bosom so mesmerizing. His gaze kept straying in that direction, marveling at the pair of lush breasts that had been concealed all this while under a baggy buckskin shirt.

Tempting, he thought, and then realized that this intimate situation was probably a mistake. On the other hand, she could use a little fresh shaking up. Just to keep her in line. His intended warning had absolutely nothing to do with a concern for her, because of course her welfare was unimportant to him. That decided, he was ready to answer her challenge.

"Is that all the gratitude I'm going to get for saving your overdressed little hide from that dragon out for blood?"

Callie hiccoughed and then scowled up at him. "Overdressed?"

"As a Christmas tree. And I don't suppose you know what that is, do you, my sweet little ignoramus? But take my word for it, you look like one."

She tossed her head so that her gaudy eardrops flashed. "Mr. Hawkins reckons I look just fine. He told me so."

"Yes, the saintly Gabriel wouldn't have the courage to give you the truth. But I do, and I say you look like a Christmas tree. One with too many trimmings." He sniffed suspiciously. "And what's that smell? Is it supposed to be perfume?"

"Whus wrong with my perfume?"

"It's about as subtle as the rest of you." He chuckled. "There it goes again, that little nose of yours twitching in indignation."

Callie hated it when he used words like *subtle* and *indignation*. Words she didn't understand but which she was convinced weren't meant to be flattering. "You turn me loose, ya buzzard! I ain't aimin' t'go on dancin' with you!"

In response, his arm tightened on her waist like a steel band. Under her anger it amazed her that he could manage to partner her so effectively with one arm in a sling. She vaguely wondered if the poignant strains of "Barbara Allen" had something to do with that. It was such a beautiful waltz.

"Not yet," he insisted. "We haven't decided whether that outfit would benefit from some lighted candles perched on the flounces."

"I tol' ya that Mr. Hawkins—"

"And I told you he lied to you," he said swiftly, "even if he is a preacher. As for the women . . . they aren't glaring at you out of envy but out of disapproval."

It was one thing for him to insult her appearance, but Callie wouldn't stand for his attacking Gabriel again. "Yer the one who's a black liar. Mr. Hawkins is pure an' decent an'—an'—"

"Honorable?" One of Linc's thick black eyebrows elevated sardonically. "Yes, I'm sure he is. That's why he's let all these drunken louts ogle and paw you tonight." Why did it aggravate him that she'd been displaying herself for every lusty male gaze on the wagon train? "Not that you don't deserve it after your profane performance with them."

There he went again, Callie thought, using one of them fancy words. Didn't seem right that a snake like McAllister had knowledge of words like that.

Well, she was as good as he was, even if she didn't have his book-learning. She proved it by defending herself with a haughty, "I ain't been nothin' but a lady all evenin'."

He laughed caustically. "And I believe in fairies and Oregon Freedom Day."

He shook her with that one. "Whatcha mean?"

"Sugar, those maneuvers you've been practicing with your partners are about as ladylike as Oregon Freedom Day is a genuine holiday. Oh, don't worry. I'm not going to tell anyone. I don't give a damn what this wagon train chooses to celebrate."

Callie had been fearing this. Drat him for being the one to find them out! "Listen, Pearl knows lots o'things, an' Pearl says—"

"Pearl Slocum invented Oregon Freedom Day for tonight the same as she invented you. She's a harlot, maybe a well-meaning one, but a harlot just the same, and she's got you dressed up and behaving like one yourself because she doesn't know any better."

"That ain't—"

"True? Oh, but it is, Callie, and it's about time somebody told you before you cause a riot. What do you think is going to happen if you keep on encouraging these men like you've been doing? They already consider you available for some wild sport."

"I ain't encouragin' nobody."

"Oh, for—" He exhaled loudly in exasperation. "What do you call this then?"

Sliding his arm out of the sling so it wouldn't be in the way, he hauled her up roughly and tightly against his chest. Before she could object, he began to slowly rub his hard body against her breasts. As a demonstration of blatant seduction, it was a success. As an exercise in self-control, it was an enormous failure.

Linc's reaction was immediate and unexpected. Her softness was so hot, so tantalizing, that a wanton flame licked through his gut and traveled to his groin where he could feel himself instantly aroused. He fought a desperate urge to stroke her breasts until her nipples went taut in response to him, and an even more untamed desire to lower his mouth and taste her naked flesh.

Callie Burgess, of all people! Hell, she was nothing but a brat! What was wrong with him, anyway?

Callie was equally stunned by her own reaction. Nothing like this had happened when she'd pressed herself against her other partners. This sudden roaring in her ears! Her sensitive breasts going all tender and swollen with an unexplained yearning! A weakness and a willingness seeping through her insides, as if—

This was terrible! Nature must be playing a trick on her! That's all it was! Nothing else could explain such sinful feelings being awakened in her by Lincoln McAllister, the man who was her sworn enemy!

Callie had hated him before this. Now her hate was intensified by this cruel joke, almost like the one her body had betrayed her with when she'd been made to bathe him, only this time worse. Why had she ever permitted him to dance with her?

"Turn me loose!" she demanded, trembling with a combination of anger and fear. "Turn me loose, ya cur, and don'tcha ever touch me ag'in!"

Linc, equally shaken by an intimacy that had backfired on him, was happy to oblige. Releasing her, he worked his arm back into the sling. Oblivious to the other dancers eddying around them, they stood there gazing at each other for a few seconds in a smoldering silence.

Then, with a lopsided smile, he lifted his good hand to his forehead and tossed her a mocking little salute. Swinging around, he squeezed his way through the dancers back to the safety of the sidelines. Never before, not even in his misguided military career, had he been so relieved to retreat from a campaign.

Left behind on the dance floor, Callie stood there slightly swaying from side to side as she struggled with her bewilderment. What on earth was the matter with her? She felt weak in the knees, and her head was swimming. Maybe what she needed was another cup of that punch.

"How 'bout you finishing up this one with me, Callie?"

"Huh?"

"The 'Barbara Allen.' They're still playing it. You're free now, ain't you?"

He had appeared suddenly at her elbow. She turned her head and tried to focus on him. It was Caleb, the one with the moustache he was so proud of. "Oh, sure, sure," she told him with a swift desperation. Anything to put that alarming encounter with Lincoln McAllister behind her. She would show McAllister it hadn't mattered.

She went into Caleb's waiting arms. They danced in silence, and she was so distracted that for a few seconds she failed to realize that he was squeezing himself against her bosom. When she did become aware of his action, a warning went off inside her fuzzy head. It wasn't altogether clear. She just knew that she couldn't submit herself to this kind of treatment ever again.

"Whatcha doin'? Stop it!"

"You liked it before."

"Well, I don't now." Damn McAllister for spoiling everything!

"Sure you do," he said eagerly.

He tried again to rub himself against her. When she attempted to push him away, he laughed and resisted. Furious now that he and the others had no more respect for her than McAllister had implied, she doubled up a small fist and smacked him so forcefully against his chest that he stumbled back into one of the other couples. The hothead he fell against, fueled by the spiked punch—as were most of the young rowdies by now—was in no mood to regard the collision as an accident.

"You bastard, who you shovin'?"

"Bastard yourself!"

For the life of her, Callie couldn't remember afterwards who delivered the first punch or exactly whose jaw it connected with. She just knew that all out of nowhere fists were flying in every direction. A *lot* of fists, because the other bucks had gleefully joined the fray. Those fists were accompanied by masculine obscenities and wild yells and feminine squeals and screams.

Callie stood there in the middle of what had become a wholesale brawl, helpless and distraught as she watched her beautiful evening being destroyed.

"Stop this!" shouted a familiar rich voice. "Stop it at once, I say!"

The Reverend Gabriel Hawkins fought his way through the battling warriors. Callie glowed as she realized he was coming to her rescue. He never made it. A set of misdirected knuckles caught him squarely on the nose. He went down, spurting blood from his nostrils.

No longer helpless, no longer anything but outraged that these clods had dared to attack her beloved, Callie abandoned all pretense of ladyhood and tore into them with a ferocious vengeance.

"Lunkheads, jackasses!" she howled, blistering the air with her curses. "Time a body taught-cha some manners!" Which was precisely what Callie intended to accomplish as she furiously swung, slugged, and slammed at whoever got in her way.

Linc, calmly observing the scene from the sidelines, saw no reason to get involved. Where Callie was concerned, he'd had quite enough contact for one evening. Any further encounter would have been downright risky. He was still recovering from the latest one.

Besides, he rather enjoyed the sight of her savagely defending her precious Gabriel Hawkins, who was still pinned to the ground. As a matter of fact—

Linc ducked to avoid a flying missile, which crashed into the side of the wagon where he'd been leaning.

—As a matter of fact, the little wildcat was quite impressive. To her credit, her opponents seemed to be getting the worst of it. Their startled faces and staggering bodies were receiving her blows on all sides, although—

Linc dodged another bottle that sailed in his direction.

—Although her appearance suffered as much

punishment as her adversaries. Her cherished scarlet-satin gown was torn and bloodied, and her hair hung in wild ringlets, beads spilling from her necklace, an eardrop missing, makeup smeared. Poor Callie.

Linc grinned.

No, the evening wasn't a social success. On the other hand, in the absence of fireworks, he would have to say that the spectacle of Callie Burgess made quite an interesting climax to this so-called celebration of Oregon Freedom Day. He, for one, would certainly remember it.

Chapter Four

Callie groaned, holding her throbbing head between her hands as she sat curled up in a tight ball outside the tent she shared with Pearl. That was as far as she'd been able to crawl last night when she'd still been able to function. This morning every movement was agony. Just raising herself into a vertical position on the blanket where she had spent the night was excruciating. Every muscle in her limbs objected to the effort.

"Pearl," she croaked, "ya s'ppose a body could die just by wishin' fer it?"

"Whyn't ya try this instead?"

The redhead handed her a cloth soaked in cool water and vinegar. Squeezing her eyes shut against the blinding glare of the sun fresh over the horizon, Callie applied the pad to her brow. It was soothing but hardly the relief she prayed for. Remembering Pa and all his mornings-after, she guessed she would be suffering like this at least until noon.

Standing over her, Pearl thought sympathetically, *She sure is a mess. Black eye, scraped nose, and a beauty of a swollen lip. And that's just what I can see.*

Callie cautiously opened her good eye and looked up at her. "Know sumpthin', Pearl? I think somebody sneaked hard likker inta that lemon punch."

"You just figgered that out, did ya?" Pearl said dryly.

"Wish I'd knowed. I ain't got no head at'all fer likker. Wonder I didn't pass out straight off. I'm sure sorry fer the dress bein' ruined."

"Don't matter."

Callie was silent for a moment, contemplating the situation. "Truth is, Pearl, I'm havin' me a tough time rememberin' all that did happen. Guess I got a bit carried away, huh?"

"Ya might say that."

"I don't mind 'bout the others, but—" Her face puckered with mortification. "Well, Mr. Hawkins. He's gotta be thinkin' sumpthin' awful 'bout me."

"Oh, I wouldn't worry none 'bout it."

Callie opened the other eye and gazed at her pleadingly. "Pearl, I can't stand it. He's just gotta know how sorry I am, an' bein' in no condition t'go t'him myself . . ."

"Fergit it. He's likely already fergiven ya. He's a preacher, ain't he?"

Pearl had no wish to approach Gabriel Hawkins, either on behalf of her friend or otherwise.

Jean Barrett

There was something about the reverend that made her uneasy when she was near him, though she didn't understand why. She just knew that she preferred a limited contact with him.

Callie sighed. "Reckon I don't have a call t'ask it. Not when ya already been so good t'me. But, see, Pearl, the thing is . . ."

"What?"

"Well, I ain't never had a sister, or a female friend neither," she confided. "Leastways, none I trusted t'tell things to. Yer the first, so I reckon I'm just a bit eager 'bout that. Ya gotta be patient with me 'til I learn not t'overdo it."

There she goes again, Pearl thought. *Choking me all up with her gratitude. How am I s'pposed to turn her down when she keeps gazin' at me like a puppy dog?*

"If it takes me carryin' yer excuses t'Hawkins t'make ya quit lookin' so pitiful," she said brusquely, "then it seems like I ain't got a choice."

"Oh, Pearl, that's awful good o'ya!"

"Ain't it, though."

She had been boiling water over the fire in order to brew their morning coffee. Now, not wanting to delay her errand, she removed the pot from the tripod. Breakfast would have to wait until her return. She started to leave, but Callie stopped her with one last pathetic plea.

"Pearl, 'bout last night . . . what did I go an do t'make it all so bad? I been tryin', but I can't seem t'figger it out."

"Weren't you what made the mistake, honey lamb."

"Huh?"

"Look, quit worryin' 'bout it. Ain't that head o'yours already got enough t'bust it?"

Me, thought Pearl as she left their wagon and went in search of Gabriel. *I'm the one what got it wrong.*

She saw that now. How she had used all of her skills to turn Callie into an alluring female. And she had succeeded, because if there was thing Pearl knew, it was seduction. The men on the train had been wild for Callie, all but the one man she was so desperate to please. Why had she failed on that level? Pearl wondered.

But she guessed the answer to that was pretty clear. Apparently, the only variety of femininity that would appeal to someone like Gabriel Hawkins had to come equipped with ladyhood. That had to be the explanation.

Pearl frowned. She couldn't help Callie to win what she so fiercely desired. Sure, she could turn her into a woman, but she had no idea how to make her into a lady. She had no experience whatever with that particular state. It was hopeless.

Seemed like the rest of the camp shared her depressed condition. Crossing the corral, Pearl noticed that the atmosphere was pretty subdued this morning. She'd already heard that they wouldn't be moving on until tomorrow in order to give the wagon train a day of recovery from last night's unfortunate turn of events.

Feeling a pair of eyes on her, Pearl stopped

and turned her head. Lincoln McAllister, the only one who didn't seem to be suffering any consequences from the celebration, was seated on a stool complacently cleaning his gun.

He had been watching her. But then, he was always watching her with that dark, intense gaze of his. Pearl knew what he wanted, but she had no intention of giving it to him or even admitting that she had it. Not when it had already cost at least two lives.

McAllister worried her. There was too much mystery about him. Like that daguerreotype he kept hidden in his pack. She'd caught him once staring at it with a peculiar yearning expression on his lean face. But he'd shoved it out of sight before she'd had a chance to glimpse its subject.

No, she didn't trust McAllister, even if he had helped to defend the wagon train against the gang that had attacked them. Which was another thing that troubled Pearl. But at least those men who'd wanted her had been licked. There had been no further sign of them in all this time, so hopefully that was the end of it. McAllister was another story. He was still here and likely to remain. Well, she'd handle him when the time came. At this moment she had other business on her mind.

Pearl ignored Linc and went on looking for the Reverend Hawkins. She found him standing by a lone cottonwood tree on the bank of the Platte. He was gazing across the broad, muddy river at a small herd of buffalo that had come down to the water to drink.

It was unusual to find the preacher unoccupied. He was seldom anything but busy seeing to the welfare of his charges. Since he seemed unaware of her presence, Pearl took the opportunity to eye him critically.

She had to admit Gabriel Hawkins was probably the best-looking male she'd ever met, which made Callie's longing for him understandable. Pearl herself preferred her men to be of the rougher variety. And definitely without saintly qualities.

She was about to clear her throat to announce her presence when he spoke with a gentle note in his deep voice. "Magnificent beasts, aren't they?"

So he had known she was here. "I can admire 'em," Pearl agreed. " 'Long as they keep on that side o' the river."

He turned to her with that smile Callie was forever in raptures about, a briskness in his voice this time. "What is it, Pearl? Is Tom Callahan asking for me again?"

"Far as I know, the wagon master is restin' peaceful. It's, uh, another matter."

"Yes?"

"Callie," Pearl said. "She's ashamed 'bout last night. Fears yer thinkin' the worst o' her and asked me t'come bearin' her apologies."

"They aren't necessary, Pearl. It was an unfortunate episode, and I think everyone is as anxious as I am to put it behind us."

"Good o' ya. But," she added with a quick loyalty, "ya oughta know it was me what turned Callie out like that. Thought I was doin' right by her."

83

"You've been a good friend to her, Pearl."

"Just so ya know she ain't the one t'blame for what went wrong."

"It's probably my fault as much as anyone's. I should have been less worried about Tom Callahan and more observant about the celebration."

"Well, so long as ya understand . . ."

Pearl started to go, but he stopped her. "Tell Callie to forget all about it and that I regret I wasn't able to dance with her."

"She'll be pleased t'hear that."

"For that matter," he went on, "I'm sorry I missed the opportunity to share a dance with you, Pearl."

She stared at him. There was a funny look in his pure blue eyes, as though maybe he expected something from her. She couldn't imagine what, and she was so surprised that she didn't know what to say. She merely nodded and turned away, finding her way back to the circle of wagons.

When she reached the camp, Parthenia Smyth came out to confront her, a righteous expression on her prissy face.

"Well, I warned you, Pearl Slocum, didn't I? And look at the result. Last night was a disgrace. But then, I don't know why I should be surprised when this whole journey has been nothing but one unpleasant scene after another. Primitive conditions, ill-mannered boors to conduct us, attacks from roving brigands. To say nothing of the endless dust. I fully expect to be treated next to a plague of locusts."

"Ya tryin' t'tell me I'm t'blame fer dirt and grasshoppers?"

"No, but you are responsible for last night. You and your little protégée. Her conduct was deplorable."

Pearl was in no mood for a lecture from Parthenia Smyth. She had her tongue all set to blast the woman with a few choice expressions guaranteed to send her scurrying back to her wagon, hands over her flaming ears, but Pearl never fired those expressions. She was prevented from doing so by the sudden inspiration that seized her.

Why not? she thought. And wouldn't it be just the perfect solution to the problem? Providing, of course, she could persuade two contrary females to attempt it.

She smiled at Parthenia with a smug sweetness. "Now lookee here, Miz Smyth, instead of grievin' over the situation, maybe what ya oughta do is correct it."

Parthenia scowled at her. "What on earth are you talking about?"

"Yer a teacher, ain'tcha?"

"I am, though why I ever agreed to travel by wagon train all the way to Oregon just to—"

"Then maybe," Pearl quickly interrupted before she detoured them with another series of lengthy complaints, "it's time ya practiced it."

"Just what are you proposing?"

"Callie wants more'n anything t'be a lady. Ain't her fault I ain't got what it takes t'turn her into one."

"Are you suggesting that I instruct Callie Bur-

gess in the refinements of ladyhood? The notion
is preposterous!"

Pearl sighed. "Course, if you ain't up to it either . . ."

"I am an *excellent* teacher. And you, Pearl Slocum, are a sly creature. You don't deceive me
by trying to appeal to my vanity. On second
thought, however, it does present an interesting
challenge."

She considered the plan for a few moments,
and then she nodded brightly. It was the first
time Pearl had ever seen Parthenia Smyth look
pleased about anything.

"You may inform Miss Burgess that I am prepared to offer her the benefit of my knowledge."

"What!" Aching body or not, Callie's reaction
was a thunderous one. "Are ya crazy, Pearl?
Wantin' me t'take lessons from that ol' dragon!"

"Honey, it's the only way. I can dress ya up in
silks an' ribbons an' tell ya how t'go 'bout plea-
surin' a man's body, but I can't tell ya how
t'please his mind. I see that now. Gabriel Hawkins ain't gonna look at ya lessen yer a lady he
can respect."

"But ya said he forgives me fer last night. Ya
said he was real sorry he missed dancin' with
me."

"Dancin' ain't marryin', an' if that's what yer
aimin' fer . . ."

"Course it is, Pearl. Ya know that. But a
lady . . ."

"Only way t'be his equal."

Callie thought about it. The prospect of one

day being Gabriel Hawkins's wife, his partner and his equal, thrilled her. And if the method for achieving that was to wear the skin of ladyhood, then she was prepared to don it.

There was another argument in favor of those lessons. She was certain to meet her old friends, Agatha and Cooper Delaney, when she reached Oregon. She longed for their approval, would hate for them to see just how sadly her education had suffered since those early days when Agatha had tried to school her.

Oh, Pa had made an effort to send her to the local schoolhouse back in Horizon. With what she'd learned from its master and remembered from Agatha's teachings, she had managed to acquire the rudiments of reading and writing. But not much else. It seemed as if she'd spent most of her time whaling the daylights out of her fellow pupils, who had constantly ridiculed her because of Pa's manure business. By the fourth grade, tired of defending her poverty, she had given up and dropped out. Now here was an opportunity to correct all that.

"All right, Pearl, I'll do it. But there's one thing what scares me."

Pearl scoffed at her misgivings. "What? That you ain't smart enough? Because ya are."

Callie shook her head. "Not that. It's havin' t'change. I ain't so sure I wanna lose the ol' me. She's all I know, an' could be I won't like a new Callie."

Maybe it was that fear that made her lessons a terrible struggle. Or perhaps it was because Parthenia Smyth was so demanding a teacher. Or that, after spending long days in the saddle scouting for the wagon train, Callie was too weary to benefit from their sessions when the train made camp late each afternoon.

Whatever the explanation, she found the road to ladyhood a difficult one. No matter how hard she tried, its graces and refinements seemed to deliberately elude her. But Callie, once committed to a battle, was a stubborn warrior. She had sworn to be a lady for Gabriel, and a lady she would be! Still, she wished the fight wasn't such a discouraging one.

There was an added reason why her progress was so perpetually frustrating. Lincoln McAllister. The skunk never lost an opportunity to make his oh-so-nonchalant appearances at her lessons. And always, *always* he managed to destroy her concentration with his diabolical observations.

"There has to be an explanation for this, uh, peculiar exercise," he said solemnly on the occasion when Parthenia had her out in a flat area away from the camp. "Ah, I see. You're learning how to walk."

Parthenia had dusted the ground with flour, marking out a thin, straight row. Callie, wearing the bare hoops again, only now balancing a book of correct etiquette on her head, was attempting to travel along the white guideline. No lofty tightrope could have been more challenging. Miss Smyth insisted that, with head up, eyes forward, she glide to her destination with the minimum activity of her hoops. No provocative sashaying this time, as she had unfortunately learned from Pearl.

"Go away!" Callie snarled.

Parthenia clapped her hands to command her attention. "Ignore him, Miss Burgess. Come now, once again. Only this time let us try to be more demure."

It was no use. McAllister's presence unnerved her. Callie stumbled, and Lincoln chuckled.

"Been sampling that lemon punch again, Miss Burgess?"

"*Mr.* McAllister," Parthenia frigidly ordered, "you will please remove yourself from this scene at once."

Lincoln departed, but he reappeared the following afternoon with another cynical offering. He found the two women seated at a makeshift table consisting of several boards slapped across a pair of sawbucks. They were engaged in, of all things, a tea party.

Parthenia eyed him with disapproval as he lounged against the side of her wagon, a crooked grin on his bold mouth. "What, back again, Mr. McAllister?" She rose majestically to her feet. "You will be gone by the time I return with a fresh supply of boiling water. Continue with your practice, Miss Burgess. The art of correctly taking tea in polite society cannot be overemphasized."

When she had sailed away with her empty kettle in the direction of a campfire, Linc parked himself on the stool she'd occupied. Callie glared at him.

"Musta missed hearin' of it," she said sarcastically.

"What?"

"The invite sent out for you t'join this party."

"I never bother with formalities like that, Callie."

Little finger extended with exaggerated daintiness, she picked up her tin cup as though it were fine bone china. "You," she said with a haughty sniff, "ain't got no demeanor."

"Ah, *demeanor*. The word for the day."

Parthenia was endeavoring to build her pupil's vocabulary by daily introducing her to some impressive new word. Once Callie had conquered the word, and to the exasperation of the whole wagon train, she would insert it like a parrot in every conversation, often incorrectly. She must have really loved *appropriate,* because Linc remembered how she'd driven them all crazy with that one. The fresh game she and some of the boys had supplied for the camp was *appropriate*. The oxen were *appropriate*. Even the damn weather was *appropriate*. It had taken Parthenia herself to finally turn her off with a crisp, "Miss Burgess, you are being *in*appropriate."

Callie sipped delicately now from her cup of tea. "Yes, and you ain't got it."

"Uh-huh. How about your preacher? Reeking with demeanor, right?"

" 'Course."

"Even at the Oregon Freedom Day dance when a fist to the nose sank him?"

Callie banged her cup down on the boards, all

delicacy abandoned. "You take that back! Mr. Hawkins ain't a coward, like you been sayin'! Yer the coward! Stood by an' never lifted a finger when they was fightin'! He was brave an' tried t'stop 'em."

"Yes, he's no physical coward anyway."

Callie wasn't exactly sure what he meant by that, but it had the ring of another insult. She gazed at him in loathing. He was no longer wearing a sling. Pearl had removed it this morning.

"Appears like yer arm is all better, McAllister," she said maliciously. "No reason fer me not t'shoot ya now."

"None at all." He rose from the table. "Except that your precious Gabriel Hawkins needs me to guide this wagon train."

She stared after him as he wandered away, whistling cheerfully. Damn him, he was right! With the wagon master still ailing, he was indispensable. No one else had a certain knowledge of the trail. Meanwhile, Callie continued to have murder in her heart. Because Lincoln McAllister seemed to grow more infuriating with each day.

For the next few days, the trail presented so many problems for the wagon train that McAllister was too busy to taunt her. But he struck again on an afternoon shortly after.

Callie had hoped to be safe from him by choosing a spot well removed from the activity of the camp, but he managed to find her where she was perched on a large, flat boulder.

"All alone? Where's the formidable Miss Smyth today?"

This time Callie was ready for him. Using Parthenia's example, she coolly ignored him and forced herself to concentrate on the open book in her lap. Miss Smyth had told her to study the volume while she nursed a severe headache. But Callie's reading wasn't on a level with the language in the book. She found it difficult.

Hoping her silence would discourage Lincoln, she refused to answer him. When he didn't go away, she steeled herself to resist another of his verbal assaults. But he surprised her.

"Relax," he said, his tone almost friendly. "I'm too weary to be anything but harmless today."

She could appreciate that. They were still paralleling the Platte River, which would be with them to Fort Laramie and beyond. But the drier country with its strange sandstone formations and tough buffalo grass was more of an ordeal for the caravan. The trail was gradually ascending now, and the climb was hard on wagons and animals alike. Two of the wagons had broken down today, causing delays while they were repaired.

After dealing with that, as well as a couple of quarrels arising from strained tempers, McAllister was understandably tired. But harmless? She doubted that. She had even more reason to be wary when he companionably settled himself beside her on the boulder. Callie didn't like his nearness. There was something alarming about the male heat from his solid body that was so close, it almost touched hers. She refused, though, to give him the satisfaction of detecting her panic.

He eyed the book in her lap. "Are you wearing it today or reading it?"

She didn't respond, but Linc could feel her stiffen. He guessed he didn't blame her. He'd been pretty hard on her since the night of the dance. With good reason. The startling temptation she had been for him that evening had forced him to change his sparring contests with her. They had become a form of self-defense. A necessary method of proving to himself that Callie Burgess was nothing more than an immature little pest. Not a woman, not a real danger to him.

Still, it wouldn't hurt for him to be pleasant to her for a change. He made that effort by inquiring harmlessly, "What's the subject for today?"

She didn't trust him, of course.

"Show me, Callie. I promise I'm interested."

She hesitated. Then, thawing slightly, she reluctantly held the book up for his inspection. He read the title on the spine. "Ah, *The Deportment of a Young Lady in Society*. I guess that's important, huh? Deportment, I mean."

She looked at him with an expression of superiority on her urchin's face. " 'Course. Miz Smyth sez a person o' any real class has gotta have *de rigeur*. That's French, see."

"I know what it is, Callie. I'm half Creole."

"Yeah, New Orleans," she suddenly remembered. "Hey, what you wanted fer down there?"

He frowned. "How do you know about that?"

"I heard things in Independence."

"I'll bet you did."

"Guess that means you ain't gonna tell me."

"Oh, I don't mind your knowing," he said casually. "I'm wanted for killing my brother."

She gasped, shrinking away from him on the boulder. "I knew you was a low-down, black-hearted villain, but t'murder yer own flesh an' blood—"

"Don't be a fool. I said I was *wanted* for killing him, not that I *did* kill him."

He could see she was eager for the details, probably wanting to strengthen her silly conviction that he'd taken the lives of her father and Bud Colby. But Linc had no intention of discussing his demons.

"We were talking about your education, not my fugitive state," he reminded her. "So, she's teaching you French now, huh? Kind of like putting the cart before the horse, isn't it?"

Linc had contempt for Parthenia Smyth's pretentious methods of instruction. In fact, this entire campaign to turn Callie into a lady was nonsense. How could she be so ignorant, so naive, to actually believe that she could win the shallow Gabriel Hawkins by— Well, the whole thing irritated him, though he couldn't understand why he should waste good energy being annoyed by something that actually benefitted him. Because, as he'd earlier realized, with Callie kept so busy striving to interest the preacher, she would have no time to take potshots at him with that fool rifle of hers.

Linc had proof of that when she was willing to be diverted from the question of his guilt by the more immediate subject of her education.

"Lot you know," she sniffed. "A lady has 'er

some French 'cause it gives 'er di-dis—" She struggled with the word before she got it out. "—Distinction. Yeah, that's it, *distinction.*"

"Now, see, I think there's far more useful knowledge for a lady dying to appeal to the man of her heart."

Callie, unable to resist the problem of fascinating Gabriel, was immediately intrigued. "Bein' what?"

Lincoln shrugged. "The skill of an irresistible kiss, for example. Miss Smyth give you, uh, any advice about that?"

"Don't be daft."

"No, of course she didn't. But being a man, I know what it takes to please one of us. And believe me, Callie, we all of us without exception appreciate a lady's sweet kisses."

"You funnin' with me ag'in?"

"Perfectly serious. I'm not talking about some awkward little peck on the cheek either. No, this sort of kiss has to be thorough and accomplished to impress someone like Hawkins. You have experience with that sort of kissing, Callie?"

To her regret, Callie had to admit to herself that she didn't. Not that she hadn't been curious about kissing, even eager to experiment with it. But the boys back in Horizon hadn't considered her feminine enough to engage in that activity. Oh, there had been that one clumsy encounter behind the chicken coop with Buck Sawyer when she'd turned fifteen. Only it had been so embarrassing that neither them had cared to repeat it.

Lincoln shook his head, looking sorry for her. "I can see you haven't. This isn't good, Callie. What are you going to do when the preacher takes you in his arms some starry night, gazes down at your pink lips, and pleads with you to—Well, the result doesn't bear thinking about."

Callie bit one of those pink lips and looked anxious. "Reckon I'd git it all wrong, huh?"

"What do you think, when a man expects the woman he desires to be a competent kisser? Hell, Callie, you've got a real hole in your education."

"Ain't nothin' I can do 'bout it."

"No, I suppose not. It's a shame, too, because I could offer some helpful suggestions. If, that is, I weren't the last man this side of the Mississippi you'd want sharing his knowledge with you."

Callie squirmed on the boulder, struggling with indecision. She sure didn't want McAllister getting the wrong impression, that she was softening toward him or anything. But she'd be a darn fool to miss out on any advice—especially his. A man like him, who'd been everywhere, probably'd had more than his share of women and knew plenty about kissing. The skunks always did.

In the end, however, it was the exciting image of Gabriel planting his mouth on hers that convinced her.

"Let's not be so hasty here, McAllister. Understand, I ain't fergivin' ya a thing, but reckon I can hear what ya got t'say."

"If you're sure . . ."

"Said so, didn't I?"

96

Linc spread his hands in a gesture of mock resignation. "In that case, scoot around here so that you're facing me. That's right, I need a full view of your mouth. It's all in the technique, understand. Now let me see you pucker up."

Callie pursed her lips. "Like thith?"

"That's awful. You look like you're ready to suck an orange, not receive a man's kiss. Just part your mouth a bit, and try to look like you're all breathless for him."

Callie pumped air in an approximation of passionate longing.

"Are you drowning? Because it looks like it."

"It's hard," she complained. "I keep worryin' where the noses go so's they don't bump."

"That takes care of itself."

"How?"

"By angling—" He broke off, looking hopeless. "Look, this just isn't any good. I'd have to demonstrate with you to show you how it works."

The words hadn't left his mouth before the question flashed through his brain: *What in sweet hell are you doing?*

This was Callie Burgess! He was actually proposing to kiss Callie Burgess! Up to this moment he'd merely been playing another of his gleeful games with her. But maybe he needed to kiss her. Needed to prove to himself once and for all that the impact of their intimate contact the night of the dance was nothing but a freakish error of nature. Right. A kiss would firmly establish for him that she had about as much sex appeal as his horse.

He looked at her, and he could see she was

stunned by his outrageous suggestion. She could hardly choke out the words. "You sayin' what I think yer sayin'?"

"Wouldn't mean anything, Callie. It's just in the interest of your education. But if you'd rather not . . ."

Maybe, she thought slowly, maybe it wouldn't be such a bad idea. A kiss would show her how mistaken she'd been in her hateful arousals when she'd bathed him and danced with him. Why, even if such a kiss was instructive, it was bound to be an unpleasant business.

Callie knew this had to be true just by the scent of him. He smelled faintly of sweat and animals from his long day of work, nothing like the heavenly aroma she associated with Gabriel. She figured McAllister would taste no more sweet than he smelled.

Nor was there anything appealing about that sardonic face of his with its expressive black eyebrows, sharp nose, and those curious pointy-topped ears that in her mind defined him as Lucifer in contrast to her Archangel Gabriel. No, there was only one thing about McAllister that worried her. His wide, sensual mouth. She gazed at it, shivering at the thought of it fastening on her own mouth. It had to be an illusion, that inviting mouth, because she was certain there was nothing more than a brute wearing it.

"All right," she informed him grimly, "let's git on with it. What do I do here?"

"To start with, you can stop looking like I'm going to strangle you, though I admit I've been tempted to do just that on a couple of occasions. Relax, Callie."

Her interpretation of his instruction was to squeeze her eyes shut and to brace herself where she sat on the boulder.

"Oh, for the love of—Okay, just keep still. This won't hurt."

She started when suddenly two hands framed her face to hold it steady. They were very large and very strong hands but surprisingly gentle.

"Now we tip your head slightly just so. And my head goes here."

She knew how close he was for she felt his breath against her face. It was warm and dauntingly masculine.

"Callie," he whispered.

"What?" she croaked.

"Part your lips a little."

"Oh."

She obeyed, keeping her eyes tightly closed, thinking she would be more secure in a state of blindness. She was wrong. In the next instant his mouth was on hers. He was kissing her! Slowly, softly. And, dear God, was that her kissing him back?

The sensations were unexpected and terrible. Terrible because they were both shattering and blissful as his mouth did wicked things to hers. Urgent things involving his busy lips and his even busier tongue. She was shocked when that tongue, deepening the kiss, invaded her mouth, playing with her own tongue. Oh, it was a thorough kiss for sure, raw but pure with pleasure!

Only this wasn't the way it was supposed to

be! He wasn't supposed to feel like this, taste like this! All hot and wet and thrilling so that her senses rioted on her!

Sanity finally fought its way to the surface of her brain. Feeling betrayed, both by him and her own treacherous emotions, she placed her hands flat against his hard chest and shoved at him in fear and anger. For a second he resisted. Then, to her relief, he lifted his mouth from hers and leaned away from her. When she found the courage to open her eyes, he was staring at her with the devil's own smile on that sinful mouth of his.

"Damn you, Lincoln McAllister!"

Linc was silent. He had no defense. How could he when he'd made a serious mistake? What had ever possessed him to suggest such a fool thing? And the worst of it was, gazing at that desirable mouth of hers, still damp and swollen from his kiss, he wanted to taste her again.

Well, it wasn't going to happen. Not now, not ever. Whatever rich vein of passion he had struck under her rough, immature surface, for the sake of his own soul and the woman he loved, he refused to mine it. He hated himself for his lust, because that's all Callie could ever mean to him when it was Anne he longed for in his heart.

Which, he thought with his little smile of self-mockery, makes me the bastard here, not Gabriel Hawkins. At least the reverend had a good excuse for failing to have the courage to discourage Callie's interest in him. He obviously didn't want to hurt her. Whereas he, Linc, didn't care about anything but obtaining what he'd joined this wagon train for.

And since Callie Burgess threatened that objective with both her rifle and now her sweet little mouth, he made a promise to himself to handle her again like the nuisance she was. Starting now.

"That mean you aren't interested in an advanced lesson?" he asked. She glared at him murderously. "No, I guess not."

Chuckling, he got to his feet and headed back to the camp. Callie gazed after him with fresh loathing, still shaken from the explosive kiss they had shared.

How could she have been so stupid, so weak? She couldn't stand it! She'd bust if she had to keep this inside her.

Chapter Five

Callie didn't keep it inside her. She told Pearl all about it over supper that evening. It was embarrassing to disclose an episode that had been so shameful, but she couldn't help it. The intimacy she'd shared with McAllister had been eating away at her ever since it happened, and she just had to get it out.

Pearl wasn't easily shocked, but she wasn't exactly calm about Callie's revelation either. "Girl, are ya out of yer lovin' mind? This is Lincoln McAllister yer talkin' 'bout. Didn't I tell ya there's something dangerous 'bout that buzzard?"

"I know ya did, Pearl, but he went an' tricked me inta it."

That wasn't altogether true, and in a corner of her heart Callie knew it. But she just couldn't admit, even to herself, that she had willingly participated in the event. A confession like that would be as good as acknowledging the inexplicable fires McAllister had ignited in her. And that would contaminate what she felt for Gabriel, a love that was fine and pure and far above anything the contemptible McAllister could ever deserve from a woman.

Pearl gazed at her suspiciously. "You certain ya ain't harborin' no secret hankerin's fer McAllister?"

"Oh, no, Pearl, I hate 'im! Hate 'im so bad," she rashly confided. "I plan t'put a bullet in his heart soon as the wagon master is fit t'guide this here train ag'in."

"That so? A mite extreme, ain't it, fer a man's stickin' his tongue in yer mouth?"

Pearl didn't believe her. Callie realized that the only way she could convince her was to tell her the truth. Pearl was a good friend. She felt she could trust her.

"I got me a better reason 'n that. Lincoln McAllister deserves t'die 'cause he killed my pa an' his friend, Bud Colby."

This time Pearl was shocked. "Where'd you ever git a wild notion like that?"

"It's true." She told the redhead the rest of it—how McAllister had been caught with his gun still in his hand standing over the fresh bodies of her father and Colby, how the crooked sheriff of Independence had let him get away with it because they'd once been friends in the army, and how Callie had tracked McAllister to this wagon train, vowing to punish him.

"Honey lamb," Pearl said to her patiently, "ya ever stop t'consider the reason the sheriff in Independence let 'im go was 'cause maybe he didn't do it?"

"No, Pearl, he did it all right."

"Uh-huh. Why?"

"Way I figgered it," Callie explained solemnly, "an' I asked around t'be sure, is Pa and Colby took big winnin's off McAllister in this here card game in a saloon. So McAllister follows 'em back to Colby's hotel room where they argues over it, an' McAllister shoots 'em."

"An' that's yer explanation?"

"Well, yeah. See, Pa could be kinda sharp when it come t'cards, an' he was feelin' lucky that day when he brung a load of manure inta Independence. I ain't sayin' he cheated," she hastily added in her father's defense "but McAllister musta figgered he did."

Pearl knew that Callie had it all wrong. Though she had no way to prove it, she knew who had killed Hank Burgess and Bud Colby and why. Her knowledge was dangerous, however; it was the reason she had fled from Independence. Keeping that secret now, in view of what Callie had just shared with her, made her feel guilty. But Pearl was too fearful to reveal it, even to her friend. She could try to reason with Callie, though.

"I can't say as how I got any use fer McAllister myself. He's a slippery rascal, hidin' something. But murder?" She shook her head. "I don't see that in 'im."

"But it's there, Pearl. He got himself kicked out

o' the army fer sumpthin' bad, an' he's wanted down in New Orleans fer killin' his own brother. Said so himself."

"Don't mean he did it."

But Callie was stubbornly determined to believe the worst, and no amount of argument would talk her out of her conviction. "He's got t'pay when the time comes, Pearl, but don't you go an' tell any o' the others. Don't want 'em tryin' t'stop me."

"You be careful," Pearl warned her severely. "McAllister ain't exactly the kind o' man t'stand still while you go an' execute him."

"Oh, I'm up to him," Callie boasted.

"Sure ya are, but you make me a promise."

"Like?"

" 'Fore you go puttin' lead in 'im, ya come an' tell me first. Hear?" That was as far as Pearl was willing to go to save McAllister. She wasn't ignoring the possibility that he was in cahoots somehow with the men who had shot Colby and Burgess. After all, didn't all of them want the same thing?

"Guess I can manage that much."

Callie drained her coffee cup and went off to see to her horse. Pearl was cleaning up after their supper when Gabriel Hawkins stopped by the wagon.

"If it's Callie ya want, Reverend, she's off lookin' after Apollo."

"Actually, Pearl, you're the reason I'm here."

Once again the handsome preacher had surprised her, and she was immediately wary. "Me?"

105

"Yes, I'd like to discuss something with you. Uh, may I sit?"

She indicated the camp stool Callie had vacated, and he perched on it. She waited for him to speak, offering him no encouragement.

"I've been watching Callie at her lessons with Miss Smyth," he said in his deep, rich voice, "and thinking how commendable it is that she's working so hard to prepare herself for a better life in Oregon."

Not a notion of why, Pearl thought in wry amazement, wondering what it'd take to make him see the real reason Callie was going through fits to turn herself into a lady.

"And it's occurred to me, Pearl" he continued, "that you also might like to improve your education. I believe Miss Smyth already has her hands full with Callie, but I would be happy to undertake your lessons myself."

Pearl gazed at him in astonishment. "Lessons? Me? *You?*"

"Why, yes, I believe I'm qualified to instruct you."

Her eyes narrowed. "You tryin' t'tell me, Reverend, ya mean t'reform me? Because I gotta warn ya, preachers have tried it before, an' they ain't liked the results."

He shook his head. "I promise you, this has nothing to do with soul-saving, though of course as a man of God I am ready to offer you spiritual advice should you ever want it. But I would never impose it on you."

"Then what're we discussin' here, Reverend?"

"Equipping you with some of the cultural advantages that will help you with your new life in Oregon."

He assumed that, like the other women on the wagon train, she was headed west for no other reason than to make a fresh start for herself. Pearl couldn't help it. She burst out with one of her bawdy, belly-deep laughs. "That's mighty nice o' ya, Reverend, but in case ya ain't noticed, Pearl Slocum ain't raw material fer refinin'."

He wasn't offended. "I think you misjudge yourself. I think you're capable of far more than you credit yourself for."

"I appreciate the vote of confidence, but I believe I'll keep me the way I am."

"If you should change your mind—" He got to his feet, a warmth in his blue eyes that she found oddly disarming. "—I'm here for you. Don't forget that, Pearl."

His blue eyes lingered on her for a second, and she knew there was no mistaking the challenge in them. Then he turned and walked away, his fair hair like molten gold in the glow of the setting sun. Pearl, sensing the curious gazes of her neighbors, felt the need to get away from the wagon train to where she could think in private. Gabriel Hawkins's offer disturbed her, though she couldn't say why.

Drawing a shawl around her shoulders and slipping away from the camp, Pearl followed an antelope path that wandered along the floor of an arroyo where the creek bed at this season was as dry as powder. Summer's long twilights guaranteed her plenty of daylight, though she didn't plan to go far. The arroyo was quiet and

107

peaceful, a good, secluded place to think.

Hawkins's offer. Pearl wondered if it bothered her for the same reason Callie had been initially reluctant to accept lessons from Parthenia Smyth. A fear of losing her identity, of becoming someone she couldn't cope with or wouldn't like. Was that why she was so resistant? Or was there another reason she had yet to recognize?

But what difference did it make? She wasn't on this wagon train to escape her past. She was here simply because it had provided her a quick, convenient refuge.

Or was she being dishonest with herself? Most likely she could have found somewhere else to run and hide. Someplace a lot less demanding than the Oregon Trail. So why had she impulsively joined the train? An unacknowledged desire deep down inside her to leave behind her old life and its ways? A need, like the reverend believed, to start over again new and clean in the far west?

She came to an abrupt halt on the path, laughing at herself for such crazy notions. "Pearl Slocum, yer a prize fool. Women like you don't change. They just go on to the next fancy house, the next customer."

Her laughter bounced off the steep walls of the silent arroyo, and that was when she realized she was a fool in more ways than one. She had walked too far. The gully had deepened without her being aware of it, making the shadows heavy and unfriendly.

Suddenly uneasy with the lonely spot, Pearl decided it was time to go back. And that was when it happened. From behind a huge boulder, where he'd been hidden several yards in front of her, appeared the figure of a man. Burly and bearded, he wore a wide grin that she could tell was a mean one even in the fading light.

Pearl picked up her skirts and swung around, intending to get out of the arroyo as fast as she could, but her path was blocked by a second man, who had managed to sneak up behind her. Trapped!

This one was skinny and hairless, with a pistol in his hand that meant business. He gestured with the weapon, silently ordering her to approach his partner, who was waiting for them by the boulder. Pearl had no choice but to obey. She had never been so scared in her life, but she was damned if she'd let them see her fear.

"Well, now, Ike, I call this real polite," the first said in a gravelly voice as they reached him. "Didn't need t'invite 'er. She just marches right out here nice as ya please t'join us."

"Sure, Judd, real nice, real nice," Ike agreed in a thin, piping voice.

How could she have been so careless about her security? Pearl wondered. Walking away like that from the protection of the wagon train. She should have known these polecats wouldn't give up after their failed raid. They must have been shadowing the train all this time, watching and waiting for a chance. And she had stupidly given it to them.

"Who are ya?" Pearl demanded boldly. "What d'ya want?"

Pearl knew exactly who they were. Judd Parsons and Ike Ritter, the men who had killed Bud Colby and Hank Burgess. The enemy from whom she had fled back in Independence. Her pretended ignorance wouldn't fool them, but she was desperate and needed to buy time.

"Think mebbe ya heard of us, Pearl," Judd, the obvious leader of the two, said with a menacing softness. "Think mebbe ya know just what we're after."

"Don't know what yer talkin' 'bout."

" 'Course ya do, Pearl." Judd thrust his brutish face close to her own, so close she could smell his sour breath and see the gap in his teeth when he grinned at her again. "See, yer lover man, Colby, got real careless drinkin' in that saloon. Bragged on what he knew that was gonna make him rich. Sly enough, though, t'keep back the important part. Said he trusted that only with his special woman."

"Wouldn't give it up either when we tried t'part him from it in that hotel room," Ike squeaked. "No, sir, wouldn't give it up. Tried to pull guns on us, him and his friend, and what choice did we have?"

"Real shame," Judd said, nodding in mock regret. "Left us nothin' t'do but look up Bud's special woman. That's you, Pearl. Thing is, time we found just who ya was, you'd up and left town."

"Guess she musta heard we was lookin' fer her, Judd. Guess she musta."

"Yer crazy," Pearl tried again to bluff them, knowing if she gave them what they wanted they would only kill her afterward.

The bluff didn't work. She felt the muzzle of

the pistol shoved against the side of her head.

"That's right, Ike. Need t'remind her she ain't bein' smart."

Pearl decided it was useless. If she didn't give them what they wanted, they'd only torture it out of her. Maybe if she shared Bud's secret they'd let her go.

"Listen," she said, trying to look unworried. "Suppose I give ya what yer after. How do I know yer gonna let me walk outta here?"

Judd shook his head. "It don't work that way, Pearl. See, first yer gonna tell us, and then yer comin' with us. Just so we know ya didn't lie 'bout it."

Then, when they reached their objective, they would kill her. Pearl had no illusions about that. But anything could happen along the way. Anyway, there was nothing else she could do.

"Ya can get this gun outta my face if ya expect me t'talk business."

Though she didn't realize it until seconds later, her request saved her. The instant Judd nodded to his partner to lower the pistol and Ike complied, leaving Pearl no longer a target, a shot rang out from the top of the gully. Ike squealed in pain as the bullet grazed his thumb. The pistol jumped out of his hand, landing several feet away in the dust.

"All right, gentlemen," a familiar voice commanded them cheerfully, "let me see you back away from her. Hands in the air, if you please. That's right, nice and easy. Pearl, are you waiting for an invitation to get that gun?"

Pearl retrieved the pistol from the ground.

Jean Barrett

Once she had it in her possession, the tall figure above them lowered himself over the edge of the arroyo. He was no more than a dark form in the gray light, but Pearl didn't need to see his face to know she had Lincoln McAllister to thank for her life.

He had tucked his long-barreled Colt into his belt in order to clamber down the rough side of the gully, and Judd Parsons and Ike Ritter seized the opportunity to turn with the speed of weasels and flee up the arroyo into the dusk. They were immediately out of sight, and a moment later came the pounding of horses' hooves that rapidly dwindled in the distance.

By this time Linc had reached Pearl at the bottom of the arroyo. His tone now was considerably less than cheerful. "What made me suppose that a woman who was fool enough to wander out here on her own would have sense enough to keep them covered with that pistol until I could join her? Or didn't it occur to you that it might not be a good idea to let them get away?"

"I'm not Callie, mister. I wouldn't know which end t'fire. Here, take the thing." She handed the pistol to him. "And if yer done roarin', I'll say I'm obliged t'ya."

"Yes, well, you're just damn lucky I got worried when I noticed you weren't in camp and that one of the women remembered seeing you head in this direction. How much did those two get out of you before I caught up with you?"

"Don't need t'fret none 'bout the mission funds," she said blithely. "I told 'em the truth, that I got no idea where the strongbox is on the wagon train."

"Strongbox, my ass. Come on, we both know what they want."

Pearl regarded him in silence.

"All right, so I want it too, but there's a difference. I didn't kill Bud Colby and Hank Burgess to get it, and you know it."

She did know it, but she still didn't trust McAllister. In her opinion he was likely as greedy as Parsons and Ritter.

"Look," he said, "you could never handle this on your own. I'll cut a deal with you. Tell me, and I'll do the rest. Then I'll see to it that you get a fair share of the money."

His offer was an attractive one. What he failed to realize was that Pearl wasn't interested in anything but surviving. And her shrewd instinct told her that, with what was at stake, anyone could be her enemy.

No, maybe McAllister wasn't a killer, but there was the possibility that he was in league with Parsons and Ritter and that this little scene in the gully had been staged to trick her into talking. All right, so it was a remote possibility. But she still feared that if she ever revealed the secret Bud had shared with her—and damn him for telling her—her life would be worth nothing.

Linc's argument was a different one as he tried one more time to convince her. "As long as you keep this thing to yourself, you're in danger. Those two won't give up, Pearl. They'll be back."

Pearl had thought of that herself, and it worried her. But not enough to break her silence.

"Okay," Linc said, "I can see you're going to be stubborn about it. For now I'll respect that, but sooner or later you'll trust me. You'll have to or be threatened by Parsons and Ritter all the way to Oregon." He took her arm. "Come on, let's get out of here before it gets any darker."

Pearl was grateful for his protection as he escorted her away from the arroyo. By the time they reached the wagon train, she'd made a decision about the problem that had sent her off into the twilight. She would accept no lessons from Gabriel Hawkins. Ultimately, it wasn't the education he had offered her that she objected to. It was the teacher himself. Nor did she care to examine that objection. It simply existed, and that was enough for Pearl.

For Callie it was another story. Her lessons from Parthenia Smyth continued as the wagon train moved on. Her progress would have been difficult under the best of circumstances, but with the brutal conditions the caravan faced in the long, hot days that followed, it became a torturous challenge for both teacher and pupil.

They traveled now across a rough, treeless terrain strewn with the bleached bones of buffalo. People and animals alike suffered from swarms of vicious gnats. Worse were the endless clouds of alkali dust that blistered parched skin, inflamed cracked lips, and stung irritated eyes.

The dryness was a perpetual problem, shrinking the wood of the wagons so that iron tires fell off wheels, spokes pulled out of hubs, and shrieking axles demanded frequent lubrication from the tar buckets suspended from every tailboard.

Bad as it all was, there was no further trouble from Judd Parsons and Ike Ritter. But only Lincoln and Pearl, who knew the two of them must be out there somewhere watching the wagon train, could appreciate that. The others, unaware of the existence of human enemies and dealing with increasingly stressed tempers, were grateful for nothing.

Parthenia Smyth was certainly not in a thankful mood as she directed a session with Callie where they were camped for the night in sight of the massive formation known as Courthouse Rock. She was tired from their arduous day on the trail, her patience strained by the restless mood of her pupil.

"Now do pay careful attention this time, Miss Burgess, while I once again indicate them for you." She began to point, one by one, to the objects from her personal belongings that she had ranged along the board erected on a pair of sawbucks. "Purse, gloves, fan, handkerchief, small bottle of scent, brooch, locket, and coral necklace. The brooch may be worn with either the locket or the necklace but not both at the same time. These are the accessories suitable for a young lady. *No other,*" she emphasized.

Callie gazed in disappointment at the dull collection on the board. "Don't seem like very excitin' jewelry, Miz Smyth. Not like what Pearl give me t'wear night o' the dance. Don't see no pot o' rouge neither."

Parthenia's mouth tigtened in disapproval. "That is the whole point of this exercise, Miss Burgess—to demonstrate the value of a tasteful simplicity. Or have you forgotten the disaster of the evening in discussion? A lady does *not* paint her face, color her hair, or wear vulgar jewelry."

"But she does git t'put on perfume, right?"

"With restraint and only if it is a delicate fragrance, yes."

Callie eagerly eyed the bottle of scent on the board. It was the only item in the collection that appealed to her. She thought it was a pretty little thing, with its cut crystal sparking in the sunlight. "Can I smell it, Miz Smyth? Please?"

"You are much too easily distracted, Callie." She sighed in exasperation. "Oh, very well."

Removing the stopper, Parthenia held the scent under her nose. Callie inhaled it with an expression of joy on her face.

"What's it called, Miz Smyth?"

"It is a French scent known as *Céleste*. That means heavenly."

"It sure is." The fragrance was familiar. Callie was convinced it was the same wonderful perfume she had been given in her childhood. She was sorry when Parthenia returned the bottle to the board.

"Now let me look at you." Parthenia stepped back to survey her. "M'm, it is not a very exact fit, but it will serve."

Callie was disgusted with the dress that Miss Smyth had lent her. It was as boring as the jewelry. But Miss Smyth had insisted she couldn't feel like a lady unless she dressed like a lady, so for this afternoon's lesson she had traded her buckskins for skirts of prim gray cotton.

"Have we everything for our rehearsal?" Parthenia scanned the collection on the board. "Ah, no. We are missing the *sal volatile*."

"What's that, Miz Smyth?"

"Smelling salts. A lady of fashion is never without them."

It was useless to try to convince Miss Smyth that she'd never fainted in her life and had no use for smelling salts. Miss Smyth insisted on returning to her own wagon to fetch her container of *sal volatile*. She left Callie at Pearl's wagon, where they had met for today's lesson to take advantage of Pearl's precious pier glass, which was propped against one of the large rear wheels of the wagon.

"You may practice with the fan in front of the glass while I'm gone," Parthenia instructed her before she departed. "And remember to be demure, Miss Burgess. *Always* demure."

When she was gone, Callie took up the fan and stationed herself before the long mirror in its fancy gilt frame. Pearl and the other women were down at the river doing laundry, and most of the men had accompanied them. Callie felt free to admire the effect of her swirling skirts as she pirouetted and swayed, all the while languidly fanning herself. She was so busy with her reflection that she failed to realize she wasn't alone.

As the caravan's acting wagon master, Linc felt responsible for the safety of the equipment. His chief concern these days, with the trail punishing the wagons so severely, were the frequent breakdowns. In an effort to avoid such delays, he had begun to personally check the underpinnings of every schooner after each day's trek.

And that's how Linc was involved this afternoon, silently examining the running gear for soundness while stretched out on his back under Pearl's wagon, where he had crawled from the neighboring covered wagon. He saw no reason to make Callie aware of his presence. In fact, he preferred to ignore both her and her silly posturings in front of the pier glass.

Callie Burgess had become a definite headache. Ever since that insane kiss, there had been a tension eating away at him, and he knew she was the cause of it. Plain lust, of course. There was no other explanation for it. It maddened him that the ridiculous creature could arouse such an appetite in him. But since he had no intention of involving himself with her, either on that level or any other, he chose these days to avoid her as much as possible.

She need never know he was down here, witness to another of her absurd lessons with Parthenia Smyth. He would finish his inspection and then quietly slither away to the next wagon. That was what he planned—until he shifted on his side to investigate a brake shoe and found himself gazing at a pair of shapely female legs.

Those legs were only inches from his nose. *Bare* legs. Holy mother, she wore no drawers under those skirts, which she had raised to her knees as she pranced back and forth in front of the mirror! Linc was transfixed.

Callie's legs were every bit as surprising, and as enticing, as her breasts. Against his will, Linc found himself admiring trim ankles and the rounded flesh of smooth calves. His imagination ran wild when he pictured what must exist up there in the secret darkness above those white calves. The blood flowed instantly to his groin, creating one terrific and very painful hardness.

Linc could swear he didn't make a sound as he swallowed past another tightness in his throat. Nothing like a groan. But something must have come out, because the legs directly in front of him froze. Then the skirts dropped down over them, like a stage curtain in mid-performance. The next thing he saw was a face hanging upside down as Callie discovered him under the wagon. Her face was flushed with outrage.

"You!"

"Uh, Callie, there is an explanation."

Not that she was in any mood to hear it, he realized as she spat at him an explosive, "Come on outta there, ya Peepin' Tom!"

His position was much too foolish to exhibit any degree of nonchalance, never mind dignity, but Linc attempted both as he emerged from under the wagon and came to his feet to face her. "If legend is to be trusted, I believe Tom had a much more entertaining view of Lady Godiva."

Callie didn't know what he was talking about. She glared at him, her green eyes afire.

"Though I will admit," Linc added, "that you do have a pair of pleasant limbs."

Pleasant? Hell, he was still hot from imagining what they would feel like wrapped around him. He didn't dare to think about the juncture of those legs or the promise of what was contained there. He couldn't help wondering, though, if that untamed russet hair on her head was matched elsewhere.

"My limbs ain't none o' yer business, Lincoln McAllister."

"They are when they're shoved into my face without petticoats, pantaloons, or stockings."

"Ya can keep that vile tongue t'yerself. An' my unmentionables ain't yer concern neither."

He couldn't help himself riling her further. "Tell me, Callie, does Miss Smyth know you're naked under those skirts? Or did she recommend the state as beneficial to your training?"

By now Callie was so red in the face that Linc knew she was nearly strangling on her own anger. She expressed her rage with a murderous, "Ya can count yerself lucky my rifle ain't t'hand 'cause, wagon master or not, I'd put a bullet in ya where ya stand."

"Don't let a little thing like that stop you," he challenged. "Here, help yourself." He had his Colt strapped to his hip. Sliding it from its holster, he slapped it into her hand. "Come on, Callie. You're always bragging what a crack shot you are. Here's your opportunity to prove it."

Callie gripped the revolver, finger on the trigger, as she lifted it to the level of his heart. Her hand trembled, something that shouldn't have happened. She was always cool and steady with a gun in her fist.

"What are you waiting for?" he taunted. "You couldn't ask for a better target."

Damn him! And damn Pearl for committing her to that promise. Otherwise, she'd put lead into him without hesitation. Wouldn't she?

Linc chuckled softly. "No, I guess not."

He was laughing at her! Standing there all relaxed and sure of himself, convinced she didn't have the guts to shoot. She'd show him!

Callie's frustration was so enormous that she had to fire the revolver or explode. She squeezed the trigger and had the satisfaction of seeing the utter surprise on McAllister's face as he yelped and leaped aside. There was a shattering sound as the bullet struck glass.

"You little fool!" he yelled. "You almost killed me!"

He didn't understand that her shot was a wild one on purpose; she'd turned the gun at the last moment. If she'd seriously meant to drill him, she would never have missed. How dared he think her markmanship was so poor that—

And then she saw it, and her grim expression crumpled with the sudden realization of what had happened. Pearl's cherished mirror! That was what her bullet had found and destroyed! The glass lay in silver shards on the ground!

She was so blind by now with wrath that she couldn't accept her own blame. The fault was all McAllister's.

"Friggin' bastard!" she roared, pitching the revolver to the earth. "I *will* kill ya! With my bare hands!"

If Callie had made any progress whatever in

the direction of ladyhood, she shed it all in that moment as she launched herself at Lincoln in unrestrained fury. The impact of her small body colliding with his was so unexpected, so startlingly strong, that the breath was punched out of him with a loud "Oof!"

They went down in a tangle of arms and legs. Callie, stretched full length on top of him, pummeled him with her small, determined fists, all the while cursing savagely.

Linc never felt her fierce blows. With their struggle having hiked her dress up almost to her hips, all he could suddenly feel was the sweet, naked flesh of a pair of incredibly soft thighs. Nor was he able to hear her curses over the pounding of his own blood. His hardness, which had diminished when he climbed out from under the wagon, escalated into a raging arousal.

His hands, pinned down by her weight, fought themselves free. Self-defense should have been his motive, but he obeyed a more powerful instinct when his liberated hands reached behind her, clasped her buttocks, and squeezed her down against the heat and hardness of his groin. Compelling her, at the risk of his soul and sanity, to feel his desire.

Callie had never understood exactly what Pearl had meant when she'd repeatedly warned her that Lincoln McAllister was a dangerous animal. She understood it now, fully, clearly, and with a sense of instant alarm. It wasn't McAllister the killer she had to fear. It was McAllister the seducer.

Her fight became a ferocious one, no longer

driven by a need to punish but only to get away. But the harder she squirmed and swore, the more relentlessly he hung on to her, laughing now like a fiend. Callie was dimly conscious, as they rolled over in the dust, of shrieks that weren't her own and a pair of feet dancing around them. But she was too busy tussling with McAllister to identify them as belonging to a scandalized Parthenia Smyth.

It was only when those feet were joined by a larger, booted pair, along with a thundering male voice demanding their immediate attention, that awareness penetrated. Callie managed to break away from McAllister and sit up. Her face flamed with mortification. Oh, no, not Gabriel! Anyone but Gabriel!

The preacher stood over them, his handsome features taut with the cold anger of disapproval. And something else. Something that bore urgency.

McAllister was also sitting up, but to Callie's disgust there was a cynical little smile on his face instead of the shame that should have been there. "What's the matter, Reverend?" he drawled. "Have we shocked you?"

"The behavior of both of you would have been reprehensible under any circumstances, Mr. McAllister, but it is particularly offensive in this moment."

"And why is that, Reverend?"

"Because," Gabriel replied, wiping the smile from Lincoln's mouth with his solemn announcement, "Tom Callahan has just died."

Chapter Six

"Oh, P-Pearl," Callie blubbered. "It's j-just awful!"

Pearl gazed at her in disbelief. She had never seen Callie in this kind of emotional state. In fact, she didn't know she was capable of such copious tears, which were streaming down her cheeks as she sat hunched on the camp stool, too miserable to eat the breakfast Pearl had tried to urge on her.

"Well, now"—Pearl cleared her throat, awkward with the situation—"I didn't figger you knew Tom Callahan good enough t'take on like this over his passin'."

"I didn't. I—I'm not."

"Then if ya ain't grievin' fer his burial yesterday sunset, what *are* ya grievin' fer?"

"I *am* right sorry he passed on," she admitted, then paused to wipe her sleeve across her dripping nose. "An' Miz Smyth had no call t'be hateful an' say I wasn't. Why, didn't I go an' help pile all those rocks over the poor man's grave so's the animals wouldn't dig 'im up after we move on this morning?"

"Yeah, you was real respectful when he was laid t'rest."

"Miz Smyth don't think so. Miz Smyth said I was indecent an'—an' undeservin'. Said a lot o' mean things when she come stormin' over t'me while I was washin' up just after first light."

"Those bein'?"

"That me and McAllister was hopeless bar— barbarians. That we was *all* a bunch o' barbarians."

"And that ain't good, huh?"

"N-no. An' there's more. She said she'd had enough o' us an' Oregon, which I don't see 'cause we ain't even got t'Oregon yet so how'd she know she don't like it? But that ain't the worst. The worst is she's leavin' us."

Pearl set the coffee pot she was holding on the tripod and stared at her. "Now how can she go an' do that?"

Callie bobbed her head emphatically. "It's true. Says she hates the west an' is goin' home. Says when we reach Fort Laramie in a week or so, she's gonna sit there until a party comes through headin' back east, an' she's goin' with 'em. Says she's made up her mind an' won't be talked outta it. An', oh, Pearl, what am I gonna do? Lessen I have her teachin', I'll never be a lady!"

The realization brought on a storm of fresh

tears. Pearl left the fire and knelt in front of the stool, trying to comfort her. "Honey lamb, don't take on so. There's other ways."

"No, there ain't, Pearl." She struggled to compose herself, hiccoughing softly and wiping again, this time at her wet cheeks. "I'm seein' my last hope go with Miz Smyth. Now I'll never stand a chance with Gabriel."

Pearl had no answer. She was afraid that what Callie said was true.

Callie, sniffing, sat up straight. Her face hardened with anger. "It's all that varmint McAllister's fault. If Miz Smyth hadn't found us wrestlin' like that in the dirt, I wouldn't be losin' 'er."

"Maybe. On the other hand it appears t'me she's just been waitin' fer an excuse t'pull out, an' if it hadn't been this here, she'd o' found some other."

"No, Pearl, McAllister is t'blame, an' I oughta shoot him in his tracks. Only now," she said mournfully, "I can't 'cause with the wagon master gone fer sure, ain't no one else t'pilot us."

"Kind of a mess."

"That's fer certain." Callie rose from the stool with a deep sigh. "Guess it's time I was saddlin' Apollo an' headin' out fer the day. Uh, Pearl?"

"Yeah?"

"I'm real sorry 'bout the mirror."

"Me, too. It was right handy fer lettin' me know I can still turn a man's head. 'Course by the time I git t'the end o' this trail, I figger there won't be anything worth admirin'. Sure is tough on a woman's looks."

Callie was too unhappy to smile. Pearl

watched her go off to her horse, hoping she would get over her disappointment.

It didn't happen. Callie's spirits failed to improve over the next two days as the wagon train continued on toward Fort Laramie. She handled her scouting duties conscientiously, but she was cheerful about nothing.

Pearl was worried. She couldn't stand to see her friend like this, distraught and silently heartbroken. Pondering the problem, she decided that Callie had had a door opened for her with those lessons. Maybe no more than a brief crack, but enough to let her glimpse wonderful possibilities on the other side. She would never be satisfied now unless she was given the chance to reach for them. Callie just had to be able to walk through that door to ladyhood.

Pearl went to Parthenia and tried to persuade her to resume the lessons, but Miss Smyth hadn't softened in her decision. She was returning east at the first opportunity, and that was the end of it. Not for Pearl. She was determined now that Callie should be educated to ladyhood. Which meant if Parthenia wouldn't teach her, then someone else must.

Who? But there was no one else on the wagon train qualified to instruct her except Gabriel Hawkins himself. Pearl seriously considered him. After all, hadn't he offered similar lessons to her? But in the end she knew he was out of the question. The mature Gabriel already viewed Callie as little more than an exasperating child. If she became his pupil—providing Callie would even agree to such an arrangement, and

Pearl had her doubts about that—he would always see her as that child. No, if Callie was ever to appeal to him as a woman, then she must emerge full blown as a lady.

But with both Parthenia and Gabriel eliminated, it was hopeless. Of course, it wasn't hopeless, and Pearl knew it. She just didn't want to acknowledge the candidate that had been there all along. Detestable on some levels maybe, but there was no denying it. Under that hard surface of his were cultured origins, and he probably had the kind of brain capable of sharing them.

Still, the whole notion was so preposterous, so outrageous, that Pearl emphatically rejected it. Until the early evening of the second day when, exhausted after a couple of sleepless nights and her long day in the saddle, Callie lay down and cried herself to sleep. That did it. Pearl couldn't take any more of Callie's suffering, but her surrender wasn't a happy one. Her pots and pans suffered a rough banging as she angrily prepared their supper.

Damn it to hell, there was no other choice! She'd have to go to him. Oh, he'd agree to do it all right. Not willingly. Not by a long shot. But in the end he'd be too eager to turn her down because, naturally, she would have to give him what he wanted. No more holding back.

There were a lot of problems connected with that. She didn't like it one bit, but it was the only way. Yes, damn it to hell!

She was still silently cursing the necessity of the situation when, after supper, she managed to slip away from Callie. She found McAllister alone with the horses, grooming his big roan. He was so occupied applying a pair of brushes to the mount's sleek coat that she was able to stand there undetected in the gathering twilight. She remained silent, taking his measure.

She could see his muscles bunch as he worked. There was all the power of a black panther in that lean body of his. And probably the cruelty of a panther too when aroused. He worried her all right. Was she an absolute fool proposing to entrust Callie to him? Maybe, but Pearl's considerable experience with men convinced her that, whatever his dark history, Lincoln McAllister had a rigid code and that, once committed to a promise, he could be counted on to honor it.

He never turned his head to gaze in her direction, but he must have been aware of her presence all along because he finally asked in a low voice, "All right, Pearl, what do you want?"

"Depends."

"On?"

"The answers I get to a couple of questions." She moved closer. There was no one else around, but she didn't want to risk being overheard. "Fort Laramie ain't far now, huh?"

He went on with his work, rhythmically brushing the contented roan's smooth flanks. "Probably less than a week away, providing we have no serious breakdowns."

"An' the trail from this point on is pretty clear, right?"

"We just follow the Platte straight to the fort."

Pearl had been counting on this, along with

Ned's knowledge. The young scout, recovered enough from his gunshot wound to ride again, was already sharing duties with Callie. Ned had been over the trail before. He would know the way, even if he wasn't an experienced pilot. Leastways as far as Fort Laramie. But there was one more thing Pearl had to know.

"I hear tell this Fort Laramie is a busy place. Got men there lookin' fer work. Mebbe even a few with what it takes t'sign on as wagon master t'Oregon. That so?"

This time Lincoln paused and turned to look at her. One of those satanic black eyebrows of his was lifted in cynical amusement. "What is all this, Pearl? Are you making sure I won't be missed before you give Callie permission to shoot me?"

"No," she said with a grim-faced decisiveness, "I'm permittin' *you*, mister, t'replace Parthenia Smyth as her teacher."

His laughter was deep and rich. "When pigs fly."

"Well, they're about t'take wing, so you'd better listen."

He stared at her for a moment and saw that she was serious.

Pearl nodded. "Yeah, that's right. Callie ain't gonna miss out on her chance t'be a lady. I'm gonna see t'that. Ya got learnin', Lincoln McAllister, an' whatever it takes, yer gonna share it with her."

"Why do I have this feeling, Pearl Slocum," he said slowly, "that I'm a prospective client about to conduct business with a shrewd whore?"

" 'Cause that's what I am. Or was. But I still got what it takes t'strike a hard bargain. An' I say it's yer fault as much as Callie's that she went an' lost that ol' dragon."

"If it's guilt you're planning to use, it isn't a smart choice, Pearl. In case you haven't noticed, I'm incapable of guilt."

Which wasn't altogether true, he admitted to himself. He had been brooding about the episode ever since it happened, haunted by the scene of them tussling there in the dust like a couple of animals in heat. Why? he asked himself. Why did he repeatedly allow that little hellcat to get under his skin? Forever get both of them in trouble when he'd always been capable of a cool self-control in the toughest of situations?

"You owe her," Pearl insisted.

"This is crazy. Does Callie even know you're here? No, I can see she doesn't. No matter how desperate she is to be a lady, she'd refuse to have any part of this."

"But you won't."

"There isn't anything that could make me—" He broke off in sudden realization. "Ah, yes, the hard bargain. I was forgetting about that, wasn't I?"

"The Black Hills," she said simply.

His dark eyes glowed with excitement. Why, the Black Hills were almost directly north from here, not more than a few days away! Was it possible that all along he'd been this close to his objective? "*Where* in the Black Hills?"

She smiled at him in mock sweetness. "Guess

them Black Hills is a big place, huh? Guess a man could search ferever in there an' not come across what he wanted, lessen he knew just where t'look."

She was presenting him with an ultimatum. Either he agreed to her terms, or he wouldn't get what he so urgently sought. "Pearl," he pleaded with her. "This just can't work. I'm not a teacher. I don't have the skills or the patience."

"Find 'em."

"And what about Callie? You think she's going to sit still, all eager smiles, and let the man she hates and longs to kill instruct her in the niceties of society—whatever the hell they are?"

"Callie won't have a choice, not once she's off alone with ya."

"What does that mean?" Linc stared at her suspiciously and then groaned as a further realization seized him. "Oh, Lord help us, you intend to send *both* of us into the Black Hills! That's what all those questions were for about the train getting to Fort Laramie on its own and hiring a new wagon master once it's there."

Pearl had it all figured out. There were too many distractions for Callie on this wagon train, Gabriel chief among them. That's why her progress had been so slow. She needed to be isolated somewhere with her teacher, just the two of them and no interruptions. 'Course, with the teacher being who he was, there were definite risks in that, but before they left she meant to put the fear of God in Lincoln McAllister.

"Maybe we won't have t'hire us a new wagon master at Laramie," Pearl said calmly. "Maybe you an' Callie will get back afore the train's ready t'roll ag'in after its layover. If not, ya can catch up with us on the trail."

He nodded. "Uh-huh. One thing, though. Just how do you propose to get Callie to accompany me? Or were you figuring on me carrying her off over my shoulder kicking and screaming?"

"I reckon that bit is a problem," Pearl conceded. "But I'll manage something."

"You do that, because I don't want to be involved in that part of it."

The roan turned its head to gaze at him mildly as Linc leaned weakly against its bulk. Had he taken leave of his senses? Because it sounded to him that he had, in effect, just agreed to this whole madness. Yeah, he must be losing his mind if he intended to go off into the wilderness with, of all creatures on God's green earth, Callie Burgess. But in the end it still came down to that one simple reality. Unless he gave Pearl what she wanted, she wouldn't give him what he wanted—and he meant to have that.

"Okay, you've got me, sucker that I am. Now let's have that place in the Black Hills."

"An' have you ride out o'here without Callie?" Pearl shook her head. "You'll hear the place when you an' Callie is ready t'roll an' not afore. An' 'til then, let's keep all this between us. Don't want anyone tellin' Callie or tryin' t'stop us."

She started to leave, but Linc stopped her. "I don't know why it should matter in the least, but there's something I'd like to ask you."

"Bein'?"

"Why are you doing this for Callie? Why have

133

you been putting yourself out for her all along?"

"That's easy. She's the first decent female who ever looked at me an' didn't right off see someone she had t'avoid."

She turned and walked away through the twilight. Linc couldn't help feeling both an admiration and a respect as he gazed after her. He wondered if Callie knew how lucky she was. Friends of Pearl Slocum's caliber were rare.

The careful, secret preparations that Lincoln and Pearl undertook to ready them for the trek began early the next morning when Parthenia Smyth demanded suspiciously, "And just why, Mr. McAllister, should you think I'd be interested in selling you my rig and its contents?"

"Well, ma'am," Linc said as humbly as he could, and humility was a quality that didn't come easily to him, "I'd actually be doing you something of a favor by buying it. Most likely the only parties you'll find at Fort Laramie heading back east will be freighters. They travel light in that direction in order to make speed. If you mean to join them, they won't welcome a loaded wagon like yours."

He was stretching the truth there, but he needed her wagon. Not only was it potentially available, it was both the smallest and strongest of the schooners on the train, capable of enduring the rugged terrain of the Black Hills region.

He could afford to offer her a fair price. Linc was skillful with cards. He'd had to be in order to survive after the army discharged him without pay. Those winnings had supported him, but they were far from being the kind of money he intended to have by the end of this journey.

Parthenia was still suspicious. "But why should you want a wagon at all?"

"If I'm going to settle in Oregon," he said with bland innocence, "which I've decided to do, I'll need my own wagon and supplies. As for all the educational materials you're carrying, along with most of the personal goods you'll have to sacrifice, anyway . . . well, I figure I can get a good price for those in Oregon."

"And you say you want the wagon *now?*"

"I thought this way I could get a feel for handling the rig, see if it needs any attention in the workshops before we reach Laramie."

"And what am I to do until then?"

"Minnie Bird and Hattie Jackson would be happy to have you take your essentials and join their outfit."

Parthenia thought about what he was offering her. It was true she would need funds when she got back east until she could find a new teaching position. And if her wagon and most of its contents were only going to be a burden on the return journey, then hadn't she better part with them now?

In the end, Linc got his wagon, into which Pearl immediately sneaked certain articles of her own choosing. He also got mules to pull it. The oxen that accompanied Parthenia's rig, like all of the wagons on the train, were sturdy, dependable beasts. They were also maddeningly slow. Linc wanted the speed of mules. A team of them had belonged to the late Tom Callahan, who'd intended making a profit on them in Oregon. The man who had been caring for them since Tom's death found them to be troublesome critters and was happy to trade them for Parthenia's oxen and a cash bribe.

Linc wasn't worried about the mules. He had managed plenty of them in his army days. Callie Burgess, now, was another story. He shuddered over the certainty of the ordeal ahead of him. The only thing he had to be glad about was that it was Pearl's responsibility, and not his, to get Callie on board that wagon.

"Was hangin' on t'this, figgerin' one day t'celebrate the end o' the trail. But the way you been down last couple o' days, I say we put it t'work now liftin' you up."

The light from their late-evening campfire cast a warm, golden glow on the corked bottle that Pearl had produced from the depths of her wagon. Callie gazed at it with strong misgivings. "I dunno, Pearl. Don't seem like a good plan t'me. Spirits an' I just don't agree. 'Member what they done t'me night o' the Oregon Freedom Day dance? I wouldn't care t'repeat that."

"Honey lamb, that was the hard stuff. Lots o' folks don't have heads fer hard likker. But this here is wine. It'll just make ya feel nice an' pleasant."

Callie shook her head. "Don't think so, Pearl."

"Champagne wine," Pearl coaxed, holding the bottle temptingly toward her. "All the way from France. You ever taste champagne?"

"No, never. I heard 'bout it, though."

"It's what ladies drink. *Elegant* ladies."

Callie was immediately impressed. "Honest?"

"Sure enough."

She was convinced. "Then mebbe I'd better try me a sip or two."

Pearl meant for her to drink much more than that. Enough, anyway, to put her in a condition where she would know absolutely nothing when she was loaded into the wagon bound for the Black Hills a few hours from now. Pearl regretted her deception, hated to think what Callie would suffer when she came around, but there was no other way.

She kept telling herself, as she popped the cork and poured a generous measure of the sparkling wine into Callie's cup, and considerably less than that into her own cup, that it was all for Callie's ultimate benefit. If she didn't believe that, she would never be able to live with her actions.

Pearl watched her taste the champagne. "Good, huh?"

"Real good, Pearl. 'Ceptin' the bubbles get up my nose. Feel like I'm gonna sneeze."

"Won't when ya git past the first couple o' sips. Drink up, an' you'll see," she urged her.

Callie obediently emptied the cup and started to push it away. "Reckon I'd better stop now."

Pearl smacked her forehead with the palm of her hand. "What am I thinkin'? Clean fergot t'raise a toast. Always have t'raise a toast when yer drinkin' champagne. It's what stylish folk do, an' we wannna be stylish, don't we? Here, you'll need another few drops fer that." Before Callie

137

could object, she splashed more wine into her cup. "Here's to our arrival at Fort Laramie."

Callie was less resistant after that, though Pearl found it necessary to invent several more toasts in order to keep her cup filled.

"I'm feelin' a lot more cheerful now," Callie said with a silly grin on her face. "Real relaxed, too."

"Well, now, that's good news." But before she relaxed herself all the way into oblivion, there was something Pearl had to try to get her to understand. "Uh, you been thinkin' anymore 'bout McAllister?"

Callie frowned, puzzled over this abrupt introduction of so unpleasant a matter just when she was getting herself all cozy and warm. "Don' wanna think 'bout that skunk. Why you bringin' him up, Pearl?"

"Just been wonderin' if you'd had any change o'heart since our talk? 'Bout his killin' yer pa, I mean. Seems a shame t'wear yerself out blamin' him when he could be the lamb 'stead o' the wolf." It was going to be difficult enough for Callie to accept McAllister as her teacher. But if she went on being convinced he was a killer she was sworn to punish . . . well, that made the situation just a mite more complicated.

"I ain't changed my mind," Callie said stubbornly.

Pearl spent the next several minutes trying to soften her on the subject of Lincoln's guilt, but there was no reasoning with the girl. Pearl finally had to let it go. She had tried, and that was all she could do. It was McAllister's problem now, and God help him to deal with it.

Before midnight the entire bottle of champagne had been consumed, three-quarters of it by Callie, whose happy fuzziness had progressed to drowsy numbness and finally to a state where all her senses had completely shut down.

Pearl, covering her where she lay curled on the ground, murmured a gentle, "If this don't work, honey lamb, yer probably gonna hate me fer the rest o' yer days. But it's all I knew t'try, so ya jest gotta make it work."

Callie was still unconscious when Lincoln came to get her in the chill black hour before daybreak. He and Pearl spoke in whispers.

"Is she ready? I want to be long gone from here before the camp stirs."

Pearl indicated the sleeping figure. They didn't dare to risk a lantern, but the glowing embers of the campfire convinced Linc as he crouched down by Callie's side that the champagne hadn't failed them.

"Well, well," he said with a grin. "This is the first time I've seen that ornery little mouth closed. Looks like it'll stay that way, too, for some time."

"You just be ready fer when it opens ag'in," Pearl warned him. "She ain't gonna be sweet 'bout what we've done."

"Which is why I've put the guns and ammunition where she can't get her hands on them." He gathered the limp figure into his arms and

139

came to his feet. For a moment he stood there, looking down at her.

"What?" Pearl asked, anxious for them to be under way before they were discovered.

"Nothing. I was just surprised at how light she is." Like a child in his arms, he thought. A defenseless one. The realization aroused something he definitely didn't want to feel, which was why he added a gruff, "Let's move."

Pearl led the way through the darkness, carrying a small bag of essentials she hadn't been able to pack for Callie until she was safely asleep. Lincoln had moved his rig off into a shallow gully before the first sentries had been posted for the night. None of those guards challenged them as they left the corral and made their way to the gully. The camp was used to its members slipping off into the dark at odd hours to relieve themselves.

The mule team was in harness and waiting when they reached the seclusion of the gully. Both Lincoln's horse and Apollo were on picket lines attached to the back of the wagon. After placing Callie on a quilt at the front of the wagon, Linc settled himself on the driver's perch. Pearl passed the bag up to him. He stowed it under the board and then leaned down to speak to her.

"That's not all, I hope."

"I ain't forgot. Here it is." Removing a folded paper from inside her shawl, she handed it to him. "It ain't just words either. It's a map Bud drew out and left with me fer safekeepin'." And there were days, Pearl thought, when she'd wished he hadn't, and other times when she had seriously considered destroying the thing and putting an end to all the cruel strife it had caused. "There's a description of what yer after on the back," she added.

Linc eagerly took possession of the paper, wishing he could read it immediately. But that would have meant lighting a lantern and wasting precious minutes. It would have to wait, though he didn't question its authenticity. He knew Pearl well enough by now to trust her. And also to be concerned about her.

"Be careful," he cautioned her, tucking the map inside the top of his boot. "With Parsons and Ritter on the loose, you're still a target."

Pearl turned her head, gazing nervously into the darkness. "You reckon they could be out there now, maybe watchin' an' ready t'follow you up into them Black Hills?"

Linc shook his head. "Reptiles like that never come out before sunup. Just get yourself straight back to camp, and from now on stick close to the wagons."

There was the first hint of daybreak in the sky. The mules were growing restless. Linc released the brake on the wagon and picked up the reins. But Pearl reached up and placed a restraining hand on his arm.

"Not so fast, mister. I got a last word fer you."

"I sort of figured on that."

"Ya take care o' Callie out there in that wilderness, ya hear? 'Cause if ya hurt her in any way," she warned him severely, "or take advantage o' her—an' I guess I don't have t'explain what that means—then she won't have t'kill ya."

141

"Yes, I know. You'll kill me yourself."

"Ya can count on it."

How had he gotten himself into this squeeze, anyway? Linc wondered. Being responsible for a foul-mouthed brat's education was bad enough. But now he had to be accountable for her virtue as well. He suddenly had a terrible feeling that it would take a miracle for Callie Burgess and him to survive each other, and the Almighty didn't seem to be handing him many of those lately.

Too late to change his mind, though. He was already committed to this piece of insanity. He just hoped, if he should end up failing, that Pearl Slocum was a poor shot.

Pearl watched the wagon rumble out of the gully and turn north. When the darkness had swallowed it, she hurried back to the corral. As the first gray light streaked the eastern sky, she sat by her fire thinking. What was done was done. It was time to stop worrying about Callie and concentrate on another problem.

The camp would be stirring soon. Gabriel Hawkins was going to be mighty unhappy when he learned he had lost both his current wagon master and his best scout. She was going to have some tall explaining to do. But there was a way she could soften the Reverend's anger. Maybe.

Pearl had told Callie the night of the dance to ignore the disapproval of the other women on the wagon train. That they were jealous because the men found them alluring. But Pearl had known all along that what the women had objected to was the vulgarity of a harlot.

She could try to change all that, Pearl thought. She could try to find acceptance among the women, providing she was willing to make the effort. She didn't need to be the lady that Callie so desperately craved to be. It would be enough if she managed just a . . . well, a kind of decency.

Why not? Maybe Oregon would like a respectable Pearl Slocum. Maybe she herself would, too.

Rising from the stool, she quietly went about preparing herself. She'd saved the largest piece of the broken mirror. Using it to guide her, she washed away all traces of makeup, arranged her hair in a plain style, and changed into her simplest dress. She was ready.

Hoping her new look would demonstrate her earnestness, even if her reflection in the glass did make her want to groan, Pearl went off to find Gabriel Hawkins. It was time to accept those lessons he had offered her.

Chapter Seven

Demons had somehow taken possession of her body. Nasty little things equipped with mallets and pincers and pokers. They were gleefully chasing around inside her, using those awful devices to sting her flesh, whack at her joints, hammer at her brain. They were everywhere, and Callie had had enough of their meanness. She would have ordered them to leave her, but each time she tried to speak, she gagged on her words.

She had never been so miserable. They even made her eyelids hurt. They were scorching them with hot instruments. Figuring to shake them off, she made an effort and rolled back her lids. That's when she discovered it wasn't demons working on her. At least not on that particular portion of her anatomy. It was the blinding heat of the sun in her face.

Squinting against its glare, she judged that it was almost directly overhead. That meant it was somewhere around noon. What was she doing stretched out on her back at midday when she should have been out with Apollo scouting the trail?

There was something else up there with the sun. Looked like ribs stripped of their meat. It was only when she concentrated very hard, slowly restoring her senses, that Callie understood the ribs above her were wagon bows. The canvas cover on them had been folded back, permitting light and air inside the wagon. What was more, the wagon was on the move. She could feel it jouncing beneath her. And she really wished it wouldn't do that, because every sway and bump made her stomach lurch, cruelly reminding her—

Oh, murder! She remembered it now. All that danged champagne last night. Pearl oughtn't to have let her drink that stuff. Served Pearl right that of course she hadn't been able to rouse Callie this morning when the train rolled out, and they'd had to go and dump her in here.

Something funny about that, though. It took her another minute to decide what it was. There were no familiar calls back and forth from wagon to wagon, no creak of many wheels turning. Except for the close sounds of the wagon bearing her, she heard nothing but silence.

Lifting her head painfully from the quilt on

145

which she had been deposited, Callie peered over a mound of bags and boxes, past the bobbing heads of Apollo and the roan off the rear of the wagon. There *were* no other wagons out there! Nothing but a vast, rugged, very lonely landscape.

The same was true when she twisted her head forward. An emptiness stretched in front of the plodding team drawing the wagon. What was not blank, however, was the seat behind those mules. It was occupied by the solid shape of a broad-shouldered back just inches from her aching head.

Even though Callie was unable to see the face belonging to that back, she had a dreadful conviction that she was on her way to hell in a black chariot and that Satan himself was at the reins. She must have registered her anguish over this realization, probably with a groan, because he turned his head and looked down at her with a diabolical grin. Sure enough, it was Satan.

"And just when I thought I was going to have to bury you out here under a mound of rocks."

"Where are we?" she croaked past a tongue as thick and furred as a buffalo hide. "Where we goin'?"

"You're being taken to finishing school, Miss Burgess."

"Ya either give me a straight answer, Lincoln McAllister, or I'll—"

"What? Come on, I'd really like to know, because from where I'm sitting you look like you're in no condition to threaten anything. Well, maybe a week-old kitten."

He was right. Callie clenched her jaws together in frustration and regretted it. Even that simple action made her teeth ache, and she didn't need still another penalty for last night.

"Now why don't you just settle down there again on that quilt," he said placidly, "and when you're feeling better we'll talk."

"I wanna know what's goin' on. Whose wagon is this, and where're the others?"

He took a deep breath and answered her in one long rush. "The wagon is mine. I bought it from Parthenia Smyth. The others are back on the Oregon Trail headed west. We are headed north. That's because the Black Hills are toward the north and not the west. And along the way, if you're a good girl, I'm going to give you the lessons Parthenia had the wisdom to abandon. See, it's all very clear and simple."

Callie jerked up to a sitting position so suddenly that her splitting head seemed ready to roll off her body. "Y've kidnapped me!" she gasped.

"Don't be silly. Why would I want to kidnap the woman who's promised to send me to hell? And if you're going to blame somebody, start with Pearl Slocum. She's the one who arranged this little party. Paid me to take you off into the wilderness and turn you into a lady. Pretty funny, huh?"

"Pearl'd never give ya money t'steal me away."

"Who said anything about money? She paid me with information. Now what's wrong?"

He was staring at her face. She figured it had probably gone a strange color. Ever since she had abruptly elevated herself on the quilt, her stomach had joined her head in a violent protest. The upheaval had reached a critical stage.

"Stop the wagon!" she demanded.

"Uh-oh."

He hauled back on the reins, but Callie didn't wait for the wagon to reach a full halt. Bolting over the side, she flung herself face down in the buffalo grass where, to her mortification, she proceeded to empty her insides.

Up on his perch, Linc watched her being sick in the sand and wondered how, by any stretch of the imagination, he was supposed to turn this excuse for a female into something remotely approaching a lady. Look at her! She was a mess!

She was also suffering one beauty of a hangover. Oh, hell! Dropping the reins with a sigh, he climbed down over the wheel. By the time he reached her, she had stopped retching and was struggling, without much success, to get to her hands and knees.

Linc reached down, grabbed a handful of her britches, and lifted her bodily into the air. "Come on, sweet pea, let's get you back to your garden."

Heaving her into the wagon, he saw her settled again on the quilt. He found a cloth, soaked it in the water barrel, and was washing her face when she found the strength to mutter, "I got it figgered now."

"And just what have you figured out?" he asked, not paying much attention to what she was saying as he concentrated on cleaning her up.

"What this here is truly all 'bout. Ya don't fool me, Lincoln McAllister. Managed t'git yer hands on that strongbox with all them mission funds, didn't ya? And now yer on the run from the wagon train."

"Uh-huh, and what else?"

"Bein' helpless, ya snatched me 'long with the strongbox."

"Why?"

"Well, 'cause—'cause ya needed a hostage. Yeah, that's right, I'm yer hostage."

"No grass growing on you, is there, Callie?"

"My brain works just fine," she assured him smugly.

"I can see that. There's only one thing wrong with your explanation. That strongbox right now happens to be somewhere in Gabriel Hawkins's wagon on its way to Fort Laramie. Never mind. You're in no state to hear the real story, so we'll save it for when you've recovered. There, you're done. Any, uh, other areas you'd like me to wash?"

She started to tell him what he could do with his attentions. But as she sputtered the first words, he dropped the soggy cloth over her mouth, left her with a cheerful "You're welcome," and scrambled back onto his perch, taking up the reins again.

Callie lay there as the wagon continued on its way, too weak and bewildered to help herself. She had been so certain that her explanation was the right one. But, on second thought, it felt all wrong.

Oh, what difference did it make? All that mattered was getting away from him and returning to the others. Only she was too sick to either flee or oppose him. And all the while the wagon bearing her was moving farther away from the Oregon Trail into a rough, treeless region scoured into gullies and rocky ridges by dry, searching winds. A hostile place with a relentless sun and only the buzzards overhead for company. McAllister must have lost his mind plunging them into this wild country. Damn him, and damn that champagne for getting her into this fix!

Callie hated to admit it, but the aroma of what McAllister was cooking over the fire was mighty appealing. They were camped for the night beside a shallow stream where he had managed to spear a fish. It was the first water she had seen all day. There were trees, too. Nothing but stunted cottonwoods, but they were a welcome sight just the same.

Chunks of the fish were swimming in the pan now, together with rice and bits of onion. Considering how she had felt for most of this awful day, Callie didn't think she'd ever have an appetite again, but she was recovered now and all hollow inside. She hadn't eaten a morsel since the night before, and what she had eaten she hadn't kept down. She couldn't wait to put her mouth around the contents of that pan.

Of course, there was a problem with her craving. Acknowledging it could have Linc thinking she was surrendering the fight and that he had her just where he wanted her. But dang it, she had to put food into her belly, didn't she? She needed her strength for what she intended to do tonight.

"This is ready," he said with exaggerated nonchalance as he lifted the pan from the fire. "There's more than enough for two here, but then, maybe you're not interested. Maybe you're not ready to even look at food."

"Oh," she said with equal casualness, "I reckon I can do with a bite or two."

"Or maybe you don't want any part of something I've cooked. Maybe you'd like to get your own meal. I mean, considering I'm the enemy here, I guess I'd understand if—"

"Just dish up the grub, will ya?" Damn him for taunting her! He had to know she was starving by the way she'd been eyeing that pan.

"I think I understand," he said with a maddening drawl as he heaped a pair of tin plates with fish and rice. "You'd refuse this mess, but you don't want to wound my feelings. That's real generous of you, Callie."

He was laughing at her again. She wanted to take the plate he handed her and dump it over his head, but her traitorous stomach wouldn't permit it. Huddled on a fallen log near the fire, she eagerly loaded a spoon and shoved it into her mouth.

Mmm-hmm! Whatever the dish was called, it sure was a savory treat. And a real surprise coming from a man like him.

Her approval must have been evident because he remarked with a shrug, "I'm half Creole. We

seem to be born knowing what to do with some
herbs and a few spices."

Maybe so, but to Callie cooking had always
been a kind of baffling magic. Except for boiling
up coffee, and even that she didn't always get
right, her rare efforts in the kitchen had been
dismal failures. Pa had usually handled their
meals, such as they were. Most times they'd
taken their suppers at a boardinghouse in Horizon.

Callie looked up from her plate. McAllister
was staring at her, a funny expression on his
face. Probably hurt because she wasn't compli-
menting him. Through a mouthful of food, she
gave him a grudging, "Ain't too bad. I can manage t'get it down."

Get it down? Hell, Linc thought, she was devouring it. It was a sight that didn't exactly en-
courage his own appetite. He'd seen men in the
army at mealtimes, rough recruits in the lowest
ranks with table manners no better than raven-
ous dogs. But compared to Callie Burgess,
they'd put away their food with a dainty refinement.

She didn't approach what was on her plate.
She *attacked* it with loud slurping and smacking
and licking noises, the sauce dribbling down her
chin. She didn't seem to bother much with chew-
ing and swallowing either before the next spoon-
ful went into her mouth. How did she do it?

And how, Linc wondered, past counting how
many times he'd already asked himself this pathetic question, was he supposed to tame her?
He knew how to train and lead men, how to fight

battles against serious odds. But he had no idea how to go about civilizing a wild female who wasn't going to be happy until she could turn handsprings on his grave.

Callie lay wrapped in a blanket on her side of the dying fire, listening tensely to the sounds of the night. She could hear the soft burbling of the waters in the creek and the leaves on the cottonwood trees rustling in a faint breeze.

And by straining her ears, she could also hear the sound of McAllister's breathing. The steady, even rhythm of it told her that he was asleep. But she was taking no chances. She had to make certain he was beyond alertness, so she went on keeping her vigil, giving him time to sink into an even deeper sleep.

When she could no longer stand the suspense of waiting, she eased herself out of the blanket and got cautiously to her feet. She stood there for a moment in perfect stillness, testing the situation, fearing that if she took a single step, it would result in a sudden challenge from him.

There was a gibbous moon tonight, shedding just enough light through the trees to show her McAllister's silent shape on the ground. She thought about making sure he wouldn't awaken by finding the nearest rock and using it on him, but she resisted the temptation. Not because she had any compunction about cracking him in the skull with a heavy object. It was simply too risky. He had gone to bed with his Colt in hand, and if she disturbed him by getting close enough to deliver an effective blow, she could find herself eating a bullet.

That made her think longingly of her own Remington. She wouldn't have to be standing here considering rocks if that rifle was worth anything. But, of course, it wasn't. He had seen to that.

The rifle had been the first thing on her mind when they'd made camp and he'd mentioned something about having brought along all of her belongings. Did that include the Remington? Could it possibly be somewhere in the wagon, and now that she was feeling better, was there any chance of getting her hands on it? There was, but the opportunity didn't occur until after supper.

McAllister had settled down by the fire to study that mysterious paper he'd been keeping close to him all day.

Looked to Callie like a map. She'd caught him poring over it earlier on the wagon when she'd been too sick to care.

She still didn't care, though he'd made an effort to interest her. "You ready for that explanation now?" he'd asked.

But she didn't want to hear his pack of lies. All she cared about was getting back to Gabriel. "Uh, figgered while there's still some daylight, I'd better clean up down at the crick. Maybe see 'bout gettin' inta some duds I ain't been sick all over."

"Help yourself."

He was in no hurry then to share his story. He hadn't even glanced up from that paper when she wandered off to the wagon on the pretext of securing soap, a towel, and a change of clothes.

Her hurried search in the wagon had turned up her rifle but no ammunition. If it existed, he had concealed it too carefully for her to find. She should have known that, had there been any threat to him, he wouldn't have permitted her to come anywhere near the wagon.

That left only one option for Callie. Escape. Riding all night over a route she wasn't sure she could retrace, and hoping that by morning she would have regained the Oregon Trail, was a daunting prospect. But she was fresh after sleeping most of the day, Apollo was a dependable mount, and there would be enough of a moon to light the way. Callie was confident she could manage. Providing she could steal away from McAllister. It was time to make that effort.

Scarcely daring to breathe, she took a careful step forward. A twig snapped under her heel, sounding like a shot in the quiet darkness. Callie froze. No reaction. McAllister never stirred. Blessing her luck, she crept off toward the wagon.

Earlier, when she'd used the excuse of washing herself at the stream, she'd managed to gather together several essentials which she'd buried at the back of the wagon. They were waiting for her now—a canteen of water, a bit of beef jerky to sustain her on the long ride, and the bridle for Apollo.

She had decided against a saddle. It'd take too much time lugging and cinching it, and she needed to hurry. Needed to be long gone before he was aware of her absence, though if her luck held, he'd sleep on until daybreak, and by then she'd be so far away he'd never manage to recover her. Anyway, it wouldn't be the first time she'd ridden bareback.

McAllister had staked out the two horses on their picket lines, along with the mules. They were browsing on buffalo grass when Callie reached them. By this time shreds of ragged cloud were veiling the face of the moon, making it difficult for her to see what she was doing. That, and Apollo's reluctance to accept the bit after she released him from the picket line, had her almost as nervous as the horse.

"What's wrong with ya?" she whispered as he blew noisily through his nostrils and tried to edge away from her. "Those mules spookin' ya?"

Seconds later, with the bridle finally in place and secured, Callie swung onto his back. "All right, Apollo, let's make tracks."

Reins in hand, she dug her heels sharply into his flanks. Apollo responded, not by springing forward but by bucking violently—so violently and unexpectedly that, without a saddle and its stirrups to contain her, Callie went sailing over his head.

There was a loud whump as her body collided with hard earth. She lay sprawled there, dazed and uncomprehending. Then the moon came out again, lighting the scene, and she understood Apollo's emphatic objections. She could see the taut leather and the buckles binding his back legs. He had been hobbled! That sonofabitch, McAllister, had hobbled her horse!

"Now, you didn't expect me to go and trust you without a single precaution, did you?"

McAllister was here! He must have been awake the whole time and followed her, never making a sound. He'd probably stood there and watched from the shadows, laughing.

"Ah, you did, didn't you? You actually thought I'd shut my eyes and just let you ride away." He shook his head in mock regret. "Callie, Callie, when are you going to learn I made a promise not to let you go?"

What she needed in this second, needed more than anything, was to feel her knuckles connecting with that arrogant nose of his. She would have answered this need, too, except she couldn't move, other than to flail her arms helplessly. Just like a fish out of water flopping its useless tail. She couldn't talk either. The impact of her fall had punched the wind out of her.

"Trouble?" he said, coming forward and hunkering down beside her.

She could manage to gasp no more than an infuriated, "You—you—"

"Yes, I know. I'm worse than a bastard. I'm your personal version of the Antichrist. Anything hurt?"

She still couldn't answer him, except with a murderous glare. But Linc decided she was probably healthy enough otherwise. "Never mind, you just got the wind knocked out of you with that fall. You'll inflate again once we get you back to the fire. Can you walk? No? Well, then . . ."

No choice about it. He'd have to carry her. She

tried to express her feelings about that when he scooped her up and got to his feet, but all that came out was a frustrated wheeze.

Linc stood there for a moment with Callie in his arms, experiencing those same conflicted emotions he'd known the other morning when he'd brought her to the wagon: a strong awareness of her helplessness and an unwanted need deep inside him to protect her.

The feeling then had been very brief, but tonight it was stronger, less easily conquered. And it was accompanied by other unwelcome sensations down in the area of his groin. A stirring of desire prompted by the alluring softness of her shapely little bottom nestled tightly against him. The warmth of her flesh sent his blood rushing to that region, an action that robbed his brain and made him light-headed.

It had been different those other times she'd aroused him back on the wagon train. The close presence of their fellow travelers had provided a kind of safety net. But out here he was entirely alone with her.

Linc knew that in another few seconds he was going to be in serious trouble if he didn't find some means of resistance. That was when he thought of Pearl and the promise he had made her not to touch Callie. So, okay, a deal was a deal, but damn it, this one had too many complications attached to it, the worst being the temptation of this little hellcat he'd gone and made himself responsible for.

He also thought of Anne, sweet, wonderful Anne, and it was her image that saved him. It permitted him the necessary self-control over his arousal to stride swiftly back to the fire and dump Callie on her blanket. He was relieved to have her out of his arms. He just prayed she hadn't broken anything, because he absolutely refused to risk touching her again.

She certainly didn't seem hurt now that she'd managed to recover her wind. She sat up on the blanket and blasted him with a few of her favorite curses, the ones she saved for extreme situations. He let her get it all out before he told her just how it was going to be.

"Look, you don't like this arrangement, and I don't like this arrangement. But we're going to live with it, and somehow, even if it means we have to walk through fire, we're going to make it work. Yes, because I gave my word to Pearl. And since Pearl went to a hell of a lot of bother on behalf of the friend she loves, and is probably making herself sick with worry about you right now, if I were you I'd demonstrate a little gratitude for her sacrifice and start cooperating."

"Stop saying that! Pearl ain't done no such thing!"

"You're going to go on punishing yourself about that, aren't you? All right, believe what you want. But do it by wrapping yourself in that blanket and letting both of us get some sleep, because you're not going anywhere tonight."

He didn't add: "Or any of the nights to come." But Callie knew that was what he meant. Hateful as it was, she had to face it. He would never let her escape. She was trapped and, even worse, dependent on him. Stranded here in the wilderness with—he'd said it himself—the Antichrist.

159

Chapter Eight

Callie intended to tell Linc just what he could do with his breakfast. She really did. Only it was oatmeal that he was heaping into those two bowls. A thick, rich oatmeal sprinkled on top with brown sugar so dark that it resembled chocolate. *Brown sugar*. Callie absolutely relished the syrupy flavor of brown sugar, particularly over properly cooked oatmeal.

Anyway, she was awfully hollow inside. Her stomach was rumbling, demanding food. Probably a result of all her effort last night that had come to nothing. It made a body weak.

"This is ready," he said, indicating that she should help herself to one of the bowls.

Callie hesitated. She ought to resist. Ought to make things as difficult as possible for him.

"What are you waiting for?" he wondered, taking possession of his own steaming bowl.

Oh, drat! She'd just have to be difficult about something else. Grumbling over her own vulnerability, she snatched up the bowl like a starving dog pouncing on a bone.

Of course, he chuckled about it. "Feeling a little cranky still this morning, are we?"

She didn't answer him. She was too busy stuffing hot oatmeal into her mouth. What didn't go down leaked in little brown dribbles out of the corners of her mouth, but Callie was oblivious to that as she gulped and gobbled. Leastways until she looked up and caught him watching her with an expression of disbelief on his angular face.

She stopped with a loaded spoon halfway to her mouth. "What?"

"Didn't either Pearl or Parthenia Smyth ever say anything to you about your eating habits?"

"Don't s'ppose Miz Smyth ever saw me eat, an' Pearl never mentioned it." She scowled at him. "What's wrong with the way I eat?"

"Probably nothing, if this was a barnyard and that was a trough you were gorging from instead of a bowl."

"Are you sayin' I got the manners of a—"

"You haven't got any manners at all when it comes to food, Callie. And since I'm supposed to be teaching you how to be a lady—" He set aside his own bowl and approached the log where she sat. "I guess table manners is as good an area as any to begin your first lesson."

He was insulting her! She was outraged! "I ain't

takin' any lessons in table manners from you, Lincoln McAllister!"

"Are you certain of that?"

"This here is how sure I am!"

She started to defiantly shove the spoon of oatmeal into her mouth, but he was too quick for her. Before she could stop him, he had grabbed the spoon out of her hand and the bowl from her lap. "Then you won't be needing these."

"Ya friggin'—Ya give those back t'me!"

His response was to turn and dump the contents of the bowl into the fire, an action which she regretted because she was still hungry, but she couldn't let him know that.

"This is how it's going to work from now on, Callie," he proceeded to calmly inform her. "I'll continue to cook the meals, but if you plan to share them, you'll listen to my instructions and start eating like a civilized woman instead of a she-wolf falling on a buffalo carcass. Is that clear?"

"I told ya, there ain't gonna be no lessons. And ya can just stuff yer fancy cookin'. I don't need it. I'll git my own meals." It was a reckless promise considering her deplorable lack of culinary skills, but Callie was sure that she would manage just fine.

"That's good, because you won't be getting so much as a taste of mine. Unless, of course, you change your mind."

"I ain't never gonna be that desperate."

"Easy to say when you've just filled your belly with the better part of a bowl of breakfast oatmeal. Let's see how you feel about it come dinnertime. And stop eyeing that pantry box on the wagon. It's closed until our next camp. We're loading up now and moving on."

"Moving on" meant another long haul over the dreary plains with their endless stretches of parched grasses and dry buffalo wallows. Callie thought it was bad enough that she had to experience this monotonous landscape at all. What made it worse was having to share it with Lincoln McAllister in such physical intimacy.

Had it been possible, she would have traveled on foot, which was how most members of a wagon train did cross the country. But oxen were slow and mules weren't. She couldn't have kept up by walking. Nor did McAllister trust her to ride Apollo. And since he had to drive the mules from his perch on the wagon, he insisted that she occupy the board with him. It wasn't a very generous seat either, which meant she was squeezed up against him, all too aware of his hard body with its disturbing masculine warmth.

Callie would have preferred enduring the situation in a stony silence, but he gave her no quarter in that area either. It didn't matter that she stubbornly refused to respond to his conversation because he talked anyway, asking and answering his own questions. Talked without letup in that rumbling drawl that abraded her nerves with its perpetual cheerfulness.

"Haven't gotten around to explaining our little trek yet, have I? What do you say, Callie? Is this a good time to make you wise?"

Actually, she wanted very badly to know just where they were going and why. But, more importantly, she longed to know when she would be permitted to rejoin Pearl and Gabriel. She thought about that all the time, but she wasn't going to admit it. McAllister had enough advantages over her already.

"I think it is," he said. "I think you should hear all about it. Can you see them up there, Callie?"

He was referring to the Black Hills. They were in sight now for the first time. A range of low, ancient mountains thickly forested with the dark evergreens that gave them their name. Of course, those mountains were still a long way off on the horizon. At least another day and a half from here.

"That's where we're headed, Callie. There's something waiting in the Black Hills. Something worth a fortune to the man who finds it and brings it back.

"What did you say, Callie? Am I that man, and is this what it's been about all along? The murder of your father and Bud Colby? Pearl Slocum running away from Independence? That attack on the wagon train back in Kansas? Yep, that's just what it's been about."

Callie trembled in impotent fury, her hands clenching into tight fists that longed to strike out at him. He was practically confessing to her that he'd killed her pa. Her rage must have been apparent because he turned to her with a wry little smile.

"No, Callie, I *didn't* shoot them. That was the work of those men who led the raid on the wagon train. See, they also want what's up there in the Black Hills. What? You still don't believe me? Then how about I tell you a story? You like stories? This is a good one. It's all about your father's friend, Bud Colby, and something he learned."

Linc paused to shift himself into a more comfortable position on the seat, his hip nudging hers in the process. She was sure it was a deliberate action. He never lost an opportunity to make her uneasy. She would have moved away from him, only there was nowhere to move. She was on the edge of the board now.

"Now where was I? Oh, right, Bud Colby. Well, Bud had this brother who was a trooper stationed at Fort Kearny."

Callie knew about Fort Kearny, located back on the Platte. The wagon train had already passed through that post some time ago.

"Turns out," Linc continued, "that the brother did something to help out a Lakota Indian who turned up at the fort. What that was I don't know, and it doesn't matter. But it must have been pretty good for the Lakota to go and express his gratitude by telling the trooper where he could find what was hidden in the Black Hills since the Hills are sacred to the Indians of the plains, especially the Sioux and the Cheyenne.

"Are you still with me, Callie? Good, because it gets a little complicated here. Seems the army had its own reason for wanting what's up there, except they could never manage to locate it. But now Trooper Colby knew just where and what, only being no fool, he kept it to himself. Before he could go after this fortune, though, he got sick and was transported home to Independence.

"What's that, Callie? Right, he shared his information with his brother. That was just before he died with whatever ailed him. Naturally, Bud was eager to get to the Black Hills, but he didn't have the funds to travel there. This is where your father and I come into the story."

He paused again to guide the mule team around a rough stretch on their lonely trail.

"What you have to understand, Callie," he went on, "is that there is nothing secret about the existence of this treasure. It's been talked about for years along the Oregon Trail. So when Bud had too much to drink and bragged about it in that saloon where your father visited him, it wasn't news. But his boast about his brother's knowledge was."

Callie squirmed with tension on the seat. Against her will, she wanted now to learn the rest, even though it was probably all lies. But she kept her silence, refusing to offer him any encouragement. Not that he needed any.

"His killers were in that saloon and heard it, and I was there and heard it. Okay, I admit I wanted to share in the riches. That's why I involved Colby and your father in that card game, and why I let him win just enough to show him there was more where that came from and that I was willing to finance his trek to the Black Hills, providing he made me his partner. And that is also why I went to his room afterwards, to make my offer in private."

Callie, no longer able to contain her seething emotions, burst out with an angry, "Bud Colby turned ya down, didn't he? An' that's when ya shot him and my pa!"

"I couldn't have, Callie," he told her soberly. "They were already dead when I got there."

"So ya keep sayin'."

"Yes, I do say it, because this is how it was. The door was ajar when I got there, and I could feel there was something wrong. That's why I drew my gun before I went into the room. The maid found me like that, standing over their bodies. But my gun hadn't killed them because it had never been fired, and the sheriff could see that."

"Yeah," she said bitterly. "It was a couple o'strangers without names what killed 'em."

"They have names. Judd Parsons and Ike Ritter. And they know what happened in that room. I can only guess, but I think they must have tried to force Colby to give them his secret, and when Bud and your father drew on them instead, they shot both men. Then they went looking for Colby's lady friend, because that drunken fool, Bud, had mentioned in the saloon that she was the only one he'd trusted with the location of what we all wanted."

"I s'ppose next yer gonna say his woman was Pearl?"

"And you wouldn't believe that either. Sorry, Callie, but it's true. It's also true that, before they could identify and track her down, Pearl heard they were looking for her. And being what she was, experience had taught her never to count on the law to protect her, so she cleared out of Independence with the wagon train. When I finally learned where she'd gone, I went after her, and so did Parsons and Ritter. End of story, Callie."

"It's a crazy story! Why, if it happened like that, Pearl woulda told me 'bout it."

"No, she wouldn't. She was too scared to tell anyone what she knew until I could give her something she needed. Lessons for you, Callie."

He was trying to trick her. Trying to convince her again that Pearl was responsible for her kidnapping. That the only friend she'd ever trusted had actually arranged for this insane treasure hunt.

"Hidden riches," Callie grumbled. "What? Bags o'silver? Gold?"

"Uh, not exactly." There was a gleam in his black eyes, as though he was about to enjoy surprising her. "This treasure happens to be a live one. *Humanly* alive, that is."

She stared at him. "Huh?"

He chuckled at her expression. "Got your earnest attention this time, have I? Well, now, Callie, that's fine, but I'm afraid this demands another story."

"I heard enough stories from you!" She faced forward, mouth compressed into a thin, tight line as she proceeded to ignore him.

"Well, if that's how you want it . . ."

They rode in silence. The only sounds were the creaking of the wagon wheels and the soft jangle of the chains on the mule collars. Callie withstood the suspense for several minutes, and then she could no longer bear it.

"Reckon ya might as well tell me. You'll likely give me no peace 'til ya do."

Her careless tone would have fooled no one, but Linc was willing to let her keep her pride. "You sure do know me, Callie."

"Reckon I do," she said smugly.

"Uh-huh. And I'm grateful you're willing to put up with my tales. Have to keep us entertained somehow until we get there. I mean, it's not like we have anything else to talk about, what with you refusing lessons from—"

"Just get on with it, will ya?"

Collecting his thoughts, he began the story in a solemn voice, but the gleam she didn't trust was still in his eyes. "Once upon a time in the Old West there lived an Indian maiden. Uh, in this case that means about a dozen years ago, and actually she was a half-breed. Anyway, this maiden had a little boy she dearly loved, and when he was about three years old, his evil white father took the child away from her and sent him to live with other people in the wilderness. She was heartbroken, but before her son's wicked father could tell her where he had hidden the boy—as he'd promised to do if she obeyed him—he died with his secret."

Callie recognized a fairy tale when she heard one. She would have dismissed it as just another fantastic fiction McAllister had concocted, except this time it stirred a dim connection from a distant past.

"This half-breed and her boy," she asked him.

169

"They got names? Ya know their names?"

"They have names. She's Magpie, and he's Daniel. Or he was called that."

Hearing them jolted Callie's memory, bringing it all back. Or as much she knew, anyway. After all, she had only been a young child herself at the time, and the situation had never been entirely clear to her.

Lincoln could read the sudden excitement on her face. "You recognize the names, don't you?" he said in wonder. "You know about this already."

"Maybe. There was this here woman called Magpie on the wagon train I went out t'Oregon with in 'forty-one. An' she did say she had her a little boy she lost name o' Daniel. Duke Salter. That was the father, an' as bad as they come. He didn't want our train t'reach Oregon an' he tried t'force poor Magpie inta stoppin' us. That's all I remember. Tell me the rest," she urged Lincoln.

"This is what I know," he said. "Magpie stayed on in Oregon and made a new life for herself after Salter's death. Married a farmer who was a good husband to her. But she never stopped yearning for Daniel. She'd meet every wagon train that arrived at Fort Vancouver, asking for word of him."

"I kind o'recollect that. Awful sad, 'cause she never heard anything."

"Not until a few years later. A woman on one of the trains had encountered a small boy along the trail that fit Daniel's description. He was living with the Cheyenne, being raised as one of them."

That must have been long after she'd returned to Missouri, Callie thought. "What then?"

"Nothing. Magpie kept hoping, but she didn't have the resources to recover her son. Not, anyway, until her husband went off to the California goldfields in 'forty-nine. He was one of the very few who struck it rich. He also lost his life there, which left his widow enormously wealthy. So now Magpie was able to offer a sizable reward for the safe return of her son, but there was still no result. After that one sighting, Daniel just seemed to vanish again. Since then, the reward has grown along with Magpie's desperation until it's a small fortune. Beginning to make sense now, Callie?"

"Yer after that reward!"

"Exactly, and I'll get it, too. Daniel is a young man now, about fifteen years of age. Old enough to have gotten into trouble, which is how his existence gained attention again and why he's hiding out in the Black Hills. Army wants him for killing a trooper. The Indians claim he was protecting his Cheyenne sister from rape. Knowing as I do some of the rabble to be found in the ranks, they're probably right. But of course," he added with a bitter note in his voice, "the army isn't interested in listening to the Indians."

"Then how ya gonna git this Daniel to his mother out in Oregon, providin' ya can even find him?"

"Oh, I'll find him. The map and directions Pearl turned over to me are pretty specific. And I'll know him when I get there, because I have a description of him. Can't be anyone else in that place his age and with a crescent moon birthmark on the side of his neck. As for getting him safely to Oregon . . . well, I'll manage that, too."

There was a steely determination in his promise that Callie found awesome. "This here reward must be an awful big one."

"Twenty-five thousand dollars big, Callie."

She stared at him in astonishment. Twenty-five thousand dollars! Why, there wasn't that much money in the whole world! No wonder men were getting killed for it.

"Guess yer aim is t'be rich, huh?"

Linc could hear the sarcasm in her voice, but he didn't bother to enlighten her. His reason for wanting that money was as private as it was vital, and he meant to keep it that way. "What man doesn't?" he asked dryly. "Do you blame me?"

Callie didn't answer. She didn't know what to think anymore. Everything he had told her sounded so convincing. Could the whole thing be true then? Even that he hadn't killed her pa and Bud Colby? It was all so confusing, but for the first time since she had struck out on the Oregon Trail with revenge as her grim intention, Callie was uncertain of Lincoln McAllister's guilt.

The more she thought about it, the more she was resolved to know one way or another. She decided there was a way to find out, at least about why they were on this trek. If she could find the box of mission funds concealed somewhere in the wagon, it would prove that her initial accusation was right and all the rest nothing but an elaborate lie.

Callie found an opportunity to search the

wagon when they stopped at noon to rest the stock. Linc, busy watering the animals in the pool of a muddy creek, didn't object to her excuse for staying behind.

"Like to rummage in them provisions fer a bite o'lunch," she said.

That much was true. After the episode with the oatmeal at breakfast, she was still hungry. She managed to find a hunk of hard cheese and a handful of dried apricots, which she crammed into her mouth. They weren't very satisfying, but she didn't have time for anything more filling.

While she chewed, she rapidly went through the entire contents of the wagon, this time interested in something other than her rifle or ammunition. But nowhere was there any sign of stolen mission funds, which shouldn't have surprised her since he'd permitted her to be alone in the wagon.

She did, however, turn up something equally revealing. There was an old carpetbag containing her personal possessions, as well as several other articles that might be useful to her. Earlier, McAllister had claimed it was Pearl, and not him, who had packed for her. She hadn't believed him. Not then. But now she couldn't deny it, for at the bottom of the carpetbag, carefully wrapped in a handkerchief, was a pair of fancy gold and silver eardrops. They were the same eardrops Callie had admired in Pearl's elegant jewelry collection and which her friend had lent her the night of the dance.

Callie held them gently in her hand, touched

Jean Barrett

by their presence in the bag and knowing that
McAllister couldn't possibly be responsible for
them. Only Pearl could have included the eardrops, maybe as a kind of message of reassur-
ance to her. So it was all true. Pearl had sent her
off into the wilderness with McAllister.

How could she have betrayed Callie like that?
Turned her over to her father's killer? No, that
wasn't right. Pearl would never do any such
thing, which meant she had to be convinced of
McAllister's innocence. Callie reluctantly recognized that much. She just wasn't ready to accept his innocence for herself. There were still
too many things about the Antichrist that she
didn't trust. His cooking, however, wasn't
among them.

He managed that afternoon to shoot a prairie
hen for himself. When they made camp that evening, she went through the torture of watching
him as he slowly roasted the plump bird on a
spit over the glowing heat of a fire he fed with
buffalo chips. The chips were plentiful on the
plains, and they made an excellent fuel.

The sight of the golden-brown hen, with its
dripping juices promising a tender, succulent
meat, was tempting enough. But the aroma, en-
riched by whatever magical liquid he basted the
meat with, drove her crazy. With breakfast, such
as it had been, only a dim memory and lunch
practically non-existent, Callie was famished.
What's more, McAllister knew it.

"Plenty of chicken here," he said casually. "I'd
be happy to share it. Providing, of course . . ."

He didn't finish. He didn't have to. They both

knew that the only way she would ever get to taste that hen was by agreeing to his lessons in table manners. Well, it wasn't going to happen.

"Ain't interested," she sniffed with a haughty lift of her stubborn chin. "I'm fixin' my own dinner here, an' it's gonna be real tasty."

Beans and bacon. It was familiar fare on every trail in the West. Not as appealing as prairie hen maybe but filling, and any fool could manage it. Except for her, as she sadly learned when she ended up burning the whole mess. It tasted awful. She could hardly swallow the stuff, but she had to put something into her belly.

"Too bad," he said, his black eyes laughing at her as he watched her trying to be nonchalant about her disaster while he feasted on his own moist, perfectly cooked meal.

Bastard! she thought, shoving into her mouth the blackened beans and bacon all pasted together and smelling as bad as they tasted. But she would show him! She was never going to give in to him! *Never*, no matter how often he tempted her!

Never lasted until the following morning.

Crawling out of her blanket at sunup, Callie wondered what she could possibly fix for her breakfast that she wouldn't destroy. Linc was already up and had the fire going and water boiling for coffee. His "good morning" to her was exasperatingly cheerful, hers in reply the mutter of someone who has accepted a truce while hating the necessity of it.

She stood by the fire sniffing the tantalizing

aroma of coffee and eyeing him as he busied himself mixing up mysterious ingredients in a deep bowl. She tried not to wonder or care what he was cooking for himself.

Callie still had no idea what she was going to do about her own breakfast when she came back from the creek after washing her face and hands. The Antichrist was whistling merrily, and when she saw that he had removed a tin of maple syrup from the traveling pantry and was greasing an iron skillet, she understood his preparations, and her stomach howled in protest.

Flapjacks! Why, everybody back in Horizon, Missouri, knew that her fondness for flapjacks was something next door to sinful. And here was Lincoln McAllister going to make them, dripping with maple syrup, too, just as if he knew flapjacks were her particular weakness. It wasn't fair!

The coffee, anyway, was something he was willing to share without payment. She helped herself to a tin cup and sat watching him, practically drooling as he poured a measure of the thick batter into the skillet and placed it above the fire.

By the time she put away most of the coffee in her cup, the first flapjack was ready, all golden brown and promising to be melt-in-your-mouth delectable. Callie's eyes hungrily followed the skillet as he lifted it from the fire. Then, to her horror, he flipped the flapjack out onto the ground.

Forgetting herself, she cried out in disbelief, "What'd ya go and do that fer?"

Thrill to the most sensual, adventure-filled Historical Romances on the market today…

FROM LEISURE BOOKS

As a home subscriber to the Leisure Historical Romance Book Club, you'll enjoy the best in today's BRAND-NEW Historical Romance fiction. For over twenty-five years, Leisure Books has brought you the award-winning, high-quality authors you know and love to read. Each Leisure Historical Romance will sweep you away to a world of high adventure…and intimate romance. Discover for yourself all the passion and excitement millions of readers thrill to each and every month.

SAVE AT LEAST $5.00 EACH TIME YOU BUY!

Each month, the Leisure Historical Romance Book Club brings you four brand-new titles from Leisure Books, America's foremost publisher of Historical Romances. EACH PACKAGE WILL SAVE YOU AT LEAST $5.00 FROM THE BOOKSTORE PRICE! And you'll never miss a new title with our convenient home delivery service.

Here's how we do it. Each package will carry a 10-DAY EXAMINATION privilege. At the end of that time, if you decide to keep your books, simply pay the low invoice price of $16.96 ($17.75 US in Canada), no shipping or handling charges added*. HOME DELIVERY IS ALWAYS FREE*. With today's top Historical Romance novels selling for $5.99 and higher, our price SAVES YOU AT LEAST $5.00 with each shipment.

AND YOUR FIRST FOUR-BOOK SHIPMENT IS TOTALLY FREE

IT'S A BARGAIN YOU CAN'T BEAT! A Super $21.96 Value!

LEISURE BOOKS A Division of Dorchester Publishing Co., Inc.

GET YOUR 4 FREE* BOOKS NOW—
A $21.96 VALUE!

Mail the Free* Book
Certificate
Today!

4 FREE* BOOKS ❧ A $21.96 VALUE

Free Books Certificate

YES! I want to subscribe to the Leisure Historical Romance Book Club. Please send me my 4 FREE* BOOKS. Then each month I'll receive the four newest Leisure Historical Romance selections to Preview for 10 days. If I decide to keep them, I will pay the Special Member's Only discounted price of just $4.24 each, a total of $16.96 ($17.75 US in Canada). This is a SAVINGS OF AT LEAST $5.00 off the bookstore price. There are no shipping, handling, or other charges*. There is no minimum number of books I must buy and I may cancel the program at any time. In any case, the 4 FREE* BOOKS are mine to keep—A BIG $21.96 Value!

*In Canada, add $5.00 shipping and handling per order for first shipment. For all subsequent shipments to Canada, the cost of membership is $17.75 US, which includes $7.75 shipping and handling per month.[All payments must be made in US dollars]

Name _____

Address _____

City _____

State _____ *Country* _____ *Zip* _____

Telephone _____

Signature _____

If under 18, Parent or Guardian must sign. Terms, prices and conditions subject to change. Subscription subject to acceptance. Leisure Books reserves the right to reject any order or cancel any subscription.

(Tear Here and Mail Your FREE* Book Card Today!)

Get Four Books Totally
F R E E* —
A $21.96 Value!

(Tear Here and Mail Your FREE* Book Card Today!)

PLEASE RUSH
MY FOUR FREE*
BOOKS TO ME
RIGHT AWAY!

Leisure Historical Romance Book Club
P.O. Box 6613
Edison, NJ 08818-6613

AFFIX
STAMP
HERE

"The first one is never any good. It's just to kind of season the pan."

He went back to whistling "The Blue-Tail Fly," pouring more batter into the skillet. Callie's gaze fastened on the flapjack that had landed only inches from where she sat. It was calling to her, and what was a little dirt? She checked on McAllister. He was ignoring her, occupied with frying up the next flapjack.

Callie leaned down, but before she could snatch up the abandoned flapjack and stuff it into her mouth, his boot came down on it, grinding it into the dust.

His "uh-uh-uh," had the tone of a parent cautioning a naughty child.

Callie wasn't a child. She was a woman. And a damned angry one. She looked up into his face, all ready to scorch him again with another stream of obscenities. But instead, she caved in. Her traitorous stomach simply couldn't take anymore.

"All right," she shouted. "I'll learn yer damn-fool table manners! Just gimme one o' 'em flap-jacks!"

"You don't get one without the other, Callie. Come over here to the table."

She had no choice. Not if she wanted to eat. While he rescued the second flapjack before it burned, she scooted her camp stool up to the board on its pair of sawbucks. She watched him with a wary eye when, turning from the fire, he slapped two tin plates on their makeshift table, accompanying them with tablewear and a cou-

177

ple of red-and-white checkered napkins he produced from the basket of utensils.

Napkins, of all things. Why, nobody on the trail used napkins. Nor, most of the time, did they park themselves at tables. They simply hunkered down somewhere with their plates on their knees.

"Why d'I need this?" she demanded, fingering the napkin suspiciously.

"Come on, Callie, you know what a napkin is for. Didn't Parthenia Smyth have you using one that day the two of you were swilling tea?"

"Thought that was just fer real refined things like tea parties."

"And what do you think society wipes its collective mouth with the rest of the time?"

"Back o' the sleeve? It's just as good. Anyways, I ain't seen *you* goin' around afore this dabbin' yer mouth with napkins."

"Just put the damn napkin where it belongs, will you?"

Linc turned back to the skillet, adding more batter for a second flapjack. He was no longer in a mood to whistle. None of this was going to be easy, was it? Not if she kept challenging his every instruction. In addition, he was dealing with the damage of Parthenia Smyth's silly affectations when all Callie needed were the basics. Yeah, and just how would he manage those? He thought of Anne. Anything he knew or really appreciated about women came from Anne. Anne would be his model then.

Linc was more hopeful when he turned away from the fire again to serve the flapjacks. Then he saw Callie with knife and fork eagerly raised in either hand and the napkin tucked into her neckline, its folds hanging down the front of her buckskin shirt. She looked like a mountain man ready to assault a buffalo steak.

"Not there. In your lap."

"Ya said t'put the napkin where it belongs, and this here is where I seen folks at the boarding-house back in Horizon put theirs. When they used 'em at all, that is."

"Take my word for it. Ladies don't wear their napkins under their chins. And ladyhood is what you've been longing for, isn't it?"

Callie was no longer certain of that. Not if it meant Lincoln McAllister being in charge of the process. Still, at this moment she was more interested in satisfying her appetite. With a resigned sigh, she transferred the napkin to her lap.

"Next step," he said, placing a steaming flapjack on each of their plates and seating himself across from her. "Now watch me." After helping himself to the maple syrup, he picked up his knife and fork and began to demonstrate, cutting the flapjack into bite-sized pieces.

"I ain't a baby. I know how to slice up my food." Snatching up the tin of syrup, she drowned the flapjack and began to hack it into chunks.

"Smaller," he commanded.

Callie's eyes darted to his plate. "Yer pieces ain't so dainty."

"They're the right size for a man."

"Why should it be different for a man?"

"It just is. I don't make the rules."

Heaving another sigh, she complied. But now the pieces seemed so ridiculously small to her that the only way to get a hearty mouthful was to load up her fork. But when she swiftly stabbed four pieces at once, he objected to that, too.

"One at a time, Callie. Nobody's going to take them away from you."

"Oh, jeez."

It seemed like a waste of time to her to eat one at a time, but she unloaded her fork and tried again. This time she managed to get some of the flapjack inside her. Shutting her eyes, she savored the heavenly taste his sorcery had concocted.

"Now," he said, "wait until you've chewed and swallowed it before you go after the next bite. And use your napkin. You've got syrup dribbling down your chin. There, much better."

It was better until she got to her third piece, which she spat out onto the ground with a loud, "Phooey!"

Linc put his head into his hands. "Now what?"

"There was sumpthin' hard in it. Like mebbe a pebble got stuck in the batter. Did ya want me t'go an' swallow that?"

"No, Callie, but the next time use your spoon or your napkin to remove it from your mouth."

"Why?"

God help him, he was going to strangle her!

He didn't, and they managed to get through the rest of the meal, but both of them were exhausted by the end of it. Still, she had made progress, so maybe, just maybe . . .

Chapter Nine

Callie read the words slowly and carefully. They were difficult for her, partly because the movement of the wagon kept jiggling the book in her lap. But mostly it was because her limited schooling made reading at any level a struggle.

"Thee mouse ran up thee clock. Thee clock struck one. Thee mouse ran down. Hickory, dickory—" She interrupted the painful flow to complain sharply to Linc beside her, "This don't make sense."

"It's not supposed to. It's a nursery rhyme. And why do you keep reading *the* as *thee?* You're not a Quaker."

" 'Cause that's the way we did it back at the schoolhouse in Horizon."

"Just how many grades did you complete in that schoolhouse, Callie?"

181

She shrugged. "Went through the fourth grade, an' then I quit. But not 'cause I was dumb," she defended herself proudly. "Pa needed me to help 'im with the business, see."

She was obviously sensitive about that, Linc thought. Well, what she lacked was certainly no fault of her own. She had clearly sacrificed opportunity for the sake of her father and their survival. His realization of that triggered a rush of compassion. The feeling was unexpected, and it was also unwelcome. Wisdom told him to preserve a complete detachment where Callie Burgess and her education were concerned, but that was becoming less easy to manage.

"Go on," he urged her. "Read the next rhyme for me."

She shut the book with a decisive snap and tossed it into the interior of the wagon behind them. "Fergit it. I ain't practicin' no more first-grade readin'. Don't see what it's got t'do with ladyhood anyhow."

Here we go again, Linc thought. What had made him think that the hard-won success of her lesson in table manners was reason enough to go on to another area of her education? Plainly, it wasn't. All right, he'd try a different subject.

"Then let's talk about speech, because it has everything to do with ladyhood. And yours, Callie, needs work. A *lot* of work. Sometimes I think you know better and that the sloppy stuff coming out of your mouth is simply the result of stubbornness. But you've got ears as well as a tongue, and if you'd use them to listen to how the language is supposed to be—"

"Mister," she cut him off furiously, "ya can take yer friggin' complaints 'bout my reading' an' talkin' an' put 'em where the sun don't shine!"

"Callie, listen to me—"

"No! Table manners, that was it! Didn't agree t' nothin' else when I struck that friggin' bargain with ya!"

Frigging again. One of these days he was going to cure her of that damn word. Yeah, along with turning her into a lady. Or at least an approximation of one. How? He didn't know, but he felt that somewhere there was a key that fit her, and if he could just find it and unlock her . . . Right, but until then she was in no mood to absorb anything.

"We'll give it a rest, Callie," he said gently.

If she appreciated his reprieve, she didn't express it. She sat facing forward on the wagon seat in rigid silence. The day wore on as they covered the long miles. By midafternoon they were nearing their destination.

The mountains ahead of them rose up suddenly from the plain, their ancient domes thickly forested with dark pine, silver birch, and quaking aspen. Between the high ridges were lush green meadows fed by rushing streams.

Callie had thawed enough by then to remark companionably, "Sure are a purty sight."

"Pahá Sápa," Linc said softly.

"What's that mean?"

"Hills that are black. It's the Sioux who gave them that name."

"How far we got t'travel inta them hills?"

"A long way, up toward the northern part of the range."

He had yet to tell her just exactly where Daniel was hiding in the mountains. Probably didn't trust her to know, Callie thought sourly. Well, it didn't matter none to her. Except she wouldn't mind seeing Daniel restored to his mother. She had liked Magpie and felt sorry for her loss. Yep, she'd be glad to contribute to that part of this fool trek.

"Leastways," she said, "we got us some pleasant country t'ride through."

"Damn unfriendly country, is what it is."

She glanced at him sharply. Oh, jeez, now what was he getting them into? "How so?"

"Remember what I told you, Callie? How the Black Hills are sacred to the Indians? They don't appreciate outsiders like us violating them. That's why Daniel went to them, because he felt he'd be safe there from pursuit."

She gulped in alarm. "Lord love us! Ya mean t'tell me we're in trouble if the Indians catch us in there?"

Linc chuckled. "I wouldn't worry about it, Callie. They wouldn't dare fool around with a rough customer like you."

The storm seemed to come up out of nowhere, an angry bruise on the horizon in one minute and then in the next masses of dark clouds burying the summits. They were in the mountains themselves by now, traveling along a narrow fold while lightning and thunder rolled from peak to peak on either side of them. The mules and horses weren't happy about the display, but under Linc's urging they plodded onward.

As bad as the pyrotechnics were, the rain was worse. The black clouds discharged a hard, steady downpour, as though a sluice had burst.

"There's a couple of rain ponchos back there," Linc had directed Callie when the first drops fell. She'd managed to find them, and they put them on, but neither the ponchos nor their wide-brimmed hats were of much use in a soaker like this. Within minutes they were drenched.

After a few miles the winding defile widened, opening into a flat, grassy valley. A stream bisected the valley at its upper end. "There's a ford there we have to cross," Linc said, heading them in that direction.

But a discouraging sight met them when they reached the banks of the wide stream. Swollen by the rain, it was already an impassable torrent, the fording place swallowed by the racing waters.

"We won't be crossing this," Linc said grimly. "Not until these waters go down, and there's no telling when that will be."

"Any way t'go 'round it?" she asked anxiously.

He shook his head. "Not according to the map. This is the route, and I mean to stick with it. We'll just have to sit it out."

"In all this here rain? Appears there ain't gonna be a letup, and it's comin' on night."

"You're right. We'll have to find shelter.

Maybe up there. I noticed it as we crossed the valley."

Callie peered through the rain in the direction he indicated. Off on their left, partway up the slope of a mountain, a roof peeked through a grove of pine. It was a surprising sight in all this wilderness.

"Ya think that's a cabin?"

"If it isn't, I'm going to be disappointed."

Callie didn't share his enthusiasm. A cabin meant people, and in this forbidden region that could translate into *unfriendly* people. But she voiced no objection when he turned the wagon. The climb to the pine grove wasn't as difficult as it appeared. There was a track of sorts, and they followed that.

Something occurred to Callie as they neared the grove. "Indians don't raise cabins."

"No, they don't."

"Then who built this one?"

"I'm guessing a fur trapper. Wouldn't be any settlers in this country."

The wagon reached the pine grove and stopped. In front of them, overlooking the valley, was a rough log structure. It evidenced no sign of life.

"Abandoned," Linc said. "But let's be sure."

The rain was still falling as they climbed down from the wagon and cautiously approached the cabin. Linc had his hand on his Colt, ready for whatever might confront them. Callie, close behind, thought how much better she'd feel if her own rifle was loaded and in her arms.

Her apprehension proved unnecessary. There

was no answer to Linc's hello, and when he spread the plank door inward and they looked into the gloom, they could see the place was no longer occupied. Nor had it been in some time, if the cobwebs and dust were any indication.

"Trapper, huh? Thought ya said outsiders weren't welcome in these hills."

"Well, he's gone, isn't he?"

Callie glanced nervously over her shoulder. "Ya mean the Indians mighta killed him?"

"Relax. A lot of these trappers have Indian wives, which is probably why his temporary presence here was tolerated. By the looks of the place, it wasn't meant for more than a couple of winters of fur gathering."

Callie could see that was true. Even by the standards of the wilderness, the cabin was a mean one—a single, cramped room with a dirt floor and a few crude pieces of furniture. But Linc was willing to accept what it offered.

"The roof doesn't leak, so we'll keep dry." He rubbed his hands together in satisfaction. "Yeah, you and I are going to be cozy playing house here, Callie. Come on, let's get our things from the wagon before it gets dark."

Two things bothered Callie as they transferred necessary supplies and belongings from the wagon to the cabin. McAllister, who'd been on fire to reach Daniel since the start of their journey, didn't seem to be fretting over this delay. Then there was that sardonic remark of his about the two of them playing house.

Didn't make sense, though, that she should be worried about their being caught here when

187

they'd already spent two nights alone on the trail. But that had been out in the open, and this was different. She would be sharing a confined space with a man she loathed but who had the power to inflame her senses. A forced intimacy that was nothing but dangerous, even if he had joked about it.

Linc misunderstood the glances she cast in his direction. She looked miserable. Probably because she was sopping wet and cold.

Once they had their gear inside, he indicated a primitive stone fireplace with wood stacked to one side. "We both need to get dry. Why don't you try to coax a fire in that thing while I stake out the animals for the night?"

He was outside and on his way through the rain to release the mules from the wagon, when it occurred to him that Callie would feel less uneasy about their situation here if she had her loaded rifle at hand. He didn't think there was much of a risk in returning it to her. Not at this point, not when she was entitled to a means of self-protection in this place.

He didn't lose any time acting on his decision. Before seeing to the stock, he retrieved her ammunition belt from where he had hidden it up in the underpinnings of the wagon. Then, helping himself to her Remington from the interior of the wagon, he went swiftly back to the cabin.

Wearing a grin on his mouth in anticipation of her surprise, the rifle in one hand and the belt in his other, Linc kicked the door open, strode into the room, and rocked to a halt. He could feel his grin sagging into a silly droop as Callie whirled around at his entrance with an audible gasp. This happened at the same time as shock slammed into his gut, taking his breath away.

She hadn't waited for a fire to get dry. She had chosen a more immediate method. Callie Burgess, the little roughneck in grubby buckskins, had stripped every damp garment from her body. What had emerged from under that male garb, however, was no roughneck, but a mature woman in all her naked splendor.

The entire sight of her as nature had molded her was riveting. Creamy skin as smooth as silk, a pair of lush, rose-tipped breasts that made his mouth go dry, hips softly rounded, and at the juncture of her thighs a dark triangle of curly russet hair that would have cost a confirmed celibate his self-control. And Linc was no celibate. He had never been so powerfully aroused.

Or so frustrated. He remembered a few other seductive encounters with her back on the wagon train, particularly that fiery kiss they'd shared, but she'd always been covered then. Or nearly so. He'd never imagined that behind that clothing would be female flesh this alluring. And, sweet Jesus, he wasn't supposed to touch it. He'd promised Pearl she would be safe with him.

He knew that the image of her like this would be burned into his brain, though it couldn't have lasted more than a few stunned seconds before Callie recovered herself. Snatching up the dry shirt she'd been about to change into, she held it protectively in front of her.

"Whatcha doin' back here?" she challenged him, her face turning almost the shade of her hair. "Thought ya went t'take care o' the animals."

"That was the plan. But then I figured," he said dryly, placing the rifle and belt on the floor like a pair of offerings, "you might appreciate having these. What do you think, Callie?"

"That you'd better take yerself outta here 'fore I use 'em on ya."

"That's what I thought. Uh, the next time you might warn me before you go raw."

"An' you might knock on that door, but just now I wanna see it closin' on ya."

He obliged, backing away out into the yard and wondering, as he shut the door, how he was going to stand spending the night with her. Or, for that matter, all the other nights to come.

Callie wondered the same thing herself, which was why she made certain they bedded down after supper on opposite ends of the cabin. It was a secure enough arrangement, especially since she kept her loaded Remington close beside her. Even so, she spent a restless night, unable to forget the unmistakable bulge of pure lust in McAllister's trousers. Or how a treacherous flame had curled inside her belly when his gaze devoured her nude body.

Callie awakened the next morning to the sound of rain drumming on the roof. That didn't seem like a good sign. Linc, who was already up and had been out checking on the animals, confirmed her fear when he entered the cabin.

"I had a look at the stream," he reported, removing his hat and poncho and shaking the excess water from them. "It's overflowing its banks. We won't be crossing it today, and if this rain doesn't clear off soon maybe not tomorrow either."

"Ya mean we're stuck here?"

"Looks like it," he said, moving to the fireplace to get breakfast under way.

The prospect of being cooped up with him in this cabin for another two days made her as nervous as a cat. McAllister didn't seem worried about it, though. He was already engaged in that damn early-morning whistling of his as he dug around in their provisions. What did he have to be so cheerful about anyway? She was afraid to ask.

They were finishing up breakfast when he said, "Looks like we've got nothing but time on our hands. What do you say we fill it?"

Just what was he suggesting? The look she sent him must have been a very suspicious one, because he laughed.

"Well, that might be an interesting way to pass the morning, too. But, no, Callie, I'm not suggesting this time that we play house. What I'm proposing is that we play school."

"Lessons ag'in," she said in disgust. "Ain't I improvin' on my table manners like ya wanted? Ain't that enough?"

"No, it isn't. I told you we need to clean up that speech of yours. Why do you keep fighting me? This ladyhood thing is what you've been wanting, isn't it?"

"Not from you."

She refused to discuss it and left the table. But

there was nowhere to go and nothing to do. While he seemed perfectly content with their confinement, reading one of the books in the collection he'd purchased from Parthenia Smyth, Callie spent her time wandering aimlessly around the room or standing in the open doorway, gazing at a dismal sky that continued to drip. By midmorning she was so bored that she could no longer stand her idleness.

"All right," she relented, joining him at the table. "Got t'occupy myself somehow, so it might as well be yer way. But I warn ya—"

"I know," he said, closing the book he'd been reading and tossing it on the table. "If I don't measure up as a schoolmaster, you'll let the air out of me with that rifle of yours. Sit down there across from me."

When she'd seated herself opposite him, he picked up another book from the stack. Callie could see it was the volume Parthenia Smyth had given her to study that day back on the wagon train. *The Deportment of a Young Lady in Society.* "This is what we're going to do," he said. "I'll read you a few passages at a time and then question you on the contents. Not because I think anything in this tome is probably worth more than a yawn. It's the way you express your answers that I'll be listening to and correcting. We're trying to refine your language, remember." He opened the book. "Ah, here's a chapter that ought to appeal to you. *Courtship and Marriage.*"

"Just read, will ya?"

He did, and they spent the next hour and a

half in what amounted to an exhausting battle of wills between two very determined people. To Linc's growing irritation, she questioned everything.

"What's that mean?" she would ask. "This givin' the mitten to the man ya been sparkin' with?"

"It means," he would try to answer patiently, "that you no longer want him to court you. It's just an expression. And stop dropping your g's. It's *giving* and *sparking*, not givin' and sparkin'. I know it isn't easy, but concentrate."

And to Callie's own annoyance, his demands were relentless. "No, not *ain't*," he would remind her, almost shouting the instruction. "Wipe *ain't* out of your vocabulary. How many times have I got to tell you it doesn't exist? Now try again."

"It *isn't* necessary," she would say carefully, conscientiously, "t'have a chaperone when courtin'—uh, court*ing*, but in the best o' families it's rec-recommended."

"Better, but not perfect," he would respond. "Let's keep working on it."

The morning stretched on, their tensions increasing. But that wasn't because of the stress of the lessons themselves, not entirely. It was because of their deepening awareness of each other on a level other than teacher and pupil—but neither of them wanted to confront that particular issue. An explosion of some kind, however, was inevitable.

"I'm wore out," she finally complained, sagging in her chair.

"So am I, but what has that got to do with it?

193

Now answer the question. What is a levee, and what's the proper form of invitation to it?"

"I don't care."

"Neither do I. Personally, I think society is vastly overrated, but since you're so eager to join it—"

"It's not for me!" She sat up straight again in her chair, restored to a fresh energy by his serious error. "I ain't learnin'—" She stopped to correct herself. "I'm not learning t'be a lady fer me. I'm learning for Gabriel."

Linc's insides clenched at the mention of the preacher's name. If he didn't know better, he would have said he was jealous. And why did he keep having this ridiculous urge to kiss that rebellious little mouth of hers? He resisted those emotions, but he could justify his honest anger with her.

"Let's get this straight," he said, slapping his hand down on the surface of the table. "If you want to improve yourself, that's fine, that's commendable. But if I'm going to help you to change, then it's got to be for you. Not for me or Pearl and certainly not for Gabriel Hawkins. Only because Callie Burgess wants it for herself. Otherwise—"

"What?"

"You can find someone else to give you lessons in ladyhood."

She scraped her chair back and surged to her feet, blistering him with her rage. "Then ya know what ya can do with these friggin' lessons o'yours, dontcha?"

Fists planted on the table, Linc got slowly to

his own feet and leaned toward her with a warning in his dark eyes. "And that's another thing. I want you to stop using that word."

"Or?"

"There'll be consequences."

"That so?" She came around the table, stretched up on tiptoe, and shoved her face into his. "An' just how d'ya figger on stoppin' me? By cuttin' my tongue out maybe? Well, ya don't scare me, McAllister, an' I'll use it all I want. See? Friggin', friggin', frig—"

She never managed to issue the last of those defiant *frigging*'s. It was smothered when his mouth crashed down on hers, effectively silencing her.

Callie was so stunned by his action that she swore her heart stopped beating in her chest. By the time she felt it pumping again furiously, she was aware of his arms around her, clasping her so tightly to his hard frame that she couldn't breathe. Or was it his kiss that robbed her of all air?

It started out as a punishing kiss, his mouth grinding savagely against hers, but it quickly escalated into something so thoroughly sensual, so pleasurably demanding, there was no way Callie could fail to respond.

Her mouth opened without will, maybe just to emit the low moan trapped in her throat. Whatever the reason, Linc took it as an invitation. His tongue entered her mouth, probing, seeking, and at last finding its mate in her own tongue, which curled around his in welcome even as her arms wound around his strong neck.

195

As he deepened their kiss, his wet, velvety tongue possessing hers, Callie inhaled the essence of him and wondered how she could ever have associated unpleasant smells and flavors with this man. Because nothing could have been further from the truth. Both the scent and the taste of him were all hot and male, irresistible, something she couldn't get enough of.

She was mindlessly savoring them when she remembered why she had convinced herself they were certain to be detestable. It was because at the time she had been comparing him to Gabriel Hawkins. And that was when Callie realized with a terrible jolt that she was betraying the man she had sworn to love. Wrong! Wrong and wicked!

Oh, Gabriel, I've gone and done it again. And I'm so sorry, so awful sorry.

As though the situation wasn't already bad enough, McAllister had to go and make it worse. She felt his hands skimming the sides of her breasts, ready to stroke their heavy fullness. That was when she acted. She frantically used all of her strength and will to free herself of his devil's spell.

Linc could see how shaken she was after she tore her mouth from his and staggered back out of his arms. He was shaken himself. When was he going to learn to control this damn carnal appetite of his? Of all the fool mistakes to go and repeat!

His voice was hoarse as he moved a step toward her, trying to apologize. "Callie—"

"Ya stay away from me!"

"We should talk about this."

"No!"

To prevent that, she turned around and fled from the cabin, racing out into the wet. He let her go. It was probably better like this. They needed to be apart for a little while, give themselves space in which to recover. He had really done it this time. But the serious problem here was his unholy desire to hold her again, to feel her sweet little mouth on his.

Linc sank down at the table, prepared to hold his head in his hands and groan. Better still, he ought to go and bang his skull against one of those log walls, see if he could knock some sense into it. He did neither, because after a few minutes he realized something. He would have to go after her and bring her back. He couldn't let her wander out there on her own. It was too dangerous.

Oh, murder. She was nothing but trouble.

Slipping a poncho over his head and strapping on his Colt, he left the cabin. The rain had lightened to a thin drizzle. Even so, without protection, Callie would be sopping in no time. That realization prompted another muttered curse from him as he tried to determine which direction she might have gone. There was no sign of her, which meant he could search for hours and not find anything.

But Linc was in luck. The rain-softened earth revealed her footprints, which in the bare patches were as clear as signposts. He followed them up the side of the mountain, where she had picked up an animal track. The path climbed through the dark spruce trees that were so common in the Black Hills.

He stopped once to call her name, but there was no response. Knowing her stubbornness, that didn't worry him. If she'd heard him, she probably refused to answer. What did concern him was the distance he'd traveled without overtaking her. He must have come almost a mile up the mountain. Where did the little witch think she was going?

A moment later he stopped again, his heart feeling as though a fist had suddenly squeezed it. This time he had cause to be alarmed. Her footprints were still there in the mud, but they had been joined by others emerging at this point from the forest. He and Callie weren't alone on the mountain.

A quick examination of the impressions disclosed the essentials. There were a number of them, which meant a party of some kind. He even knew who they were. The prints were those left by moccasins. It wasn't a good discovery.

There was only one thing that Linc found the least bit encouraging as he sped up the path after them. The prints overlapped Callie's, which meant their makers were following her but hadn't yet caught up. But once they did—

He refused to finish that fearful thought or to consider what he was going to do to rescue her. All he knew for certain was that he had to reach her. She was completely unprotected because, of course, she had left the cabin without her rifle.

He didn't know whether to damn Callie for her carelessness or himself for letting her out of his sight. It was probably a toss-up. And what did it matter? he thought as he quickened his pace.

Linc was winded by the time the spruce cover ended and he came out into the open. And there was Callie standing on a flat spur of rock overhanging the valley below. Her back was to the long drop, her small, neat features wearing a startled expression as she faced the band grouped in a semicircle several yards in front of her. Either by accident or by design, they had her trapped on the spur of granite.

There were five of them, and they were armed with lethal-looking bows and arrows. There was nothing friendly in the stony gazes they directed at Callie.

Chapter Ten

Fort Laramie was the busiest post on the Oregon Trail, which was why Judd Parsons and Ike Ritter were able to be there without drawing attention to themselves. As long as they were careful to avoid their enemies, they were able to lose themselves in the swarms of fur trappers, freighters, Oglala Sioux, and emigrants camped in the meadows outside the high adobe walls.

But the risk of recognition within the confines of the fort itself was much greater. There was less chance here to escape notice. And this is what worried Ike, who hurried with his crablike shuffle to keep up with Judd moving purposefully toward the gates of the post.

"Don't like goin' in there, Judd," he complained nervously. "Don't like it. What if McAllister or the Slocum woman are hangin' around in there in plain sight? Could make real trouble if they spot us first. Real trouble."

Judd, squinting against the morning sun, refused to be intimidated by the sight of the formidable blockhouse towering over the open portal ahead of them. "That's a chance we gotta take," he snarled, "so just quitcher wailin'."

The wagon train had arrived at the fort late yesterday, Judd and Ike not far behind it. There had been no further opportunity on the trail to get at Pearl Slocum and what she knew. Nor did it seem likely that they'd be able to snatch her here at Laramie, where she was surrounded by people. But Judd had been casually asking questions in the camps where they had mingled last night and this morning, and he'd learned something promising from a rough trader with bad teeth.

"Yeah, I spoke with someone from that train," the man said, spitting tobacco juice to one side. "Name o' Parthenia Smyth. She's askin' around fer a party t'take her back east. Can't say enough bad 'bout that outfit what brought her here. Hell, I thought I'd never git away from her. One o' those women who makes it her business t'find out everything, an' then won't let ya go 'til you know it, too."

"That so?" Judd permitted himself to look mildly interested. "Maybe I'll look 'er up, see what she's offerin' t' hire us. What's she look like?"

"Can't miss 'er. Staked out a bench fer herself in a corner o' the post yard. Just keep yer eyes peeled fer a female with a stick up her rump."

Parthenia Smyth, Judd thought as he and Ike joined the stream entering the gate. If the trader was right, it could be she would be willing to provide them with useful information. It was worth a try.

There was a lot of noisy activity in the enormous quadrangle, most of it centered around the post store. Judd could hear the clang of hammers in the workshops where wagons were being readied for the trail. He and Ike scanned the faces on all sides, but there was no sign of McAllister or Pearl Slocum.

They found Parthenia Smyth on her bench mending a garment in her lap. The trader's description of her was an apt one. She had a rigid spine and the kind of glacial eyes that looked like they didn't favor much of anything. That was obvious in the way she gazed with disdain at Judd's thick-waisted, burly figure and then with even less approval at Ike's skinny frame and bald head. There was a risk that she'd identify them as members of the band that had attacked the train back in Kansas, but Judd didn't think it likely.

"I assume," she said with a haughty sniff, "that you have a reason to approach me."

"I heard, ma'am," Judd said, affecting humility as he stood before her with his hat in his hand, "that you was wantin' t'return east."

That thawed her a little. "I am. Are you telling me you represent a caravan able to accommodate me?"

"Might be I could put you in touch with the

right party," he said evasively. "If yer willin' t'meet their terms, that is."

"Funds are no problem," she assured him. "I sold my rig and most of its contents. I was glad to be rid of them, just as I will be glad to turn my back on the west."

Judd stroked his beard and nodded sympathetically. "Shame the country didn't agree with ya. Or mebbe it was the company ya traveled here with."

That opened her up all right, just as he'd hoped. She put aside her mending and leaned toward them with an injured expression on her prissy face. "Irresponsible, the lot of them. It's a wonder we arrived here at all without a wagon master and only one scout left to us."

Judd looked appalled. "No wagon master, ma'am?"

"Oh, we started out with an experienced pilot, but he died on the trail. The man who replaced him was a scoundrel. And then Lincoln McAllister left us, too, taking our other scout with him. Though how that silly young woman could be defined as a qualified scout—"

"Ran off an' left ya flat, did he?" Judd interrupted, jabbing his partner in the ribs with his elbow to silence him. Ike had started to squeal at the mention of McAllister's name.

"On some fool's adventure," Parthenia said, "and my rig went with them."

"Just vanished in the night, huh? Where ya s'ppose they went to?"

"I don't have to suppose," she said smugly. "I *know*. I was settling my things in another wagon

203

when I overheard that Slocum woman pleading
excuses to our leader. Of course, they weren't
aware that I was there on the other side of the
canvas."

"Didn't want anyone else knowin', huh?"

"Naturally not, since it was obviously all her
doing."

Judd shook his head. "So she's the one what
sent 'em off to—Where did ya say they was
headed?"

"Oh, somewhere up to the north end of the
Black Hills. She didn't say exactly, and what
does it matter? It's all nonsense anyway. Now
about this party going east . . ."

Judd left Parthenia Smyth with a vague promise about seeing what he could arrange on her
behalf. Ike was all excited as they made their
way out of the fort.

"No real need now fer us t'risk grabbin' Pearl
Slocum, is there, Judd? No real need."

Judd didn't answer until they were out in the
open again. He stopped on the track and gazed
northward. Some distance off behind the post
were dry, treeless ridges. And beyond them,
even farther away, stretched the Black Hills.

"Hidin' their heads in all them clouds," Judd
observed. "Must be havin' a spell o'bad weather
up that way. But we ain't gonna let that stop us,
are we, Ike?"

"Nosirree. An' if we don't beat McAllister to
the prize, we can always take it away from 'im.
Hell, Judd, I can smell that reward money already. Yep, smell it already."

The time had come for Judd to tell his partner

the truth he'd been withholding. "Well now, Ike, that's not exactly how it's gonna work. See, the party who staked us has got somethin' else in mind. Somethin' that's gonna be worth a lot more t'us than splitting that there reward money."

And he told him what was going to happen and why.

Linc had only a sketchy knowledge of the plains Indians from his army days. He thought these five braves might be Lakota, but he couldn't be certain. Tall and lithe, they wore banded leggings above their moccasins and loose-fitting leather shirts decorated with beads and porcupine quills.

It didn't look like war garb anyway. Since the Black Hills were rich in such game as elk, white-tailed deer, and bighorn sheep, this was probably a hunting party. That much was encouraging, but it didn't mean these warriors were in a mood to tolerate a white presence in sacred lands.

Linc realized that he and Callie were in danger and that he had to act before both of them ended up on the floor of the valley far below. He had to persuade this band that they were in the mountains on a peaceful mission. But how? He knew only a few words in the Algonquian tongue, and the language of these people must be Dakota. But maybe he could make them understand his English.

They were aware of his arrival on the scene, watching him silently and without expression as he slowly approached the spur of granite. Linc knew that if he made the slightest threatening gesture, there would be an arrow in his chest before he could even think about reaching for his Colt. He took care to keep his hands upraised, palms flat in the universal sign of friendship.

Linc was aware of Callie gazing at him in openmouthed surprise when he reached the group. He avoided looking at her. The Indians didn't move. They continued to eye him as he spoke to them carefully, solemnly.

"My woman and I respect the sacred hills. We are stopping here only until the rains end. Then we will travel on to the north and leave these lands as we found them. If you let us go in peace, I promise you we won't return."

He went on in this vein for another moment or two. He had no idea whether they understood a single word of his English, but his earnest tone must have sounded convincing. They were silent when he was finished, and then, to his vast relief, they exchanged brief mutters, the leader grunted something at him and made a sign of good will, and then he led his band off into the forest.

When Linc and Callie were alone again, she rounded on him. "Whatcha mean, *yer* woman? I ain't yer woman!"

"You're welcome, Callie."

"Oh, I coulda taken care o' myself all right. I didn't need you flyin' t'my rescue."

"Yes," he said dryly. "You looked like you had

the situation under control. You might at least pretend to be grateful."

"Why? I don't need any man's protection."

"No? Well, you need someone looking after you. Just look at you. Dripping wet, mud on your knees, a smear on your chin. What did you do? Fall down?"

"I—"

"You're pathetic. Those Indians must have wondered why I was even bothering about you. What were you doing way up here, anyway? Contemplating suicide from this ledge?"

"You—"

"Or maybe just admiring the view. If you're through with the scenery, then, let's get you down to the cabin and into something dry."

"I ain't through," she said obstinately, "and I ain't going anywheres with you, Lincoln McAllister."

"It's, 'I am not through, and I am not going anywhere with you,'" he corrected automatically. "And yes, you are, because if you don't come without an argument, I'll sling you over my shoulder like a side of beef and carry you down the mountain. It's a position I promise you won't like, Callie. Not when it'll put my free hand within easy reach of your backside, which this palm of mine is just itching to spank. So, have we settled this issue, or do I go into action?"

"Try it, an' there's a part o' ya, the *private* one, that'll be hurtin' real bad." She lifted her chin to a haughty angle and started around him. "Just so happens it suits me now t'go back to the cabin. Wanna check on Apollo."

"Uh-huh. Careful, it's slick-looking here, and if you miss that first step, it's a long way to the bottom."

It wasn't necessary for him to place his hand in the small of her back and guide her off the spur of rock. Both of them understood that, but it happened just the same. Callie hated to admit it was a pleasing sensation, that his protective touch sent a sudden jolt of warmth up her spine.

His proprietary handling of her all the way down the mountain was just as oddly satisfying. He fussed at her like a stern father, cautioning her where to step on the path while lecturing her about the idiocy of her flight from the cabin.

Nor did his scolding let up once they were safely back inside the cabin. He made her sit on a stool. Then he got a towel from their supplies and began to dry her thick russet hair, scrubbing at her untamed masses so ferociously that her scalp ached.

"No poncho, no hat," he muttered. "You're trouble, Burgess. You need a full-time keeper."

Callie offered no further complaint, accepting his attentions in complete silence. She had never had anyone worry about her in this way before, not in a long time anyway, not to this degree. And the truth was that his caring, rough as it was, felt good. But it was all an illusion. It had to be, because in reality she was nothing more than a burden he resented. That was why she finally resisted when, finished with her hair, he ordered her to change into dry clothes.

"No. I'll sit by the fire t'dry. That's just as good."

"That'll take forever. Change," he insisted.

She lifted her head and looked him straight in the eye. "I ain't—" Catching her error, she went on to inform him with a smooth, mature authority she had never demonstrated before, "I'm not a child, McAllister."

"No," he said softly, "I guess you're not."

The realization caught him with all the force of a fist in the gut. Why had he never acknowledged it before? That Callie Burgess was a woman under those buckskins. Not just because she had a woman's fully developed, alluring body but because she possessed all those elusive feminine qualities that a man finds impossible to define and just as hard to resist.

Seeing her in this new way aroused a sudden tender longing in him. And at the same time a warning went off inside his head. This was another mistake. This was dangerous.

Linc moved away across the room, swiftly putting distance between them. He settled at the table with one of the books. They didn't talk, and he tried to avoid looking in her direction. But he couldn't help being aware of her. She had dragged her stool over to the fire and sat there, gazing quietly into the flames.

From time to time he glanced up from his book, checking on her. And each time he was amazed all over again by his discovery of her womanhood. She was all grown up, independent, capable of her own decisions, and at the same time so damn forlorn and vulnerable looking sitting there like that, she made a man want to put his arms around her and hold her.

This has to stop, he ordered himself.

It was impossible to concentrate on reading. But since it was past midday and time for another meal, Linc was able to busy himself fixing lunch. He was hunting through the provisions for the box of salt when he found an article he'd forgotten about tucked down in a corner and carefully wrapped in a cloth to protect it.

Removing the object, he gazed speculatively in Callie's direction. He had been saving it as a surprise, having acquired it with some vague notion of rewarding her with it when she made an impressive progress with her lessons. That hadn't happened yet, but why wait? He owed her this.

Getting to his feet, he crossed the cabin. She had just settled on the stool again after adding wood to the fire when he leaned down and placed the gift in her lap. Callie looked at it and then up at him, her expression bemused.

"What's this?"

Linc, suddenly feeling awkward, cleared his throat before answering her in a husky voice. "Call it an apology."

"Fer?"

He shrugged. "I've been pretty hard on you, especially this morning. Uh, look, if you don't want it, I'll understand."

"How'd I know I don't want it 'til I seen it?"

He watched with uncertainty as she unwound the cloth that bound it. When it was revealed, the cut crystal of the small bottle winking in the firelight, she stared at it for a few seconds in

210

disbelief, expressing her pleasure with a soft, "Oh, my."

He'd been caught in an act of uncharacteristic generosity, but Linc decided it was worth all his embarrassment to see the delight on her face. "It's the perfume, *Céleste*. I bought it from Parthenia Smyth."

"I know what it is, but how'd you—"

"Oh. Well, that day I was, uh, under the wagon I heard you going into raptures over it."

"An' ya got it 'specially fer me?"

"Let's say I've been keeping it to celebrate your entry into ladyhood."

It didn't matter to Callie that she was still a long way from graduation. She was too touched by his gift to care, as well as too busy removing the stopper and sniffing at the contents. "It's as heavenly as I remembered."

"Why don't you put some on? That's what it's for."

She was shocked by his suggestion. "I couldn't. Not dressed like this. It'd be—why, it'd be wicked."

He chuckled over her exaggeration. "I see what you mean. In that case, why don't you just change into something appropriate? Pearl anticipated your transformation into ladyhood, you know. There are all sorts of female garments over there, though where she expected you to wear them up here in the wilderness is beyond me." He nodded toward their gear stacked in the corner.

Hugging the precious bottle of *Céleste* to her breasts, Callie gazed with both longing and uncertainty in the direction of the boxes.

"Go on," he urged. "You don't want to waste this opportunity."

She was so eager to try the perfume that she needed no further convincing. Rising from the stool, she went over to the corner, carefully placed the bottle of *Céleste* to one side, and began to investigate the boxes that Pearl, bless her, had packed for her. There were several dresses—some had belonged to Pearl and the rest had been purchased from Parthenia Smyth, who was closer in size to Callie.

By the time she had selected the necessary garments, Linc had rigged a blanket over a line in another corner of the cabin, where she could change in privacy. While she slipped behind the screen, he went back to fixing their lunch, amused over the mutters of frustration he heard on the other side of the blanket as she struggled with hooks and buttons. Then there was a long silence. He was beginning to think she had gone to sleep back there when she emerged from the screen.

Linc would have said Callie Burgess wasn't capable of shyness, but shy was exactly what she was in that moment as she stood there, anxiously waiting for his reaction. It was the first thing he noticed about her. And then he noticed all the rest.

For once she had chosen something that was in no way flashy—a simple muslin dress whose green sprigged full skirts suited her russet hair and green eyes. He had never realized her waist was so tiny, her bare arms dimpled at the elbows, or that a pair of breasts could be so enticing when concealed by a modest neckline.

What was it he had discovered about her earlier? That she possessed all those elusive feminine qualities a man found so hard to resist. But she'd been wearing the buckskins then. Now, in this dress, those mysterious womanly qualities that managed to infuriate a man at the same time they fascinated him became intensified, robbing him of his tongue.

She was waiting for his approval. He finally managed to give it to her, making it genuine without behaving like the fool he was dangerously close to becoming. "Too bad we're not riding in a carriage in New Orleans, Callie. You'd turn the heads of society looking like that."

"Sure enough?"

"Sure enough. Hell, you've turned my head."

She could feel herself blushing with pleasure over his admiration. Only that didn't make sense. It wasn't as if he was the first man who'd ever admired her. Plenty of male eyes had followed her the night of the dance. But this was different. Maybe it was the dress itself. In this particular dress she was experiencing something she'd never known before, a femininity that made her feel all soft and vulnerable and wistful.

"Are you wearing the perfume?"

"Yes."

"Well, get over here," he teased, "where I can get a whiff of it."

She obediently crossed the room and stood before him close enough to reveal the scent.

Linc inhaled in appreciation. Why was it, he wondered, that perfume in a bottle was just that—perfume in a bottle? But on a woman it became something bewitching.

This scent was familiar, he suddenly realized. It painfully reminded him of Anne. Was *Céleste* Anne's fragrance? He had no idea, but it was an unsettling possibility.

Callie could tell he was disturbed. "What's the matter? Don't it smell right?"

"It smells like a lady, an extremely pretty one," he assured her warmly, and he could see that pleased her. He firmly put the image of Anne out of his mind and offered Callie his arm. "May I escort this lady to lunch?"

She giggled over his gallantry and called him a fool, but she enjoyed the attention of being led to the table and having her chair held out for her. No male had ever before made a particular effort to behave like a gentleman with her, and even if it was all in humor it made her feel special.

When they were both seated, and she had dutifully remembered to place the napkin in her lap, she said to him, "I ain't—haven't thanked ya for the perfume. That was real decent of you."

"You're welcome."

"An', um, thank you for comin' t'my rescue this mornin' on the mountain."

"You're welcome."

"Though," she added hastily, preserving her pride, "I woulda made out all right on my own."

"No question of it."

Callie began to eat the meal he set before her,

but she had no real awareness of her food. Cornbread and some kind of a pudding—both excellent, but she was unable to concentrate on them. She was too absorbed in being amazed by the man seated across from her. It didn't seem possible that Lincoln McAllister could be capable of kindness and gentleness. Yet, he had offered both since her flight up the mountain. It was all very bewildering. And at the same time exhilarating.

"You want to try the lessons again?" he asked when they had cleared their lunch away.

After this morning's blowup he thought she would refuse, but she agreed without hesitation. To his further surprise, her progress as they worked again to improve her speech was smooth and rapid. What had suddenly turned her from a reluctant pupil into a receptive one?

It took Linc a few minutes to understand, and then it came to him all at once. By accident he'd discovered the key he'd been searching for to unlock her obstinate mind. It was extraordinary, and yet so simple. When he treated her like a woman deserving respect and affection—in other words, a lady—she responded like one. But if this was such a wonderful breakthrough, why did it make him feel guilty, as if he were taking unfair advantage of her?

Callie, too, was conscious of the new level in their teacher-pupil relationship. Of how thoughtful and patient they suddenly were with each other. What she didn't realize, at least not so that she noticed it, was that Gabriel Hawkins had completely gone out of her head, just as though he no longer existed. She wasn't laboring to be a lady for Gabriel. She was striving to please the man who sat across from her. And there was the problem, because while the session continued, with the rain pattering on the roof, their concentration slowly, steadily ebbed until neither was certain anymore what the other was saying.

"What was it ya called it?" she asked him softly.

"What?" he answered blankly.

"Um, that word ya—*you* just read?"

"Oh. Shivaree," he said politely. "It's called a shivaree." There was a long silence before he remembered to prompt her. "You're supposed to explain it to me in your own words, Callie."

"Am I?" She hesitated. "What was the question?"

"Uh, I forget. Something about a shivaree and when it's appropriate."

"Yes, that's right. A shivaree is ser—" She struggled with another unfamiliar word. "—Serenading a newly married couple."

"Good."

"It's a nice custom," she said in a dreamy voice.

"What is?"

"Serenading that couple."

The lesson had reached a stage of complete inanity by now, their questions and answers making no sense whatever. Laughable, had they been in a state to be anything but solemnly, hypnotically aware of each other. They sat there at opposite ends of the table, gazes locked in a slow, deep discovery that had nothing to do with education and everything to do with desire. It was almost frightening.

It *was* frightening, Callie decided. How could she hate this man in one minute and then turn around in the next and feel like this about him? This unbearable longing to have him hold her, touch her, possess her body with his?

Their dialogue had dwindled away to a long, expectant hush. The only sounds were the monotonous rain on the roof and the hiss of the dying fire. Linc's dark, intense eyes continued to hold hers. But he made no physical contact with her, though she silently willed him to reach out for her, ached for it.

When she could take no more of his restraint, Callie submerged her pride and got to her feet. She came around the table. "Push back," she ordered him.

"What?"

"Push yer chair back from the table."

When he mindlessly complied, she boldly settled herself on his lap. She felt him flinch, as if a hot flame had seared him, but he didn't push her away.

"Now," she said, her meaning altogether clear, "I want you t'take the next step in teaching me t'be a woman."

"Callie, you don't know what you're saying."

"I reckon I do all right. Go on, show me what it means t'be a real woman." Her hands lifted and began to stroke his lean, angular face.

Her touch was like warm silk, so instinctively sensual that he fought for self-control. "Callie,

217

no," he pleaded, his voice thick and raspy. "You'll regret it."

She ignored him and went on caressing his face. "I want my education t'be complete, and probably this here will make it the most complete it can be. How can I feel like a woman without it?"

"This is a mistake. I swore to Pearl that you'd be safe."

"I will be safe. I'll be safe in your arms." Her hands framed his face. She leaned in close, her voice low, barely a whisper. "Teach me, Linc. I trust you t'teach me what I need t'know."

His frustration by now was so great that he could no longer contain it. With a groan of anguish, he hauled her tightly against his chest and crushed his mouth on hers.

Callie's appetite had been awakened by his previous kisses, but they hadn't sufficiently prepared her for this hungry assault where there were no more denials, no longer any barriers. His mouth devoured hers, demanding and receiving her full attention.

His kiss, wild and feverish, ignited something deep inside her yearning to be fulfilled. It was only after his first urgent release that his raging mouth gentled. The kisses became tender and very thorough as his tongue slowly probed every corner of her mouth, encouraging her to experiment with her own tongue. He must have liked the results because she could hear him moaning again in his throat.

"You," she said, fighting for air when his

mouth finally lifted from hers, "are a very good teacher."

He grinned, his voice hoarse. "That's because I have very good material to work with."

"Can we go onto the next lesson?" she purred, looping her arms around his neck.

"I'm not sure you've mastered the first one," he said, angling his mouth across hers again. For the next several minutes, he introduced her to other versions of the kiss, some as fiery as what came earlier, others involving his teeth and lips nibbling playfully on hers.

Though Callie was trembling by the time he was finished, she was eager to continue. "The next lesson," she implored.

He placed his hands against her breasts, letting them rest there, his manner turning sober with concern. "Has any man ever touched you like this before, Callie?"

"A boy or two back in Horizon," she assured him. But their awkward fumbles had never felt this hot, this pleasurably intimate.

"But it never went beyond that," he guessed. "I promise to be gentle, Callie."

And he was as he cupped her breasts in his big hands, testing their fullness. Then his long fingers began to fondle her through the muslin until her breasts were heavy and swollen, their rigid buds straining against her snug bodice, begging for release.

Linc accommodated her, his hands sliding around to her back, his skillful fingers working swiftly at the fastenings of her clothes. Before she knew it, her breasts had been freed of all

219

restraints. He gazed at them for a long time, his black eyes so slumberous and seductive that she shivered with anticipation, her nipples puckering in the cool air.

"Cold?" he murmured. "Let me warm you."

She wasn't sure what to expect until he dipped his head. His mouth closed around first one nipple, then the other, his tongue swirling and tugging. Skyrockets went off inside Callie's head. She arched her back to give him better access to her breasts, pressing herself against him, her fingers digging into his scalp as she greedily sought more of his sweet torment.

He gave her more, suckling until she cried out for relief. "I can't take this," she gasped. "I want—"

He raised his head. There was no mercy on his face. "What?" he demanded. "What do you want, Callie? Tell me. You have to tell me."

She sagged against him, feeling his hardness strained against her bottom and knowing he was equally inflamed. "Everything," she implored him. "I want everything."

"Then let me give it to you."

She clung to him as, supporting her back with one arm and sliding his other arm beneath her knees, he rose with her from the chair and carried her to the fireplace, where one of their thick blankets was rolled up at the side of the hearth. He nudged the blanket with his toe, and it unwound on the floor like a magic carpet inviting them on a fantastic journey.

"This is the ultimate lesson," he promised after depositing her on the blanket and stretching out beside her. "Are you certain you want to undertake it?"

"Yes," she replied without hesitation.

"Then let it begin."

He proceeded to remove the rest of her clothes, garment by garment, then quickly stripped away his own things until the both of them lay face to face as nature had intended, man to woman, woman to man, their naked flesh ruddy in the glow of the fire, raw with need.

"Touch me, Callie," he commanded.

Her hands, shy at first, began to explore him, learning the shape and textures of his awesome body—his hard shoulders, his surprisingly sensitive nipples peeking through an expanse of black hair, his lean belly and hips, his muscled thighs. Then, her hands growing bolder with confidence, she dared to clasp the engorged shaft rising from his groin.

She had never realized it was so vulnerable an area for a man. He shuddered as if in unbearable pain and gripped her urgently at the hips. And for the first time she understood with wonder the power a woman is capable of.

Needing to demonstrate his own power, he touched her in return, his hands stroking, caressing, squeezing gently. His mouth was as active as his hands, capturing her own mouth, his tongue sweeping its interior. Then suddenly his fingers were on that secret place between her thighs, and she drew back in alarm.

"What—"

"Easy," he whispered. "Just let go and trust me."

She willed herself to relax, and within seconds his fingers were doing slow, exquisite things there that had her wet, whimpering, and writhing. One of his fingers located the nub within and began to slowly, steadily massage it. Callie, biting her lip, felt her self-control slipping away as something intense and wonderful began to build inside her.

"Linc," she murmured.

"Shh," he soothed.

A moment later, just when she thought she could endure no more, her body was gripped by a series of spasms. They were blinding, incredible. He held her tightly through her release, and when the last wave had subsided, he asked her softly, "You all right?"

She swallowed and managed to answer him weakly, "Fine. It were—was lovely, but—"

"What?"

"Is that all?"

He turned very sober then. "No, sweetheart. We've just come to the best part, but it's going to be uncomfortable for you at first, maybe even a little painful."

Callie blushed. "I'm not all that ignorant. I know about . . . well, a woman's virginity."

"I just wanted to give you the chance to be sure before it's too late. See, Callie, it's going to be next to impossible for me to stop once I, uh—"

"It's all right. Go on," she urged him.

"I'll try not to hurt you."

He was true to his promise as he positioned himself between her thighs, but there was no way he could relieve her of this strange, not unpleasant ache of her first time with a man. She bucked when she felt his great hardness probing the petals of her womanhood. But Linc was patient with her until she accepted him.

Callie could feel the pressure mounting as he sought entrance, murmuring words of encouragement to her with each of his slow, persistent thrusts. She felt a sharp, brief stinging sensation that made her cry out as he penetrated the barrier, and then, to her wonder, she realized he was completely buried, filling her with his length.

"All right?" he checked with her again, giving her a moment to adjust to him.

"Yes."

"That's good, because I've got to tell you this feels so great that I just have to . . ."

The rest he said with action, not words. He began to stir inside her, his hips lifting and sinking with each of his deep strokes. What followed for Callie was a blur of mindless, rapturous sensations as she participated in the performance, her rhythms answering his, her legs and arms clasping him, her mouth issuing wanton little cries of joy.

"Callie," he groaned as he carried her with him to the pinnacle and then over the top in a surging, radiant release.

When she surfaced at last to reality, he was beside her, holding her close to his body with its sheen of perspiration. "How do you feel?" he asked, concern in his tone.

She was a little tender down there, a little

sore, but it was unimportant. "Like I have the best teacher in the world."

Linc smiled, shoving aside the guilt and the unhappy realization that Pearl Slocum was going to have his head for this. What did it matter after what he'd just experienced? Callie Burgess was a sensation!

He wouldn't even let himself think about Anne.

Chapter Eleven

The skies cleared in the night, and by midmorning of the next day Linc discovered that the
waters had subsided in the stream.

"The ford is open for crossing again," he reported eagerly on his return to the cabin. "We
can be on our way."

Callie's reaction irritated him. She made no
complaint about leaving, but he thought she
looked disappointed. Linc worried that she
might have attached some romantic sentiment
to their interlude here when all he wanted to do
was distance himself from the place.

Guilt, of course. He could no longer hide from
it in the light of a new day, and it soured his
mood. He fought the terrible struggle of loving
the woman back in New Orleans while lusting for
the body of his traveling companion. He knew

he shouldn't touch her again, but after their fantastic sessions yesterday afternoon, and again last night, he didn't think he had the will to resist her.

The worst of it was, he feared hurting Callie. Hell, face it, he already had. Maybe that was why, once they were in the wagon and rolling again, he made such a conscientious effort to resume her education. If he had to hurt her, at least he could leave her with this much.

Linc didn't know if it was the weather that was responsible for the change in her lessons. The skies were blue again, the sun pleasantly warm, the air fresh after the long rains. Or maybe it was the scenery. It was magnificent on all sides—towering crags of granite furred with dark spruce, meadows edged in silver birch, spectacular waterfalls. Once they even glimpsed a herd of wild mustangs thundering along a ridge, a sight that thrilled both of them.

Whatever the explanation, just being on the trail north again in pursuit of Daniel lifted their spirits to such a degree that Callie's progress was remarkable. Not that his breakthrough with her yesterday didn't also account for a great deal of that. With the barriers finally lowered, she greedily demanded and absorbed every scrap of knowledge he fed her. It was astonishing how quick her mind was now that it was receptive.

Linc was glad, thinking once again that if he could give her a chance at a better life for herself, then maybe their eventual, inevitable parting wouldn't be so wrenching when the time came.

There was something else that emerged from those intense lessons. Something that greatly surprised him. Linc discovered that, all other motives aside, he experienced joy in watching her rapid growth and knowing he was responsible for it. The pride of a teacher for the success of his pupil. He'd never believed himself capable of that kind of satisfaction. Amazing.

It was late in the afternoon, with the shadows of the lonely mountains lengthening, when he began to realize there might be a serious flaw in all this wonderful logic. He had been correcting Callie's pronunciation of the more difficult words as she read aloud to him the rules of polite society.

"What is it?" he said when she suddenly stopped in the middle of an easy sentence and looked at him. "Oh, I know. It's that part about saying *limb* instead of *leg* in mixed company and referring to a bull as a *gentleman cow*. It is damn silly, isn't it?"

Callie shook her head. "Not that. I was only wonderin' . . ."

"What?"

"See, I know I just touched the surface, so t'speak. I got an awful long way t'go. Years o' learning, I guess. Things like history and geography and I don't know what-all. But what I've done so far, like working on my speech—" She paused, a little breathless, and gazed at him anxiously. "Does it please you, Linc?"

There was such an appeal for his approval in

those wide green eyes that Linc had an immediate, uneasy feeling that neither the weather nor the scenery, nor for that matter the quality of his teaching, were responsible for Callie's enthusiastic progress. He regarded her suspiciously. Was it possible, just *remotely* possible, that Callie Burgess either consciously or unconsciously was transferring her affections from Gabriel Hawkins to him?

He thought about that. She'd been so smitten all along with the illusion of Hawkins and his perfection that, even if he, Linc, was the first man she'd ever been physically intimate with, he doubted her heart could be disloyal to the preacher. And the possibility scared the hell out of him. Where their emotions were concerned, women had such funny notions about sex. He had to set her straight.

"Callie, remember what we talked about? How you're doing all this, not to please Gabriel Hawkins or me or anyone else, but only you? That's important to remember, that you need to be true to yourself. Do you understand?"

The green eyes blinked at him. "Oh, I know that. I just wanted t'hear you say it."

She put it so blandly, without a trace of distress, that he was deeply relieved. It was all right. His ego had simply been imagining she was falling in love with him, that was all.

But it was less easy for him to be convinced of that when they were camped that evening near a hot spring. All day, when he hadn't been concentrating on her lessons, Linc had thought of nothing else but Callie's luscious little body and how much he wanted it under him. He couldn't stop himself from lusting for her, and she seemed just as eager for another bout of lovemaking when they turned in for the night.

Clothes hastily shed, they came urgently together on the blanket they shared. The sex was wild and all-consuming, and to his gratitude there didn't seem to be any emotional issues connected with it. It was what followed that troubled him.

Linc was lying on his back, sated and limp while Callie, propped on one elbow, hovered above him. The firelight revealed a mysterious little smile on the mouth he had been plundering for the last half hour with his marauding tongue.

"Is there something I should know?" he murmured.

The forefinger of her free hand reached down and began to investigate the features of his face, taking special interest in the areas Linc had always wryly regarded as the more interesting aspects of his structure.

"It's this here sharp nose and these pointy ears," she explained. "They're the devil's own, y'know. Makes you look downright wicked."

He chuckled. "I'm afraid I can't take credit for them. They're a family trait with the McAllister men, maybe because there's Satan's blood somewhere in the line. It wouldn't surprise me."

Her finger moved on, playfully tracing the long scar on his jaw. "Didn't get this from your ancestors, did you?"

"Ah, that. No, that's a gift from a Mexican saber that just missed cutting my throat."

"The Mexican War?"

"Yes."

She sobered. "That saber have anything to do with why the U.S. Army parted company with you?"

Linc could feel himself tensing. This wasn't something he liked to talk about. "No, that was another occasion."

She sensed his reluctance. "It's all right. You don't have t'tell me."

But he knew she was curious, and what did it matter? "It was a brutal war, Callie, although what war isn't? I was involved in some pretty savage fighting. Well, that's what I was trained for, and as long as it was army to army, I accepted it. Couldn't do that, though, when it came to this one Mexican village."

"What happened?"

"The village was accused of hiding an escaped Mexican general, refusing to surrender him. I was ordered by my commanding officer to take my men and destroy the village and to shoot every adult male in the place, and any woman or child who interfered. I couldn't do it. This wasn't honest combat. It was an atrocity against people who were already so poor, they were close to starving."

His description of the cruel situation sickened Callie. "And you were—what's the right word?"

"Court-martialed for disobeying orders. I was a West Point officer, so that made it worse. The outcome was no surprise. I was stripped of my rank and dishonorably discharged. End of my fine career in the U.S. Army."

"But that was wrong of them! Terribly wrong! How could something like that happen?"

He was startled by her outrage on his behalf. "It happens all the time, Callie. Besides," he teased her, "I find you rushing so fiercely to my defense like this a little ironic. What happened to the hellcat who vowed to put a bullet through my heart because she was convinced I'd killed her father?"

"Oh, that," she mumbled, suddenly embarrassed.

"Yes, *that*."

"Well, a body can be wrong, can't she?" She peered down at him sharply. "Are you laughing at me, Lincoln McAllister?"

"Of course not. I'm just being happy I no longer have to go around worrying that my next breath is going to be my last."

Her face softened. "I was a fool to ever think you could be a cold-blooded killer. Not you. Not a man who's so decent and—and so, well, caring and all," she said rashly.

There it was again, that warning bell sounding in his brain. What was she telling him? That she'd changed her mind about him because she'd fallen in—No, he refused to name it. His imagination was just being all cockeyed again, that was all.

Nevertheless, he had felt much safer when she wasn't being so forgiving of him. Because when she was like this, she made him nervous, questioning his conscience once more. It was probably the worst thing he could do to silence his guilt, but he obeyed his impulse, dragged her down, and began to kiss her again.

It seemed to work. She expressed no more tender feelings about him, and by morning his concern lifted again. They were back to being teacher and pupil as they continued their journey. But by the end of that day, Linc realized with a jolt that he could no longer pretend she wasn't in love with him. Or at least that she imagined she was, which was just as bad.

This time it caught him by surprise, though he told himself afterward that he should have understood what was happening when she'd begun to question him like that.

They had made camp earlier than usual, agreeing that the animals needed to rest and that they would find no better spot than this grassy hollow with its pool of clear water. It was an excuse for another session of ardent love-making, and both of them knew it. But neither one of them could seem to help themselves.

There was still plenty of light in the sky afterward, and that was when she sat up on the blanket and turned to him, asking shyly, "Linc, do you like the way I look?"

His hand drifted down her firm back, coming to rest on the curve of her hip. "You haven't heard any complaints, have you? This area is especially appealing."

"No," she said a little impatiently, "I don't mean that. I mean—"

"What?"

"I want more than to talk right. I want to look right. That's part of being a lady, too."

"I guess."

"Things like clothes and hair and such."

"Sweetheart, if you're suggesting what I think you're suggesting, then you need another teacher. Preferably one in skirts."

"But you know what's right," she insisted. "You come from that sort of world."

"Callie, you look just fine the way you are."

"Maybe out here, but I wouldn't fit in with any real society. I know that much from my time back home where they looked down on the likes of me. And that was just ol' Horizon, Missouri, which wasn't much of a society. No, Linc, I need t'know. Please tell me."

"All right," he relented, "but I warn you, I was never all that observant about female fashions. Anyway, considering it's been some time since I've been around the people they do matter to, what little I know is probably already *out* of fashion. But I guess there are certain things that always follow the basics. So where do you want me to begin?"

"Clothes," she said promptly. "What do ladies wear that makes them ladies?"

He thought about it for a few seconds. "That dress you wore back at the cabin to try on the perfume—that was a good example."

"It was? And what's an example of a real bad dress?"

He didn't have to think about it this time. "The one you wore the night of the Oregon Freedom Day dance, although I have to admit that strictly from a male point of view it had, uh, certain qualities that were mighty interesting."

She ignored the obvious reference to her bosom and considered his comparison. "It wasn't respectable 'cause it wasn't simple enough, right? Guess I learned that much from Parthenia Smyth."

"It's usually better to go with simplicity," he agreed.

"What about bonnets?"

"I don't know. I think the fashions in them change with the seasons, sometimes sooner. I do remember that paisley shawls are popular with the ladies."

"And how about hair?" She combed her fingers through her heavy russet mane. "What would a lady do with this?"

He angled his head, studying her hair. "It suits you just like that, all thick and untamed and hanging down your back. Wild like you are when we're—"

"Linc, be serious!"

"I'm trying to, but you distract me with all that sweet flesh."

She grabbed an edge of the top blanket and dragged it up to her chin. "Go on."

"Um, I guess a lady would part it in the middle, smooth it back over her ears, and coil the rest in a net at the back of her neck."

Callie frowned. "This hair of mine has a mind of its own, but I reckon I could manage that. No curls?"

"Yes, in the evenings for parties. Probably ringlets at the sides and the back piled up toward the top of the head."

Excited, Callie let the blanket slip in order to

poke through the carpetbag close beside her. She came up with the gold and silver eardrops Pearl had tucked into the bag for her. Their ornate pendants glittered in the light as she held them to her lobes. "And these would look elegant with that kind of 'do, wouldn't they?"

Linc offered no judgment, but his face must have betrayed his opinion of the gaudy eardops. Callie lowered them with a sigh. "So these are bad, too. What isn't?"

"Something plainer, maybe with pearls."

Then simplicity was the rule even with jewelry, Callie realized. Yes, Parthenia had tried to teach her that as well, and she had failed to absorb it. But she was absorbing it now, adding up everything Linc had described for her and totaling it into the image of what he regarded as a refined lady. That sedate image was very important to Callie. She couldn't do much about trying to achieve it here in the wilderness, but once they were back with the wagon train . . .

"Are we through, I hope? Because I've got to tell you, sweetheart, I'm beginning to feel like an ass dealing with this stuff."

She startled him by exuberantly throwing her arms around his neck. "But you won't feel like one," she promised him. "Not once I get the chance to turn myself out for you like the ladies you admire. Then you'll see how glad you'll be. Oh, Linc, I can do it! I can be that kind of lady!"

And that's when Linc knew. Knew with a certainty he could no longer deny, no longer pretend was just his imagination. What had been happening between them was for Callie not just pleasurable sex. It was far more complicated than that. The little fool had gone and convinced herself she was in love with him. He could feel it in the way she clung to him, hear it in the giddiness of her voice. He had been a fool to think otherwise. A damn fool!

Shaken by the realization, Linc wondered what he was going to do about it. How was he ever going to make her understand that she'd fallen in love with her teacher, not him? And that it was impossible for him to feel what she felt? Impossible because—

Oh, hell, how could he have been such an idiot to get them into this mess? What had ever made him imagine that he could sleep with a woman as young and vulnerable and inexperienced as Callie and it wouldn't result in something serious like this? And why, oh why, hadn't he controlled his lust for her in the first place? Now all he could do was fear the outcome while praying she wouldn't grow impatient waiting to hear him express his feelings for her and end up impetuously declaring her undying love.

He should settle it now with the truth, but he was a coward. He couldn't bear the pain of such a scene, of seeing her anger and heartache and knowing he was the cause of it. So he put it off, hoping that he would figure out some way to soften the blow. But he knew that sooner or later . . .

"This is as far as we go," Linc announced shortly before noon the next day.

Callie looked around. He had halted the rig in

a deep fold between the mountains. A tumbling stream fed the narrow valley, which was lush with trees and grass.

"Then we're here?" she asked, surprised because she saw no signs of occupation.

Linc, bending over the small map, shook his head. "I meant this is as far as we go with the wagon. We still have some miles to cover, but the way from here is too rough for the wagon. We'll have to leave it and ride the rest of the distance on our horses, which, in case you've been wondering, is why I brought them."

"What about the mules?"

"We'll turn them loose. There's plenty of water and grass to keep them in the area, but if they should wander off . . ." He shrugged. "Well, no choice about it. We'll just have to hope we can round them up when we get back."

" 'Less a party of Indians happens by and rounds them up for us. Which means," she pointed out, "we're risking the wagon and all that's in it, too."

"We'll park the wagon out of sight behind all that buffalo berry over there. It's the best we can do."

Eating a quick lunch, they saddled the horses and filled their saddlebags with as many supplies as they could carry. Within a half hour they were on a rugged, stony track climbing into the hills.

"Where's this taking us?" Callie asked.

Linc pointed toward the rocky flank of the mountain above them. "Up there."

"To a certain spot? You never did say."

He nodded. "The Indians call it the Cave of the Crystals. They regard it as even more sacred than the Black Hills themselves, which is why Daniel is hiding out there."

If he's still there, Callie thought. But she kept the thought to herself, knowing how much Linc was counting on finding the boy.

The track grew steep and narrow, forcing them to ride single file. Linc led the way with Callie following him on Apollo. Conversation was difficult now, so she addressed her own thoughts. They were pleasing thoughts, as was the sight of the subject of them. Even from the rear, he made her light-headed with his broad shoulders, straight back, and narrow hips.

When had it happened? At what delirious moment had she fallen in love with Lincoln McAllister? Sometime back at the cabin, she supposed. Probably when he'd first made love to her on that long, rainy afternoon, his body branding hers. The enthralling memory of it would stay with her always.

A much less simple question was: *How* had it happened? It didn't seem possible that all out of nowhere her hated enemy should become the man whose arms she wanted to be in forever. That the very things she'd detested about him, those satanic eyebrows and ears, that lean, angular face with its mocking grin, should now be so precious to her. It was insane and wonderful at the same time, and she was still dazed by it.

But she was afraid to tell him how she felt. What if he didn't return her love? Oh, but he must! Anything else would be unbearable.

Of course, this was the wrong time for any declaration of love. Callie could see that. But once the problem of Daniel had been dealt with, once they were on their way back to the Oregon Trail, surely then . . .

Huge boulders reared their heads on either side of the wild, rutted track, which had become less easy to follow, dwindling to a thread. Rock walls seemed to enclose it now, making the route even more remote. There was a lonely silence about the place, its only sounds the clicking of the horses' hooves on the hard surface of the stone, echoing hollowly.

Callie began to feel uneasy, as though she were violating something forbidden to her. It was a feeling she couldn't shake, maybe because she sensed hidden eyes on her.

They hadn't spoken in some time. But Callie, no longer able to stand it, finally whispered a taut, "Feel like I'm being watched."

"We *are* being watched," Linc murmured calmly over his shoulder.

"Then oughtn't we—"

"No. Any challenge or unfriendly action would be a mistake. Just keep riding, and don't look around. Act like you have nothing to be afraid of."

Easier said than done, Callie thought nervously, but she tried to obey. She kept Apollo moving and her gaze straight ahead. All the while she could feel those hostile eyes on her, and she worried they were riding into a trap.

The strain was unendurable by the time they

rounded a bend and crested a rise. Here the track ended on a natural terrace tucked against the sheer side of the mountain. The flat area was the size of a small field and dotted with low, sprawling junipers. There was no one in sight. The stillness persisted.

"We walk from here," Linc said, dismounting from his roan.

Callie slid from Apollo's back and started to reach for her rifle, but Linc stopped her.

"Don't touch it," he warned her. "We'll leave the guns here. I don't want him to think we've come in anything but peace."

Callie thought it was a mistake not to arm themselves, but she didn't argue about it. She joined Linc on a footpath that crossed the wide terrace, meandering through the ragged junipers. She didn't have to ask him where they were going. Ahead of them was a dark gap in the wall of the mountain. It had to be the entrance to the Cave of the Crystals.

"Shouldn't we go and hail him?" she asked Linc.

"Why? He knows we're here."

Callie had never felt so vulnerable as they approached the cave. In a gravelly area outside its opening she could see the blackened remains of a campfire. There were no other signs of occupation.

Reaching the cave, they peered into its yawning, silent depth. Areas in the walls and ceiling flashed like polished mirrors in the slanting sunlight, evidence of the crystals. It was a spectacular sight. Beyond was blackness.

Callie, hating this eerie stillness, was waiting for Linc to suggest their next move when there was a sharp crack from somewhere behind them. A bullet pinged into the rock framing the cave opening, biting off a chip of it. It struck within inches of Callie's hand. Uttering a little yelp of alarm, she started to swing around to confront their attacker. But Linc's hand on her arm restrained her.

"If he wanted to kill us, we'd both be dead by now. That was just a warning. Go easy and turn slowly. Keep your hands open and away from your sides."

Callie did as he asked, turning with him until they were both facing away from the cave. She found herself covered by a rifle in the steady, capable hands of a lithe figure several yards away in the junipers.

He was tall and as slender as a sapling, with long, straight black hair and a skin that, though browned from the sun, was more white than Indian. He couldn't have been more than fifteen years old, but even from here Callie could see that he had all the dignity and solemn bearing of an adult. They had found Daniel.

"What now?" Callie wondered as the young brave continued to train the rifle on them, his body as motionless as a rock, his face wearing no expression whatever.

"I'll need somehow to explain who we are and why we're here," Linc said, keeping his gaze on the figure who wore buckskin leggings and a single eagle feather in his hair. "Which won't be easy, since I don't know his Cheyenne name, and

241

I have only a smattering of the Algonquian language of his people."

Without even a brief hesitation and in the coolest of voices, Daniel called to him, "Then try the white man's tongue, and the name is Sky Wolf."

Was it her imagination, Callie wondered, or did that blank young face register just a hint of amusement at the sight of their startled expressions?

"You speak English," Linc said in wonder and relief. "And damn good English at that."

Sky Wolf was silent for a moment. Then his bare shoulders sketched a shrug. "A white trapper stayed with my people last winter. He talked, I listened." With no change of tone, he went on swiftly, "You trespass on sacred land. What do you want here?"

"Put down that rifle," Linc requested, "and I'll tell you everything."

Sky Wolf wasn't persuaded to do anything but keep the rifle where it was.

"Look," Linc said, "you can see neither one of us is armed. I promise you we're not here to capture you or convince you to give yourself up. All we want to do is talk to you."

Sky Wolf slowly lowered his weapon, but he kept a firm grip on it as he cautiously approached them. He stopped a few safe feet away from them. He was close enough now that Callie could see on the side of his neck the crescent-moon birthmark that identified him as Magpie's long-lost son. She could also see the look of wariness in his dark, handsome eyes.

"Talk," he demanded, "and if I don't like what you say, then my rifle will answer for me."

"My name is Lincoln McAllister," Linc told him, "and the woman is Callie Burgess. There's another name you need to hear. *Daniel.* Do you remember it?"

"Why should I?" But Callie thought there was a sudden flicker of interest in his gaze, as though Linc had stirred a dim recollection.

"Because it's your name, Daniel. The one you were born with."

The young man was prepared to deny it. His mouth tightened in both anger and uneasiness. "I am Sky Wolf, and I am Cheyenne," he insisted proudly.

"Only by adoption," Linc said. "Your father was a white man, and your mother is half white, which makes you nearly all white yourself. But you know that already, don't you? I think you must have always known it. Maybe that's why you were so willing to be taught English from that trapper, and why it was so easy for you to learn what must have been your first tongue."

"And *your* tongue speaks lies. You think I don't know that you try to trick me so that you can drag me back to one of your forts?"

"Where the army wants to punish you for killing the man who attacked your Cheyenne sister. Yes, Daniel, that might be why I'm here—to collect a bounty on you if I bring you in. Only that isn't the reason why I've come to you."

The youth's mouth curled in a sneer. "Are you here to help me then? Is that what you expect me to believe?"

"You *will* benefit, and in more ways than you can imagine. But I won't lie to you. I have my own selfish purpose in finding you. Can I show you what it is?"

"Where?"

Linc turned sideways to clearly reveal the pocket in his jean trousers. "It's here in my pocket. You can see there's no bulge that might mean a gun or a knife. It's just a paper."

"Take it out," Daniel commanded. *"Slowly."*

Raising the rifle again, he watched suspiciously as Linc withdrew the thick printed paper, unfolded it, and extended it toward him.

"Here," Linc said, "look at it for yourself."

Daniel stared at the paper in Linc's hand, making no effort to accept it. It was Callie, always sensitive about her own deficiencies, who immediately understood.

"Don't you see that's no good?" she murmured to Linc. "He wouldn't have learned to read." She snatched the paper out of his hand and held it up so that Daniel could see for himself. Above the bold print was the sketch of a small boy with a crescent moon birthmark. "It's meant to be you when you were little, Sky Wolf. Will you let me tell you what the paper says?"

Daniel nodded, and Linc offered no objection either. He could see that the boy was inclined to trust Callie more than him.

She turned the paper around again in order to translate it for Daniel. It was creased in many places, evidence that Linc must have been carrying it for a long time, though he hadn't mentioned it to her.

"This is what you call a circular, Sky Wolf," she explained carefully. "They get passed from place to place over great distances when men are hunting for what they can't find on their own. But this here circular was printed long before you were wanted by the army. It asks for your safe return to the woman who gave birth to you. It promises white man's money to anyone who brings you back to her."

"A *lot* of money," Linc added. "A much greater reward than anything the army might be offering."

The youth was silent for a moment; then he said gravely, "And you want this money, Lincoln McAllister."

"I do. Now will you let me tell you the whole story, and you can decide for yourself?"

Daniel, still wary but plainly interested, nodded. Seconds later the three of them were seated cross-legged on the ground, though Daniel sat apart from them and vigilantly kept his rifle resting across his knees. He listened without comment as Linc earnestly explained how he had been taken from his mother when he was three years old and placed in the care of the Cheyenne. How the grieving Magpie had searched for him all these years without result. But now, as a wealthy widow in far-off Oregon, she offered an immense sum for his recovery.

When he was finished, Callie leaned forward, adding a gentle, "I crossed on a wagon train to Oregon when I was little myself. Your ma was with us, Sky Wolf. I remember how sad she was

245

over your loss and how nothing mattered to her but to find you again."

Daniel said nothing. Did he believe them, or did he think the story was nothing but a fantastic fairy tale?

Linc placed his hands on his knees and spoke to the youth in urgent tones. "I know what you must be feeling at the thought of coming with us. You'd be leaving the Cheyenne behind and going to a mother you don't remember. The Cheyenne have been your people all these years, and their life is the only one you know. But consider this, Daniel. You can't hide out here forever, and you can't go back. You risk your Cheyenne family if you try, because the army won't stop hunting for you and they'll punish your people if they're caught helping you."

"And in this far-away Oregon?"

"You'll be safe, and you'll be free. No one is going to look for you out there. Anyway, your mother is so rich that she may be able to clear your name."

"And," Callie said softly, offering what she considered the most important argument of all, "you'll be loved."

Daniel gazed at her, as though only her plea had made any impression on him. "Wait," he said.

Without another word, he laid down his rifle, got to his feet, and moved off to the far side of the shingled terrace, where he mounted an enormous boulder that looked out over the vastness of sky and mountains.

"What's he doing?" Callie wondered, puzzled

by the sight of Daniel standing straight and tall on the boulder, his head stretched back as he looked toward the heavens.

"My guess is," Linc said, "he's addressing the spirits of the Cheyenne, asking for their advice."

Callie watched the young figure on the boulder while they went on waiting outside the mouth of the cave. He remained motionless, as though in a deep trance. After a moment they began to discuss him again in low, anxious tones.

"He left his rifle behind," Callie said. "That's a good sign, isn't it?"

"That he trusts us now, yes. But it isn't a decision to come with us."

"There's the English he learned from the trapper," she reminded him.

"That's in our favor," Linc agreed. "It could mean he was eager to connect with the white man's world, that something inside him sensed he didn't really belong to the Cheyenne. Or it could mean nothing."

They weren't to know until long, suspenseful minutes later when Daniel finally left his lookout and returned to them. Getting to their feet, they faced the young man.

"I will let you take me to Oregon," he informed them casually. "But there is a promise you must make me, Lincoln McAllister."

"What? Name it."

Daniel glanced at Callie, a gleam of boyish humor in his dark eyes. "This great reward you will get from my mother for bringing me to her . . ."

"Yes?" Linc encouraged him.

"You will share it with your woman here."

Callie and Linc exchanged looks of complete surprise. Of all the things Daniel might have asked for, this was the most unexpected.

Callie waited for Linc to make his strong objections to such a proposal. But to her astonishment and pleasure, he agreed to what Daniel asked without hesitation.

"Consider it done," he said. "She deserves a generous portion of the reward."

It wasn't the money that made Callie suddenly light-headed with joy. The money in itself was unimportant. What did matter was the tender smile that accompanied Linc's unhesitating pledge to share it with her. She was certain that here at last was evidence of his love for her.

Chapter Twelve

"Slocum, there's no question about it," Pearl told herself bluntly. "You're being a prize fool."

She had no reason to turn and eye with regret the mass of the adobe fort on its eminence behind her. No reason not to join the tall figure waiting for her on the path below. But she couldn't seem to rid herself of this nervous reluctance to be alone with Gabriel Hawkins.

Until now, her daily lessons with the preacher had occurred in the vicinity of other people, first on the wagon train and then inside the post itself after their arrival here at Fort Laramie. This afternoon, however, Gabriel had asked her to meet him for a walk along the banks of Laramie Creek. He had so surprised her with his request that she'd agreed before realizing her error.

This was a mistake. Innocent stroll or not,

there was something threatening to Pearl about the two of them going off by themselves. A suggestion of intimacy she didn't trust.

Plain nonsense, of course, she lectured herself again. Why should she be uneasy in the company of the gentle Reverend Mr. Hawkins when she'd dealt with scores of men in her career in the most familiar of terms? Why should this particular one trouble her so?

Maybe the answer to that had something to do with the smile he greeted her with when she arrived at the stream where he waited. It wasn't just a warm smile. It was a very personal one. And suddenly, looking up at him, she was far too conscious of his dazzling good looks. Damn it all, a clergyman had no business being so handsome.

Pearl was unreasonably annoyed with both him and herself, hating her feeling of awkwardness. She was *never* awkward with men. To disguise it, she hid behind her old breeziness.

"Well, padre, what am I working on today? How to behave like a lady without society guessing I'm not? Or how to talk like the new schoolmarm in town?"

"I thought we'd take a rest from the lessons this afternoon, Pearl. Just use the opportunity to get to know each other a little better."

She didn't like the sound of that.

"You don't object, do you?" he challenged her.

"I don't reckon there's any harm in it," she lied, not wanting him to know he worried her.

She waited for his questions, knowing he must be curious about her past, but he was silent as they strolled side by side along the bank of the creek. It was a shallow, sluggish stream, which wasn't surprising in this arid landscape with its thin, parched grass. There were a few stunted ash trees and several cottonwoods at the edge of the creek, but the range of dry ridges behind the fort was barren.

Pearl was far too concerned about her companion, however, to pay much attention to the scenery. She supposed his closeness was understandable since the path they walked was very narrow. Still, he made her uncomfortable with his long silence and the way he turned his head from time to time to eye her. When he finally did speak, his abruptness startled her.

"You've changed in these past couple of weeks," he said, pausing to observe her critically.

Pearl nodded. "I expect it's my hair. I haven't been coloring it, so it's going back to its natural brown. Not as attractive as the red, but I reckon it's more respectable." She didn't add that she'd also stopped painting her face and was dressing more conservatively. She assumed these were obvious differences, though he hadn't mentioned them. Silly of her to hope he approved of them. What did it matter?

Gabriel shook his head. "I'm not talking about any physical change. I'm talking about all the progress you've made with our lessons."

"I should hope so. I've been working da—uh, real hard to improve myself."

"Do you like the new woman you're becoming, Pearl?" he asked her earnestly.

251

She thought about that for a minute as they moved on along the path. "Yeah, I think I do."

"I'm glad, because I wouldn't be happy about the growth you're making unless you, yourself, are pleased with it." He hesitated. "But there is something I'd like to know about the old Pearl."

Here it comes, she thought, trying to tell herself she had no reason to be disappointed in him. He was going to ask her how she'd become a prostitute. Men always did sooner or later, and she would always provide them with one of the brazen or flippant responses that were her stock in trade.

But once again Gabriel surprised her, taking her breath away with his slow, solemn question. "Have you ever been in love, Pearl?"

"What?"

"Love. Have you ever been in love with any of the men you've known? Bud Colby, for instance."

Pearl had been forced to trust Gabriel with the story of her flight from Independence in order to explain McAllister and Callie's absence from the wagon train. She'd shared it all, including her affair with Colby, and been relieved that the preacher hadn't judged her. The only thing she hadn't told Gabriel was Callie's love for him. That was her friend's secret, and she wouldn't betray it.

Gabriel was waiting for her answer. Pearl wasn't sure she had one. She thought about Bud Colby. His death had been a shock to her, but there had been no time to mourn. She'd been too terrified for that and far too busy hiding herself on a wagon train bound for Oregon. And since then? Well, Bud had been a good friend, and she did miss his fun-loving ways all right. But the truth was, Pearl had never been as serious about Bud as he'd been about her.

"No," she said, realizing for the first time in a kind of wonder that she'd never been serious about any of the men who'd passed through her life. "I never have, come to think of it. Too busy practicing love to ever feel it, I reckon."

She should have known Gabriel's response would be totally unexpected. The man was forever surprising her. Even so, he left her speechless and confused when he uttered a fervent, "I thank God for that."

She came to a stop on the path and turned to stare at him. That was when she realized she was actually trembling. What on earth was the matter with her? There had never been a man Pearl Slocum couldn't handle with aplomb and a quick jest. Why should this one, who ought to have been the most harmless of all, be any different? But he was, and vastly so.

Gabriel, too, had come to a stop and was facing her. "Why, Pearl?" he asked her in a soft, low voice that sent a shiver along her spine. "Why are you afraid of me?"

She was discovering that he had an uncanny ability to sense her feelings, and it alarmed her. "Me?" she croaked, forcing a laugh that would fool no one. "You've got the wrong woman, padre. There isn't any man I'm afraid of."

"In that case," he said with an easy confidence

she wouldn't have believed him capable of, "you can't mind being alone with me."

Pearl looked around, suddenly realizing that they were absolutely alone. The fort was out of sight behind them. They were standing at the edge of a green meadow fed by the creek. There were wild roses here. They made her intoxicated with their delicate fragrance. Or was it the blond, handsome figure who had moved so close to her that she could feel his warm breath on her face?

"And," he added in a seductive whisper, "you can't possibly mind my doing this."

Before she could stop him, or even decide whether she wanted to stop him, Gabriel's arms slid around her waist and drew her tightly against his chest. When her lips parted in an effort to win her release, his mouth covered them.

His kiss was so deep and thorough, so stunningly passionate, that she lost both the ability and the desire to demand anything. All she could suddenly think about, all she could feel or want, was the heady taste of him as his mouth took possession of hers. The experience was so potent, so all-consuming, that it shocked Pearl. It was as if all those countless other men in her life had never existed, as if this kiss was her very first one.

What was happening here? How could a clergyman be capable of such intense lovemaking? But then, as she was so swiftly learning, Gabriel Hawkins refused to fit the role in which she had cast him.

For a mindless, exhilarating moment, Pearl totally involved herself in the kiss, savoring the sensation of his eager tongue playing with hers, relishing the strength of his arms possessively clasping her body to his. And then all at once the image of Callie rose in her mind.

Guilt, sharp and overwhelming, struck her like a blast of icy wind. How could she? How could she permit herself to be kissed by the man Callie loved? Even worse, even more disloyal, she had enjoyed every aspect of the intimacy. With all the strength she could summon, Pearl severed their kiss, thrusting herself out of Gabriel's arms.

"No," she pleaded. "No."

He ignored her objection, declaring urgently, "Now you know why I thanked God you never felt love for a man. It's because I want to be the first and only man you ever love."

"You're crazy. I don't love you. I can *never* love you." Her claim lacked conviction, and she knew it. This, then, was why she had been afraid of him all along, why she had resisted any treacherous closeness in their relationship. But how could she have failed to see exactly what was happening?

"Why?" he persisted. "Just because I'm a man of the cloth?"

"Yeah, that's it," she said, snatching at the argument. "That's just it, Reverend. You don't want me that way. You *can't*. Why, you just see me as a challenge, the bad woman to be reformed for her past sins."

"You're wrong, Pearl. None of that matters to me. Maybe it should, but it doesn't."

"It will," she insisted. "What do you think will happen if we go on this way? Do you think your followers will continue to believe in you if I end up to be the woman at your side?"

"Let me worry about that."

"You're blind, Gabriel. They'll crucify you."

"People can be understanding, Pearl, if you give them the chance. They'll forgive you for your mistakes, whether you ever embrace my faith or not. And, yes, I hope you will one day, but if you can't—"

She cut him off with a bitter laugh. "Forgive? You don't know what you're talking about. I've got a past nobody can forgive, and maybe it's time you heard it."

"Pearl—"

"No, listen to me," she raced on, hoping to shock him into being sensible. "I had an old man who walked out on us when I was still in diapers and never looked back. My mother took in washing to keep us from starving and slowly drank herself to death. I was on my own by the time I was fourteen. In order to earn a living I went into service. I became a housemaid for a wealthy family in St. Louis, but I was good looking and the randy son of these people wouldn't let me alone. I tried to avoid him, but his mother caught him trying to paw me one day. I was discharged without a reference. She told all her friends I was a lewd person not fit to be employed. Do you know what that means for a young girl without skills, Gabriel?"

"Yes, I think I do," he said solemnly.

"It means," she went on wildly, as though she

hadn't heard him, "she has only one way to survive. Well, I wanted to survive, so I got tough and chose that way. An old story, huh? The oldest one in the world. Nothing new about it, but I bet this is the first time you ever heard it from the woman you want to make your own."

She was still laughing, but there were tears in her eyes. "My dearest," he murmured, "it doesn't matter. Whatever you became, your goodness was always there. That's all I care about, and that's what I love." He tried to put his arms around her to comfort her, but she wouldn't let him.

"Oh, Gabriel, you're such a fool! Of course it matters. You've never brought up your own past, but I've heard things from the others on the wagon train. They say you came from a rich and important family in Philadelphia. It's true, isn't it? So what does that make you and me?"

"Yes," he admitted, "my people are an old, prominent Philadelphia family. But did they also tell you I'm an outcast from that family because I turned to the church instead of obeying their plan for me to marry the right girl and join the family shipping firm?"

"No, I didn't know that."

"Pearl, don't you see? We're both of us putting our pasts behind us to start all over again. That's what the west is all about, a place for people to renew themselves. That makes us equals, Pearl, with nothing standing between us that really matters."

He had met her every objection with arguments more powerful and persuasive than her own. That left her with only one weapon. She had sworn not to use it, but in her desperation she had no choice. She could only pray that her friend would forgive her.

"Oh, but there is," she said, her voice hoarse with emotion. And she went on to tell him all about Callie's unshakable love for him and how at this moment she was sacrificing her very identity for that love.

Nothing had shocked Gabriel—until now. He stared at Pearl in disbelief. Then, recovering himself, he uttered an oath that would have stunned his congregation, following it with a fiery, "This is ridiculous! Callie Burgess is nothing but a child!"

"You haven't looked, Reverend, or you would have seen a woman desperately in love."

"All right," he conceded, "about this I have apparently been blind. But you can't expect me to be serious about Callie being an obstacle to us."

"Maybe not, but *I'm* serious about it. See, Reverend, there's something you need to realize about me. Whatever I've done or been that might have been wrong, there's one thing I hung on to no matter what. If I care about someone, *really* care about them, like I do Callie, I make sure I'm loyal to them. And I won't lose that, because in the end it's really all I have to give."

"Pearl, be reasonable."

"I won't hurt her, Gabriel. I *can't* hurt her."

"Don't do this to us," he begged her.

"There's nothing to say. I—I'm sorry, that's all."

And Pearl left him there on the path and hurried back toward the fort. Heartsick with regret, she was climbing the slope toward the main gate when it occurred to her that if she had tried hard enough, *really* tried, she might have put an end to this mess by convincing Gabriel that she didn't care for him in the way he wanted and never could. A simple, direct solution. Only it wouldn't have been the truth. And that was when, with a deep, wrenching anguish, Pearl realized just how much Gabriel Hawkins did matter to her and how hopeless their situation was.

"And now," Daniel announced importantly to a pleased Callie, and an even more pleased Linc, "I will gather up my belongings from the cave, and we will make the journey to this Oregon."

"Well, at least the first part of it. Which," Linc said hopefully, as they accompanied Daniel toward the mouth of the cave, "will be a lot easier if you happen to have a horse of your own."

The young man snorted in scorn, informing them proudly, "A Cheyenne is not a brave unless he is mounted on his own pony. He is not far from here. We will go there when—"

He never finished telling them where his horse was hidden. There was a sudden, sharp crack. Daniel staggered, then righted himself, clutching at the side of his upper arm. Callie saw with horror blood begin to seep between his fingers. The boy had been wounded! That crack had been the sound of a rifle! Someone was shooting at them!

She started to whirl around to seek out their attackers, but Linc drove both her and Daniel into the cave, shouting an urgent, "Take cover!"

The concealed rifle barked again, but by then they were safely within the dimness of the cave, the three of them huddled on the floor behind a barrier of rock projecting from a side wall.

"Daniel's been hit!" Callie said, already busy examining the young man's injury.

"How bad?" Linc demanded, checking around a corner of the rock to see if their attackers were making any attempt to follow them into the cave.

Callie peered at the arm in the murky light. "The bullet just grazed him, I think," she reported thankfully when the boy himself didn't answer, "but sure is enough blood."

"See if this will help." Linc tore the bandana from around his neck and passed it to her, all the while keeping his eye on the mouth of the cave.

Daniel offered no objection and didn't so much as flinch as she bound the flesh wound, though she knew she must be hurting him in her clumsy haste to halt the flow of blood. When she was finished, she looked into his face and was chilled by the cold, steely look in his eyes. That was when she realized his gaze was directed not at her but at Linc. Why was he angry with Linc?

"Not a sign of anyone in the clearing out there," Linc muttered, "and nothing now but silence."

"Could they have cleared off?" Callie wondered.

"Not likely."

And us pinned down in here without our guns, she thought in helpless frustration. What good were her sharpshooting skills to them when Linc had made her leave her Remington with her horse? He, too, was unarmed, and Daniel had left his own rifle out there in the open. To try to reach it now would be asking for death.

The same thoughts must have occurred to Linc because he turned his head, asking a quick, "Daniel, have you got any other weapons here in the cave?"

The young man didn't answer. That was when Linc saw the accusing look in his eyes and understood it.

"No, Daniel," he promised him solemnly, "we didn't lead the troopers here to capture you. I don't know who it is out there, but this isn't an arranged ambush, and I didn't lie to you."

The two men held each other's gazes for several tense seconds, and then Daniel slowly nodded, his trust restored. "There is no other weapon," he said.

"Then we're in a real fix. We have to figure out some way to—"

Linc's grim assessment of their situation was interrupted by a shout from their hidden enemy. "You in there, McAllister? We want the boy! You send him out t'us, an' nobody gits hurt! An' if yer real peaceful-like 'bout it, you an' the woman can go! My word on it!"

Another voice, this one more shrill, added, "Ya got two minutes t'think it over, an' if ya don't show with what we want, then we're comin' in t'git it. Comin' right in."

Linc, recognizing the two voices, muttered a curse. "Judd Parsons and Ike Ritter! How the hell did they manage to track us here?"

The vipers who killed Pa, Callie thought. She had an angry reason now to regret even more deeply the absence of her Remington.

Daniel was puzzled. "Who are these men?"

"A couple of nasty critters," Callie explained to him, "who also want the reward money your ma has offered for your return."

"By killing me?"

Linc frowned. "No, that doesn't make sense. I suppose they must have been trying to eliminate me and hit you by mistake. Still, that was a damn careless risk for something so valuable to them."

"One minute t'go, McAllister!" Judd Parsons's booming voice called out to them. "What's it gonna be?"

Daniel got to his feet. Linc, misunderstanding his intention, grabbed at him. "Daniel, no! You can't go out there to them! They're killers, and we can't be sure just who they were aiming at!"

Daniel again expressed his scorn with a quick, "Lincoln McAllister, you are wasting this minute of time they talk about. I am going in the other direction, and if you are wise you will both come with me."

Callie understood him. "There's a back door to this cave?"

"Two ways out on the other side of the mountain."

"Well, why didn't you say so to begin with? Wait a second, your arm—"

"No longer bleeds. Hurry, before they understand we have slipped away."

Scrambling to their feet, Callie and Linc followed Daniel as he swiftly led the way into the depth of the cave. She wondered how, without a torch, they could possibly find their way in the blackness. But after a few seconds of trotting close behind Daniel, she realized the darkness wasn't complete. Light was stealing in from somewhere, enough to permit them to pick their way along the twisting passage. She understood its origin when, rounding a corner, they encountered on the floor a pile of broken rock over which they had to clamber. Through the ceiling above it penetrated a bright shaft of daylight from the outside.

"A cave-in," Linc said.

"There are others," Daniel said. "Many of them."

The realization that this mountain inside which they were traveling was susceptible to such action made Callie nervous. She didn't appreciate the possibility of being buried in here by a sudden collapse over her head of several tons of rock.

Daniel, observing her uneasiness, teased her with an unconcerned, "Do not worry, Callie Burgess. I will ask the mountain to fall instead on these men who hunt us."

And just where were Judd Parsons and Ike Ritter at this moment? Callie wondered, listening for the echoing slap of running feet behind them. Linc and Daniel must have been asking themselves the same question because they, too, had paused to listen, straining to detect any sound of pursuit. There was nothing but silence, but Callie knew that their enemies must have learned by now they had fled into the depths of the cave. And if Parsons and Ritter weren't already chasing after them, they would be soon enough.

Linc also had to be worried about that. "Let's keep on the move," he urged. "I don't want to think of one of those rifles going off in here if they catch up with us."

Callie knew that he meant the reverberations could cause another cave-in, maybe a serious one. Shuddering, she hastened after Daniel.

As he'd indicated, there were other cave-ins along their route, happily none of them major and a good many of them allowing further daylight to enter the passage. The openings were too small and too high overhead to permit any exit for them that way. But the crystals for which the cave was named, clustered thickly on walls and ceiling, trapped the welcome glow from these light holes, creating shifting rainbows in their prisms. It was a beautiful, almost magical sight, although there was an eerie quality to it.

Daniel, thoroughly familiar with the route, never hesitated. But when the winding passage began to resemble a labyrinth, Linc expressed his misgiving. "You sure there's another way out of here?"

Daniel smiled. "A prairie dog never has just one hole," he assured them.

Meaning, Callie thought, he'd made sure he couldn't be cornered before he ever hid out here. The real evidence of Daniel's cleverness, however, was yet to be demonstrated.

Seconds later Callie heard the sound of running water and wondered if she was imagining it. But the sound grew to an unmistakable roar, and when Daniel led them into a vast, hollow chamber lit by still another shaft of light, she discovered the source.

They found themselves on the edge of an underground stream, a torrent that raced into a cataract on one side of the chamber, which plunged down into a yawning, wicked blackness that made Callie shiver.

"We cross here," Daniel said, indicating stepping-stones that bridged the stream. "Be careful to go just where I go and no other. The waters are bad."

She could believe that, Callie thought, eyeing the dark, wild current as she cautiously followed his lead with Linc bringing up the rear. There was an almost straight path across the swift stream, the upthrust boulders there offering surfaces that were generous in size and perfectly flat. It seemed like a natural, safe choice, and she wondered why Daniel led them on a much less direct crossing off to one side, where the surfaced rocks were smaller and more treacherous. But there was no time to ask questions.

When they reached the other side, Callie saw that the chamber divided into two passages.

"Which way?" Linc asked, checking over his shoulder. There was still no sign of their pursuers.

"Both ways lead out of the mountain, but that way is longer," Daniel said, indicating the passage on the right.

He led them into the left branch, and Callie

wondered about his choice. The floor was uneven, the ceiling so low that it forced them to bend over from the waist. In other places the gallery narrowed to such closeness that they had to squeeze through the gaps.

Feeling claustrophobic, Callie was about to ask Daniel how much farther they had to go when he stopped abruptly in front of her with a grunt of unhappy surprise.

"What is it?" Linc asked, coming up beside them.

"That," Daniel said. "It was not here when I came this way before."

The light was almost nonexistent in this area, so it took a few seconds for them to clearly discern what Daniel indicated. There was a fresh pile of rubble blocking the route. It extended from wall to wall, reaching all the way to what was left of the ceiling. The passage was a blind one now, sealed completely by this latest cave-in.

"No way around it and no way over it," Linc muttered.

"We must go back to the other one," Daniel said.

Turning, they swiftly retraced their steps to the fork in the chamber. The time they had lost was their enemy. They learned just how serious an enemy when they emerged from the gallery. Their pursuers had caught up with them. Judd Parsons and Ike Ritter stood on the other side of the underground river, rifles leveled at them.

"Well now, Ike, ain't this nice?" The brutish Parsons chuckled above the rush of the stream.

"Don't have to go on chasin' 'em. No sir, they come right t'us."

"Sure did, Judd," Ike squealed. "Sure did."

Callie clenched her hands into fists and glared at the villains, wishing there would be another cave-in, this time over their vile heads. But nothing so convenient occurred.

"Don't just stand there. Come on over an' join us," Parsons invited, motioning with his rifle for them to cross the river.

Daniel, who had shrunk back against a wall of the cavern, slid down the rock until he was sitting on the floor. "Come for me if you want me," he called weakly. "I have no more strength to fight."

Alarmed, Callie knelt beside Daniel. He was moaning now, clutching his bandana-wrapped arm where blood had reddened the cloth. Was it fresh blood or from earlier?

"Move away from 'im!" Parsons thundered.

"No," Callie refused. "Can't you see he's hurt? That bullet o' yours struck him."

"I want that boy sent across here t'us," Parsons demanded.

"You heard him," Linc shouted. "If you want him, come and get him!" And he moved protectively in front of Callie and Daniel, shielding them with his body. His clear intention to sacrifice himself if he had to made Callie's heart swell with love.

Parsons cursed violently but lowered his rifle, prepared to cross the river. "Cover them, Ike," he directed his partner.

Restraining her anger, Callie turned away to

check Daniel's arm. When she leaned close, peering anxiously into his face that had been strained with pain mere seconds ago, he met her gaze with a cheerful wink that astonished her. He followed the wink with a brief, conspiratorial nod in the direction of the river behind her.

Callie twisted around in time to witness the result of Daniel's cunning. He had used the excuse of his injured arm to lure Parsons into crossing the river. And with good reason. Parsons, of course, chose the direct route across the stream, not knowing it was a trap.

Callie didn't know that either until the burly Parsons reached the second stepping-stone. When he placed his considerable weight on the stone, it teetered at a precarious angle, revealing that it wasn't a solid boulder but a thin flag balanced on a narrow stem of rock.

Bellowing in outrage, arms flailing, the hapless Parsons tried to save himself by leaping to the next stepping-stone. But that, too, had been rigged by Daniel at some time during his stay in the cave to defeat any possible enemy in pursuit of him. There was no way the fleshy Parsons could save himself when he landed on it. The flag upended, spilling him and his rifle into the raging torrent. The water was far deeper than Callie had imagined.

The icy river closed around Parsons, the powerful current tugging on him as he managed to cling to the stem of rock. Spitting out water, his gun snatched away by the current, he screamed for his partner to rescue him. Ike Ritter gaped at him for a few helpless seconds, then hopped out onto the first safe boulder. But Parsons was out of arm's reach, leaving Ritter no choice but to extend the barrel of his rifle for his partner to grasp.

And that was when Linc, after casting a swift grin of approval in Daniel's direction to let the youth know he was impressed by his resourcefulness, acted. Bending down, he scooped up a rock, took aim, and whipped it across the stream.

The small stone struck Ritter in the side of his head, destroying his balance. Ike followed his partner into the water, the rifle that Parsons had just managed to clutch the muzzle of torn from his grip.

While Callie watched in horror, their bodies were swept away by the relentless current. The cataract claimed the two men, tumbling them over its edge and into the throat of the black hole that swallowed them.

Except for the sound of the unforgiving waters, there was a silence in the chamber. Linc ended it with a question for Daniel. "The river— where does it come out?"

Daniel shook his head. "I do not know that it does."

"Then we're rid of them. How's your arm?"

Daniel picked himself up from the floor and made a scoffing sound to show them that his weakness had been no more than a pretense. "Now we will go find our horses and ride to Oregon," he said with determination.

As he led them away from the chamber, Callie looked back over her shoulder at the cruel black waters of the river. Linc slid an encouraging arm around her waist.

"Forget about them," he said. "They can't possibly have survived."

Chapter Thirteen

"This is the plan," Linc instructed Callie and Daniel as they stood with him near the freshwater spring where they had made camp the night before. "You two will stay here with the wagon, just like we agreed, while I ride back into Fort Laramie. If I learn our wagon train has left the post, then we'll know we have some hard traveling to catch up with them."

Linc suspected that was probably the case. Although their journey from the Black Hills had been an easy one, the necessity of circling around the fort and recovering the Oregon Trail on its western side in order to avoid contact with the army had cost them time. Besides, they'd been gone for so many days now that, unless extensive repairs to the wagon train had delayed it at the post, it would have moved on.

But Linc had to make certain of that. Traveling on their own all the way to Oregon would be much too risky, so they needed to hook up with the train again.

"And what if we can't catch up to them?" Callie wondered.

"You forget how much faster our mules are than their oxen. We'll overtake them." But Linc knew that wasn't what worried her. She was unhappy about separating from him, even for a day or so. He tried to comfort her with a teasing, "Meanwhile, you and Daniel have a good spot to wait for me. There's the spring right here, our old friend the Platte River nearby, and Register Cliff over there to entertain you if you get bored."

"Or," Callie said, "we could count the wagon ruts in the trail. See if they'd tell us how many emigrants have passed this way over the years."

"That's the spirit. Walk with me to my horse."

She left Daniel at the spring and accompanied Linc to where his saddled roan waited for him. Hating for him to see how much she was going to miss him, even for a matter of hours, she looked away as they stood by the roan, gazing at Apollo and Daniel's pinto grazing with the mules in the early-morning light.

But Linc read her despair. "Look, sweetheart," he spoke to her gently, "it has to be this way. We can't leave the boy alone, and we can't take him into Fort Laramie. The place is crawling with soldiers."

"I reckon."

She wasn't arguing with him about it. Then,

damn it, why did she make him feel so guilty? But Linc knew that guilt had nothing to do with his departure. He just didn't want to examine the reality of their relationship, which had grown more complicated for him with each passing day. And more painful, even in those ecstatic moments when he couldn't resist her. He'd have to answer for that guilt one of these days, but right now . . .

"Callie," he said, lowering his voice as he glanced in Daniel's direction. "The boy likes you, and you're good with him. Take care of him while I'm gone. I want to be sure we deliver him safely to Oregon."

Hearing the sudden seriousness in Linc's tone, she searched his face. "What is it?"

"I don't know. It's just that I'm not convinced Parsons and Ritter weren't trying to kill him back at the cave, except it doesn't make any sense. Just look out for him, that's all. I don't want anything happening to him. Besides being worth a fortune to us, I've grown pretty fond of the boy."

"He'll be all right. Remember, I'm a crack shot."

Linc grinned. "I know. That's why I'm leaving you here and not me. C'mere. I want this to be a proper good-bye."

He held out his arms, and she went into them willingly, tilting her head back for his kiss. He dipped his head down, his mouth covering hers quickly and possessively. The heat ignited from their fusion was so compelling that Callie knew, if it continued much longer, they would be in

273

danger of embarrassing themselves in front of Daniel. But it was always like this whenever they came together, urgent and explosive.

Linc, too, recognized the danger and reluctantly lifted his mouth from hers. "With any luck," he reassured her, "I should be back here by nightfall or early tomorrow."

Callie clung to him, knowing she was being weak about this parting but unable to help herself. "You take care of yourself, you hear?"

A moment later he was in the saddle and riding off into the morning sun. Shading her eyes against its glare, she watched him until he disappeared from view.

Daniel, amazingly insightful for a fifteen-year-old boy, came and stood beside her, offering a comforting, "It is good sometimes to miss someone deeply. Then the joy of their return is all the sweeter."

She turned her head and smiled at him. "Cheyenne wisdom?"

He shook his head and grinned at her. "Daniel's wisdom."

Callie laughed. She had learned to appreciate the young man during their journey from the Black Hills. When he wasn't telling her about his life with the Cheyenne or asking questions about his mother, he kept her entertained with his gentle humor.

"And what does Daniel's wisdom say today about the wound in his arm?"

"That Callie Burgess should not be concerned." He offered the arm for her inspection, indicating that it was healing rapidly and cleanly and was no longer in need of a dressing. Then, satisfied by her approval, he cast his gaze in the direction of the enormous sandstone formation known as Register Cliff. "That strange rock is calling to us," he said with a gleam in his eyes.

Callie knew that, ever since their arrival here at twilight yesterday, Daniel had been curious about the carvings in the side of the cliff. He was eager to examine them up close, but she suspected his proposal to visit the site was also prompted by a desire to divert her from Linc's absence. She couldn't ignore such kindness.

"Then let's answer it," she said.

Crossing the shallow swale along which the Oregon Trail passed, they approached the bulk of the high cliff. Daniel was silent for a long moment, gazing in wonder at the countless inscriptions cut into the soft rock of the cliff's face.

"What are they?" he asked her.

"The names of settlers who passed here on their way west. Guess that's why they call it Register Cliff."

"All of them names?" he wanted to know as they strolled along the base of the cliff, admiring the carvings.

"Well, no. Some of them are messages."

"What do they say?"

"Oh, things like when they were here and where they came from and where they're going."

Watching him as he reached out a hand, his forefinger slowly tracing some of the letters that were both a mystery and a fascination to him, Callie had a sudden inspiration. "Daniel, would you like to learn how to read? Then you could

275

make out some of the words for yourself, at least the simple ones. I could even help you to carve your own name in the rock. We have nothing else to do all day."

He turned his head to stare at her. "You could show me this reading in one day?"

"Well, not all in one day. It takes time and practice. But we could make a good beginning at it."

Why not? she thought. Why couldn't she teach him some of the things Linc had been teaching her? At least the basics, anyway. Linc had said her progress was remarkable.

Daniel was silent for a moment, thinking about her proposal. Then he nodded with his usual restraint, but she could tell he was enthusiastic about it. "It will be good for me to know this reading and writing when I get to Oregon."

They went back to their camp. Callie left Daniel to clear up the breakfast things and check on their stock while she climbed into the wagon to fetch the essentials she would need for his instruction. She found everything but the primer Linc had used with her in those first days. She hadn't seen the little book since then because her reading skills had improved so rapidly that she had graduated to more challenging materials. But she knew the primer had to be somewhere in the wagon.

When it didn't turn up after a frustrating search, Callie wondered if Linc had tucked it into his pack and forgotten about it. He was traveling light on his errand into Fort Laramie and had left the bulky pack behind. It was there in the corner where he had tossed it.

Callie eyed it, knowing it contained most of his personal belongings. But under the circumstances, she didn't think he'd mind her hunting through it for the primer.

Dragging the pack onto her lap, she undid its leather straps, lifted the flap, and emptied its contents. The primer was there. She rescued it and was sliding all the rest back into the pack when she caught the faint whiff of a familiar scent.

Céleste. For a moment Callie wondered if the perfume had somehow leaked inside Linc's pack before he had presented her with the small crystal bottle she treasured above any other possession. She looked through all the articles for a spill, and that was when she found it.

A handkerchief. Fine linen edged with lace. Plainly a lady's handkerchief, and to it clung the unmistakable traces of *Céleste*.

Even before Callie let herself be aware that the handkerchief contained something flat and hard, that its folds were arranged so neatly and carefully that the object underneath must be precious to its owner, she felt herself go rigid with denial. All but her hands, and they were trembling as she unwrapped the handkerchief, not caring now that she was violating Linc's privacy. She had to *know*.

The parted linen revealed a small daguerrotype inside a frame studded with tiny seed pearls. Callie gazed at the image of the woman in the daguerrotype, feeling sick. Not because she was so beautiful, which she unquestionably was with her delicate, aristocratic features, wide eyes, and fair hair, but because she was so immediately familiar to Callie.

Oh, yes, she recognized this flawless creature. She had met a much rougher version in herself, or at least in the woman Linc wanted her to be. There was everything here that he had described for her as the ideal woman and worked so diligently for Callie to match. The paisley shawl draped around a pair of frail shoulders, hair parted in the center and smoothed back over her ears, pearl drops in her ears, all of them reflecting elegant manners.

Why, even the *Céleste* perfume belonged to this woman. It had to be her handkerchief, her fragrance scenting it. And Linc kept both the handkerchief and the daguerrotype because they were beloved to him. So beloved that he had striven to model Callie after the original.

She could no longer deny the obvious. Couldn't try to comfort herself with the possibility that this angelic creature might be a blood relation to Linc, because there was no remote resemblance to him. No, whatever the identity of this woman, she was someone far more important than a sister.

Unable to bear looking at the daguerrotype any longer, she wrapped it again in the handkerchief and stuffed it back into his pack. But the image and the scent remained with her. *Céleste*. Callie hated it now, promised herself she would never wear it again.

Picking up the primer, she sat there clutching

it tightly in both hands, her eyes misting with heartache and a painful jealousy. But those emotions were replaced by humiliation as she angrily wiped the tears from her eyes. Callie suddenly remembered all those wanton nights she had spent in Lincoln McAllister's arms. Nights when she had been as eager for his lessons in lovemaking as his lessons in ladyhood, and every bit as anxious to please him.

Her face burned with shame as she thought about it. How she had naively convinced herself that their teacher-pupil relationship had progressed to something so sublime, so wonderfully sensual, that it must represent their deep love for each other. Instead, whenever Linc had kissed her, whenever they had come together so passionately as man and woman, he must have been thinking of *her*. Wanting *her* in his bed and not Callie.

She felt a terrible sense of betrayal.

"Callie Burgess, have I lost you?"

It was Daniel outside the covered wagon. He wanted to know what was keeping her.

"Coming," she answered, her voice sounding numb in her own ears.

Gathering up the teaching materials, she left the wagon. Daniel gazed at her face as she joined him. He knew something was wrong, but she was grateful he didn't press for any explanation.

They went and sat by the spring, and she made every effort to concentrate on his reading lesson. He was a quick learner, and as the hours passed he mastered the essentials.

Chalking letters on the small slate as they

279

worked, Callie tried not to think about her anguish. Tried to tell herself that maybe she hadn't been an immature fool, that there might be an innocent explanation for the daguerrotype. And that she was judging Linc before he had a chance to explain himself.

All right, she would give him that opportunity. If only this long day would end, if only he would return . . .

"Our wagon train pulled out of Fort Laramie less than a week ago," Linc reported.

Hungry from his long hours in the saddle, he paused to swallow another mouthful of the beans and bacon Daniel had fixed. "I figure," he went on, "that we just missed them. "They couldn't have passed through here more than a couple of days ago. We shouldn't have any problem catching up."

Linc had ridden into camp just before sundown. Now, in the first stages of twilight, the three of them sat huddled around the fire with their supper plates. Not that Callie had any appetite. All she could do was gaze at Linc's lean, angular face in the firelight, as though she were seeing it for the first time, and restlessly wait for the meal to end so that she could speak to him in private.

"Oh, I almost forgot," he said, apparently unaware of the unbearable tension she was experiencing. "They did manage to pick up a new wagon master at the post. Man by the name of Hal Jamison. I think that's right."

"Were the troopers there?" Daniel asked him. "Do they still search for me?"

"No one was talking about it," Linc assured him, "so I think we're safe from pursuit."

Daniel, bless him, must have sensed her need to be alone with Linc. He rose after pouring coffee for them, announcing his intention to go back to Register Cliff before darkness fell. "I would see those carvings again. This time I will know what some of the letters say."

When he was gone, Linc hastily downed his coffee and then said abruptly to Callie, "All right, what's wrong?"

"You did notice, then."

"How could I not help noticing? I left here this morning with a fierce kiss, and I return to something not much better than a polite nod. Did something happen while I was gone?"

In answer, Callie got to her feet and went to the wagon. She returned a moment later bearing the daguerrotype. "This happened while you were gone," she said, placing the daguerrotype in his lap.

Linc gazed down at the daguerrotype and then up at her, his face tight with anger. "You went into my pack?"

She had already told him about the reading lessons. "I was looking for the primer," she said, "and that's where you'd put it. Were you ever going to tell me about her, Linc?" He didn't answer. There was a sudden look of guilt on his face. "Never mind. You can tell me about her now. Who is she?"

For a moment she didn't think he was going

to respond. And then, broad shoulders slumping in an expression of defeat, he told her. "Her name is Anne McAllister."

Callie shut her eyes briefly in pain. "Your wife?" she asked dully.

"No, of course not. I'm not that much of a bastard."

"A relation then?" Maybe, after all, she *was* his sister. Or a cousin.

"By marriage, yes. She was my brother William's wife."

"The one you're wanted for killing in New Orleans?"

"Yes."

"Did you kill him over her?" she asked. "Is that why you carry her picture with you everywhere?"

"Oh, for the love of—Haven't I already told you I never killed anyone? And stop standing there over me like an avenging angel. If you've got to know the whole miserable story, then at least sit down while I tell it."

Callie sank reluctantly on the camp stool next to his, instinctively knowing she wasn't going to like what he was about to tell her but forcing herself to turn to him with a hoarse-voiced, "Okay, I'm listening."

But he didn't immediately begin his explanation. She could see by the expression on his face just how difficult this was for him. Well, it was every bit as difficult for her, and she was in no mood to offer him any sympathetic encouragement. She simply waited.

"Anne and I grew up together in New Orleans,"

he said, struggling for the words. "Our families were very close. We played together as children, and later on . . . well, uh, there was an understanding between us."

"You were sweethearts, you mean," Callie said, hating the accusing tone in her voice but unable to help it.

"I guess that's the word for it. Only our families thought we were too young to marry. Also," he admitted, "I was a bit wild in those years. Hell, maybe more than a bit. Anyway, her parents weren't sure they approved of me for Anne. That's when I went off to West Point."

"Why?" Callie demanded. "To show them you were good enough for their daughter?"

"Something like that," Linc mumbled.

"Let me guess," Callie said. "By the time you came back from West Point, Anne was married to your brother."

"She had every intention of waiting for me, but both our families insisted that Will was right for her. Her father demanded that she marry him."

"And you and Anne came to be sorry she didn't wait for you," Callie said bitterly. "That's what happened, isn't it?"

"Whatever we felt, we had no choice but to forget about each other. It was too late for us, and I had my career in the army waiting for me."

"So you went off to war. But you didn't forget about her, did you, Linc?"

He didn't deny it. "I tried to stay away from Anne and Will when I went back to New Orleans. I figured I'd only embarrass them. I'd been dishonorably discharged. I was a social outcast, even from my own family, who ended up wanting no part of me."

"But you couldn't stay away from her."

"Anne needed me. My saintly brother turned out to be the worst kind of husband for her, an abusive drunk who went through both his money and hers at the gaming tables."

"You went to her then," Callie said, insisting on knowing the whole truth no matter how much it punished both her and Linc to hear it. "And your brother found you together. That's what happened, isn't it?"

"I was comforting her," Linc defended himself. "Just that, nothing else. But he'd been drinking, and he was in one of his dirty moods and wouldn't listen. He threatened Anne with a gun, and when I tried to get it away from him . . ."

Linc didn't go on. He didn't have to. Callie could visualize the scene for herself. William McAllister had been accidentally shot during the struggle and died. "Didn't anyone believe your story?" she asked. "Did all of them call it murder?"

Linc shrugged. "New Orleans society can be damned unforgiving. They remembered the wild reputation of my boyhood and the disgrace of my court-martial and that my own family was against me. I knew I didn't stand a chance."

"So it was either hang for something you didn't do or save your neck by getting out of town."

"I had to stay free. I had to find a way to help Anne. She's existing in near poverty with no one to turn to. Since the scandal, not even her family will have anything to do with her. I'm all she has, and I swore to myself I wouldn't rest until I found a way to make her life comfortable."

There was such caring desperation in his voice that Callie's heart sank a little deeper at this evidence of just how much the lovely Anne McAllister meant to him. "Which," she said unhappily, "is what this reward for Daniel's return is all about. That's it, isn't it, Linc? You'll send the money to New Orleans to support your brother's widow."

"Don't look at me like that, Callie. You know nothing about her. Anne isn't like you, tough and independent. She's a gentle creature whose life with Will was such a hell that it's left her in a fragile state of health."

"And you love her very much, don't you?" she said, hating to finally put it into words but knowing she couldn't avoid the full truth.

"What difference does it make? They have long memories in New Orleans. I can never go back."

"Yes, I can see just how much you love her. And how hopeless it all is for you, because you'd never let her join you so long as you're on the run, even if her health did allow it. That's just the way it all is, isn't it, Linc?"

"Callie—"

"But," she continued, ignoring his effort to stop her, her voice a little frantic now as she confronted him with the final, awful reality, "if you couldn't have what you really wanted, maybe you'd settle for a copy, even if it would be a poor substitute for the original. I'm still learning, but those are the right words, aren't they?"

"What are you talking about?" he growled.

"Her." She stabbed a finger in the direction of the daguerrotype. "You tried to make me over to be like Anne McAllister. Same hairstyle, same clothes, same jewelry, even the same perfume."

"Are you crazy? I never tried to model you in Anne's image."

She wasn't listening to him. She was too wounded to listen. "Only it didn't work, did it? Because I can never be like her. I'm too rough for that. But I could be good enough for a"—She struggled for the right words to express it—"a temporary sport in bed."

"Callie, stop this!" He tried to reach for her, wanting to hold her, wanting to ease the hurt, but she pulled away from him.

"No!" she said vehemently as she felt the silly tears sliding down her cheeks. "No, don't!"

Linc sat back, feeling helpless. "All right, maybe I did try to turn you into a version of Anne's ladyhood, but I didn't do it with any conscious intention. Callie, I never meant to hurt you."

"I reckon you didn't hurt me as much as I hurt myself. I've been a real fool, haven't I? All along I've been that blind, immature brat you once said I was."

"Damn it, Callie, don't underrate yourself like this. You've come a long way since those days."

"Not far enough. Leastways, not grown up enough to see that you never felt about me like I came to feel about you."

She held her breath, longing for him to tell her otherwise. But all he could do was gaze at her, stricken into a helpless silence by a charge he was unable to deny.

She released the air she was holding in a long, shuddering breath. "Guess you couldn't help that, though," she said forlornly. "Not loving your Anne like you do."

He stirred then, leaning toward her earnestly. "Look," he pleaded with her. "I'll probably never see Anne again. But you and I . . . well, we can still be together. There is a magic between us, Callie, and if we can share that much, then—"

"In bed. That's where the magic was, and it was nothing but a lie. Sure, you liked all those wild nights with me, but it was another woman you were longing for. And if we went on, I'd always know that the only reason you were with me was because you can't have what you really want. Well, that's just not good enough, McAllister."

Impatiently wiping the tears from her cheeks with the back of her hand, Callie got to her feet. "Tell me something," she said, the old fire back in her voice as she looked down at him. "Was that share of the reward money you promised me just so you could make peace with your conscience? Because it sure wasn't offered for the reason I figured."

"It wasn't like that at all. And if your pride is about to throw that share back in my face—"

"Oh, don't worry about that." She cut him off with a brittle little laugh. "I plan to keep every dollar of it. Way I figure it, I've earned it."

He surged to his feet, angry with her now. "Don't say that, as if you went and sold your body to me."

"That's what it amounted to, isn't it?" she asked, abruptly turning away from him.

Daniel was returning from his visit to Register Cliff as she brushed past him on her way to say her customary good night to Apollo. Twilight had dwindled into darkness, but the glow from the campfire revealed the puzzled expression on the boy's face as he glanced from Linc to Callie, knowing something deeply unpleasant had occurred between them. She offered no explanation.

But she could, and did, talk to the handsome chestnut gelding seconds later as she stroked his velvet-soft nose. "You know it doesn't make sense, Apollo. I couldn't have lost him when he was never mine to lose in the first place. So why do I feel like somebody just took away the best part of me?"

The next few days were an ordeal for Callie as they pushed on toward the wagon train somewhere ahead of them. Not because the trail was difficult or because the long hours of hauling from first light to sundown were exhausting. It was the unbearable strain of Lincoln McAllister's company when all she wanted was to be far away from him, out of sight of his face, out of range of his voice. Both were constant reminders of an ache that didn't want to go away.

But in the forced closeness of their necessary situation, there was no way to avoid him, though she tried. She spoke to him only when it was essential and kept her distance as much as possible. To his credit, Linc respected her privacy, keeping his distance. Or else he simply didn't care any longer. Either way it hurt.

Hurt so much that she came to a decision. Her struggles for ladyhood had brought her nothing but unhappiness. She'd been far more cheerful when she'd been the old Callie. So why not just go back to that easier personality? Which was just what she recklessly and obstinately did.

Linc said nothing on the morning that she cursed out one of their contrary mules who'd tried to run off in the night, smoking the air with all the obscenities that had once been her favorites. And he held his tongue when she reverted to her grubby appearance and rough manners.

Even her sloppy speech brought no comment, though it seemed to bewilder the usually stoical Daniel when she chattered a bright, artificial, "Shore will be good t'see ol' Pearl ag'in when we git t'them wagons. Heck, I reckon even them stuck-up peahens what useta hang 'round Parthenia Smyth will look just fine t'me."

Linc went on preserving his silence. Until, that is, the evening meal, when Callie shoved a large chunk of buffalo steak into her mouth, the juice dribbling down her chin as she smacked her lips and chewed noisily. Then, putting down his own plate, he murmured a quiet, "Excuse us, Daniel," grabbed Callie by the arm, and dragged her off behind the wagon.

"What in sweet hell," he challenged her angrily, "are you doing to yourself?"

"I'm bein' me, Callie Burgess, that's what, an' lemme go!" She jerked her arm free, but he kept her pinned against the side of the wagon.

"No, you're *trying* to be her, but it isn't working. That Callie is gone forever."

"Don't know what yer talkin' 'bout."

"Yes, you do. This performance of yours is all about punishment, isn't it? You're trying to punish either me or yourself or both of us."

"That ain't so!"

He ignored her objection. "All right, maybe I need to be punished. But you don't. Give it up, Callie. Stop trying to go back to what's no longer there. Because whatever happened between us, however much we're both suffering for it, you deserve to be all you can be. And that means going forward, hanging on hard to the new Callie with or without me."

"I don't need you t'tell me who I am," she informed him coldly, and she pushed past him and went back to the campfire.

She knew, though. Underneath her defiance and her swagger, she knew he was right. It was all an act, and it was increasingly difficult for her to maintain it. She had worked so hard to lose her rough manners and poor speech that somewhere along the way correct manners and speech had become a natural part of her, together with a hunger to advance her education, to progress even beyond what she had attained already. Now, ironically, she found herself laboring to copy the old Callie. But that Callie, just as he'd said, had slipped away forever. It was Lincoln McAllister who'd done that to her, damn him!

He'd taught her ladyhood, just as he'd taught her how to love. All right, she determined, if she could learn to fall in love with him, then she ought to be able to learn to fall out of love. Maybe it had all been a delusion springing from her old naivete, anyway. Something she'd convinced herself was real but which actually was nothing but sex, the result of a man and woman thrown together like that. But how could she be sure, how could she ease this anguish?

It was Daniel who unknowingly helped her, observing perceptively the next morning as she helped him with another reading lesson in the back of the swaying wagon, "You no longer pretend to be a woman who acts like a man. Good. I like you better as you are now. Won't there be ones on the wagon train who will also like this Callie?"

Gabriel, she remembered, grasping at the hope offered her by the sudden image of the gentle preacher. Until Linc had mesmerized her with his compelling sexuality into forgetting all about him, Gabriel Hawkins had meant everything to her, her very reason for struggling to achieve ladyhood. Could Gabriel matter like that again, cure her of Lincoln McAllister?

The preacher was honest and good, pure in a way Lincoln could never be. But, oh, she thought with a deep sense of guilt, she had been unfaithful to the devotion she had once sworn to Gabriel in her heart. Wronged him by giving herself to that devil, Linc. Could she ever redeem herself of that?

Gabriel. Was he her future, after all? This she couldn't know until she was with him again, introducing him to the new Callie Burgess. But he was a possibility that made her long for them to catch up with the wagon train—if for no other reason than to escape the closeness of Linc. Being back with the train would mean other people to distract her, Pearl among them, and a chance to distance herself from Linc. Yes, rejoining the train was the solution. It just had to be.

Callie clung so desperately to this certainty that it was with sweet relief when, on a late afternoon three days after leaving Register Cliff, they topped a hill and saw below them the familiar circle of wagons camped on the banks of the North Platte.

Chapter Fourteen

Callie flung herself off Apollo's back and into Pearl's outstretched arms. The two women proceeded to greet each other with hugs, whoops of joy, and simultaneous bursts of wild chatter.

"Honey lamb, you had me worried sick!"

"You're a treat to these dust-sore eyes, Slocum!"

"I was beginning to think the savages got you!"

"I haven't seen another female since we left the train!"

"I prayed you'd forgive me for sending you off with McAllister like that!"

"What's been happening since I've been gone? I want to hear everything!"

"Please say you have!"

"Huh?"

The two women broke off, stared at each

other, and began to laugh, realizing that neither had heard a word the other was saying.

"No more talk," Pearl insisted. "Here, I want to get a good look at you." She held Callie away so that she could properly inspect her. After a long moment of silent scrutiny, she nodded decisively. "I'm not just imagining it. You've changed."

Callie smiled self-consciously. "No wonder. My hair hasn't seen a comb since sunup, I'm covered with trail dirt, and I'm drooping with exhaustion."

Pearl shook her head solemnly. "It's not looks."

"I guess you mean the way I talk."

"Yeah, I noticed that. Like a real lady. McAllister's teaching . . . it worked then, huh?"

"You couldn't ask for a more refined female in buckskins," Callie said lightly. "Parthenia Smyth would be proud of me."

"That so?" Pearl, frowning, went on gazing at her. "Know what I think, honey lamb?"

"What, Pearl?"

"That it's a lot more than talk and manners. You went and grew up while you were gone, didn't you?"

"That's crazy, Pearl."

"No, it's not. I see a woman now, not a girl. Just what happened between you and McAllister while you were out there?" she asked suspiciously.

"A lot of lessons and almost losing our lives getting Daniel," Callie said evasively.

Pearl looked toward the corral of wagons

where the campfires were sending spirals of smoke into the air. "Where are McAllister and the boy?" she wondered.

"He took Daniel to meet Mr. Hawkins and the new wagon master." Afraid Pearl would begin asking questions again about Linc and her that she was in no mood to answer, Callie swiftly changed the subject. "Look, I want to know about you. You're different, too."

Pearl put a careless hand to her head. "I reckon it's the hair. I'm letting it go back to its natural color. And I'm dressing more quietly these days. Well, I have to be respectable for Oregon, don't I?"

"But that isn't all of it. I can hear from the way you—" She stopped in sudden realization, then went on with an accusing, "Pearl Slocum, you've had some lessons yourself! Why? Who?"

"From Mr. Hawkins," Pearl said, looking embarrassed about her admission. "Figured if you were going to improve yourself, maybe I ought to try some of the same medicine. And since he was pretty upset about my sending you and McAllister off like that, I, uh, sort of made peace by agreeing to have lessons from him. They're to help me start over in Oregon."

"That's real fine, Pearl. So Gabriel was upset about me, huh?"

"Well, sure. You might know he would be."

"How upset, Pearl?" she asked her friend anxiously. "Did he miss me while I was gone? Did he *say* he missed me?"

"We all missed you, honey lamb. Oh, wait 'til I tell you about Parthenia Smyth. She couldn't

295

find anyone to take her back east along the trail. She got so frantic about it that she paid a band of friendly Indians to carry her up to the Missouri River to catch a steamboat. You never saw such a sight as that high-nosed old dragon leaving Fort Laramie perched on a travois, of all things."

Pearl crowed with laughter at the memory, and Callie joined her, although she was puzzled. Pearl had seemed awkward when explaining about Gabriel, using the Parthenia Smyth anecdote to abruptly change the subject. But she supposed it was understandable. After all, Pearl had never been particularly fond of the preacher.

It was late afternoon of the next day before a frustrated Gabriel finally managed to find Pearl alone. The caravan was again camped on the banks of the North Platte, which would continue to parallel their route to the Red Buttes in sight of the Rocky Mountains beyond.

Pearl was cooking a stew for the evening meal when Gabriel, ignoring her objections, drew her behind the wagon. Its cover provided momentary privacy, and he was very much in need of that.

"You've been avoiding me," he complained.

"I've been busy nursing Minnie. She hasn't felt well."

He brushed aside her excuse. "We haven't had a moment together since Callie and McAllister turned up yesterday. She's been eyeing me all day with this expectant look on her face. It's unsettling. When are you going to talk to her?"

"There hasn't been time yet."

"Pearl, didn't you finally agree the night before they rolled in that you *would* speak to her? She needs to be told about us."

Pearl shook her head unhappily. "I changed my mind again. I can't do it. I can't hurt her like that. If you could have heard her when she asked about you . . . Gabriel, she loves you."

He made a sound of impatience. "But that love isn't real."

"It is for her."

"And what about our love?"

"I—I don't know."

"Well, I do, and it's got me wild. I can't go on like this, with you holding me off because of some stubborn loyalty that's wrong for all three of us." His voice softened. "I've missed you since they came back. I need to be near you, Pearl."

There was such a tender look in his blue eyes gazing down at her that Pearl weakened. "I know. I—I've missed you, too."

Gabriel needed no other invitation. His arms started to slide around her waist, but Pearl held back. "No, we can't. What if Callie should—"

"Don't worry. She's busy with another of Daniel's reading lessons on the other side of the corral." Not waiting for another objection, he drew her into his arms with a low moan of pure desire. "Oh, Pearl, Pearl, I want so much more than just this, but right now I'll settle for one kiss."

She wanted to resist him. Knew she *ought* to resist him. But it felt so good being in his arms, so absolutely right that, in spite of all her self-promises, she surrendered to her own longing. Head back, eyes closed, she waited for his mouth to cover hers.

But Gabriel didn't kiss her. His warm breath on her face was suddenly withdrawn, then rushed out again in a startled hiss. At the same time his body stiffened against hers. Pearl's eyes flew open, searching his face. His handsome features registered guilty surprise. His gaze was not on her but on something behind her.

Seized with alarm and dread, Pearl knew even before she pushed him away and twisted around what she would find behind her. She was not wrong. Callie had come unexpectedly around the corner of the wagon and discovered them. The young woman stood there, shock and disbelief on her face.

There was a long, frozen moment of silence during which none of them either spoke or moved. Then, with a painful little sound that expressed both despair and accusation, Callie swung around and fled the scene.

Feeling sick over her betrayal, Pearl started to go after her, but Gabriel caught her arm, holding her back. "Let me go," she rasped. "I have to go to her."

"No," Gabriel said. "No."

"You don't understand," she pleaded, her voice frantic. "She needs—"

"I do understand," he cut her off, his tone insistent. "And what she needs is to know the truth, and she's going to hear it from me. It's time I stopped being a coward about this situation. I should have spoken to her long ago."

"But—"

"No arguments about it, Pearl," he said severely. "I want you to trust me to handle it."

She gazed at him with worry and uncertainty. But there was a look of such strength and decisiveness on his face, qualities that Pearl wasn't used to finding in the men who passed through her life, that she relented. It was with relief, in fact, that she laid this heartbreaking problem on his broad shoulders.

"All right," she murmured. "But you be gentle with her, Gabriel. Promise?"

Gabriel found Callie down by the river. There was a lone cottonwood there close on the shore, a huge old warrior of a tree that had died and fallen years ago. Its upper boughs, still intact, poked up from the waters themselves like skeleton claws. But the massive, upended trunk rested on dry land. Callie was perched on its weathered gray surface, staring out over the muddy river. She glanced up at him when he arrived on the spot. He had thought to find her in tears, but her eyes were dry. Nor, to his surprise, did she object to his appearance. Quite the contrary.

"There's plenty of room," she said, indicating the space next to her.

She was actually inviting him to join her! "You sound as though you were expecting me, Callie."

She nodded. "I figured either you or Pearl would come."

He settled beside her on the wide trunk and turned in bemusement to consider her. No anger, no hysterics, no wild emotion at all, just this quiet acceptance of his presence. This wasn't the Callie he remembered, the untamed, eager girl overly anxious to please him. She had changed dramatically in a matter of a few weeks.

Gabriel cleared his throat. "Will you let me tell you about Pearl and me?"

"I reckon you'd better do just that, Reverend."

She listened without interruption, her eyes trained on the river again as he proceeded to explain to her how he and Pearl had become very close during their shared lessons on the trail and at Fort Laramie. How he had cared for her even before then and how they had both come to fall in love, in spite of Pearl's every effort to resist him.

Callie made no comment when he was finished. Worried about her silence, he added a soft, pleading, "We never meant to hurt you. It was something we couldn't help, and Pearl is heartsick that you went and found out about us in that way. You mean a great deal to her, Callie."

Her gaze still on the river, she murmured, "Then you knew all along how I felt about you?"

He shook his head. "I'm sorry, but I was blind about that. I didn't guess until Pearl told me back at Laramie. Don't blame her for revealing your secret. She was desperate for arguments of why she and I shouldn't be together."

Callie nodded. "And none of them worked."

"No," Gabriel admitted, and when she was silent again, he leaned toward her with an unhappy sigh. "How much do you mind about Pearl and me? Is it so terrible for you, Callie?"

She turned her head to regard him. Mind about Gabriel? Did she? She searched his face, frowning, and she realized all at once that she was no longer dazzled by the reverend's male beauty. That the sublime love she'd once experienced for this fair-haired man had never been anything more than an illusion, a girlish infatuation she'd shed when a dark-haired devil had introduced her to womanhood. And that what she had lost in the moment of discovering Pearl and Gabriel together was not Gabriel himself but the hope he had represented. The hope of using him to exorcise Lincoln McAllister from her heart. But she couldn't clutch at that hope now.

It was no use then, Callie thought miserably. She could no longer pretend, no longer combat the obvious. This man seated beside her was decent, caring, everything a woman was supposed to want. But she didn't want him. She wanted the man who didn't have those polite qualities, the man who excited and challenged her at every level. She wanted Linc and his love, but she couldn't have them because they belonged to another.

Poor Gabriel. He was waiting for her response, suffering over her hesitation. "No," she promised him, "I don't mind. I'm real glad for you and Pearl. It's just that it was so unexpected." She forced herself to smile at him reassuringly. "I guess maybe because you and Pearl are kind of an unlikely couple, huh?"

But then, Callie thought sadly, so was the idea of Linc and her unlikely. Not just unlikely but absolutely hopeless. She thought about that as she went on sitting there in the warmth of the sinking sun after Gabriel left her to hurry back to Pearl with his happy news.

Linc could never give her his love, even though she would always love him. She was prepared to accept that now. But without him, what else did she have?

The answer was an obvious one. Linc himself had provided it by insisting during their lessons that, if she was determined to change, then it should be for her own benefit, not because of Gabriel or anyone else. That much Linc had honestly given her, teaching her she was worthwhile in her own right.

Yes, she had herself. She didn't need either Gabriel or Linc to survive. Difficult as it would be without the man she loved, she could and must go on alone, build her own life. Where, how? Callie didn't know, but when she got to her feet and turned her back on the river, she realized that she had some hard decisions to make about her future.

"I was as surprised as you are," Gabriel said, "but I promise you, it's all true. Why, Callie actually gives us her blessing."

Pearl couldn't believe it. "She wanted you, and now you're telling me that she doesn't want you anymore?"

"It's this new maturity she's acquired. I have to say I'm very impressed by it."

Pearl shook her head. "There's something funny about all this."

Gabriel took her hands. "Dearest," he pleaded

with her, "don't let's question it. Not now when we're finally free to be together."

He was so eager that Pearl had neither the heart nor the will to oppose him any longer. Not when he took her in his arms and kissed her with such elated passion that she forgot everything but their long-denied desire for each other. And certainly not later when night fell and the two of them slipped off together into the darkness.

On a rough blanket under the stars, away from the wagon train and with only the sound of the flowing river to disturb them, Gabriel abandoned all caution and made love to her. A slow, exquisite love that inflamed her senses and convinced her there was no other man in the universe but this one.

Long before the cold light of morning, wrapped in his arms there on the scratchy blanket, she knew that she belonged to Gabriel Hawkins—body, soul, and for always. As for Gabriel's shocked followers . . . well, she guessed they'd just have to get used to the idea of Pearl Slocum as the preacher's life partner.

Callie had made up her mind.

Forget Oregon, forget that reward money waiting out there. She really didn't need or want it. Not when it meant having to be daily in sight of Lincoln McAllister on the long trek that was still ahead of the wagon train.

She was going home, back to Horizon, Missouri. All right, maybe there wasn't anything there now but the pathetic little farm Pa had left her. But given time, she was confident she could make something of it. At least it was familiar, and Linc wouldn't be close by to agonize over. She needed to put distance between them, hundreds of miles of distance. Yes, this was the right thing to do.

Daniel didn't think so. "But who will teach me the reading and writing if you are no longer with us?"

"Ask Linc. He's very good at giving lessons." She couldn't help the cynical note that crept into her voice.

The young man shook his head mournfully. "It will not be the same without you."

"Oh, Daniel, don't look like that. You'll forget all about me when you get to Oregon. You have a wonderful life waiting for you out there."

"But we are friends, Callie Burgess."

"I'll always be your friend, even when I'm far away," she promised. "You have to realize, though, that this is something I have to do."

But she could see Daniel wasn't convinced of that. Nor did Pearl understand her decision when she told her.

"Callie girl, you can't be serious! This is the dam—" She caught herself with a mumbled, "Got to watch this tongue of mine now that I'm a preacher's woman."

"Try, this is the darndest thing you ever heard."

"It isn't. It's the *damndest*. There I've said it, and it's true. Why, honey lamb? *Why?*"

Callie still couldn't bring herself to explain to Pearl about Linc. The subject hurt too much for discussion. "Well, Pearl," she said instead, "I only joined this wagon train to punish Lincoln McAllister for killing Pa, and now that I know it was Judd Parsons and Ike Ritter who shot him, there's no longer a reason for me to stay. I guess, after all, I belong in Horizon."

"And here I was figuring you'd make your home in Oregon. Well, hel—uh, heck, Callie, I counted on you standing up with me when Gabriel and I get married out there."

"You're going to be married?"

"Yeah, can you see Pearl Slocum as a bride?"

"You'll make a beautiful bride, and you don't need me beside you. All you need is your proud groom."

Pearl sighed. "I reckon you know what you want to do, but I still don't understand it."

Even Gabriel came to her. "I wish you'd change your mind, Callie. But if you insist on returning to Missouri, then at least do so in the company of other travelers."

"That much I can promise you, Reverend." Though she needed to get far away from Linc, Callie recognized the danger of trying to cross those hundreds of miles on her own. "We're bound to meet up soon with some emigrants who've turned back or freighters going east. I'll hook up with them."

One by one the company approached her about her intention. She listened to all of them, answered their concerns politely, and obstinately refused to change her mind. The only one she would not to talk to was Linc himself, though he tried. He came storming up to her with an angry, "We both know you're only doing this because—"

Before he could say more, she cut him off with a fast, "I want you to keep all of the reward money. I expect you'll need every bit of it for Anne." That was all she could bring herself to say before she fled from his presence.

After that brief, painful encounter, she couldn't wait to join a caravan destined for Missouri. But the days passed, stretching into weeks, and nowhere on the trail did they meet a single party headed in the opposite direction. Callie tried to silence her frustration by keeping as busy as possible. When she wasn't working with Daniel on his lessons, she occupied herself by improving her own education, reading every book that was available on the wagon train. But the endless waiting nagged at her nerves, making her moody and tired in a way she'd never experienced before.

To her relief, Linc didn't try to speak to her again, respecting her privacy. But though she managed to keep out of his way, she couldn't avoid seeing him. His physical presence was a constant reminder of a yearning she could never hope to satisfy. Even a glimpse of him at what was supposed to be a safe distance would make her poignantly aware of all she was striving to forget—the sensual timbre of his voice calling out a command, the shape of his strong hands coiling a rope, the way his rangy body moved as he strode from wagon to wagon. All of it haunted her, straining her patience at every turn in the trail.

If only, oh, if *only*, they would sight another company making for the east. But there was no release for Callie in that form.

And then it didn't matter anymore because suddenly, stunningly, everything changed.

On a cold morning along the Bear River, with the mountains towering majestically north of the trail, a worried Pearl went in search of the missing Callie. She had slipped away from camp at first light and failed to return.

Come to think of it, Pearl thought, there had been several unexplained morning absences this past week or so, with Callie either skipping breakfast altogether or picking at a small helping of oatmeal before disappearing. Trouble? Maybe an illness?

There was another possibility, but Pearl refused to consider that. Not until, alarmed, she finally located Callie on her knees behind a thicket of willows at the river's edge. She was wiping her mouth after having just emptied the contents of her stomach. Pearl helped her to her feet and sat her down on a flat boulder.

"I'm all right now," Callie objected. "It always passes, and then I'm fine the rest of the day."

Pearl stared at her, fearing the worst. She confirmed it after asking Callie several questions, the first being when she'd had her last flow.

"Honey lamb, I wish it weren't so," she concluded unhappily, "but it looks to me like you're standing behind a baby."

Callie wasn't surprised. She nodded slowly.

"Yeah, I kind of figured that's what's been ailing me."

Pearl didn't have to ask who the father was. There could be only one man responsible for Callie's pregnancy. And heaven help her, how could she she have been so blind? But she'd been so distracted by her involvement with Gabriel that she had failed to see all the signs. She, Pearl Slocum, whose business had been the intimate relations of male and female.

It all made sense now—Callie's sudden and complete disinterest in Gabriel, the strain between her and McAllister since their return from the Black Hills, even the war between them before then. The kind of battles a man and woman fought when they were powerfully attracted to each other and refused to acknowledge it. She'd missed that, too, in her fears over Judd Parsons and Ike Ritter.

Pearl called herself every kind of fool, because of course this mess was all her fault. She'd sent them off together into the Black Hills, where the inevitable had happened.

"Just wait until I get my hands on that buzzard!" Pearl muttered. "He promised me that—"

"No! You're not to say a word to him, Pearl. I—I'm as much to blame as Linc is. More so."

Pearl sank down heavily on the boulder beside Callie and gazed at her as still another awareness seized her. It wasn't Callie's newly acquired refinement that had so puzzlingly altered and matured her. It was something else.

"Sweet mother," she whispered, "you went and fell in love with him."

Callie smiled at her glumly. "Pretty stupid of me, huh?"

"I suppose it was those hot black eyes of his."

"It was more than that, Pearl. A lot more than that." No longer able to keep it to herself, Callie told her everything that had happened during their trek to the Black Hills, including her bitter discovery of the woman Linc loved back in New Orleans.

"She can go to blazes!" Pearl flared. "It's you who's carrying his child. He's got to do right by you, and if you won't go to him about marrying you, then I will!"

Her face stone-hard with determination, Pearl started to get to her feet, but Callie put a restraining hand on her arm. "You will do no such thing, Pearl Slocum. Baby or no baby, I have no intention of marrying Lincoln McAllister. Oh, I have no doubt that, once he knew, he'd rush both of us off to your preacher. Then after the vows were spoken, he'd spend the rest of his life trying to be a good husband, only his heart would always belong to another woman. And I won't live with that, Pearl. I can't!" she said fiercely.

"But he has to know about the baby."

"No! I tell you I won't have him marrying me for all the wrong reasons. He's *not* to know. None of them are to know, including Gabriel. You have to promise me that, Pearl."

Pearl shook her head with deep misgiving. "I'll keep your secret, but this is all wrong. Look, why don't you just talk to McAllister? He's been trying to speak to you ever since he heard you meant to leave the train. He keeps coming to me about it, asking me to get you to listen to him."

"It's only his conscience talking for him. I learned that even the devil has one. Well, he can live with it."

"Dear heart, I love you like a sister, but you are one mule-headed critter. You can't have a baby and raise it all on your own."

"Yes, I can, and I will!"

"How, without a husband or money?"

"I don't need a husband, and I'll have plenty of money. There's my share of the reward money for Daniel. Looks like I'll have to swallow my pride now and accept it."

"Which means you'll be going on to Oregon with us after all. Hallelujah for that! 'Course," she pointed out, "it also means you won't be keeping this secret of yours. Not once you start to show."

"Being I'm in the early stages, that won't be for a long, long time. Not until we're in Oregon, and by then I'll have decided just what I'm going to do and where I want to go."

Pearl expelled her breath in a long sigh. "Honey lamb, I sure hope you know what you're doing."

Callie was confident that she did know exactly what she was doing, and never mind that she would be an unwed mother facing the censure of society. That was a concern she would face later on. All that mattered right now was having the funds that would enable her to raise her baby in comfort. A baby that was already precious to her.

Placing a hand protectively over her stomach,

she solemnly promised herself that she would love and cherish this child. And, yes, it would love her, even if its father did not.

"Why, Callie's simply changed her mind, decided that she'll go on to Oregon after all."

That was what Pearl told the others on the wagon train. They all accepted it. No one bothered to question her about it. No one, that was, except a puzzled Linc.

"Why, Pearl? Why this abrupt change of heart?"

Pearl fixed him with a steely glare. "Because she'd be a fool to toss away her share of the reward money, and I guess she's finally come to realize that."

Yes, Linc thought, he was glad about that. Her flat refusal of the money had been troubling him, along with all the rest. "I wish she'd talk to me about it. I don't suppose . . ."

"No, that's something she hasn't changed her mind about. So you just forget about it, Linc Mc-Allister, and let her be." Pearl wanted the satisfaction of adding that he'd already done enough damage to Callie, but of course she didn't dare mention a word on that particular subject.

Linc walked away, realizing that Pearl was right. What could he say to Callie that hadn't already been said? Why hurt her with further words of remorse, which in the end was all he had to give? Both of them were miserable enough as it was.

After that he kept out of her sight whenever he could. But his conscience continued to gnaw at him in the days that followed. Not just about Callie but all the rest—Anne, what had happened in New Orleans, his fugitive existence.

In the end, out of all this tangled, unhappy mess, one thing became very clear to Linc. He knew with a grim certainty that he could no longer stand the meaningless existence of a drifter. Whatever the outcome, it was time for him to go back to New Orleans and face his accusers. And he wanted to see Anne again. *Needed* to see her. Yes, even if they hanged him for it.

It was a straightforward, determined decision. Once they reached Oregon, he would collect his portion of the reward money and arrange a passage for himself to New Orleans.

The problem of Callie was not so easily resolved. Nor did he, or Callie herself, have any further opportunity to deal with either that or any other personal issue. None of the members of the wagon train did, for they were now entirely occupied, mind and body, in surviving the rigors of the Oregon Trail.

The route had been rugged enough before this, but the far western part of the trail was an ordeal that challenged the caravan at every level. Day after day, week after week, they were confronted by raging rivers that had to be crossed, endless sun-scorched sage flats that tested the endurance of both men and animals, and brutal mountain ranges that punished spirits and weary bodies alike.

Oregon. Callie was desperate now to reach it. Conscious of the life growing inside her, she convinced herself that everything would be sorted out once she got there. It would be her chance to put the pain of Lincoln McAllister behind her, to start over again. Oregon. If only they would reach it. . . .

Chapter Fifteen

The hues of early autumn were tinting the wooded hillsides when the wagon train neared its final destination in western Oregon.

Callie, riding beside Daniel near the head of the caravan, asked him, "How do like it so far, this land that's to be your new home?"

Daniel didn't immediately answer. She watched his face as he slowly, thoughtfully scanned the wilderness on either side of the trail. "It is very different to the place I knew," he finally said. "Here everything is so green, it hurts the eye, but it is good."

Callie had forgotten how incredibly lush the evergreen forests were in this mild, humid climate with its towering firs and spruces, its lofty, mist-clad mountains, its deep blue waters. It was the Oregon she had once loved, and yet there had been changes in the intervening years.

Ferryboats no longer carried arriving emigrants on the last stage of their journey down the Columbia River to Fort Vancouver. The old fur post had lost its importance when that route had been replaced by the Barlow Cutoff around Mount Hood. It was along this trail that they were traveling now, and by nightfall they would reach Oregon City on the Willamette River. It was the gateway for the fertile Willamette Valley, where the emigrants would settle, and Callie had been told it was a thriving center.

"And you, Callie Burgess," Daniel solemnly asked her, "how do you like this place you have come back to?"

What *was* she feeling? A mixture of conflicting emotions actually. Relief that they were here at last. Excitement tempered by anxiety. And a certain forlornness that she didn't care to examine.

Before she could answer Daniel, a shout was raised from the front of the train. "Riders approaching from the west!"

No one on the caravan was surprised. Their advance scout, Ned, had gone ahead to Oregon City to announce their immiment arrival. This was probably some committee that had come out to welcome them. But the man and woman who appeared on horseback were nothing so ordinary as that.

It was Linc, accompanied by a beaming Ned, who led the eager couple on foot down the line of halted wagons to where Callie and Daniel had dismounted.

"This here," a pleased Ned introduced the

pleasant-faced, well-dressed man who smiled at them warmly and doffed his beaver hat, "is Mr. Wendell Gates what I met up with in Oregon City."

"And this," Linc said soberly, "is his wife, who has waited twelve years for this moment."

Except for a single, startling streak of white in her black hair and a few lines around the eyes, the slender woman had changed remarkably little since Callie had last laid eyes on her. But even if she had never met Mrs. Gates before, Callie would have recognized her. She and Daniel shared the same handsome, proud bone structure.

So she's married again, Callie thought as mother and son stood gazing at each other while Wendell Gates slid a supportive arm around his wife's tiny waist, for she seemed in danger of fainting. But only for a moment. Then, drawing away from her husband's protective arm, and with a cry of joy, Magpie rushed forward and folded Daniel in her embrace.

Callie, witnessing the emotional reunion, couldn't help the thickness in her throat. As she watched, the other members of the wagon train gathered around with grins and noisy congratulations. Through their ranks, her gaze suddenly met Linc's. For a few brief seconds they shared in silence the satisfaction of having brought Daniel safely back to Magpie. Then, knowing with a wrenching anguish that it was all they could share, she turned away.

* * *

Linc didn't try to meet her gaze, or to approach her, at the party celebrating Pearl and Gabriel's wedding in Oregon City three days later. Callie, however, was conscious of him on the other side of the crowded ballroom of the sprawling inn that overlooked the Willamette River.

He leaned negligently against the wall, an untasted punch cup in his hand, as he idly watched the dancers on the floor. She remembered him looking just like this, with almost the same sardonic expression on his face, at another dance long ago on the trail. Except the sight of him that memorable evening hadn't caused her heart to swell or to miss a beat as it did now.

Pearl, always sensitive to the pangs she was suffering, slipped away from her groom and came to where she stood by the windows. "You and I have come a long way, haven't we, honey lamb?" she said softly.

Callie understood to what she was referring. Pearl looked as radiant as any bride was supposed to look in a tasteful gown of ivory silk. Callie herself wore a simple dress of cream-colored muslin with dropped shoulders that showed her bosom to advantage, and full, tiered skirts. Even the flowers in the bun at the nape of her neck were subdued in color and size. All very different to the garish wear that once would have appealed to both of them.

"Yes, Pearl, we sure have."

She said it with as much enthusiasm as she could muster, but her gaze, straying again in Linc's direction, betrayed her.

"We had to invite him, Callie. We couldn't leave him out."

"No, of course you couldn't. It's all right. I—I really don't mind."

Pearl hesitated before telling her friend what she had learned. "You won't have to keep running into him for much longer. I hear he's trying to get passage on one of those ships that sail down the coast and stop at Panama."

Callie knew about the route, which permitted travelers to cross the narrow isthmus and board other vessels voyaging to eastern ports. It was an alternative to the overland trails and had been created to permit a faster, although more expensive, access to the California gold fields, where Magpie's first husband had made them rich before losing his life.

"He's, uh, got New Orleans in mind as his destination," Pearl added.

Callie's heart plummeted. So he was going back to *her*. Well, in the end it was all for the best, wasn't it, since that was just where he wanted to be? She could feel Pearl anxiously watching her face.

"I had to tell you, hon. Couldn't let you hear it from someone who wouldn't have understood. You going to be all right?"

Callie, steadying herself, summoned a smile. "Sure, Pearl, I'm going to be fine. I—I just need to find me a way to keep busy until he's gone, that's all. You know, kind of take my mind off things. I've been feeling useless anyway since we got here. Not used to being idle. Look, you don't worry about me. You get back to your husband.

He's looking real impatient over there."

Callie didn't know whether Pearl spread the word about her need to be occupied or whether there was something in her attitude that suggested she was available and willing. Whatever the explanation, she suddenly had all manner of offers.

It was Agatha Delaney, the tall, regal woman who had once been like a mother to Callie, who approached her first.

"I know I keep telling you this, Callie, but I will say it once more. We are so pleased to have you with us again." She paused, her kind gaze admiring Callie in her cream-colored muslin. "And so very proud of you."

Oh, Aggie, Callie thought with a pang of guilt, I wonder just how proud of me you'd be if you knew I'm more than three months gone with a baby? Eventually, of course, Agatha, as well as everyone else, would have to know. But so far, except for a slightly thickening waist that was in no way evident with stays and full skirts, her pregnancy remained a secret. She and Pearl had suspected that several observant women back on the wagon train had speculated about her condition, but if so, they'd buzzed about it only among themselves.

"Now that you are here," Agatha went on, "do you have any plans for yourself?"

"Nothing definite. Not yet."

"Then, until you do, I was wondering . . ." Her gaze wandered lovingly in the direction of her big husband, Cooper, who was busy on the other side of the hall settling a dispute between their lively son, Matthew, and their daughter, Miranda, who was a year younger than her brother.

"Yes?"

"Well, it is Cooper, you see. What with the ranch and all our other interests in the valley, he is sadly behind in the accounts. I do what I can, but until I can find a replacement for that wretched Parthenia Smyth, I must occupy the position she was to have taken, teaching at the school. I know that you do not need the money, since Magpie is to settle that generous reward on you, but you were always so excellent with math, dear, even when you resisted all your other subjects, that—"

"Are you trying to hire me?"

"Only if you are interested. Do think about it."

Callie promised Agatha that she would.

The second offer occurred a few minutes later. It came from Meg Owen, the lovely, raven-haired owner and hostess of the inn. Her devoted husband, Archer Owen, operated two steamboats, one on the navigable portion of the Willamette and another along the Columbia River into which the Willamette emptied above Oregon City.

Callie had stopped by the table where Meg was serving punch to compliment her on the sumptuous wedding cake.

Meg laughed. "Oh, heavens, don't thank me. It's all Toby's doing. He's pure magic in our kitchen."

Toby Snow. How could Callie have forgotten about him? The gangly young man, with a British accent and an eccentric taste in flamboyant clothes, had spent the last few days rushing in and out of the room where Pearl and Callie were being fitted for their dresses, urging them to sample and approve the refreshments he was preparing for the wedding party. Toby had come west on one of the Delaney wagon trains with the Owens. He was both their friend and the chef at the inn.

"You're lucky to have him," Callie said, thinking of her own sad efforts in this area.

Meg's face clouded. "Yes," she confided, "but we may lose him. Toby has gotten it into his head that he would make a good lawyer. He's been spending so much time reading law over at Judge McGruder's office that I'm finding it difficult to cope without him."

"But he was here for all the wedding preparations."

"Oh, yes, he's been excited about that, but come tomorrow when everything is routine again . . ." She broke off to consider Callie, a gleam of sudden inspiration in her blue eyes. "I understand you're at loose ends, not decided yet about your plans. I don't suppose . . ."

It was Callie's turn to laugh. "Don't even think it. I'm a disaster around kitchens."

"No, I wasn't going to suggest that. I can handle the cooking myself if I just had someone reliable at the desk to welcome the guests and keep the records. It would only be until I can find a replacement for Toby, providing he does permanently leave us."

Callie gave Meg Owen the same response she

had given Agatha, that she would think about it and let her know. But the truth was, neither of the offers of employment suited her. She didn't want some confined situation where she would have to work closely with people who would end up asking her questions that, no matter how well-meaning, she didn't care to answer.

But there was a third offer that did appeal to Callie. It came from Magpie and Wendell Gates several moments later. Linc was nowhere in sight by then; presumably, he had returned to one of the inn's tiny bachelor cottages that she had heard he was occupying. His absence enabled her to move freely around the ballroom without the risk of encountering him.

She was enjoying the sight of Pearl and Gabriel lovingly toasting each other, and trying not to envy their bliss, when Magpie and her husband joined her. The couple seemed interested at first in nothing but an exchange of pleasantries.

"What, not dancing, Miss Burgess?" the jovial Wendell said in greeting.

Callie had, in fact, declined a number of invitations, her mood far too restless to concentrate on even a simple measure. "I've been too busy visiting," she said by way of an excuse.

"And those skirts just made for waltzing," Magpie said, admiring her gown. "All very becoming, even the flowers in your hair."

"They're refreshingly fragrant, too," Wendell added.

Callie smiled. "Thank you, but the flowers are artificial, and the fragrance comes from my perfume. I'm afraid I have a weakness for perfumes."

"Is that so? It seems to me I heard there's a shop in town that offers a selection of interesting scents. But maybe you've already investigated it."

Callie shook her head. "I haven't had time to do anything but help with the wedding, but I would like to see the town."

It was an opening for Magpie to say, "Daniel is also eager to explore." She gazed across the room in the direction of her son, who was patiently suffering the adoration of Molly, the eldest of the two Owen children. The little girl was attempting to teach Daniel the basic steps of a polka. "Unfortunately," Magpie went on with regret, "he isn't at all happy about discovering Oregon City in the company of a watchful parent. But the thought of him wandering on his own makes me very nervous."

Callie gazed at the woman, thinking that she, too, had somehow, over the years, acquired refinement. Her wealth must have been responsible for that, or perhaps this second husband. "But why should that worry you?" she asked. "Daniel is perfectly able to take care of himself. After all, he lived all alone in the wilderness."

Magpie shook her head. "I'm afraid for him."

It was Wendell Gates who explained it to the perplexed Callie. "Daniel is the heir now to a great fortune, and that makes him vulnerable to all manner of scoundrels. Brutes like those you and Mr. McAllister prevented from snatching him back in the Black Hills."

"Judd Parsons and Ike Ritter are dead," Callie pointed out.

"Ah, but there are always villains, aren't there? And if this Parsons and Ritter planned to demand a ransom for Daniel—let us say for an amount far greater than the reward offered for his safe return, which I believe may have been their intention—then others could attempt to kidnap him for the same purpose."

"Yes," Callie said, "I see what you mean."

"We don't want to restrict Daniel," Magpie continued, "but we would feel better if he had some form of protection, at least until next week, when we return to our ranch upriver."

"But surely there's a sheriff here who could provide that."

Wendell shook his head, informing Callie in an undertone, "Our local sheriff is not very effective, I'm afraid." He paused for a second and then, after a sheepish little laugh, admitted, "I confess, Miss Burgess, that we flattered you for a purpose. We need you for Daniel, you see."

Magpie took up the appeal. "With so much to thank you for already, I hate to ask, but there is no one as qualified. We know how much you care for Daniel, and we've been told that you can outshoot anyone."

"And, of course," her husband promised, "we would provide a generous salary. Please tell us that you will, Miss Burgess."

Callie looked from Wendell to Magpie. They were asking her to be Daniel's bodyguard. That's what it amounted to. It seemed to her at first like a rather absurd proposal, but when she thought about it . . . Yes, why not? It was only temporary, and it would keep her occupied and out in the open, both of which suited her purpose. Moreover, she and Daniel were already used to each other.

There was also the attraction of that generous salary. Even though she would have her share of the reward when Magpie's bank made the funds available in another day or so, she would need all the money she could accumulate to raise her baby. And that was another thing. Her pregnancy was no obstacle. She was blooming with health.

"Consider me hired," she told the Gateses. "Providing, that is, Daniel has no objection."

Daniel didn't, and the next morning, with a small but dependable pistol tucked inside her purse, Callie called at the Gateses' handsome town house to collect him. Together they set off on foot to explore Oregon City. Both of them were impressed by what they saw.

It was a prosperous, rapidly growing community with most of its activity concentrated along the busy riverfront. New buildings were sprouting everywhere, both in the city and in the two villages on the western bank. There were already gristmills, sawmills, and churches keeping company with taverns, a brickyard, and stores of every description—all of them supporting a lively traffic.

But Daniel grew restless as they sauntered along the main street, peering into shop windows. It was the forty-foot-high Willamette Falls he was eager to visit. He made no objection, though, when Callie stopped in front of a millinery in a narrow, two-story structure located between a newspaper and printer's and a doctor's office.

There were bow windows on either side of the front door. In one of them were arranged hats of every description. But it was the display in the second window that excited Callie. There, on dainty, lace-trimmed shelves, was the most irresistible collection she had ever beheld. Perfume bottles in all shapes and sizes. Gorgeous bottles in blue and amber and pink glass, with silver and gold stoppers.

"This must be the shop Wendell mentioned! Oh, Daniel—"

Her young companion sighed with resignation. "Callie Burgess, if we do not go in there, you will never forgive me. But flowers are better."

Callie didn't agree with that, not once they entered the shop and her nostrils were greeted by a delicate fragrance as lovely as the woman who wore it. Slender and graceful, with an abundance of black hair in strong contrast to a porcelain-white complexion, she came from behind a counter to welcome them in a low voice that bore traces of a French accent.

"Yvonne Sabay at your service, madame. Do you wish to see a hat? I have an excellent selection."

Callie shook her head. "It's the perfumes that interest me."

Her enthusiasm must have been evident because Mademoiselle Sabay's dark eyes widened in pleasure. "Ah, you share my passion for scents. So rare in this place where nothing seems to appeal but the usual rosewater."

"I'm not sure exactly what I do prefer myself," Callie admitted. "I seem to love them all."

"Then we will find out which suits you best. This way, please."

Mademoiselle Sabay led them to another counter at the side of the shop. Its surface was crowded with small crystal bottles. "This one perhaps."

Callie saw the label as Yvonne started to reach for it. *Céleste*. She hadn't worn it since learning about Anne McAllister. Nor would she ever wear it again. "Not that one," she said quickly. "I—I've tried it before, and it doesn't agree with me."

"No? Well, there are many others."

Callie sampled them all in the next several minutes, discovering in the process that her pregnancy seemed to make her particularly sensitive to the fragrances. Never had she indulged herself in such a feast of scents—verbena, jasmine, patchouli, sandalwood, sweet olive.

"Perfumes are like music," Yvonne informed her. "Each is created by a blending of notes—the sweet, the mild, the spicy."

Callie was fascinated. "You know everything about it."

Yvonne smiled. "I should. It has been my family's business for generations." She went on to tell Callie that one of her ancestors had created a special formula for Marie Antoinette in his

Paris shop. That was before the revolution drove her people out of France. They'd settled in the West Indies, but political unrest there had brought Yvonne Sabay to Oregon. "And now I try to create custom perfumes for Americans who are more interested in hats."

Callie was impressed. "You make the perfumes yourself? Right here in your shop?"

"Yes, of course. I have my own small laboratory upstairs. Would you care to see it?"

Callie glanced at Daniel. He'd been silent all this time, but she could tell he was growing impatient.

Seeing her hesitation, Yvonne coaxed her with a tempting, "I think both of you would find it very interesting."

"Just for a few minutes, Daniel?" Callie appealed to him. "Then we'll go on to the falls."

"A few minutes," he agreed.

Yvonne Sabay led them through a curtained doorway into a back room. There was a table there under a window. On it were decanters and trays of labeled vials containing various fragrant oils. She dismissed the area with a wave of her hand. "Those are nothing. The real work is performed upstairs."

Opening a door, she invited them to precede her up a steep, narrow stairway. Callie, just behind Daniel, suspected nothing until they rounded a corner at the top and entered a bare room. Bare, that was, except for the two men who had been waiting for them in the shadows, revolvers in their hands.

Instantly alarmed, Callie started to draw the

pistol from her purse, but the burly leader of the pair growled a warning. "Wouldn't if I was you. We'd have both of ya drilled 'fore you could get off a shot."

When the two figures emerged from the dimness into the light of the single, tiny window, guns pointed at them, Callie gasped. Daniel, also recognizing them, went rigid with shock.

"See ya ain't forgotten us," chuckled the leader as he leaned forward to snatch the purse out of Callie's hands.

Judd Parsons and Ike Ritter! They had managed to survive that cataract in the cave! Had followed them here to Oregon!

"I'm right pleased by that, too. Ain't you pleased, Ike?"

"Sure am, Judd. Sure am," Ike squealed, producing several lengths of rope as his partner continued to cover them.

"Turn around, both o'ya," Judd snarled. "Hands behind your backs."

Callie and Daniel had no choice but to obey the command. When she faced the other direction and found Yvonne Sabay standing there in the doorway watching the scene with an impassive expression on her gardenia-white face, Callie damned herself for an incautious fool. Daniel was her responsibility. She had been charged to protect him, and instead of remaining alert, she had permitted them to be lured into this startling trap. And all because of her weakness for perfumes.

While Ike busied himself tightly binding their wrists, Judd moved close to Callie's side, so close that she could smell his sour breath as he taunted her.

"Wasn't very friendly o' you folks leavin' us fer dead back in that cave. Nosirree, not friendly at'all. 'Course we didn't die. See, that ol' underground river went an' spit us out far down the mountain where it come to the surface. I mean, we was battered some, Ike and me. Took us days t'feel better, but we made it aw' right."

He shoved his bearded face into Callie's, displaying the ugly scar that slashed across the top of his cheek from the corner of his eye to his ear. "Only you all left me with sump'n t'member you by. An' Ike here has got him a limp that'll never go away. Figger we owe you, an' looks like the time has come t'pay that debt."

Before he could elaborate, Yvonne interrupted him with a nervous, "Stop playing your foolish games. I want them both out of my shop as soon as possible."

"You know the orders," Judd barked at her. "We don't move 'em 'til we got the cover o' night. Meantime, they stay right here."

Uttering a sound of disgust, the woman turned on her heel and retreated to her store below.

"That's right," Judd chortled. "Me and Ike, we got away, but you two ain't gonna be so lucky."

As proof of that, he and his partner shoved Callie and Daniel down into a dark corner of the room, where their ankles were lashed together, their bodies roped by the waist to a pair of upright beams, and gags thrust into their mouths. Then the two men went away, locking the door behind them.

Questions swarmed through Callie's mind. Orders? Orders from whom? And how had Yvonne Sabay known all about them beforehand, which she must have if she'd been able to arrange this ambush? What was it all about? A kidnapping for ransom as Magpie and Wendell Gates had feared? Or something far more diabolical than that? Callie couldn't forget what Linc had suggested back in the Black Hills. That Judd Parsons and Ike Ritter weren't trying to recover Daniel but to kill him. Why?

But there was something more urgent than answers. The need to escape before Parsons and Ritter returned. Callie tested the bindings on her wrists. The rope, thin but strong, cut cruelly into her flesh. Useless.

Meeting Daniel's gaze, she could see by the frustrated expression in his dark eyes that he was having no more success than she in his struggle to free his hands. They were helpless, which made it a crazy time for her to suddenly start thinking about Linc. But that was exactly what she did do with both longing and regret.

"You've got one hour to be on board with your luggage," the grizzled captain informed Linc, squinting into the afternoon sun to measure what was left of the day. "If you're not here, we cast off without you. I mean for us to be laying off Fort Vancouver before full nightfall. Come sunup tomorrow, we load our cargo of furs and make for the open sea."

"Understood," Linc said.

The time was no problem for him. He had only

a few belongings to pack back at the inn and his bill to settle. And since his portion of the reward money had already been delivered to him this morning, that left him with no other business. Except to say good-bye to Callie, and perhaps that wasn't a wise thing to try, not even by letter. Better for both of them maybe to just end it in silence, cleanly and swiftly.

He was still undecided about that when he came away from the vessel after having secured his passage, still suffering pangs of guilt over the whole unhappy affair. It was in this mood, as he started away from the riverfront, that Gabriel Hawkins found him.

"What are you doing down here, padre?" Linc challenged with a wry grin. "Thought you were supposed to be on your honeymoon."

"I'm been hunting for you, McAllister. Pearl thought there was a chance Callie and Daniel might be with you."

"I haven't seen either one of them since your wedding yesterday." That was when he noticed that the expression Gabriel wore was not that of a carefree bridegroom. "What's wrong?"

"They're both missing. They left the Gateses' house together first thing this morning to see the town. Callie promised to have Daniel back before noon."

Linc frowned. "And that was hours ago."

Gabriel nodded. "Magpie is frantic, and perhaps with good reason." He went on to explain how Magpie and her husband, fearing the possibility of kidnapping, had hired Callie to protect Daniel.

Linc had to agree that the situation didn't look good, not when he knew how reliable and capable both Callie and Daniel were. "Has the sheriff been notified?"

"The man is totally incompetent. He appears to know only how to deal with saloon brawls and the occasional purse snatching. We've been searching on our own and asking questions, but no one has seen them since early this morning. Nor does anyone seem to recall just where they were last seen." He gazed appealingly at Linc. "We need you, McAllister."

Linc glanced at the ship that was supposed to carry him to Panama. It looked as though he wouldn't be sailing on it, after all. He had no hesitation about that, knowing he'd never forgive himself if he blithely departed while Callie and Daniel were missing and maybe in serious danger. But he was angry about the necessity of his decision.

Damn little nuisance! She was still involving him in her sorry predicaments. And just when he'd hoped to bring an end to it all, giving both of them a chance to recover from each other. He definitely needed that chance after the wedding celebration yesterday, which he never should have attended. Seeing her in that creamy, breast-revealing gown had fired his blood all over again. He hadn't dared to come anywhere near her. She was a temptation he had to put behind him. Only now . . .

"All right, Hawkins," he said grimly, "exactly where have you and the others looked so far?"

"Up and down every street and byway in town.

And we've talked to all the shopkeepers. We're heading over to Willamette Falls now. Someone remembered Daniel was eager to see it, and if that's where they went and there was an accident . . ."

Gabriel murmured a quick prayer against that possibility, but Linc didn't share his concern. Daniel, raised as a Cheyenne, was as surefooted as a mountain ram, and Callie would have been equally careful at any great height.

He sent Gabriel off to join the others, intending on his own to cover the town again. There was a chance the searchers had overlooked something. He was still angry as he struck off along the main street, refusing to admit to himself just how sick with worry he was.

Moving from shop to shop, he talked to the store clerks again, questioned people in the street. None of them had any information about the disappearance of a woman and her young companion. Even the newspaper office, whose business it was to be observant, had nothing encouraging to offer.

Linc had just come away from the newspaper and was passing the millinery shop next door when something caught his attention. Backing up, he looked again at the display in one of the bow windows. Perfumes. All manner of perfumes. It was then he remembered; for Callie, perfumes were like blossoms to a bee. If she had discovered this display, nothing could have prevented her from entering the shop.

The woman who rose from behind the counter as Linc came through the front door of the place had an aristocratic bearing and black hair piled on her head.

"And how may I serve you this afternoon, monsieur?"

"I'm looking for a woman and the young man who was with her. They may have been here earlier." And he told her about Callie and Daniel.

"I have already been asked about them," she informed Linc. "And I tell you what I said before. I was very busy with customers this morning. If they were here, they left without a purchase so I did not notice. I am sorry, but this is all I know."

Was he imagining it, or did the woman seem evasive? "While I'm here, I'll just look around a bit."

She seemed annoyed by that, but she nodded politely. "As you wish."

He took a slow turn around the store, inspecting the merchandise. Hats and perfumes. He was wasting his time. There was nothing to be learned here.

Linc was on his way to the front door when he heard it. A loud thump above him, as if something heavy had been overturned up there. Or as if a pair of feet had been banged down on the floor boards. This time, when his gaze met the woman's, he knew he wasn't imagining it. She was decidedly nervous.

"I have a cat upstairs," she said with a little shrug. "She is always upsetting something."

The noise came again, as though to deliberately draw attention to itself. Linc made up his mind. "Maybe Kitty's in trouble. Maybe she needs our help."

And before the shopkeeper could stop him, he was on his way to the back regions of the shop, brushing through a curtained doorway. The woman ran after him, protesting vehemently, "Monsieur, those are my private quarters! You have no right!"

Linc cast his gaze around the room behind the curtain. "Where is the stairway to the second floor? Here?"

There was a door at the side. When he yanked it open, it revealed a flight of stairs. He was starting up them when something hard and heavy crashed down on the back of his skull.

Chapter Sixteen

He was dead, and this was hell.

Linc was convinced there could be no other explanation for his situation. It certainly felt like hell with his body stretched out on some painfully hard surface, his head throbbing. And it looked like hell as he permitted his gaze to shift carefully from side to side. A faint, flickering light revealed the deep, black pit into which he had been cast. The hot glow originated from high overhead. Yep, those had to be the flames of Hades.

"McAllister," he rasped to himself, "your sins have caught up with you, just like everybody promised you they would."

Lucifer heard and answered him out of the darkness. "Not yet, but we were beginning to think we'd lost you for good."

Except it didn't sound like Lucifer, and the hand placed on his brow sure didn't feel as if it could belong to a horny-skinned devil. It was much too pleasant for that.

"You were unconscious for hours."

"Callie?" he whispered, beginning to remember.

"Yes, and Daniel is here with us."

There was a rustle off in the blackness as the young man scooted himself across the stone floor to join them. Linc, struggling to sit up, realized that a rough woolen blanket separated him from the dampness of that floor, if not its bruising hardness.

"Oh, murder, my body feels like I was thrown into this hole. *Head first,*" he emphasized with a groan.

"No," Callie informed him, "they lowered you down with ropes. They were being careful, because they said you had to be able to walk when the time came. Don't ask me what they meant by that."

Daniel grunted. "They were not so gentle with us. They made us climb down a long ladder and then pulled the ladder up afterward to make certain we stayed here."

"Who are *they?*" Linc demanded. "And just where is *here?*"

"Judd Parsons and Ike Ritter," Callie said, adding after his exclamation of surprise, "That's right, they survived and managed to follow us here to Oregon. The light is from their campfire up there." She pointed to the ruddy glow that seeped through the opening somewhere above their heads. "And *here* is some kind of deep cave on a mountainside."

"With no back door like my cave in the Black Hills," Daniel said with a finality that meant he had already investigated. "And no way to climb out."

There was a glum silence, which Linc ended with an impatient, "The two of you have to do better than that. Let's hear all the rest of it, starting with how Parsons and Ritter got their hands on you." He paused to rub the swelling on the back of his skull. "Damn! That woman must have hit me with a boulder."

"A candlestick," Callie said. "She gloated about it afterward. Don't you think you'd better lie down?"

"I've been lying down. Right now I need to hear a story, so let's have it."

Callie launched into an account of all that had happened since she and Daniel had entered Yvonne Sabay's shop that morning. When she finished, Linc reviewed certain portions of her explanation in order to be clear about them.

"All right, so Parsons and Ritter were waiting there to grab you. But what connection does this Sabay woman have with those two miserable excuses for humanity?"

Callie shook her head. "I'm not sure, but something was said about all of them following orders."

"Meaning," Linc surmised, "that someone else, who hasn't revealed himself yet, is in charge of this kidnapping."

"It looks like it," Callie agreed. "And whoever

he is, I think Yvonne Sabay is his mistress. There was some sarcastic remark from Parsons about how her man would be proud of her. This was after she'd knocked you out and they'd carried you upstairs and were tying you up."

Linc nodded. "Where, like you said, the three of us remained until night. And then we were carried out the back door and tossed into a covered cart and brought—where?"

"It was too dark to tell once we'd left town. All I know is that we came through country that was wild and uninhabited."

"How far, and in what direction?"

"Miles, and I don't know what direction."

Daniel supplied that information. "Toward the hills where the sun rises. I could tell from the stars out the back of the cart."

"So we were brought east, probably into the Cascades. And they knew about this cave and had the ladder waiting, which means this was all arranged beforehand. And now we're being held down here like animals in a pit. But why and for how long?"

" 'Til morning," Callie said. "That much they told us before they sent us down the ladder. 'Til morning when someone is supposed to come."

"Probably the bastard who planned this little party. And what do you want to bet Parsons and Ritter have been in his pay all along? That's why they were trying to snatch Daniel in the Black Hills. Well, whoever he is and whatever he wants, we can't just sit here waiting for him." Linc shoved himself to his feet. "We have to find a way out of this hole."

Callie and Daniel watched him in the feeble light, saying nothing as he circled the area searching for a means of escape. They knew he wouldn't be satisfied until he'd learned for himself what they already knew. That the walls, slick with dampness, were sheer before they curved inward toward the ceiling, making it impossible for them to scale. That the only opening was high in the center of that ceiling, and outside it were two vigilant men armed with rifles.

"You're sure there's no other exit?" Linc finally asked.

Daniel, huddled beside Callie, explained how he had carefully felt his way through the blackness. The cave was a small one, and although there were three short galleries that branched off this single chamber, all of them ended in solid rock.

Cursing in frustration, Linc dropped back onto the blanket, knees drawn up to his chest. "It's not entirely hopeless," he said after a moment of thought. "They're searching for us back in town. Maybe they'll pick up the trail."

"I'm afraid we can't count on that either," Callie told him dismally. "Parsons and Ritter laughed about it, how a false trail was being laid in the other direction."

"So the bastards anticipated that, too," Linc muttered.

Callie, gazing at him in the gloom, knew how much he hated his state of helplessness. She felt it as well, sharing his desperation.

After a moment, she fumbled for a flask at her side. "There's water here. They gave us that,

341

along with three blankets. I guess they mean for us to stay healthy while we wait for whatever is supposed to happen."

Linc accepted the flask she held toward him and drank from it deeply. There was a long silence in the cave after he returned the flask to Callie, each of them occupied with forlorn thoughts. Nothing interrupted the stillness but a slow, muted plopping sound off in one of the dead-end passages where water, seeping through the rock, dripped from the ceiling.

In the end, with a yawn that announced his exhaustion, Daniel crawled off to a dry corner of the chamber, curled himself into his blanket, and promptly went to sleep. A fatalist like many of his Cheyenne brethren, Daniel accepted what he couldn't alter. Linc envied him.

The cave was dank and cold. He wasn't surprised when he noticed Callie shivering. "This blanket isn't enough," she complained, huddled within its inadequate folds. "I had a shawl, but they took it away from me."

"Probably used it, or parts of it, to lay that false trail. Let's see if I can help."

Before she could object, he shifted himself against her side. Using her blanket as a cushion under them and his as a cover, he wrapped them inside a cocoon where they shared each other's warmth.

This is not a wise arrangement, Callie thought.

Not wise at all, Linc thought.

She considered drawing away from him, but the comforting heat of his body pressed against hers was irresistible.

342

He wondered about surrendering both blankets to her and then putting distance between them. Yeah, that was what he ought to do, escape the temptation of her soft nearness. Only he couldn't bring himself to do that.

It was the wrong place, the wrong time for yearnings like this. They both knew that. But there never had been either a right time or a right place for the sweet ecstasies they'd shared, and they knew that, too.

"We're not going to survive what's going to happen tomorrow, are we?" Callie whispered at last.

"It doesn't look good for us," Linc admitted.

Then what difference does it make what happens tonight? Callie thought. If she was to die in the morning, and her baby with her, unthinkable though that was, then she wanted one last time to find joy in the arms of the man she loved.

Linc must have felt entitled to answer the same need. That was why he turned to her suddenly, reaching for her in the darkness with both his arms and his mouth. Her willing lips welcomed his as she squeezed against him, losing herself in his embrace.

Their kiss was long, deep, and compelling. So compelling that she forgot they weren't alone until his mouth finally lifted from hers.

"We can't," she said hoarsely. "Daniel—"

"We'll find a spot where we won't disturb him," he promised her eagerly.

Untangling them from the blanket, he rose, caught her hand, and tugged her to her feet. Then, scooping up both blankets, he led her off

into the depths of one of the galleries. It was inky
black in this part of the cave, but by feeling their
way they located a little alcove where they
would be secluded.

Linc spread one of the blankets for them on a
level section of the floor. They sank down onto
its woolen surface still warm from their bodies.
His breath on her face was equally warm, telling
her how close he was.

"I need to see you," she said.

"Sweetheart, without a light I'm afraid that's
going to be a problem."

"No, this way."

Her fingers groped through the darkness,
making contact with his face. She placed her
hands on either side of his head, holding him
steady as she leaned forward.

"My lips aren't blind, you see."

Using her mouth, Callie slowly traced the con-
tours of his face—her sensitive lips learning the
shape and texture of his eyebrows, the pointy
tops of his ears, the sharpness of his nose, the
ridge of the scar along his jaw. In the end, wanting to taste him as well as to feel him, the tip of
her tongue located his mouth, seductively, lovingly stroking its sensual width from corner to
corner.

She could hear his arousal as he raggedly
dragged air into his lungs. And she could feel it
when he captured her hand and carried it down
to the hard bulge at his groin. As further evidence, his own marauding tongue met hers in
another blistering kiss. But as thoroughly as he

plundered her mouth, it wasn't enough. Not nearly enough.

"I need all of you," he rasped.

"Yes," she said, understanding him.

Fumbling in the dark, they shed their clothes, then stretched out side by side on the blanket. The cool air drifted over Callie's nakedness, threatening to chill her. But Linc didn't permit that to happen. His lean body clasped hers, branding her with his heat.

There was the heat of his mouth as well, this time on her breasts. They were tender with her pregnancy, more sensitive than they'd ever been. She responded to his attentions with little whimpers of delight as his tongue swirled around their tight peaks.

And there was the heat of his questing fingers between her parted thighs, gently invading, enticing her with deep caresses until she was straining against him, pleading for release. He obliged her but not with his hand, for suddenly, stunningly, his mouth was down there. Callie bucked, and he steadied her as he applied his tongue to her nub, bringing her to a shattering climax.

She was still quivering with spasms when he joined his body with hers, burying his rigid length inside her with one powerful thrust. In that exquisite moment, Callie knew that nothing else mattered. Not their unresolved differences or the woman back in New Orleans or the peril that waited for them tomorrow. There was only tonight and the two of them lost in each other.

Afterwards, when the urgency had been satisfied for both of them, when they surfaced from the oblivion into which their raw desires had cast them, Linc drew the second blanket over their flushed bodies. Content with him nestled beside her, drowsy with fulfillment, Callie took pleasure in his hand stirring idly over her peaceful flesh.

She forgot the danger of such an exploration. It was not until his hand suddenly stilled on the swell of her belly that she realized how reckless she'd been. And by then it was too late.

"Callie?" There was puzzlement in his voice, and then something much more than that when she tensed under the flat palm of his hand, betraying herself. "It's true, isn't it? That's why you've filled out here. Your breasts are heavier, too, but I just thought—You're going to have a baby, aren't you? *My* baby."

It was useless to deny it. What hadn't been in any way obvious under her clothes in the light of day was now, even in total blackness, all too apparent to him. His hands could *see* it, just as her mouth had seen his face.

"Yes," she croaked.

He must have sat up, because now his voice came from above her. It was rough with anger. "And just when were you going to tell me?" Her silence was answer enough. "You were never going to tell me, were you? You would have let me sail off without knowing."

"It—it seemed best that way."

"What kind of logic is that? Damn it, Callie, didn't it ever occur to you that I had a right to know? That this life we made is my responsibility?"

"Your responsibility is waiting in New Orleans," she said quietly. "You told me as much, remember?"

"That was before, but now—"

"Linc," she interrupted him with a catch in her voice, "d-don't let's argue about it. Because none of it will matter anyway after tonight, will it?"

She was reminding him there would be no future for them to worry about since they weren't likely to be alive when tomorrow came. How could he be anything but gentle with her after that?

Linc stretched out again beside her. She didn't object when he gathered her into his arms. They were silent as he held her close. There was nothing more to be said. He was glad when she finally drifted off. At least in their last hours she would have the blessed peace of sleep.

For Linc there could be no rest. He lay there as the long hours passed, at first tormenting himself with guilt. How could he have been so idiotic, so irresponsible as to have made love to her repeatedly and not anticipated the consequences?

But remorse at this point was a worthless emotion. He switched his thoughts to the imperative problem of finding some way for Callie and the child, *his* child, to survive. He couldn't let them die. *He couldn't.*

But no matter how ferociously Linc attacked their dilemma, he could find no escape. His mind was still frantically searching when at length, in pure exhaustion, he dropped off.

The ladder came slithering down into the cave, its feet landing with a thump on the floor of the chamber. The ladder was followed by a gruff shout from the opening above.

"Come on up! And no tricks when ya git here, lessen ya want bullets for breakfast!"

Callie followed Daniel up the long ladder, with Linc bringing up the rear. The morning light when she emerged into the open was blinding after the gloom of the deep pit. Shaken from her night underground, she stood there blinking. When her eyes had adjusted to the brightness, she saw Judd Parsons and Ike Ritter covering them with their rifles.

"My, my," Parsons taunted them with one of his ugly grins that displayed the gaps of his missing teeth, "they sure do look a messy sight after bein' down there."

"Sure do," Ike agreed.

"Not fit t'welcome the company that's comin' t'call, but guess there ain't much we can do 'bout that. Won't matter after a bit, anyway."

"What company?" Linc demanded.

Parsons gestured with his rifle, pointing off toward the distance where the slope of the mountain dropped away through the evergreens. There was a rider down there dressed all in black. They could catch brief glimpses of him through the thickets of alders and native rhododendrons as he ascended the trail along a series of switchbacks, one of which skirted the rim of a gorge.

"Anyone we know?" Linc asked him wryly.

"That mouth o'yers ain't been improved with a night underground, has it, McAllister? Ya just wait."

Their wait was a long one. It took forever for the rider to reach them up the long trail. Or so it seemed to Callie as she stood there in suspense overlaid by a mounting apprehension.

When he finally rounded the last bend and rode into the clearing, Callie gasped in recognition. But Linc, close beside her, didn't seem surprised by the identity of the immaculately dressed figure who slid from his horse.

Aware of Callie's shock as he strolled toward them, he greeted her with a falsely sympathetic smile. "Yes, I know. Why would I bother to hire you as the boy's bodyguard if all along I was planning his elimination? It's quite simple if you think about it."

Linc explained it for him in a voice that was grimly humorous. "Oh, we understand all right. You were guaranteeing your innocence by urging protection for him—just in case he was abducted, which, horrors, is exactly what happened."

Wendell Gates turned his head, favoring Linc with his smile. It was a very different Wendell Gates from the one Callie had spoken to at the wedding celebration. This one was not Magpie's loving and concerned husband. The smile was that of a man who was cruel, relentless in his purpose.

"Exactly, Mr. McAllister, and I should resent you for turning up at Yvonne's shop and interfering with our intentions. But instead I find myself obliged to you."

"And how's that, Gates?"

"Why, you've just become the kidnapper, of course."

"I see, the convenient scapegoat."

"Yes, this is all much better than Parsons and Ritter here killing Daniel back east, as was originally planned, or being his unknown abductors now. This way you will be blamed for his death, as well as that of Miss Burgess, and there the matter will end."

"I assume you have all the details of this little inspiration of yours worked out and we're about to learn what they are. Just one thing, Gates. Why?"

"My wife's fortune, naturally. Oh, not for me, not ultimately. Yvonne and I have a son. Our secret, you understand. He is everything to us. And once Magpie's grief for Daniel has softened, she will be persuaded to adopt this little boy, this poor orphan needing a mother."

"Who will then replace Daniel as Magpie's heir. Uh-huh."

"Splendid, isn't it?" Wendell turned in annoyance to Judd Parsons, who was waiting anxiously at his elbow. "What is it, Parsons?"

"It's gettin' late, an' if their friends is out lookin' fer 'em—"

"Patience, Parsons. We are safe. The searchers are all on the other side of the river, where the wrong trail has led them. And I . . . well, I am the anguished stepfather on his way to Portland to beg for further volunteers in the search. Now what are you scowling about?"

Judd, lowering his rifle and leaning on it, began to complain that he and Ike hadn't been paid lately. And just when, he demanded, were they going to see some of that big money Wendell had promised them? Though Ritter kept his own weapon raised, his goggle-eyed attention was focused on the heated exchange that was developing between his partner and Gates.

Linc seized the opportunity to edge toward the inattentive Ritter. Holding her breath, Callie watched him slowly close the distance. When he was within a yard of his target, he made a lunge for the rifle. Ike squealed in alarm as the weapon was torn from his grasp.

But before Linc could train the rifle on their captors, Wendell Gates acted with lightning swiftness. Whipping a pistol from his belt, he was instantly at Callie's side, the gun pressed against her skull.

"Drop it, Mr. McAllister, or she dies here and now."

Knowing Gates was far too ruthless not to mean it, Linc released the rifle. It clattered to the ground and was quickly retrieved by its nervous owner.

Gates made a sound of irritation. "We've had enough comedy. It's time to get the job done. You and Parsons and I are going to take a walk down the trail, Mr. McAllister. There's a gorge along there, a very deep gorge. You can see the drop from here at the edge of the trail. You will miss your step at that very dangerous edge and fall to your death. When they find you, as eventually the searchers will when they give up on the false trail and turn in this direction, they will discover this in your pocket."

Satisfied that Parsons and Ritter were covering the prisoners again, he tucked the pistol back in his belt and withdrew a folded paper from inside his coat. "It's the ransom note you were on your way to town to deliver. I'm afraid, Mr. McAllister, there's only one conclusion they'll be able to draw after reading it—that the reward money you received for Daniel's return simply wasn't enough for you. As for the boy and his bodyguard whom you kidnapped"—he paused to shrug his shoulders—"I suppose in time they also will be found, but by then it will be too late. They will have died of exposure and starvation where you left them at the bottom of the cave."

Bad enough, Callie thought, that Linc would be flung to his death, but that she and Daniel would be subjected to so inhuman an end was unimaginable. Nor could Linc tolerate it for her.

"Listen, Gates," he pleaded earnestly, "you'll have what you want if you kill Daniel and me, but find a way to spare Callie. She's expecting a baby. I swear it's the truth. Let her and the baby live, I beg you."

If Linc, in his desperation for her, expected any shred of mercy from Wendell Gates, he was mistaken. Gates cast a cold, indifferent eye in Callie's direction before shaking his head. "I'm afraid that isn't possible. She's a witness. No more delays now."

He gestured for Linc to precede them down the trail, but Parsons stopped him, jerking his head toward Callie and Daniel. "What 'bout these two? Oughtn't we t'put 'em back in the hole first?"

Wendell paused to consider them with one of his brutal smiles. "No, that can wait for our return. Let them stay here and watch Mr. McAllister's dive into the gorge. That's a pleasure they shouldn't be denied. But I think they need to be tied up, just in case Ike becomes careless again. Be quick about it. I still have to give myself an alibi with the journey to Portland."

Hands bound behind them, legs trussed up at the ankles, Callie and Daniel were shoved down onto the ground in front of what was left of the morning campfire. It was a position that framed an adequate view of the gorge below.

As Linc was driven down the path in front of the armed Parsons, with Gates behind, he looked back over his shoulder. His gaze met Callie's in a poignant look that was both an apology and a silent good-bye. It was a last look that tore at her insides.

When the forest swallowed the three men, an excited Ike Ritter stationed himself at the far edge of the clearing, where he could look directly down onto the gorge. It would be some time before the three men emerged on its rim, but Ritter was already craning his scrawny neck, not wanting to miss the action.

Unable to bear the sight, sick at the thought

of what was to happen to Linc, Callie looked away. That was when she saw that Daniel, too, was looking elsewhere. But not for the same reason. Head twisted around, he gazed down at the remains of the campfire just inches behind them.

Leaning toward her, he hissed into her ear, "Do you see it? The chunk of wood there just under your hands."

By ducking her head and stretching around, Callie *could* see it—a short length of split pine with the unburned end toward her and the other end glowing where it rested in the embers.

"Take it," Daniel whispered. "Use the hot end to burn through my ropes."

"Daniel, no! Even if I managed it, I couldn't avoid burning you as well!"

He made a low sound of scorn. "A Cheyenne brave knows how to stand pain. Do it, Callie Burgess, or we will all die."

He was right. This was an opportunity that had to be seized. The *only* opportunity. She glanced rapidly in the direction of Ike Ritter. Confident that his prisoners were no threat and too far away to hear their soft exchange, he was absorbed in searching the area below for glimpses of the three men on their slow progress along the winding trail.

"Now!" Daniel insisted.

Callie acted. Her fingers strained to reach the wood. Closed around it. Maneuvered it into position, with Daniel squirming around to give her access to his wrists. She applied the brand to the bindings. Checked on the dull-witted Ritter to make certain he continued to be more interested in the gorge than in them. And prayed.

Callie didn't know whether she was searing Daniel. She dared not think about that. She could only hope that the sizzle and smell that resulted weren't flesh but simply rope. In any case, he made no sound of anguish or objection.

Minutes, maybe only seconds; the whole effort couldn't have lasted more than that, but it seemed like an eternity. A precious eternity slipping away from them while Linc was marched toward his death.

The impossible was achieved! Daniel, exerting his strength, burst from the blackened bindings and tore at the rope restraining his ankles. He was free. On his feet now, he stole toward Ritter while Callie held her breath. *Hurry, hurry before he turns around.*

Ike must have either heard Daniel or sensed trouble behind him. Alert now, he whirled with the rifle upraised. But before he could get off a shot, Daniel launched himself through the air. His head struck Ritter in the gut with all the force of a cannonball. The skinny man sank to his knees, the gun flying out of his hands. Giving him no time to recover his wind and yell a warning to his friends below, Daniel snatched up the rifle, slamming Ritter in the head with its hard butt. Ritter folded like a marionette whose strings have been cut, falling unconscious to the ground.

Callie finally released her breath. But her relief was only momentary. Gates had left his horse behind in the clearing, saddled and waiting for him. Daniel was already racing toward it, rifle in hand. She had to stop him.

"No!" she cried out. "It's too far! You'll never reach them in time! Untie me and give me the gun!"

His foot already in the first stirrup, Daniel looked back, his face registering uncertainty.

"Remember why your mother and Gates hired me," she pleaded with him. "I'm a crack shot! I can do it!"

Daniel's hesitation vanished. He flew back across the clearing, grabbed the knife from Ritter's belt, and ran to Callie. Crouching beside her, he hacked at the ropes binding her.

Her mind chanted the words again in an urgent litany. *Hurry, hurry before it's too late.*

The ropes scarcely had time to fall away from her ankles and wrists before she was on her feet and accepting the rifle Daniel thrust into her hands. Once more they tore across the clearing, this time to the edge that looked down on the gorge.

Together they searched the length of the trail where it appeared below on the rim. Nothing. No sign of the three men. Were they already too late?

"There!" Daniel said, pointing to a movement through the trees on the left.

Callie saw them then. The three figures on their slow, lethal progress to the rim of the gorge. She dropped to one knee in the position of the expert marksmen of the plains, the rifle lifted to her shoulder.

The three figures had emerged from the forest

now and were approaching the dangerous edge, Parsons driving Linc before him with his deadly rifle. Callie sighted them down the barrel of her own weapon.

I can do it. That was what she had promised Daniel. But *could* she from this distance, this angle? Never had her skill with a rifle been so crucial. There would be no second chance. She would get only one shot. One critical shot to save the man she loved, and if she missed, Gates and Parsons would destroy Linc before she could fire again.

It was Parsons she wanted, Parsons who had his weapon out and ready. She waited until they were on the rim of the gorge itself, until Parsons offered her a clear target. She could feel Daniel tensing beside her as she steadied the rifle, her finger on the trigger. Now! Drawing a quick breath, she squeezed.

The sound of the shot reverberated out over the gorge, startling the three men far below. Parsons clutched at his chest, the rifle falling from his grasp, his thick body dropping with it. Callie's bullet had found its mark.

The rest was up to Linc. Before Gates could whip the pistol out of his belt, Linc was on him with the ferocity of a mountain lion. The two men grappled there on the sharp edge of the cliff, a life-and-death struggle that ended seconds later with Wendell Gates sliding over the precipice. Linc shot out a hand to save him, his fist closing on nothing but air. Gates had already plunged to the bottom of the gorge.

Only then did Callie release the rifle she was clutching. It clattered to the ground as she buried her face in her hands with deep, wrenching sobs of thankfulness.

Chapter Seventeen

The sun was burning away an early-morning fog on the river below. Ships berthed along its front floated like phantoms in the gilded mist. Callie caught glimpses of them through the side window as she moved around her upstairs room at the Owen Inn, taking clothes out of the wardrobe and chest of drawers.

She had several choices for the day laid out on the bed. Her buckskins were not among them. She had a feeling she would never wear them again. It was time to put that image behind her.

In the end she selected a dress of woolen plaid. Its warmth would be welcome. There was a sharp chill in the air this morning, a reminder that it was autumn.

Callie was aware of the inn's stillness as she

dressed behind the screen. Even the town outside seemed quiet and lazy compared to its usual bustle—probably because the excitement of the kidnapping was over, and Oregon City had been able to return to its peaceful existence.

Wendell Gates and Judd Parsons were dead, Ike Ritter was behind bars, and no one knew what had become of Yvonne Sabay. She had taken her child and fled. Callie hadn't seen Daniel since their return from the mountains yesterday, though she knew he was fine. She'd been told he was staying close to home, comforting his shocked and grieving mother.

All the loose ends had been cleared up and made tidy. *Everything, that is*, Callie thought unhappily as she emerged from behind the screen, *but the problem of Linc and me*. That thought had been nagging at her since yesterday.

It was still gnawing at her as she knelt by the window that overlooked the back of the inn. Through the golden leaves of an aspen she could see the tiny, white-frame bachelor's cottage that Linc was occupying. There was no sign of him, which probably meant he wasn't up and stirring yet.

Callie continued to gaze at the cottage, yearning to be there. She *could* be there at this very moment, sharing its bed with Linc. He had suggested as much yesterday. She had refused, knowing it would only complicate a dilemma that had already been made difficult enough by their night of passion in the cave. Linc hadn't argued with her decision, maybe because he was too busy concentrating his determination in another direction. It was a subject he had besieged her with all the way back to town.

"We're going to be married, Callie Burgess. When all this mess is cleaned up, you and I are going to be married. Husband and wife. That's just the way it's going to be. Do you understand me?"

It was a temptation for her. He would never know just how much of a temptation, how desperately she wanted him. How she longed to say yes. But how could she when she knew his resolution was only because of the baby?

She had reminded him of his love for the woman back in New Orleans. And though he had minimized Anne's importance to him, insisting his sister-in-law no longer mattered, Callie knew it was a lie. Knew that Anne McAllister would always be in Linc's heart and that she, Callie, just as she'd always maintained, could never be anything but a poor substitute.

On the other hand, she asked herself as she got to her feet, did she have the right to deprive her child of his father and his father's name because she didn't have Linc's love? Could she stand to be a second choice for the sake of their baby, or would such a union be a terrible mistake?

Glancing again at the cottage below, Callie realized that the time had come to deal with the whole issue. The answers to her difficult questions weren't to be found here in this room but down there inside that cottage. She had been avoiding any serious discussion with Linc on the subject of his marriage proposal, fearing the result. She could no longer avoid that outcome.

Leaving her room, she headed for the stairs. She met no one in the corridor, and the inn's lobby when she descended to the first floor was equally empty. Meg Owen wasn't at the reception desk, which meant she was probably replacing Toby Snow again in the kitchen.

Callie was on her way to the front door when a young man in seaman's garb entered the inn. "Would you be the lady of the inn?" he asked her hopefully.

"I'm afraid not, but can I help you?"

Removing his cap, he scratched his sun-bleached hair in perplexity. That was when she noticed he had a letter in his other hand. "Well, I dunno, ma'am. See, I'm off this ship down at the port there. Come in from Panama, and when we docked yesterday, my captain says to me to deliver this here letter. Trouble is, we're sailing again for California in the next hour or two, and I still ain't found the fella what this letter goes to. Someone in the tavern where I stopped said to try the inn up here."

"I've met most of the guests staying here. Who is the letter for?"

The young sailor held the letter toward her so that she could see the address. But even before Callie read the name penned in a beautiful, flowing script, she *knew*. The thick, creamy paper bore the faint scent of *Céleste*. Anne McAllister's fragrance. Linc must have written to her either back in Independence or from somewhere along the trail, telling her of his destination, and her reply from New Orleans had eventually found its way to him here in Oregon.

"Yes," she said, amazed that her voice should sound so casual when she felt anything but normal. "Lincoln McAllister is here. You'll find him in the first cottage behind the inn. Just follow the path out there around to the back."

His boyish face brightened. "Much obliged to you, ma'am."

Callie felt so shaken that, when the front door closed behind him, she sank into the nearest chair. She didn't know what that letter contained, but it didn't matter. Its existence was enough to summon to her mind the image of the woman in the daguerrotype. A woman whose elegance and refinement Callie could never hope to match. She felt sick.

Seconds later she knew she couldn't go on sitting there like a coward. She had to go out to that cottage and confront reality, however harsh it might be.

Getting to her feet, she left the inn, making her way through the aspens whose yellow leaves were fluttering down on the path. The young seaman had left the door of the cottage partly open. She couldn't see him inside, or Linc either, but she could hear their voices as she approached the small structure. Hanging back below the shallow porch, she listened.

"If you'd like to pen an answer, sir, I can wait for it, 'long as it ain't past the time I gotta be back on board."

Linc had to be reading the letter, because there was a long moment of silence inside the cottage. It ended with a loud whoop of joy that made Callie feel as though her heart had just stopped beating.

"Good news, sir?"

"The best, sailor," Linc answered him, his voice excited and happy. "The very best there can be. The sweet angel in New Orleans who wrote this letter moved heaven and earth to clear my name. I'm a free man now, and I can go back there without worry whenever I choose."

"That so, sir?"

The young man clearly didn't understand, but Callie did. The reality she'd come out here to confront had just been dealt to her in the form of a hard truth. Anne McAllister had somehow managed to exonerate Linc in the matter of his brother's death. The shadows on his love for Anne had been lifted. He could go to her; they could be together without fear or restraint. It was what Linc had always yearned for.

Callie didn't need to hear any more. She turned around and hurried back to her room in the inn. She was no longer indecisive about the future. She knew now just what she had to do.

California. The young seaman had said his ship was sailing in another hour or two to California. She had visited Monterey as a child in the company of the Delaneys, had been impressed by the town and its people. It wouldn't feel alien to her, especially now that California belonged to the United States. Nor would there be anyone there who would question the legitimacy of her baby, not if she posed as a widow. Not when she had sufficient funds from her share of the reward to buy a comfortable existence for herself and her child.

Yes, California was the answer. It had to be, because if she stayed here, letter or no letter, Linc would insist they marry. He'd sacrifice everything he really wanted, pretend it didn't matter, and always be miserable. And so, ultimately, would she. It would be a poor way to bring up their child; Callie understood that now.

She had to do this for all of them, hard though it would be. It was maybe the hardest thing she would ever have to do. She couldn't weaken. She had to leave. She kept telling herself that all the way up the stairs and along the corridor to her room.

It took her only moments to pack her meager wardrobe. Penning the letters necessary to explain her sudden departure required more time and was far less easy. She wrote a quick note to Meg Owen, expressing her appreciation and accompanying it with sufficient money to cover her bill. A brief letter to Agatha Delaney followed and then one to Daniel, asking him to accept Apollo, who was stabled here at the inn. In both messages she promised to write more once she was settled.

Pearl certainly deserved to hear from her, but she wasn't there. After Callie's safe return from the mountains yesterday, Pearl and Gabriel had left Oregon City to deliver the mission funds to their destination upriver.

Telling herself she would write Pearl a full explanation after she reached California, Callie rose from the table, the letters in her hand.

There was none among them addressed to Linc. Unforgivable perhaps, but what could she say that he didn't already know? He would be angry when he found her gone, but in the end he would be relieved that she had freed him of an unhappy burden. He might even thank her.

She had to believe that, Callie told herself as she gathered up her things, or she would never find the strength to leave this room, to walk down the hill to that ship.

The lobby was still mercifully empty when she reached it. She placed the letters where Meg would be sure to find them behind the reception desk, then let herself out of the inn and headed rapidly in the direction of the river.

The ship captain was a tough Scotsman who understood exactly what she wanted when she paid for her passage and was conducted to her tiny cabin below deck. "Have no fear of it, ma'am. Your privacy aboard this vessel is guaranteed. No one gets by me or my men."

Thanking him, Callie locked herself in the cabin and sat down on the edge of the narrow bunk. It was done. She had only to wait now until the packet sailed, and she would be safe. And until then, she would not cry. She *refused* to cry. But the tears came anyway, salty and bitter.

The sailor had departed, leaving Linc alone in the cottage with his letter. It was a long letter, and he hadn't finished reading all of it when, aware that the young man was growing restless, he'd sent him back to his ship.

Linc's elation over the contents of the letter

had been so great that Anne's words hadn't been much more than a rapid blur for him. Now, his initial excitement under control, he settled in a comfortable chair and started the letter again from the beginning, this time reading with care.

Anne wrote that she'd had the good fortune to meet a prominent New Orleans lawyer. His name was Anton Carver. They had become friends, and when she'd shared the story of her husband's death with him, Anton had insisted on clearing both her and Linc of any blame connected with the scandal. This he had miraculously managed to do, even without Linc's presence in New Orleans.

By the time Anton had won a decision to reopen the case, he'd been able to locate a maid who had been in Anne's employ when her husband died, as well as two devoted men who had served under Linc in the army. All three had testified in Linc's favor, and after further investigation and a lengthy deliberation, the court had determined that William McAllister's death was an accident. Lincoln McAllister was no longer wanted for the murder of his brother.

Linc came now to the end of the letter and the section he'd not had the chance to scan earlier.

"And so, my dear Lincoln," Anne wrote, "this man who has been kindness itself in our need, who has come to mean so much more to me than just a friend . . ."

Linc blinked at her words. What was she telling him? He read on, unable to believe her final news. Anne and Anton Carver had fallen in love and were engaged to be married. *Were* married already probably since her letter had taken weeks to reach him.

Anne was sorry. She knew that she and Linc had once deeply cared for each other. She prayed that she was not hurting him, wished him every happiness, and finished by hoping that he would visit Anton and her when, and if, he ever returned to New Orleans.

And that was it. The end of a long dream, *his* dream, with a few strokes of the pen.

Linc sat there in stunned silence. It took him several moments to realize that, apart from relief over his vindication in Will's death and his considerable surprise at Anne's announcement of her marriage, he felt nothing. Not rage, not despair. Absolutely nothing. Why was that?

Gradually he came to understand. He had told the young sailor that now he could go back to New Orleans whenever he chose. But the truth was he had neither a desire nor a need to return to New Orleans, because everything he really wanted was right here in Oregon.

Callie! Dear God, when had it happened? Just exactly when had Callie Burgess sneaked up on him and stolen his heart? For it was true. He was wildly, desperately in love with that exasperating, wonderful little hellcat, and how could he have been so blind not to see it until now—to know that Anne had been nothing more than a fantasy, with no more reality for him than Gabriel Hawkins had been for Callie?

Callie had had the good sense to grow up and figure it out long ago. But Linc, fool that he was, had clung to the dream even as it evaporated, long even after he should have realized that Callie was not just real but the only woman for him. Not that he deserved her, but if he was lucky she wouldn't question that.

It wasn't too late. He could still convince her that he wanted to marry her, not for the sake of their baby, but for all the reasons he should have expressed long ago. Because he loved her, because they belonged together. Whatever it took to make her his wife he would do, because he refused to lose her.

Linc was in a state of euphoria when he left the cottage and hurried toward the inn to find Callie. It lasted until he reached the lobby, where he encountered Meg Owen reading a letter behind the reception desk. She looked up at him, her face grave, and that was when he knew something was very wrong.

They were gathered in the back parlor of the inn, Meg Owen and her husband Archer together with Agatha and Cooper Delaney, whom Meg had summoned for the crisis from their town house down the street.

Except Linc didn't think that any of the four of them really appreciated that this was a crisis. They sat there with expressions of mild sympathy on their faces, silently watching him as he paced back and forth across Meg's beloved Persian rug, venting his anger and frustration.

"Threw me off the ship!" he raged. "That damn captain and two of his deckhands! Took three of them to do it, which is why I didn't get anywhere near Callie's cabin!"

"Then you had no opportunity at all to speak to her?" Agatha inquired from where she was perched on the horsehair sofa, hands folded placidly in her lap.

"Oh, I yelled for her all right, begged for her to come out and talk to me! They could have heard me up in Portland, but she never answered, never showed herself!" Linc reached the end of the room and rounded on the four of them, his eyes like black storm clouds. "Lucky for her I never got the chance to get my hands on her! Running off like this without a single word to me! It's one thing to make up her own mind, but where does she get the right to make up mine as well?"

"Yes, it is very unfortunate, particularly so if she is in love with you." Agatha turned to her husband, who had been listening to Linc with his mouth stretched in a wide grin. "What amuses you, my love?"

"The lunacy of a man all tied up in knots over a woman. First it was me, then Archer there, and now it's McAllister's turn."

Linc scowled. He didn't see that there was anything remotely funny in his situation. He was desperate, and he tried again to make them understand that. "Don't you people realize how wrong this is? I love Callie, I want to tell her how much I love and need her. I want her to be my wife, I want to be a father to our child. Only I can't tell her any of this, because where is she?

370

On her way to California. *California*, of all places!"

"Yes, dear," Agatha tried to soothe him, "we do understand. It is just that I do not see what we can do about it."

"She really oughtn't to be sailing off to California to have her baby all on her own, though," Meg said, "even if she does have funds now to provide for herself and the child."

Agatha sighed. "I agree, but Callie has always been so headstrong. When she gets something into that willful mind of hers, it is next to impossible to make her see reason. I recall how once as a little girl she brought a fawn back from the woods, determined to raise it. We could not seem to convince her that the fawn was in all likelihood not an orphan and that it must be returned to its frantic mother."

"I also remember," Cooper drawled, "how we ended up handling it. Our neighbor, Buck Gordon, was the sheriff at the time, and we got him to pretend to Callie that keeping the fawn was illegal and that he'd have to arrest her if she didn't release it back into the wild."

Agatha nodded. "A regrettable deception, but it was necessary when nothing else would serve."

Linc couldn't stand it. Callie's ship had sailed. With every minute she was getting farther away from him, and these people were sitting here calmly reminiscing.

"I wonder," Agatha said thoughtfully.

"You got one of your famous inspirations, Aggie?" her husband asked.

"Perhaps. Judge McGruder is a friend, after all. Not always reasonable, of course, but I believe I can persuade him to act on our behalf."

What the hell was she talking about? Linc wondered.

"Although," Agatha continued, "if we are to keep Callie here with us, we must make certain of the means of getting by that captain and his crew in order to remove her from the vessel."

Linc had reached a stage of explosiveness. "This is crazy. That ship is long gone! It's probably reached the Columbia River by now! Not that I'd let that stop me, because if I thought there was a chance of catching up with it and getting aboard I'd swim after it!"

"That will not be necessary, dear." Agatha turned to Meg's husband. "Archer?"

He nodded serenely. "The *Willamette* is in port," he said, referring to one of his two steamboats. "She can outrun anything on the rivers."

"Yes, I thought as much."

Cooper leaned toward his wife. "Like to tell us now, Aggie, just exactly what you've got in mind?"

Callie hadn't failed to hear Linc up on deck. All of Oregon City must have heard the man bellowing like an enraged bull. It had taken the captain and two of his brawny deckhands to drag him off the ship. Or so the captain had claimed once they'd sailed and he'd had time to slip down to her cabin to assure her that she had nothing to worry about now. They were safely under way.

That had been hours ago, and Callie was still

trying to shake the memory of that painful episode as she stood by the single porthole in her tiny cabin, gazing out at the wake of the ship. They were on the broad Columbia River now, headed toward the open sea. And beyond the sea lay California and the new life there that she would build for herself and her child. The prospect of that future should have exhilarated her, but all she could feel was loneliness and despair.

She was doing the right thing. That was what she kept telling herself. Without that verbal talisman, her courage would have deserted her.

Callie went on idly watching the wooded shoreline sliding away on the side of the river. After a time she became aware of another vessel approaching from behind. It was closing rapidly on them. A few minutes later she could see that it was a steamboat, which explained its ability to overtake their cargo-laden packet.

She expected the steamboat to sweep on by them and was surprised when, once it was abreast of them, it slowed its powerful engines to a crawl that matched the speed of their vessel. Someone on the steamboat hailed Callie's ship. There was an exchange between the two captains which she could neither see nor hear, but after a moment the steamboat drew alongside the packet.

We must be taking on another passenger, she thought, for the thumping noises overhead told her that someone was coming on board. It was nothing to do with her. Or so she believed until a moment later when there was a rapping on her door.

Callie answered the knock and was baffled when she found the captain standing there, cap in hand and looking decidedly uncomfortable. Behind him in the passageway stood two men with dour expressions on their faces.

"Offical business, ma'am," the Scotsman apologized to her. "This pair behind me is deputies from Oregon City."

"But what has that to do with me?"

He awkwardly cleared his throat. "Well, uh, it appears they have a signed warrant for your arrest."

Callie was astonished. "Arrest! What for?"

"Theft," one of the deputies brusquely informed her, and suddenly the two of them were inside her cabin.

"What are you doing?" she demanded, outraged as they began to search through her luggage.

"Looking for what you been charged with stealing."

"This is preposterous, a stupid mistake! I haven't stol—You give that back to me!"

One of the deputies had taken possession of the carpetbag containing her most personal possessions, including her precious funds. She tried to snatch it back from him. A brief struggle ensued before she was restrained by the other deputy.

Fuming, she watched helplessly as the carpetbag was opened and the leather pouch bulging with the gold pieces that were her share of the reward was removed and inspected.

"This is it, the gold eagles she's accused of

taking. See for yourself, Captain." The deputy held out the gaping pouch for the embarrassed captain to examine.

"I didn't take that money!" Callie cried. "It was given to me!"

"That's for the court to say. You'll get your chance to speak your piece before Judge Mc-Gruder back in Oregon City."

Incredulous, Callie turned pleadingly to the captain. "You're not going to let them take me?"

"Ma'am, I don't see that I got a choice here."

And with that, she was taken into custody and removed from the packet. It wasn't until she was on the steamboat returning her to Oregon City that the incensed Callie understood what had just happened.

Lincoln McAllister! He was responsible for this unforgivable treachery! She should have obeyed her first longing back on the trail and put a bullet through him instead of falling in love with the varmint!

Chapter Eighteen

"You are *what?*" Callie thundered.

"Your legal defender, love," Toby Snow answered her cheerfully, the prominent Adam's apple in his scrawny neck bobbing like a cork on a fishing line.

Callie stared at the young man in disbelief. As a master chef, she had no problem with Toby Snow. As a lawyer, particularly one who had just announced he was here to represent her in court, she drew the line.

"In the first place," she informed him emphatically, "I don't need anyone to defend me, because I haven't done anything wrong. And in the second place, you aren't a qualified lawyer."

Or someone even remotely resembling one, Callie thought, gazing in horrified fascination at his long, bony figure. Even in their worst moments, she and Pearl had never been as garish as this. Toby was proudly clad in yellow-and-green checked pantaloons, a bilious green coat, and a silk vest that blinded the eye with its embroidered explosion of tropical flowers. No, this was definitely not her idea of a distinguished man of law.

"Close enough," he assured her happily, "for the court to appoint me your advocate."

Callie put her lowered head into her hands in abject misery. This whole thing had taken on all the aspects of a ghastly nightmare. Bad enough that she had been arrested aboard the packet yesterday, then forced to spend the night aboard the *Willamette*. All right, her quarters had been comfortable enough and her meals appetizing, although she'd had no appetite. But she hadn't been permitted to come ashore, and no one had come near her in her locked cabin.

They might as well have put manacles on me, she thought. Not that this had happened when they'd conducted her this morning from the steamboat to the courthouse, but she still felt like Oregon City's definition of a dastardly villain. And now here she was sequestered in this chamber adjoining the courtroom, awaiting her appearance before Judge McGruder and being told by Toby Snow that he was going to represent her. Well, enough was enough.

Callie lifted her head in renewed defiance. "Look, I don't care who appointed you. I don't need you. I can defend myself."

Toby shook his head, pitying her in her ignorance, and made *tsk*ing noises with his tongue.

"Love, love, it doesn't work that way. Not to worry, though. Toby shall slay the dragon for you."

"Now just a minute, I refuse to—"

They were interrupted by the bailiff, who had come to escort them into the courtroom. When Callie rose from the table where she'd been seated, Toby leaned down from his considerable height, whispering, "This is exciting. My first appearance in court."

Callie was beyond reply.

She had another shock waiting for her when she entered the courtroom. This was not going to be the simple, private hearing she'd anticipated. Every bench in the place was packed with gleeful spectators.

You'd think it was a sensational murder trial, Callie thought in disgust. Which it could very well end up being by the time she was finished with Lincoln McAllister.

Naturally, he was there, seated off to one side, the expression on his devil's face looking suspiciously smug. His dark, mesmerizing eyes met hers, holding her gaze for a long moment. If he was silently trying to tell her something, she wasn't able to read it. All she knew was that it hurt looking at him.

Why? Callie asked herself. Why was Linc doing this to her, for she had no doubt he was responsible for this infuriating farce? Why should he go to such elaborate lengths to get her back when it was Anne he loved, Anne he was free to go to now? The baby, of course. That had to be the explanation. It was his child he didn't want to lose, not Callie.

She had no further opportunity to question Linc's motives since the bailiff, impatient with the delay, was glaring at her. He led her and Toby to the front of the room and seated them at a table facing the judge's elevated bench. Then, smothering a yawn, he instructed the crowd in a bored monotone, "All rise for his honor, Judge Alban McGruder."

The spectators shuffled to their feet as Judge McGruder banged through a door behind the platform, climbed to his perch, and cast a baleful eye out over the courtroom. He was a little gnome of a man with ill-fitting spectacles under a pair of bushy eyebrows that wagged expressively. They were wagging now at a figure lounging at the rear of the courtroom.

"Jeremiah Peters, if you're gonna chaw tobacco in my courtroom, you go outside to spit. This court is now in session."

There was another rustling of the crowd settling back on the benches while Judge McGruder ducked down behind his seat of justice, searching for something. "Where's my gavel?" he demanded. "How can a body expect this court to convene without a gavel?"

The bailiff ran forward. "It *was* there, your honor."

"Well, don't just stand there. Go find me another."

The bailiff hurried away. Judge McGruder, catching sight of Toby, who was stroking his

379

long nose in solemn contemplation, beckoned him forward.

Toby approached the bench. "Your honor?"

"I gave you the opportunity to represent your first client."

"Yes, your honor. I'm grateful, your honor."

"Then what in dadblame are you doing turning up here looking like a dadblamed peacock?"

Judge McGruder had a voice that boomed. Even those in the back row couldn't miss what was meant to be a private exchange. There were loud guffaws. His honor suppressed them by peering severely at the crowd over his spectacles.

"I am wearing a conservative necktie, your honor."

There was a long silence. Toby's Adam's apple bobbed; the judge's eyebrows wagged. And Callie decided that she did not have a good feeling about these proceedings. Not good at all.

"That the accused seated over there?" Judge McGruder barked.

By now Toby's long nose was twitching as nervously as his Adam's apple. "Yes, your honor."

"Then get back to her."

Tugging at the offending waistcoat, Toby returned to Callie's side. The bailiff, out of breath, trotted into the courtroom and handed the judge the replacement for his missing gavel.

"What in dadblame is this?"

Necks craned to get a view of what his honor had just received. The instrument in his hand was a wooden cooking paddle about a foot and a half in length.

"Your honor, there isn't another gavel. Had to borrow that from the tavern next door. It's real heavy, so it should work just fine. Promised Mary Catherine Mahoney I'd return it soon as you're done with it, and Mary Catherine said to tell you be careful of the rough edge there, else you could run a sliver through your finger."

"It's wet," Judge McGruder complained.

"Well, uh, she was stirring up a pot with it at the time, but she washed it off real good."

His honor tested the paddle, whacking it on the surface of his bench. It produced a smack that resounded impressively. "All right, read the charge, and then let's move on to the first witness. Haven't got all day here, y'know."

Linc was the first witness, and after the charge against Callie was read, he was called to the stand. He ambled to the front, was sworn in by the bailiff, seated himself with a casual ease, and looked inquiringly at the judge, a half smile on his angular face.

"Wipe that smirk off your mouth," Judge McGruder ordered him, "and speak your piece."

Linc took his time, folding his hands over his stomach, stretching his long legs out in front of him, crossing them at the ankle. All eyes in the room were on him. The female ones in particular, Callie noticed. Damn him, anyway!

"Your honor," he drawled, "the reward for the return of Daniel Salter was twenty-five thousand dollars. I returned him, I was paid that reward, and when I got around to counting it, ten thousand dollars of the money was missing. Now I'm not saying that someone helped herself to that amount, but it sure looks like it. And that's all I know."

"That's what we like to hear," Judge McGruder congratulated him. "A plain, simple statement without all that clutter nobody cares about." There was a long silence in the courtroom before the judge fixed his gaze on Toby and demanded an exasperated, "Well?"

Toby gave a start. "Your honor?"

"You gonna cross-examine this here witness or not?"

"Uh, not, your honor."

"What are you doing?" Callie hissed at him. "Go after him, and make him tell the court that I never took anything and that he promised me that ten thousand dollars as my share of the reward."

"It's all right, love. Our turn will come."

Callie hoped so, but it didn't look as if it was going to happen with the next witness. He was the manager of the local bank, and he testified that he had delivered the reward money to Daniel's mother at her home. She had asked him to wait while she took the money into another room, presumably to count it. Then she had returned, handed him the sack, and requested that he take it on to Lincoln McAllister at the inn. Nothing had been said to him about any share for Miss Burgess.

Callie murmured swift instructions to Toby, sending him off with a determined, "Now you get up there and get the full story out of him."

Toby did make an effort this time. In stentorian tones, complete with appropriate gestures, he asked the bank manager if he was not aware that Mrs. Gates had retired to another room to separate ten thousand dollars from the sack in order to hold it for Miss Burgess, who was stopping at the house to collect her son for an outing that morning? And did the bank manager not realize that, when Miss Burgess arrived at the house, she asked Mrs. Gates to keep the sum for her until she returned? Or that Mrs. Gates complied with her request and that Miss Burgess finally received the money the evening after their terrifying experience in the mountains?

No, the bank manager said, he guessed he didn't know about any of that. How could he? And Judge McGruder barked at Toby, "What a lot of damn-fool questions! Haven't I taught you anything, boy?"

Callie couldn't stand it. She sprang to her feet, crying, "This is absurd! Why aren't we asking Magpie herself? Why isn't she here to testify?"

There were shocked gasps from the spectators, not because of Callie's outburst but because everyone knew that you didn't ask a recent widow in mourning to appear in public. It was unthinkable.

Toby, all aflutter over his client's breach of etiquette, arrived at Callie's side to utter a cautionary, "Uh, love, I think you've just a teeny bit demonstrated contempt for the court."

"And if you try it again, young woman," Judge McGruder warned her, banging his paddle for order, "you're apt to find yourself wearing a gag. Who's the next witness here, bailiff?"

Callie had only a rudimentary knowledge of

law, but even she knew that none of what was happening here was standard procedure for a courtroom. It didn't even approach that, what with his honor acting as judge, prosecutor, and jury all in one, while at the same time coaching the defense. The proceedings, which had already deteriorated into a mockery of frontier justice, couldn't get any worse. She was wrong.

"Mrs. Archer Owen to the stand!"

Finally, Callie thought, someone on my side.

"Now, no need to be nervous," Judge McGruder gently counseled Meg after she'd been sworn in and seated.

"I'm not a bit nervous, your honor."

"That's good, that's real good," he said, peering down at her over his spectacles. "Just tell us what you know."

To Callie's dismay, Meg testified that from the kitchen window yesterday morning she had seen Miss Burgess slipping away from the inn with her bags, leaving without a single word of good-bye to anyone. It had struck Mrs. Owen at the time as a very stealthy sort of behavior, something that could almost be defined as ... well, sneaky.

Callie was livid. How could Meg betray her with all this outrageous innuendo? And that fool, Toby Snow, made another mess of his cross-examination, failing to establish that Callie had left behind a perfectly acceptable letter of explanation for Meg.

"Our turn will come," Toby kept promising her.

But Callie had lost all faith in him, not that

she'd had much to begin with. Not knowing who her friends were anymore, she was worried in earnest when Agatha took the stand, especially since Agatha and Judge McGruder seemed to be on cozy terms.

"Cattle still a good investment, are they?" he asked her pleasantly, referring to the Delaney ranch upriver.

"Excellent, your honor. The hides are as good as gold."

"Always looking for a chance myself to invest in something sound." He adjusted his slipping spectacles. "So, Agatha, anything worthwhile to contribute here?"

Agatha admitted that she had no real evidence of Callie's involvement in the alleged theft. However, she did recall that, as a child, Miss Burgess had a regrettable tendency to be light-fingered. "I remember a certain episode regarding pastries. Apple tarts, I believe they were . . ."

It was a conspiracy! This whole comedy was nothing more than a conspiracy, and Callie had had enough. Her hard-won ladyhood deserting her, she surged to her feet with a furious, "Now just a gol'danged minute! Swiping a couple of pastries from the pantry when I was a kid doesn't make me a gol'danged thief! And they weren't apple tarts, they were oatmeal cookies! And if I had a few of them right now, I wouldn't be eating them! I'd be slinging them at—"

Toby clapped a hand over her mouth to silence her. Laughter rumbled through the courtroom. Judge McGruder smacked his paddle so savagely on his bench that it was a wonder it didn't splinter. Out of the corner of her eye, Callie saw Lincoln McAllister grinning like an ape. She promised herself that before they dragged her off in chains she would make him regret that grin.

When order had been restored, Judge McGruder peered down at Callie as if she'd already been condemned. "Looks to me, young woman, like the moment has come for me to render a decision in your case."

Toby sprang to his feet. "May it please your honor, there is a last witness to be called."

Judge McGruder scowled at him over the spectacles. "Don't tell me, boy, you've gone and saved out one of those surprise witnesses for the defense. If you have, you been readin' too many of them dime novels."

Toby gulped, his Adam's apple betraying his trepidation, but he persevered valiantly. "May I respectfully remind your honor that your honor himself taught me—"

"Yes, yes, yes," the judge relented, waving the paddle at him. "Call your dadblamed witness, and let's get this here circus over and done with."

Callie gazed at Toby with a newfound respect. "Our turn?" she whispered.

"Our turn, love." It was his moment of glory, and he executed it with a flair that rivaled a Shakespearean drama. "I call Daniel Salter to the stand!"

There were murmurs of interest in the crowd, and bodies swiveled on the benches as Daniel appeared from the chamber at the side. He had a folded paper in his hand, and every eye was on it as the young man proceeded to the front of the courtroom.

"What's that?" Judge McGruder demanded after Daniel had been sworn in and was seated on the stand.

"Proof that my client is innocent of theft, your honor," Toby announced triumphantly.

"I'll decide that. Let's have a look at it. Got to be sure it's bony-fide before I allow you to offer it as evidence."

The paper was passed up to the judge, who adjusted his spectacles and read the contents with a series of grunts that could have meant either acceptance or disapproval.

"May the witness be permitted to read it aloud to the court, your honor?" Toby anxiously asked the judge.

"Suppose he'd better before your audience out there expires of curiosity." He handed the paper back to Daniel. "Get on with it."

Daniel obeyed, reading in a clear, slow voice what turned out to be a letter from his mother.

"As circumstances do not permit me to be present in the courtroom, I appoint my son, Daniel Salter, to be the bearer of my testimony, which is as follows: I, Magpie Salter Gates, do solemnly swear that on the evening of October 5, 1852, I delivered in person to the woman known as Callie Burgess the sum of ten thousand dollars in gold. I further state that this sum was earned by Miss Burgess as her portion of the reward for the safe return of my son, that it is hers free and clear and to do with as she wishes. Respectfully, Magpie Salter Gates."

Daniel looked up from the letter and winked at Callie. There was a taut silence in the courtroom. It was ended by Judge McGruder's verdict directed at Callie.

"Guess that makes you innocent of theft, young woman."

Callie, who only minutes ago could have strangled Toby, now wanted to hug him. "Toby, you are brilliant!"

He glowed, leaning down to confess to her, "Actually, love, it was Agatha and Meg who suggested that little strategy to me, though I will say I delivered it rather effectively."

Before Callie could react to this baffling confidence, or to the babble of voices behind her, Judge McGruder banged his paddle repeatedly, shouting for order.

"I pronounced you innocent of theft, young woman," he said when he had everyone's attention again, "but I didn't say you were free to go. There's the little matter of your arrest. I understand you resisted it, and that ain't lawful." He turned to one of the two deputies who had taken Callie into custody. "That right?"

The deputy, who had been waiting in a corner, popped to his feet. "Oh, yeah, your honor, she was real uncooperative. Carried on something awful. We near had to cart her off that vessel."

"Guilty!" Judge McGruder declared without hesitation. "I sentence you, Callie Burgess, to serve thirty days in the town jail."

There was another explosion of excitement in

the courtroom. Callie was too busy being irate over this newest injustice to notice that Agatha had slid forward to whisper something into Toby's ear, which Toby relayed in a similar whisper to the bailiff.

"Another outburst in my courtroom," Judge McGruder threatened them, "and I'm locking you all in the town jail. The menfolk anyway, since we don't have facilities there for ladies. Huh, suppose that presents a problem where this young woman and her sentence are concerned. What is it?"

The bailiff had approached the bench. He leaned down, passing on Agatha's information into his honor's ear. Callie watched Judge McGruder's bushy eyebrows lift in surprise.

"Well, why didn't somebody dadblame say so in the first place? Can't go and jail a young woman when she's in a delicate condition."

An invaded beehive couldn't have buzzed with more sensation than the courtroom behind Callie. Her secret was no longer her secret.

"Well, now," Judge McGruder wondered out loud, oblivious to Callie's fuming embarrassment, "what are we gonna do about those thirty days?"

"I have a solution, your honor."

All eyes turned again, this time toward Linc who was on his feet as he boldly addressed the bench. Callie suddenly knew that she was in for more trouble.

Judge McGruder frowned at him. "I don't remember asking for any suggestions."

"You sort of did, your honor," the bailiff murmured to him.

"I did, huh? All right, state your proposal."

"I ask the court," Linc said, his eyes on Callie, "to release Miss Burgess into my custody, and I will watch over her and be responsible for her."

Expecting another uproar from the crowd, the judge grabbed the paddle, ready to pound it again on his bench. But there was absolute silence this time, every breath held in suspense.

"You tellin' me," his honor asked Linc, "that you're prepared to have this young woman serve her thirty days in your care?"

"I am."

The judge peered at him shrewdly. "You the father of her baby?" he barked.

"Yes, your honor."

"Uh-huh. And in your opinion that entitles you to look out for her?"

"No, your honor. It's because I'm in love with her."

Callie's jaw dropped. She could swear she actually felt the blood rush through her body. She just wasn't sure in which direction it was going, her head or her heart.

Judge McGruder had no further hesitation. "Good enough. Young woman, you are remanded to the custody of Lincoln McAllister for a period of thirty days. Or longer, providing he can convince you to stay." The paddle smacked. "Court dismissed."

There was a collective sigh of relief from the crowd as the judge turned to his bailiff. "Just what was Mary Catherine cooking over there with this here gavel?"

"Irish stew, your honor."

The bushy eyebrows lifted, registering considerable interest. "That so? Guess I'd better mosey next door then and return this thingamajig to her."

Callie came to her feet and stood there beside the table, too numb now to react as her friends filed past, offering warm wishes mingled with apologies for what they had regarded as a necessary scheme.

The courtroom finally emptied, leaving only Linc and Callie facing each other across its width. There was a moment of silence, and then he asked her with a slow smile that tugged at her insides, "*Can* I persuade you to stay?"

"How long did you have in mind?"

"A lifetime would be good."

"Will it be more interesting than California?"

"I think I can safely promise you that."

"What happened to the woman in New Orleans?"

"She got married."

"She did?"

"To the lawyer back there who helped her to clear my name."

"Oh. Don't you mind?"

They'd been slowly drifting toward each other as they spoke, but Callie wasn't conscious of it until he stood directly in front of her.

"Let's see if you think I do," he said softly.

She didn't object when his arms slid smoothly around her waist and drew her up against him.

And she certainly had no objection when his mouth came down and angled across hers. After that it was a question of neither approval or objection because she was much too occupied with his deep, mind-robbing kiss to give a thought to anything beyond pure bliss.

"No," he said when he finally released her, his voice raspy with emotion. "Looks like I don't mind in the least. How about you?"

"Oh, I'm just fine with it," she said lightly, which wasn't altogether true since she was still shaken by his declaration of love. "Except if you went and decided it was me you loved and not Anne—and, mind you, I'm not complaining about that. I mean, how could I when I've been off my head about you ever since the Black Hills? Then don't you think—" She paused to draw a steadying breath. "Don't you think you might have let me know it? Because if you had, it could have saved a lot of trouble here this morning."

"You didn't hang around long enough for me to tell you anything. Which is why we had to go to, uh, a little bother to get you off that boat and then make you stay in Oregon long enough to—"

"Never mind, I forgive you all. Only it was a bit extreme, even if—Oh!"

"What is it?" he asked her sharply, concerned by the sudden, startled expression on her face.

"Nothing, I—There! He did it again! Or her, as the case may be."

"What?" Linc demanded, worried in earnest now because her hand was at her stomach.

"Our baby! Isn't it wonderful? He's exercising for the first time. Or whatever it is they do to let you know they won't be ignored. Here, feel."

She caught his hand and carried it to her stomach. When the baby stirred again beneath Linc's flattened palm, a silly grin took possession of his mouth. It stayed there for a full, joyous moment before he got serious.

"That settles it. As soon as we can get Gabriel Hawkins back here to perform the ceremony, you and I are going to be married. This baby has put up with enough scandal. It's going to be born a McAllister."

"I suppose that is the best thing to do. Settling down as husband and wife, I mean."

"Damn right it is. Here in Oregon, too."

"I can accept that," she said solemnly, but her heart was singing. "Uh, what do you think you'd like to do? Here in Oregon, that is?"

"I hear the town is looking for a new sheriff."

She nodded thoughtfully. "You could be that."

"Be a chance to put to work the peacekeeping skills I learned in the army. How about you? I understand Agatha still wants that teacher for her school."

"I did enjoy working with Daniel on the trek west. I think I was rather good at it, too."

"Exactly."

"Of course, I still have a lot to learn myself, but there's plenty of time to do that while we're waiting for this baby."

"See, it's all going to turn out just fine."

"One thing, though," she warned him.

"What's that?"

"The old Callie. I'm convinced after this morning that she's still lurking there underneath the surface and is bound to pop up when we least expect her." She shook her head and sighed. "It looks, after all, like I'll never be a real lady for you, all sweet and refined."

"Now why would I want sugar all the time when I can have spice? And for a hot-blooded old varmint like me, darlin', spice is more appealing." His mouth moved toward hers again. "Oh, yeah, a *heck* of a lot more appealing."

Archer's Crossing
JEAN BARRETT

Crossing Archer Owen seems like the last thing anybody would want to do, or so Margaret Sheridan thinks. Bringing dinner to the convicted murderer is terrifying—for though he is nothing like her affluent fiancé, he stirs a hunger in her she has never known. Then the condemned prisoner uses her to make his getaway. In the clutches of the handsome felon, Margaret races into the untamed West—chasing a man Owen claims could clear his name. Margaret wonders if there is anything Archer won't do. And then he kisses her, and she prays there isn't. For if this bitter steamboat captain is half the man she suspects, she'd ride to Hell itself to clear his name and win his captive heart.

___4502-8 $5.99 US/$6.99 CAN

The Cowboys

LEIGH GREENWOOD

MATT

Matt's rough-and-tumble childhood taught him to size up a situation at a hundred paces. And to end his standoff with respectable society he knows he has to take a wife. Ellen agrees to act as a mother for the two boys he's sworn to protect, if he will be a father for the two children she brings to the union. It is a business arrangement. But nothing has prepared him for the desires the former saloon girl incites. She gentles him like a newborn colt, until he longs to be saddled with all the trappings of a real marriage. Until he understands he's found a woman to heal his orphaned heart.

__4877-9 $5.99 US/$6.99 CAN

The Agreement

Constance O'Banyon

In the midst of the vast, windswept Texas plains stands a ranch wrested from the wilderness with blood, sweat and tears. It is the shining legacy of Thomas McBride to his five living heirs. But along with the fertile acres and herds of cattle, each will inherit a history of scandal, lies and hidden lust that threatens to burn out of control.

Lauren McBride left the Circle M as a confused, lonely girl of fifteen. She returns a woman—beautiful, confident, certain of her own mind. And the last thing she will tolerate is a marriage of convenience, arranged by her pa to right past wrongs. Garret Lassiter broke her heart once before. Now only a declaration of everlasting love will convince her to become his bride.

___4878-7 $5.99 US/$6.99 CAN

Dorchester Publishing Co., Inc.
P.O. Box 6640
Wayne, PA 19087-8640

Always a Princess

Alice Chambers

The woman is a fraud if ever Philip Rosemont has seen one. And not only is she masquerading as an aristocrat, the dark-haired beauty is posing as the Princess of Valdastok— a tiny country that has been a dukedom for years! Yet though this impostor can hardly be a noblewoman, Philip has good cause to believe he will find her anything but common.

Eve Stanhope despises the aristocracy: a gaggle of scoundrels that are noble in name alone. She has few scruples about stealing their jewels. But ripping off rubies is harder than she expected, especially when she is cornered by a man who knows too much. And if kisses are illicit, the viscount is an arch-criminal.

_4867-1 $4.99 US/$5.99 CAN